The King of Silk

Joe Douglas Trent

To Fiano,

Thanks for

being patient

MuseItUp Publishing
www.museituppublishing.com

The King of Silk © 2011 by Joe Douglas Trent

MuseItUp Publishing
14878 James
Pierrefonds, Quebec, Canada
H9H 1P5
http://www.museituppublishing.com

Cover Art © 2011 by Delilah K. Stephens
Edited by Nancy Bell
Copyedited by Penny Lockwood Ehrenkranz
Layout and Book Production by Lea Schizas

Print ISBN: 978-1-926931-78-4
eBook ISBN: 978-1-926931-17-3

First eBook Edition * February 2011

Production by MuseItUp Publishing

The King of Silk

By

Joe Douglas Trent

The King of Silk is a fascinating story about a man armed with modern knowledge who is forced to explore the world centuries ago. Michael is a congenial hero thrust into an impossible situation. As the reader progresses through the novel, they are swept into the dangers and realities of a treacherous world. The book is well written and edited. The prose is clear and the story is easy to follow. Numerous colourful characters that Michael meets as he journeys to Venice and later Portugal, keep the reader engrossed in the story, turning pages to find out what happens next. – Historical Novel Reviews

Dedication

"We are like dwarfs standing upon the shoulders of giants, and so able to see more and see farther than the ancients."
Bernard of Chartres (twelfth century)

Hats off to the giants, and to my dad, Harold, the best man I ever knew.

Acknowledgements

My thanks are due to many who assisted me in the production of this work.

God, of course, is responsible for any writing talent or inspiration you may find in these pages. Rhonda, my sweet wife and hot girlfriend for better than a third of a century, encouraged and waited patiently. My mom, Cora Gail Johnson, inspired and gave feedback. Mary Andrews and all the folks at Write Right Critique Group co-labored to refine and polish.

Others, in books and online, gave me valuable insights into history and historical figures. A couple in particular stand out. Felix Fabris left us illuminating journals of his sea voyages to Palestine in the fifteenth century. If you want to learn about the Venetian silk industry during the Renaissance, Luca Molà is your man.

My editors, Nancy Bell and Penny Ehrenkranz, smoothed out the last wrinkles. And publisher Lea Schizas, the busiest woman in the world, gave me a shot.

Thanks to all.

Part One

Chapter One

Michael Patriate suppressed a smirk at the serious expression on the clerk's face. The pigtailed girl studied the magazine he pitched on the counter and glanced up at him a couple of times while he counted out one dollar bills. At a quarter to midnight and with no impatient customers behind him, he let her gawk for a few seconds.

He dropped the money next to the register and raised his eyes to the young woman. "Good picture?" His own smug likeness peered at him upside-down from the cover of *High Finance*.

The girl grinned. "Yeah," she said in a thick Slavic accent. "Very good, Mister..." She examined his name on the magazine again. "Mister Pahtriahtay."

"Thanks, it's pronounced patriot." Michael picked up the magazine and Marlboro Reds. "Remember the name—it'll be famous soon." He left her with a smile and a wink.

Out on the dimly lit sidewalk, he turned back toward the office. He should go home, but the deal closed in a couple of days, and the contract language still needed a few tweaks. Home was just a figure of speech now, anyway. He held up the magazine and admired his picture once more, then folded it under his arm.

High Finance. Welcome to the big leagues.

Michael opened the pack and lit a cigarette as he strolled past closed shops illuminated by dim security lights. Soothing nicotine relief soon flowed through his body.

Even this late, heat radiated off the buildings of Manhattan. It would be cold soon enough, but this night the mild September breeze caressed his face. He savored the warm, wet aroma of the river mixed with cigarette smoke.

Where in the world could you find another place like this?

A siren wailed from the next block. What passed for quiet in the city returned as the sound faded and Michael had the street to himself. The sign advertising Big Rich's Candy Store hung overhead, its bright red script muted under the street light.

'Try the apricot, *amico mio*,' Rich told him the first time he ventured in and sat at the corner table. The stocky confectioner hovered like an expectant father as Michael bit into the hot, tart sweetness of the flaky turnover, and beamed when he gushed, 'Good!'

He washed it down with a dark-roasted Guatemalan coffee that perfectly complemented the dessert. Big Rich's became his favorite early-morning spot, a good place to drink coffee and plan the day. Then he met Sheila there and they made it their place. He hadn't been back since...

Michael shook his head. He needed to think clearly, no distractions. He took one more glance at the sign overhead. *Wish he was open.* The sugar and caffeine would keep him running for another hour or two.

A bum huddled under the pink and white candy cane painted on Big Rich's door. Michael sneaked a look as he passed. Shadows concealed the man's head and upper torso, but the bottom of a New York Yankees logo peeked from beneath the arms crossed over his chest. Had he been there a few minutes ago? Michael hadn't seen many homeless down here since the mayor's clean-up campaign, but everybody had to sleep somewhere, he supposed. He edged closer to the curb.

He retrieved his cell phone to call Bernie and tell him about the magazine but flipped it closed instead and stuck it back in his pocket. His assistant deserved the night off. Let him sleep for once.

He turned the corner and wondered what Sheila would think about him making the cover, or if she would even see it.

When he stepped off the curb to cross the alley, a sound from the shadows froze him for a second. A quick movement from behind the trash bin jolted his feet into action.

He whirled around the way he had come and bounced off a wall. A wall with the word *Yankees* stitched across its chest.

Michael gave the guy a two-handed shove and started for the street, but something caught his collar and kicked his knees from under him. He tried to twist away as he fell, and then the world went black.

He heard himself groan and opened his eyes wide enough to observe a pair of spotless white sneakers planted on the curb inches in front of his face. In the gutter lay his magazine; his picture mocked him from the cover. A hand fished in his pockets.

Don't hurt me.

His mind replayed a photograph of an unshaven behemoth clad in a dirty orange ski cap and dingy athletic jacket despite the heat. The monster towered above him, pinning him with a crazy vacant stare.

Michael closed his eyes again and mumbled, "Just take what you want."

* * * *

An irritating chirp roused him from the awful dream. He shivered as he fumbled around for the alarm. Instead, he grabbed a handful of something cold and wet, and his eyes popped open. He recoiled from the touch and snapped to a sitting position.

A thin slice of moon highlighted a blanket of stars across an enormous black sky. He shook his head to clear his vision.

Where am I?

He sat on a bed of...grass? Grass, wet with dew. Were those the outlines of trees around him? A shadowy thought flashed across his consciousness and gripped him in a spasm of fear.

Danger. Something, someone chased him. *Run.*

He leaped to his feet and fled. What threatened him? He couldn't remember, and the realization only magnified his terror. The blues and blacks of night placed a monster beside each bush, an enemy behind every tree.

Up and down, over an embankment he scrambled. The slope flattened before Michael could react, and he ran headlong into the ground.

"Huh!" Air exploded out of his lungs with the impact.

Stunned, he gasped, anticipating the strike of his pursuer. But aside from the pounding of his heart and the rasping of his breath, he heard only silence. Somewhere close, a cricket sent out a frantic love call, and then another joined in. The pungent aroma of grass and earth assaulted his senses, but he didn't move. He couldn't take the chance.

For several long minutes, he struggled to control his breathing and remained prostrate, terrified to move or make a noise that might draw attention. In spite of the cool night air, beads of sweat ran down his face and dripped onto the earth beneath his face. When the ache in his lungs eased and no brute or beast had set upon him, he flopped over onto his back and stared into a sky just losing its stars to the impending sunrise.

He flexed his legs and arms, found nothing broken, and pressed his fingers to his temples. "Ow!" He jerked his hand away, drew a sharp breath, and grimaced. After a moment, he touched the lump again and then rubbed his fingers and thumb together. No blood, at least.

He propped himself on a stiff arm. That much worked. He rolled over on his knees and tried getting to his feet. *Whoa—not yet.*

He eased back down and shut his eyes. After a few minutes, the worst of the dizziness cleared, and he raised his head to take stock of his surroundings.

The sun sent a smattering of color and detail in advance of its arrival, revealing short green grass, brown brush, scattered trees and an occasional white flower. Panic threatened to flare again. He sucked in a deep breath. *Settle down and think.*

He tried to remember. Midnight, walking to the store for cigarettes—Michael patted an empty shirt pocket—the magazine, wishing for coffee. Then this. Nothing made sense. He searched for the cause of his blind fear this morning.

You're lost in the middle of nowhere, maybe? He sighed and tried to focus.

His gut told him to hide, his common sense said get help. He reached in his pants for his cell phone, but found the pocket barren. All his pockets were empty.

Surely, he wasn't far from a town or a house where he could call Bernie. He tried standing again; a little wobbly, but not too bad. A few feet away, a primitive road ran east and west. He squinted into the sun just peeking over the hill and set off for help.

Hours and miles later, he trudged the last few steps toward an ancient tree. The cool of the morning only a memory, its shade promised at least a temporary respite from the sweltering heat. Michael relished the protection from the sun that baked his skin. He swallowed what spit he could muster to dampen his parched throat and sat back against the rough bark, trying to clear his head enough to make a rational decision.

I have to go back.

Beyond the shade, a pair of ruts, the only break in the rolling landscape of scrub brush and short grass, led up the hill to the ridge he had just labored over. The pond lay on the other side.

When he eyed the pool an hour before, he couldn't bring himself to drink the stagnant, green liquid, but now with his tongue stuck to the roof of his mouth, he thought better of it. His stomach rebelled at the thought; help couldn't be that much further, could it? He snorted a sarcastic laugh.

That's what he had hoped the whole miserable day, but at the crest of each rise he encountered only more desolate wilderness.

If he were back at the pond, he would wade right out in the middle and fall into its cool embrace. He shook his head to snap himself out of the seductive daydream and then wished again for a cigarette. The thought came unprovoked.

Wilson.

Michael's eyes narrowed. Wes, "The Weasel," Wilson. Yes, it had to be. With the offer deadline for the PharmaCent-Nussbaum buyout looming, Wilson had moved himself and the Ransel Group into contention through a series of maneuvers Michael gave grudging admiration. Still, the deal was his to lose.

What had Wilson done? He didn't seem like a kidnapper, but one never knew how far some people might go to make this kind of money.

Well, the Weasel won't beat Michael Patriate out of this deal. When I get to a phone, I'll...

A bird chirped in the branches overhead. Michael eyed the sparrow for a moment and forced himself back to his situation.

How long before dark? He pulled back a grimy white sleeve with "MXP" monogrammed in gold on the cuff. Midnight, the watch said. Late afternoon, the sun contradicted.

Had only twenty-four hours elapsed since he remembered leaving the office? And if this was September, why did the trees and grass boast of new growth? Nothing made sense. What, who brought him to this desolate place devoid of people? *Why can't I remember?*

Michael sighed. Sitting and thinking wouldn't get him a drink. He wiped a gritty palm across his sunburned forehead and then held out his hand and stared. He had stopped sweating.

Move.

He forced himself up from the tree root seat and tried to ignore the complaints from his aching joints and sore feet. A squishy twinge on the back of his left heel announced the beginning of a blister. Even at five hundred dollars a pair, these wingtips weren't hiking shoes.

He limped back into sunlight, onto the clumpy grass growing beside the road. After a few paces his legs worked a little better. Then his situation intruded again.

What happened? Did he get disoriented and drive a hundred miles out in the sticks to run out of gas?

No, you don't get Alzheimer's before you're thirty-five.

Michael realized he had stopped walking and forced his feet back into action.

"This is nuts," he said aloud. "I'm going nuts." He raised his head and shook his fists at a raptor soaring high overhead. "Where is everybody?" he screamed at the solitary hunter. Only a buzzing insect answered. He dropped his arms in defeat.

He plodded on, passing a patch of dead grass and weeds left from the previous season. Something exploded out of the brush at his feet.

"No!" He jumped back, heart pounding. The furry creature halted behind a stone twenty feet away and watched him with a sideways, one-eyed look only a rabbit can give.

His muscles tensed. His clenched jaws threatened to pop under the pressure. "It's...a...*bunny*." He held himself in check for a moment and then scanned the landscape around him. What other creatures might rove about, especially after dark?

Launching up the slope with an eye out for movement around him, he felt again in an empty pocket. No Chapstick. No cigarettes. His two comfort habits denied, he licked his cracked lips and tried to ignore the craving in his bones.

Michael turned his thoughts to the coming night. He needed to find food and a safe place to sleep. Panic rose in his chest as he acknowledged the absence of the basics of life he had taken for granted for so long.

Desperation returned with a paralyzing grip on his chest. Danger closed in on him from every side. He leaped off the path, toward a line of trees, but the back of his shoe landed wrong on a clump of grass. A searing pain shot through his left heel and robbed him of his alarm.

"Aahh!" Michael dropped to one knee.

He sucked in a breath through his nostrils and popped his foot partway out of the shoe. Careful of the tender spot, he pulled down the sock. The sore had burst, and the shoe already worked on another layer of skin.

What else could go wrong? Slowly he let his lungs empty. *Think.*

He stared at the stinging, mutilated flesh for a moment and reached in a back pocket for the handkerchief that wasn't there. What could he use for a bandage? He grabbed the pocket on his shirt with his thumbs to tear it loose but stopped and cocked his head.

Sounds floated from the other side of the hill. Creaking, accompanied by the sound of hooves and a one-sided conversation. The thought of rescue revived him, and he drew a breath to shout but checked himself and decided to get a look first.

He jammed his foot back into the shoe, and ignoring the pain, jumped up and ran, squatted behind a bush, and waited.

A horse pulling a crude wagon topped the rise. Four solid wooden wheels bounced along in the ruts, rocking their commander back and forth in his seat.

Michael's jaw dropped. Was he on a movie set?

Dressed in period clothing from some ancient era, the driver engaged his long-eared companion in boisterous, incomprehensible, accented oratory. His free hand slashed through the air, punctuating his point.

Fear turned to amusement and Michael choked back laughter in spite of his predicament. The wagon clattered by on its way down the hill before he recovered.

"Hey!" He hopped up and chased the strange pair, favoring his sore left foot. "Hey, stop."

The driver looked over his shoulder with wide eyes, then turned and slapped his reigns at the horse's flanks. They shot away in a clamorous wake of hooves, wheels, and cargo.

"No," Michael screamed. "Come back." He hobbled down the hill after the receding wagon, but sucked in a lungful of dust and stopped in a choking fit.

Come back.

Hands on his knees, he watched the wagon go. Then the world did a funny dance and the earth rushed up to meet him.

* * * *

A horse nickered nearby. Michael opened his eyes and looked up into the middle-aged, weathered face of Jack Walters, a neighbor from his childhood. Of course, it wasn't Jack shading him from the sun, but the dark eyes reminded him of the man who always had an apple for a tow-headed kid.

"You came back," Michael croaked. The patches of bare earth and spotty grass formed warm and cool spots on the ground beneath his back.

The man stared down at him for a moment and then straightened and walked away.

"Wait." Michael pushed the words out in a rasp. "Can you help me? I'm lost. I have to get back to the office." He turned his head and watched the man leave. A blade of grass tickled his ear.

The horse grazed in the shade of the tree Michael had vacated only a short time before. The stranger pulled a jug from under a tarp covering the wagon.

Michael struggled to sit and lean on his left arm. He winced at the pounding in his head.

As the stranger walked the distance back, Michael took in his odd dress. The hat resembled an upside-down cloth bag pulled down to his ears. He wore a one-piece shirt with a kind of a v-neck and long, loose sleeves, over pants tied at the waist with a drawstring. Rough cloth, crude stitching, off-white and faded brown.

Where would you buy this stuff?

Jack, he might as well have a name, pulled a plug from the brown ceramic jug and handed it to him; then he stood back and watched with arms crossed over his chest.

The tepid water smelled like moss, but it soothed Michael's swollen tongue. He turned up the jug and drank until he had to stop to breathe and then set it on the grass between his outstretched legs.

He looked up at Jack and blew out a relieved breath. "Thanks." He nodded toward the wagon. "Have any food in there?"

His rescuer frowned and gave him a shrug.

Michael chewed a mouthful of air and swallowed.

Jack released an impatient sigh and walked away again. He returned with a bag that yielded a small loaf of bread, broke it in half and held out a piece.

He grabbed the offering and bit off a coarse hunk. It tasted worse than the whole-wheat kind Sheila bought, before the divorce, but he gobbled it down anyway.

"Wouldn't have a cell phone on you, I guess," Michael said through a full mouth.

Jack only squinted at the sunward horizon like a salesman late for an appointment.

"Yeah, I didn't think so." He took another pull on the water jug and handed it back, but before he could ask for a ride his roiling stomach demanded attention. *Don't drink the water.*

He leaned again on his arm and turned to the side, feeling a familiar acrid taste coat his mouth and wishing it away.

He rolled over on his knees and hands. All of the bread and water came back up. His stomach kept trying to expel its contents long after it had nothing left to squeeze out.

The shadows had grown long when Jack pulled Michael to his feet and helped him on the wagon. He lay on top of the covered cargo, still twisted in fruitless spasms as they jolted off. He wanted to panic at the loss of control over his body and his safety, but every bounce of wooden wheels over a punishing road threatened to split his head open and relieve the pressure inside.

Had this guy kidnapped or saved him? Michael couldn't concentrate on anything but the violence of his illness.

Sometime after dark, the wagon stopped. Michael clenched his teeth to hold back the heaves. *Thank you.*

Jack called out, hopped down, and walked away.

The smell of his own vomit made Michael want to gag again, but at least Jack had shut down this horse-drawn tilt-a-whirl for a minute. Maybe there was a phone somewhere nearby. Michael tried to snatch a moment of rest.

Presently, he heard footsteps and a pair of male voices approached the motionless wagon. They seemed to be negotiating in a language he couldn't understand.

One of the voices grew louder and floated around the back of the wagon and to the left. It called away into the darkness. After a moment, the voice's owner swung over the rails beside Michael.

Another climbed in with deliberate motions on the right while the first one, bending down close to Michael's ear, jabbered something that sounded like a question. Perhaps, "Are you all right, sir?"

He groaned and shook his head.

They slid him to the edge and helped him down, then led him toward an open door that spilled a dim yellow light onto the ground. Inside, they deposited him on something soft and still.

He closed his eyes again, grateful the heaves hadn't returned.

A woman's soft words tugged at his consciousness.

He opened his eyes at a gentle touch on his arm and squinted against the glare. The concerned look on the face haloed in lamplight pulled him away from the rest he craved.

The woman held out a cup. She persisted when Michael refused but seemed satisfied when he accepted a couple of sips of cool water. A terse male voice called from outside the door. She patted his shoulder and scampered out, leaving him alone again.

He laid his head down in the least uncomfortable position, and in the moment between consciousness and sleep, he recalled a walk down a dark Manhattan street.

Chapter Two

The cool breeze on Michael's cheek stirred him awake from a dream that left him with a nebulous longing for something lost.

No, take me back.

He opened his eyes, expecting the world to spin again, and sighed in relief when it didn't. Michael drew the scratchy blanket aside and struggled up on the lumpy bed until his breath came in heavy puffs. He leaned back against the coarse plank wall. His arms still felt like noodles, but at least they worked enough to push him up this morning.

It felt good to sit up after several days huddled in a ball, alternating between shivering and sweating like a pig. When he could focus without triggering the nausea, he examined his surroundings and groaned.

His bed, a bag stuffed with hay or grass, lay on a dirt floor packed hard with use in some kind of primitive building; not a house, but a barn or storage shed. Overhead, dense, dried vegetation covered dark wooden slats. Old manual farming tools hung on unpainted walls. Next to his bed, a pair of wooden barrels hid their unknown contents within gently curved staves, blackened with age. The crude entry door remained closed, but a board that covered the window had been pulled aside.

From his vantage, blue sky hung over a neighboring roof. The breeze carried an oddly pleasant scent of cow manure. For an instant the smell took Michael back to his uncle's farm, until he noticed the odd clothing he was wearing.

He vaguely remembered his hosts helping him change despite his feeble resistance. The brown pullover shirt and formless pants tied around his waist with a cord resembled Jack's, but were even more crude, if that was possible. The uneven hems on the sleeves and pant legs didn't quite reach his wrists or ankles. A pair of cracked leather shoes with rawhide strings laced through the hooks lay at the end of his bed.

It was too much. Michael closed his eyes and leaned his head back. His hand moved instinctively to a breast pocket that didn't exist. *A hundred dollars for a cigarette.*

After a moment, he sat up again and swept trembling fingers across his whiskered chin. Four, maybe five days growth, someone should be looking for him by now. Bernie wouldn't have waited very long to call the police and report him missing, especially with the deal ready to close. At the thought, Michael hung his head. The deal. Whatever the result, it was too late to do anything about it. All that work for nothing.

He pushed away a feeling of failure. He had prepped Bernie well enough, he hoped. Michael dragged his thoughts back to the problem at hand.

His eyes darted around the room until he spotted something familiar. In the corner beside him, the black toe of a wingtip peeked from under the blanket. He found his pants and shirt, stained but clean, folded over the shoes still coated with a layer of dust from the road. Arthur, the shoeshine man at the barbershop, would have a fit.

Michael pulled the bundle up on his lap and something rattled in the left shoe, his watch. He hadn't noticed it missing. Tuesday the nineteenth, it said. Five days.

He clasped the timepiece on the wrist his shirtsleeve didn't cover and rifled through the shirt and pants for his other belongings. The pockets were empty. His wallet and keys were missing along with his spare change.

This is unreal. I need to find out what happened.

He grabbed the barrel by its worn lip, intending to pull himself up and march outside. Halfway up, he collapsed back on the bed. He'd rest before trying again, just for a minute.

Somewhere near midday, the farmer's wife woke him as she swept in the door with a big bowl that smelled wonderfully of hot grease. *Brodo*, he remembered her saying of the thin soup she had fed him. At least it was boiled. How could he ask them, when he graduated off of the soup, to boil his drinking water, too?

I won't be here that long.

"Good morning," she said, or something to that effect.

Michael didn't understand the language, but it sounded familiar. Italian, maybe, or East European?

He sat up and smiled in spite of himself. He welcomed a visit from this woman who had cared for him. In hazy glimpses, he had taken her for fifty or sixty, but now he could see that she was younger, probably not much over forty. Her drab sack of a dress didn't help. She wore the hollow look of someone who had surrendered her youth to a harsh life. And she was short. Even sitting on the bed, Michael almost looked her level in the eye. Her appearance didn't matter, though. She brought food.

"Thank you." He reached for the bowl.

She froze and stared at his arm.

"What?" Michael followed her gaze. "Never seen a watch?"

He rotated his arm so she could get a better look and heard her gasp.

Her stricken face lost its color. Her right hand flew to her chest as she crossed herself. The left lost its grip on the bowl.

Michael caught it, spilling only a little, astonished as his host backed out of the shed with a panicked look. He jumped when she slammed the door.

The woman cried out a single word, "Alberto!" The sound of her quick footsteps died in the distance.

He mulled over her reaction. *Didn't she take it off me?* Without understanding why, he took off the watch and tied it around his neck with the wingtip shoestrings.

Soup came again in the evening, in the morning, and at noon the next day, left outside the door. Michael heard heavy footsteps arrive and leave. The woman never entered. Her husband peered in the open window a couple of times, only to scowl. Their behavior troubled him, and he considered sneaking out to look for help, but hesitated. Maybe when he felt a little stronger, he told himself.

Michael stared at the wingtips, then his ratty clothing. He put on the borrowed shoes, just in case.

* * * *

A familiar horse and wagon clatter aroused him. Michael woke, hot and disoriented, and looked around the shed to get his bearings. Light angling through the window made it late afternoon.

Jack?

The commotion stopped and a man called out.

Michael struggled to his feet and held onto a hook on the wall for support while he peeked out the window.

The farmer and his wife glared up at Jack, still mounted on the wagon. Michael couldn't hear the hushed conversation, and wouldn't have understood the words anyway, but he got the gist of it by watching the only three people he had seen in the last few days.

Jack said something and shook his head. The farmer gestured toward Michael's shed several times while he snapped off some gibberish, and then pointed up at Jack and down the road. The woman let her gaze fall to the ground. Jack nodded. He hopped off the wagon and marched toward the shelter with a grim look that put Michael in mind of young Travis on his way to shoot Old Yeller.

Michael's racing heart tried to pump strength into his wilting legs without success.

Jack pulled the door open and barked a command. Michael hesitated, unsure of what was required of him, until Jack shouted something that sounded like "Now!" and waved him out of the hut.

Michael reached down for his shoes, and Jack repeated his harsh command. Michael straightened up and looked him in the eye. "I'm taking my clothes."

Jack took a couple of steps forward and poked Michael on the shoulder with a thick finger.

His last bit of strength fled and he reeled backward. He crashed onto the bed and held up a jittery hand. "Okay."

He pulled himself up and ducked through the doorway. Jack walked swiftly across the hard, barren yard, and Michael trailed after him. Fear kept him upright, but his head was swimming by the time he reached the wagon. He leaned his back against a wheel and locked his knees to keep from falling.

Jack turned and pointed up toward the seat. Michael nodded, but didn't move, taking the opportunity to catch his breath. Jack's face turned darker and Michael hurried.

He raised his weak arms and grabbed the rail, but his hands refused to grip. Jack got under him and shoved him up face first onto the seat, then left Michael to right himself while he spoke brusquely with the farmer. Michael sat up and waved at his caretakers. They turned away leaving his gesture of thanks unacknowledged.

Jack stalked around and mounted the wagon, then jerked up the reins and slapped them on the horse's rump. Michael held tight while the seat bucked and jerked. The farmer's place could hardly recede fast enough.

The bouncing wagon jarred his pounding head, but this time he rode in the front instead of puking his guts out in back. Jack stared ahead at the dirt road and ignored him. Michael had questions, but doubted he'd get answers from this yokel, even if they spoke the same language.

The sun and the dust combined to crack his lips and stick his throat together, but this time when Jack took out the jug and sullenly offered him water, Michael eyed it for a moment and shook his head. He needed a drink, but didn't want to risk another week like the last one.

* * * *

Make it stop.

It was only a couple of hours since they had left the farmstead, but in Michael's exhausted condition if felt like days. The sun was setting, throwing slanting shadows across the washboard road, and he ached to lie down, even more than he wanted to find a phone. *Please.*

In a merciful act, Jack turned out of the ruts and parked the wagon at the bottom of a hill, then hopped down without a word.

Michael slumped on the bench and closed his eyes for a moment, relishing the stillness. When he opened them again, Jack was bent over next to the horse, almost under it.

Curious, Michael propped himself up on an elbow.

Jack held up a front hoof, studied it for a moment and went to the others and did the same. When he straightened, he patted the animal's hindquarter with an affectionate slap and then spotted Michael watching and went back to his stone-faced routine.

He unhitched the horse and replaced its harness with a rope he left draped and coiled on the ground while he stowed the gear under the wagon. He retrieved the rope and made a clicking noise; then he led the animal down a gentle slope. They disappeared over an embankment under a canopy of tall trees swaying in the light breeze. The gurgle of running water whispered through the brush.

Michael stayed where he was, wondering whether he should get off the wagon.

In a few minutes, Jack led the horse back and tied the rope to a tree; then he set about picking up scattered sticks. He broke several into short lengths, pitched them into a pile, and wandered off again.

Might as well make myself useful. Michael hauled himself upright and swung his legs over the edge of the seat. He intended to slide down and hit the step, easing himself to the ground, but his left hand lost its grip, and he swung to the right. When he planted his foot on the step, the leg buckled, and his other hand slipped. He twisted in the air for a long moment and then rolled as he hit the ground. He lay still for a minute.

"I'm all right," he said, as if anyone understood or cared. When he sat up and looked around, he saw Jack bent over to pick up another piece of firewood. "Thanks for your concern," he muttered.

He got to his knees and then his feet, clinging to the wagon for support until his head stopped spinning. He limped over to Jack's collection of twigs and branches. Clearing an area, he began to make a pile, starting with larger pieces and working up to the twigs. He wished he'd been in Scouts.

Jack returned a few minutes later carrying a pair of knotty logs and stopped when he saw Michael's handiwork. He frowned and kicked the pile of wood off the cleared area.

"Don't do that," Michael said.

Jack glanced his way, but otherwise ignored him. The man knelt and grasped a piece of tree limb with two hands to gouge out a shallow hole. He gathered twigs and leaves into the depression and then laid small scraps of branches on top. Next, larger sticks crossed in another layer. Finally, the biggest pieces sat atop the pile.

He got up and pushed by Michael without a look. From under the wagon's seat, he retrieved a small cloth bundle, untied the string binding it and rolled it out on the ground. He lifted the top panel from one edge, folded it back, and then again to reveal its contents: a rock, a strip of metal, and a pile of wood shavings.

What is that? A frown creased Michael's forehead.

Jack took a pinch of the shavings and placed them in a compact heap next to the twigs and grabbed the rock and piece of metal. He dropped to his hands and knees and lowered his head next to the firewood.

Michael took a couple of steps around him for a better view.

The man placed one end of the metal strip into the edge of the shavings pile and began striking the rock against it in a downward, scraping motion. Sparks flew from the flint and steel.

Two, five, ten, fifty times or more, Jack struck, with patience Michael knew he couldn't muster, never taking his eyes off the shavings. Once or twice, Michael thought he saw a tiny puff of smoke, but Jack kept his rhythm. Just as Michael determined there would be no campfire, Jack dropped his tools and blew.

From a tiny ember, a small flame flared into life. Jack pulled a handful of twigs over the yellow spot of light. Soon, the fire crackled, and Jack refolded the oiled cloth, rolled it tightly and re-tied it, before placing it back under the seat.

"Good job," Michael said.

Again, Jack looked away.

What do I have to do?

Farther back in the wagon, Jack dug in what must have been his food store. He returned to the fire with a water jug, knife, pan, a couple of bags, and a bottle. Jack placed the pan directly on the fire and opened the bottle. He poured enough golden, viscous liquid to coat the bottom of the pan.

The smell of olive oil warming set off a rumble in Michael's empty belly.

From the other bag, Jack retrieved a lump, further cloaked in a piece of cloth. He unwrapped a piece of dried or cured meat, cut off several slices, and placed them in the pan. The sizzle and the heavenly smell sent Michael to another place and time.

Lost in this wilderness, Michael could almost taste the *prosciutto* down at Lombardi's. He hadn't eaten solid food in a week. He hoped the stuff would stay down. The cooking food smelled like heaven.

Jack sliced off a hunk of bread and laid a couple of pieces of the ham on it. He stuck the knife in the loaf and turned away to eat.

Invited or not, Michael cut two slices of bread and made a sandwich from the remainder of the meat. A simple meal never tasted so good, but Michael's dry throat refused to push down the dry bread.

"Hey," Michael said.

After a pause, Jack turned his head.

Michael pointed to the jug, then the fire, and made what he hoped were boiling motions.

Jack shrugged, shook his head and got up, holding his food in one hand and walked to the wagon. When he came back he thrust a small pot and an empty jug into Michael's hands and walked away.

Michael wanted a cold drink, but couldn't wait that long for the boiled water to cool. He slaked his thirst with tepid water straight from the pot.

Later, Jack found some blankets at the back of the wagon, climbed up, and without a word, spread them over the cargo. He glanced over at the fire and, seeming satisfied with it, slid in between the covers on one side and turned away from Michael.

Where was he supposed to sleep? The makeshift bed looked wide enough for two. Michael felt a little stronger after eating; he figured he had just about enough strength to drag himself up onto the wagon. He found a hold for both hands, put his left foot up on the step, and took a deep breath. *On three.*

He rocked back and forth a couple of times, and then put all his effort into hauling himself up onto the seat. He lay there for a minute while he caught his breath.

Jack muttered something.

"Hi honey, I'm home," Michael said. "Sorry I'm late, but the boys wanted to go one more round, and I just lost track of time." He looked back at the unmoving bulge and shook his head.

He scooted over the seat and claimed his spot. The bed was lumpy, but it felt better than the first time he lay there. Michael shivered. In the open wagon bed they were exposed to the elements and had no protection from thieves or wild animals that could appear out of the night shadows.

An animal snarled from beside the wagon. Michael's heart raced as he imagined a panther leaping over the side rails. Jack snorted again, then shifted and eased into rhythmic snoring.

Michael took a deep breath to calm his ragged breathing. Great. He might never sleep.

He pulled his half of the covers close and drew in the moist night air. The stars winked bright against the perfect dark background. He couldn't remember ever seeing this many or so clearly. It reminded him of something...

Chapter Three

The bed creaked and groaned underneath him.

"Quit it," Michael mumbled. He opened his eyes to watch Jack disappear over the side of the wagon and land with a thump.

The sun's not even up yet.

He sat up and swore softly. After the jolting wagon ride yesterday, the fall and the hard bed, everything hurt. But he had to get down, just slower than last time. Michael turned on his stomach and eased himself feet first over the side. He held on to the sideboard and took a few cautious steps to let his shaky knees get used to the weight again.

Jack disappeared behind some bushes for a few minutes and wouldn't look at him when he came back. Michael decided it was time to set some things straight; he stepped in front of Jack and tapped his chest.

"Michael."

The two stared at each other for a moment until Jack relented.

"Baldo." He walked around Michael and kicked dirt on the still smoldering fire.

It was a start.

Michael picked up a stone from the road. "I throw the rock," he exclaimed to Baldo's back.

Baldo slumped. He stopped and turned around. "What now?" his expression said.

Michael tapped his temple. "Look." He pointed to himself and made a throwing motion before holding up the rock with a thumb and finger. He drew the words out with the action: "I throw the rock."

He turned and, with as much force as his weak arm would muster, hurled the object down the road behind them and repeated the phrase. When he faced Baldo again, the man nodded his head.

"Butto il sasso."

He tried it out and Baldo laughed, just a little. He spoke it again. Better. They spent the next hour or so learning different phrases. "I eat the food. I drink the water. I throw up."

Baldo found a sense of humor.

* * * *

Michael pulled the brim of his floppy cloth hat down against the afternoon sun. The approaching village held little interest for him. Like the others they visited during the three months he tagged along with Baldo, it consisted of a few dozen simple structures placed at random intervals.

He had been so sure when they rolled into the first one that rescue was only a phone call away, but the looks and whispers hinted at the isolation and suspicion he would find in this strange place. He stayed with Baldo because he didn't have anywhere else to go.

Forced to learn the basics of the language in order to survive, Michael was surprised at how easily he slipped into conversational...whatever this was. One could do a lot when forced to, he supposed. Of course, he got lots of practice talking to Baldo's customers.

Baldo was a trader. His clientele appeared limited to working people from farms and small villages. From his wagon he sold cloth, cooking utensils, dried plants and herbs, small tools, trinkets and miscellaneous items. Some he exchanged for barter and some for coin.

Michael kept expecting to run into someone important or find a place where he could get his bearings. But, despite his daily requests, Baldo seemed intent on staying away from anything Michael would recognize as a town or city.

Where are we? Michael wondered more than once.

It couldn't be the U.S., with no sign of modern technology anywhere. Once, driving in Wyoming, he didn't see another human for a hundred miles. Still, utility poles lined the smooth caliche road. There was nothing similar here: no cell phone towers, no paved roads, no lights at night.

Michael thought of the Amish country in Pennsylvania. The people there made a mostly successful effort to shun modern conveniences, but this bunch hadn't forsaken technology. It was as if they hadn't discovered it yet.

Where could you go to find a place this backward?

Their clothing looked like peasant costumes pulled from a movie set in the Middle Ages. Something else was odd, too. It seemed everyone here was short. Baldo looked average for a man at about five-three or four, making Michael's five-feet-eleven seem tall. He had landed far from home.

The effort to pin down his location frustrated him. Although Michael worked hard every day on his language skills, he just couldn't get through to these people. He questioned Baldo and others with whom he came in contact, asking them where he was. "Here," most said with a blank look. Others gave him names of places to which he had no reference. Most were reluctant to talk about anything from the outside and Baldo's sales suffered when people grew suspicious. Michael gave up asking.

As his language improved, Michael involved himself in Baldo's business and found he enjoyed trading a little salt for some dried beans, which he might sell the next day for a length of homespun cloth, things you hoped would turn into money someday, but were real in the moment. He gave Baldo a few marketing tips in the process, but it brought him no answers. And here they were in another dirt-poor farming community.

Baldo wound around the lanes among a set of houses. He reached a street in the middle of town before he reined the horse to a stop and set the brake.

Michael sighed and swung a leg over the side. He hit the ground and turned to loosen the rope that fastened the tarp over their goods. A bell pealed out behind him, then struck again. The third ring sent an adrenaline rush through his heart. *A church.*

He let the untied rope drop against the side of the wagon. "Baldo, I'll be right back."

Baldo came around the back. "Where are you going?"

"I'm going to see a priest. He'll know where I am." Michael noticed Baldo's shoulders droop.

"All right." Baldo turned away and worked on the tarp.

Michael forced himself not to run and set off for the church.

Heart racing, he took a deep breath and opened the thick front door. High, narrow windows with open shutters let in a few thin shafts of light. He closed the door and waited for his eyes to adjust to the darkness, savoring the contrast of the cool air against the late summer heat outside.

"Come in, my son." A disembodied voice floated from somewhere toward the front. "I'll be right with you."

The aisle separating a dozen pairs of simple, narrow pews guided Michael forward. A crucified Jesus stared down at him from the shadows when he stopped in front of the altar. From this distance he could make out the back of the robed priest at work in front of a candleholder. The shaved crown of the priest's bobbing head reminded him of saints in those ancient paintings Sheila had showed him once in a museum. Michael smiled at the thought. She always tried to enlighten him. He waited until the last candle went into place.

The priest set a box to the side and turned to Michael. "How may I help you?"

The youth in his voice surprised Michael. "I'm lost, Father. I mean I don't know where I am."

The young priest folded his arms across his chest. "Most men come here wondering where they are going."

Michael shook his head. "Right now I can't see that far ahead. I'm a long way from home, and I don't know how to get back."

"Well, then. We should try to locate your home, but first, what should I call you?"

"Sorry, Father. Michael is my name."

"Ah." The priest pointed heavenward as he spoke. "Like *Michele*, the Archangel. I'm Father Matheus. Welcome, Michael. So, where is it you come from?"

Michael suppressed a smile. This young man worked hard at being serious. "I don't suppose you have heard of a place called America?"

Matheus furrowed his brows and looked at the ceiling. "No, not America. I know a man by the name of Amerigo, but the place isn't familiar to me."

Michael sighed. He wasn't surprised at the answer, but he had hoped that it would be different. "Father, do you have a map?"

"A map?" The priest put a finger to his lips. "Yes, I believe so. Come with me."

He reminded Michael of the geeky kid in fifth grade that everyone made fun of, but he appreciated the young man's helpful attitude.

Father Matheus whirled about and darted to the back of the church, then disappeared through the door before Michael could react. He hurried to catch him but stopped and squinted against the sudden blast of sunlight.

The priest stood at the door of a modest residence a few feet from the church. "Please wait here." He disappeared inside, but soon returned with something in his hand. "Father Cremona left this when he died. He could write and read Latin, you know."

Michael accepted a scrolled piece of paper and unrolled it. Not paper; vellum or parchment by the soft feel of it. The ink outline map depicted land masses, water, and mountains. Scattered labels in something he couldn't read didn't help much. But something looked familiar.

"Here we are, I think." Father Matheus pointed to a place left of a sea that ran southwest to northeast above a long peninsula. A name lay below Matheus's finger. *Venetia*. Something about the map bothered Michael: the orientation. East pointed up. He rotated the map a quarter-turn clockwise and recognized it. *Roma* sat in the middle of the peninsula, and *Neapolis* stretched southward toward the boot heel.

Venice, Rome, Naples.

How could that be? Italy was a modern country. The map showed them maybe a hundred miles from Venice. The document in his hands started to shake.

"Are you all right, Michael? You don't look well."

"Father, what's the date?"

"August twenty-third."

Michael looked up at the priest. "No, the year. What year is it?"

"Why, the year of our Lord fourteen hundred and ninety two, of course."

Michael's knees buckled. The scenery went white.

* * * *

Baldo looked up from stowing a package on the wagon. "What's the matter?"

"I got some bad news, but I don't want to talk about it." Michael climbed up on the wagon and sat with his head in his hands.

Gone. It was all gone: the job, the money, the people, everything, along with hope. Until this moment, he had believed rescue was only a matter of time. Any minute, someone would find him and take him back home. Everything he had built his life upon had been ripped from under him behind that church.

"Are you all right?"

Michael cupped his hands over his ears to shut out the insanity that threatened to overwhelm him.

* * * *

Michael gazed up at the stars, hardly noticing Baldo's rhythmic snoring.

Italy. 1492. That's crazy.

He had never thought to ask anyone the *year*. He just hadn't considered it. A person could, in a way, travel to the future by being unconscious for a while, but to go backward?

He lay in the darkness and tried to sort things out. One day he worked and lived a sophisticated life in New York. The next he hitched a ride in a horse-drawn wagon. Some part of his awareness traced the Big Dipper sparkling in the black sky free of light and air pollution.

This had to be a dream, but Michael had never experienced one that felt like this. He ran his fingers across the worn edges of the wagon's sideboard, feeling the realness of the texture. Maybe he was dying and having someone else's twisted life flash before his eyes. Or was he sitting in a white room, selling dried vegetables to some bemused psychiatrist? The breeze that stirred his hair and the creak of the wagon when he shifted his weight seemed real enough.

But if this place was real, he would never again ride in a car, watch T.V., never hear Sheila's voice on the telephone.

"Stop it."

He hadn't meant to speak it aloud. Baldo stirred next to him. Michael looked over and held his breath until he heard snoring again.

Don't panic. Think.

Michael explored the possibilities. One: he was dreaming or somehow incapacitated. Two: he suffered from some kind of delusion. Three: everyone around him was deluded. There surely were a bunch of them. Four: he was really in the fifteenth century.

If he were dreaming or delusional, someone would wake him or give him a shot soon, so it didn't matter what he did. But if it were numbers three or four...Michael's mind kicked into business mode. How could he work this thing to his advantage?

1492, he thought again. *In fourteen hundred ninety two, Columbus sailed the ocean blue*.

Where would Columbus be now? This world was set to see a lot of change soon, assuming he wasn't dreaming or delusional.

With change comes danger—and opportunity.

The night air had acquired a chill. Michael pulled the cover over him with only his face left exposed. He thought for a while and drifted off.

His mother, dressed in 15th century peasant clothes, sat in a rocking chair and hummed an indistinct tune. On the wall above her hung a calendar that rolled months out of sight to the left and right.

Mom ceased her humming and stood up under August 1492, pointing her finger at him. "You remember they changed the calendar, because the old one wasn't quite right."

So was it really August? Or 1492?

He tried to get a closer look at the scroll, but someone had placed it too high on the wall. He climbed on a chair, and the calendar kept rising farther away. "Mom, help me," he tried to say. The words wouldn't come. He wanted to shout and then cry, but he could only struggle against this vocal paralysis. The chair slipped from under him and he fell.

He woke, disoriented, and thought himself back in his New York apartment, grateful to wake from the dream. But no, a cricket chirped nearby, and stars lined the ceiling.

Why can't I wake up from this one?

* * * *

Michael cleaned the supper dishes and put them away. He sat by the fire where Baldo rested and leaned back against the other wagon wheel. He watched the flames a moment before he spoke.

"Baldo, have you ever seen anyone like me here?"

"What do you mean?"

"I think you know. Someone out of place."

Baldo looked out into the night. "No."

Michael thought about that. Even the most remote peoples in isolated places at least saw an occasional missionary or anthropologist or government snoop.

Unless it really is the fifteenth century.

"Why did you pick me up that day?"

Baldo dropped his head just enough for Michael to notice and stared at the general direction of his feet. "You needed help."

"You didn't have to come back for me."

"I took the responsibility when I put you in the wagon." Baldo lifted his eyes again into the dark sky. "The people you stayed with were kind enough to care for you until I could return."

Michael considered what he would have done. At home, his efforts would have stopped at calling emergency services. He might have waited until the ambulance arrived. After that, it would have become a fading memory.

"Thank you." Something stirred a thought from that first week. "Why did that couple dislike me so much?"

Firelight deepened the lines in Baldo's face as he frowned. "They said you wore some kind of magic, on your arm."

His watch. He supposed it would appear as magic to a person who had never seen anything like it, second hand ticking away the time.

"Not magic, just a toy."

"Mmm-hmm." Baldo responded. "I took it off your wrist and hid it in your shoe. I don't believe in magic, but many do." He rubbed his hand back and forth on his leg as if to wipe away the memory.

"Thanks," Michael repeated. Something didn't make sense. He hadn't heard the whole story. "Why did they take me in?" It might have been his imagination, but he thought Baldo squirmed.

Baldo drew in a deep breath and released it in admission. "Your clothing. You looked wealthy."

That's it. A lost, rich guy; they had hoped for a reward. Baldo promised the couple a share and left Michael at the farm disguised in local clothing while he scouted for someone missing a wayward giant. But he didn't find anyone looking. Then he found himself stuck with this burden that couldn't even speak Italian when the farmer ran them both off because of Michael's "magic." At least they didn't knock him in the head and bury him in a shallow grave, or worse. A chill swept across his arms and back.

What if he hadn't come back for me?

He collected himself and let his friend off the hook. "Are we near your home now?"

The trader relaxed and smiled. "Not too far away. We should be back there in a week or two."

"Is that in a city?"

Baldo shook his head. "No, no. I don't go there unless I have to. Only to buy things in the spring. Too many people take advantage of you there."

Michael had no intention of spending a winter in some little village. He needed answers. "How could I get there?"

Baldo looked at Michael like he had asked how to go jump off a bridge and then looked out into the night. "In a few days we'll come to a busier road. There should be someone on it you can pay to take you. Don't worry. I owe you for sales I wouldn't have made without your help. The money will get you where you want to go."

Michael thanked him once more. Later, sleepless, he watched the stars and clutched the watch, the only solid link to his past, or maybe it was his future. The time paradox was too confusing. He could only hope his new destination promised something that made sense.

Chapter Four

Agostino

Agostino Barbarigo bristled with controlled rage as he glared around his ducal chamber. Only the elderly minister of salt commerce draped in his heavy robes moved, wiping away a bead of sweat from his cheek. None of the other six men seated around the desk stirred. Their stares told Agostino they waited to gauge his response to the council's messenger.

Well, they will hear my reply.

The Council of Ten had sent its representative with a message. The young man interrupted the meeting over the objections of Agostino's secretary, and marched in to stand in front of his desk and blurt out a message.

"You can commission all the artwork you desire, only do so with your own money." Then he bowed his head and added, "Your Grace."

Of course, the issue wasn't money or art, but power and who wielded it. Agostino filled an elected position, and his predecessors had largely been figureheads. In earlier times, that was good enough. *But not now.* The council members wanted to show him their supremacy. They should have sent one of their own instead of this lackey.

He glanced at the clock standing against the wall behind the intruder. The soothing rhythm of the pendulum called out *control, control, control*. Positioned around the clock face, the four golden winged lions, symbol of patron Saint Mark, reminded him of the power he held as titular head of the Republic. He let the clock tick ten times before he rose and focused his attention on the messenger, who by now had lost his confident pose and sneaked a glance back toward the door. Agostino's usually deep voice raised an octave when he shouted in staccato.

"I am the *Doge* of *Venice*! I will not be lectured."

"Forgive me, Your Grace." The messenger stared at his feet. "I merely bring the message. If you please, sir, the council expects your reply."

Agostino studied the poor youth. Probably not yet twenty-five, fodder for the old men of the council. He brought his voice back to its normal deep timbre.

"Tell the council that if one of them has a problem with my spending, he should come to me and we will discuss it."

"Yes, Your Grace."

Agostino dismissed the boy with a wave of his hand. "You may go now."

The messenger fled the room.

Agostino leaned over, placed his hands on the desk, and looked each minister in the eye. "Gentlemen. Is there any more business?"

Six heads shook in unison.

"Good day, then." He turned to his right. "Toma, stay."

Agostino waited until the door closed before speaking to his chief counsel, Toma Sandeo. "How did I become so impotent, my friend?" Agostino took off his red silk hat, dropped it on the desk, and sat back down at the desk. Out of habit, he smoothed his full, white beard as he leaned back in his chair.

"Toma, you were with me when I was commissioner of the army at Ferrara. I made decisions that mattered. And later as procurator, when my brother was *doge*, the powerful valued my opinions. But now I am a puppet of the council. Why did I seek this position?"

Toma nodded, his thin face locked in a contemplative frown. "I think you exaggerate. You have more influence than you admit. You do much good here."

"Perhaps, but I see things happening to us I do not like. The French and Germans grow quarrelsome, and we ignore their threat, fat with our past successes." Agostino pointed at the piece of cloth on the desk. "Venice is becoming as empty as this hat."

"Agostino," Toma said. "We seem to fight somewhere every day. We have fought for hundreds of years, and no one has conquered us."

"Yes, and look at our army." Agostino thrust his hands in the air. "What do you see? Mercenaries."

The difficulties of managing hired soldiers lay fresh in his memory, twenty-five years after the stalemate at Ferrara.

"How fiercely do you think they will fight for us when they meet real resistance? They know only kidnap and ransom and loot. They do not defend their homes or families." After a moment, "We have grown soft."

"I am not so sure." Toma sat down in a chair across from Agostino. "We handle the other states on the peninsula when we must, and our navy is the best in the world. Who can challenge us in our lagoon?"

"You can't see it either, can you?" Agostino said. *We have been through this before.*

"Toma, things aren't as they have always been. What happens when a motivated army from France or Hungary or, God forbid, Turkey comes in and cuts off our land routes? What will we eat? What can we produce on our islands? Salt and fish." He tapped a fist on the desk. "When we are forced to use our shipping capacities to bring in all of our food and supplies, our trade will suffer. We will exhaust the treasury. The city will not be lost in battle; we will give it up without a fight."

Toma held Agostino's gaze for a moment, and then dropped his eyes in deference. "Yes, I understand, but what can we do? The senate will not allocate funds for a permanent army now with no emergency hanging over their heads."

"Perhaps..." The doge peered into Toma's eyes and lowered his voice. "Perhaps we require an emergency."

Chapter Five

Michael laughed when Baldo turned north onto another road that sported two sets of ruts. *A superhighway.*

Baldo gave him a quizzical look. "What?"

Michael shook his head. "Nothing, I just had a funny thought."

Baldo shrugged and looked ahead.

As the day wore on, they met more traffic than Michael had seen in the last week, maybe two. On foot, horseback or donkey, cart or wagon, people carried personal possessions, bags and loads of grain south. Baldo waved and greeted a few people in passing, but kept his eye on home and away from the city Michael hoped would be the first stop on his way back to New York.

Late in the afternoon, they stopped under threatening skies. Baldo dragged out the big tarp and the eight square posts that dropped into slots around the wagon, the fifteenth century pop-up camper. Michael smiled the first time he saw it, but now he had to hurry. They tied it down just as large raindrops splattered off the canvas. When heavy rain beat against the temporary walls they shut the flaps from the inside. Enveloped in darkness, Michael listened to the roar and fury of the storm while Baldo rustled around. The sound reminded him of a summer afternoon when he was six.

* * * *

Michael looked up from his play on the floor of a lean-to shed tacked onto the old garage back of the house. The bright sunlight had been replaced with gloomy gray. Sweet smelling chilly air mixed with the warm breeze. He looked back at the toy truck making tire tracks in the sand when a thunderclap made his heart leap into a staccato march.

Before he could jump up, a torrent of rain assaulted his shelter. The racket drowned out the noise of the wind he could now see whipping the willow tree beside the back door of the house. Then a new sound, a few sharp raps on the tin roof, then more, and soon a solid wall of noise beat against him.

He shot to his feet. "Daddy," he shouted, but he couldn't hear himself.

Outside, little white pebbles hopped off the grass like popcorn. Leaves cut from the willow mixed with the white stuff starting to cover the yard.

A light from the house caught his attention. The back door opened and his father filled the frame. He waved and shouted something, but Michael could hear only the assault on his shed.

Michael yelled at the top of his lungs, "I'm coming, Daddy." He took a deep breath and launched himself out the doorway.

The rain flooded his eyes and made it impossible to keep his eyes on his dad. The little pebbles stung him all over, but he struggled to keep going. He caught his dad screaming something over the rain. "No, Mike...." Michael's foot hit a slick patch, and he went face down into a puddle.

Strong hands grabbed his arms and pulled him up. Something shielded him from the stings. In a moment, he was in the back door alongside his father, dripping water on the tile floor.

"Mike, I said wait there." His dad's eyes were filled with worry and concern.

"I couldn't hear you, Daddy," Michael sobbed. He buried his face in his father's chest. The thunder didn't seem so scary now.

Dad pulled him close and stroked his head. "It's okay," he said. "You're okay."

* * * *

Baldo moved something and shook Michael from his memory, but he continued to reflect on his situation.

I made sure that never happened again. Until he came to this place, he hadn't been out in a storm since high school. Other than running to or from a parked car, he hid from storms inside the safety of wood or steel. He had insulated himself. Kind of like the rest of his life.

Soon the rain eased into a shower, and he could open the front flaps for the meager light the gray clouds were willing to give up.

With no way to cook, supper consisted of cold ham and bread. Baldo hadn't said two words since before noon. Michael wondered if it was because of his determination to leave, or maybe Baldo thought he was ungrateful for the food and lodging he had received. *Whatever.* It wouldn't stop him from going to this city Baldo had talked about. He needed to start finding a way out of this mess.

Michael lay back on the bundle he called his pillow and listened. Rain drummed on the canvas and dripped into puddles forming underneath the wagon. In the morning, he stepped off into ankle-deep mud when he went to harness the horse, a routine he couldn't have imagined three months ago.

Mid-afternoon, he sighted a pair of men on a wagon like Baldo's. Baldo pointed as if to say, 'This is it,' but kept up the silent act. He reigned in when the two vehicles drew even.

"Wait here a minute." Baldo hopped down.

He and the other driver, a chubby, genial man of middle age, shook hands when they met between the wagons. The passenger, a skinny young man, remained seated but stared ahead at the road.

Michael listened to old friends laugh and talk about trade and weather and then strained to hear when their conversation grew serious and quiet. The stranger looked up at Michael, pursed his lips, and nodded.

Baldo turned and motioned for Michael to join them.

Michael jumped down and stepped over a puddle to stand before Baldo and the stranger.

Baldo nodded to the older man. "Michael, this is Papi. He's on his way to Caorle."

Papi looked up at Michael while they shook hands. "A tall one, aren't you?"

"Yes, sir."

"So you want to go to the city." Papi studied Michael's face. "Ever been there?"

"No sir, not this one. I've been to a few, though." Maybe this wasn't a good idea.

"Well, throw your things in the back, I guess." Papi cocked his head and pointed at Michael's sack. "You don't have much."

All his possessions fit in one little bag. "No, sir, not much."

"Well, climb in the back behind my boy, Gherardo, and we'll be going. I'm anxious to get there and back." Papi gave Baldo's hand one more shake; then he climbed up into the wagon seat.

Michael shook Baldo's hand. "Thank you, my friend. You saved my life."

Baldo sighed. "God keep you safe, Michael. I hope you find what you're looking for."

Michael hadn't thought much about God for a long time but nodded to Baldo and smiled. He climbed up and sat on a box behind the younger man and waved. The wagon lurched forward before Michael could change his mind. Baldo stood looking after them and grew smaller as they pulled away. Michael regretted deserting him after so many weeks together.

"Where are you from, Michael?" It was the first thing out of Papi's mouth.

He faced front. "England." He lied, of course, but if these people thought it was 1492, he would avoid giving them a place that didn't exist for them yet.

"England," Papi repeated. "Isn't that far away?"

"Yes, very far." Michael quickly changed the subject. "Uhm, I'm visiting here for the first time. Would you tell me about this city?"

Gherardo's shoulders drooped when Papi started to talk, and Michael soon understood why. He went on for hours, spinning tales his son must have had heard many times before. Michael gleaned what pertinent information he could from the volume of words and a sketchy picture of the city awaiting him began to emerge.

* * * *

Michael squirmed in his seat again. Three days of solid riding had worn the hide off his tail. He caught a glance of Gherardo asleep in the back. "Teenagers," Papi had said, or so Michael assumed from the context. The boy sulked when Papi made him give up his seat a couple of days ago and hadn't said a word since.

"So, you say the Turks overran the Greeks at Constantinople."

Papi nodded. "A sad time. The people were afraid they would come here and do the same. They still fear, sometimes."

Michael wished, not for the first time, he had paid more attention in history class, but he recognized the final stake in the heart of the Byzantine Empire. "And how long ago was this?"

Papi turned his eyes up to a line of puffy, white clouds over a farmhouse on the green hill ahead. "My father told me it happened when he was a boy. Maybe fifty years ago."

Michael couldn't remember exactly when the last remnant of Rome's dominance surrendered its grip on power, but the middle of the fifteenth century sounded right. He fell silent while he assimilated the bits of information Papi had given him.

They approached the city of Caorle, a minor port on the coast of a sea, the Adriatic, he remembered from the map, and part of a city-state style republic. The ruling city, *La Serenissima* or *Venezia*, a major trading center and maritime military power, sat at some distance to the southwest on the same coast. *Venezia* was built on a collection of islands in a protecting lagoon. Michael knew the city by the anglicized name of Venice.

Political intrigue and war sharpened relations with neighboring states. The republic had lost an ally in the Byzantine Empire. Yet, this *Serenissima* had 'overcome all obstacles,' according to Papi, and still held its position as a world leader in trade and war.

I've landed in a history book.

He had to find a way out.

42

* * * *

"We're here."

Michael woke from his nap and leaned against a sideboard. *Buildings.* They had arrived in the city while he slept. The mid-morning sun threw short shadows into the stone-paved streets.

Papi negotiated the wagon around pedestrians and carts, even some chickens a young boy chased out of a doorway. The narrow streets, lined by two and three-story buildings, reminded Michael of New York, only smaller and closer. The structures crowded against one another up to the edge of the narrow streets, and as he feared there were no utility poles.

What's that stink?

He glanced back to see a wagon wheel had picked up a glob of waste, human or otherwise; he couldn't tell.

I hope this isn't as good as it gets.

Overhead, a baby's angry cry cut through the street noise. Michael picked out different sounds: a couple fighting; an old man laughing at an unheard joke; a bird's plaintive screech. Perched on a sign advertising some business establishment, a gull pleaded for a handout.

Michael noticed something about the people wandering about. He studied Papi's outfit and compared it to local fashions. Though still antiquated, clothing here sported a different, finer cut, like work jeans compared to business slacks.

Men gave up their work shirt and pants in favor of form-fitting stockings and a longer blouse or tunic that might even be tied at the waist to form a short skirt. The few women on the street wore long, full-figured gowns instead of the utilitarian dress favored in the hinterlands.

The country boys bounced on through the city.

Michael filled his lungs with salty air when Papi reined the horse around a corner. At the end of the street, Michael spied the blue of the sea, a couple of hundred yards away.

Papi started a sharp U-turn in the intersection and pointed at a building on the corner. In contrast to the taller structures they had passed, the single-story white plaster building with broad double doors on the side featured function over form. He pulled over in front of the building and stopped.

Michael followed Papi's example and hopped down onto neatly fitted cobblestones. An odd odor emanated from the open shutters on the building, like an old market he once visited. Papi came around the rear of the wagon as Gherardo jumped out of the back.

"Well, Michael we're here. I hope your travels are successful. Come on, Gherardo, let's see what Rizzo has for us this time."

In this busy little town, Michael felt more out of place than in the field where he awoke. "Papi, wait. I need some help finding my way around."

The trader frowned. "Come on. Maybe someone here can help you." He turned and stomped up the steps, followed by the sullen Gherhardo.

Michael followed them up under the shade of the covered porch and in through the front door. The sources of the jumbled tangle of smells became obvious. A wide variety of goods sat on shelves and tables and in stacks on the floor the men walked through and around. Michael recognized bolts of cloth and folded leather in one area. In another, large bags of beans, grains, dried vegetables, and spices sat stacked on one another, open for inspection. Tools and implements adorned a wall at the far end. An open door on the back wall led to what looked like a storage area, piled high with more merchandise. Men in varying types of dress ambled around the store, shopping, Michael assumed.

Papi stood on tiptoe and looked over a display. "There's Rizzo." He made a zig-zag path toward his target.

They found the burly man with curling shoulder-length dark hair haggling with a customer. He gave his gray streaked wavy beard an occasional tug while he negotiated in a gravely voice. When he completed the transaction, Rizzo turned and showed a delighted face.

"Papi! It is good to see you, friend." He gave the trader a vigorous handshake.

"I'm sure it is after you robbed me the last time, you thief." Papi still grasped the hand. Michael couldn't tell if his face bore a grin or a grimace. "Do you have anything worth selling this time?"

"Oh, yes. Twice the value and half the cost, as usual." Rizzo looked at Papi's son and stepped forward to shake his hand. "Hello, Gherardo."

Rizzo stopped when he noticed Michael and looked up at him. "Hmm. This is a face I have not seen. A new assistant?" He laughed. "Papi, if he is a son-in-law, you will have tall grandsons."

Papi shook his head and turned back to Michael. "No, our old friend Baldo found him. He's looking for somewhere to stay. Do you know a place? He probably needs work, too."

Michael hadn't thought about a job. He realized he still thought he could call someone to the rescue. *Not likely.* He nodded. "Yes, sir."

"What can you do?" Rizzo's smile faded.

He looked around the store. "I can buy and sell things."

The amiable countenance vanished. "I do the buying and the selling here. I don't need help with that."

Michael thought on his feet, what else could he offer? Investment banker, corporate lawyer, deal-maker, IPO wizard. He couldn't see much demand for those skills. "I can keep books."

"He's Baldo's friend?" Rizzo asked Papi, who nodded. Rizzo chewed a thick lip and looked at Michael for a moment. "I tell you what. We'll see if you can keep the place clean. You sleep here and watch the place at night, and I'll keep the books."

Michael put a hand on the shelf beside him to steady himself. He had become a janitor.

Better than a poke in the eye, like his dad always said. He shook it off. "Yes, sir. Thank you." He didn't intend to stay a janitor forever.

Chapter Six

Ludovico

The servant filled their glasses again. "More, sir?"

Ludovico Sforza glanced at the empty bottle. No need opening a new one this late in the evening. The dinner guests had excused themselves and left him alone with Ercole d'Este. He didn't want the visit with his father-in-law to last long.

"No." Ludovico waited until the man backed through the door and closed it before he spoke again.

"Your daughter is magnificent, Ercole." The acting Duke of Milan turned his glass to watch its etchings scatter light from the fireplace through the red wine. Perhaps the title would become permanent soon.

"She is that," agreed the Duke of Ferrara. "Not many women her age are capable, or willing, to go to Venice to spy for you."

Ludovico smiled. His bride, all of seventeen, saw herself equal to any fine lady and hungered for recognition as a proper duchess. Venice didn't stand a chance.

"Beatrice is motivated."

Ercole nodded, then drew a breath. "Ludovico, you must do something about Gian Galeazzo. He is of age and holds the rightful claim on the duchy. He will trouble you while others listen to his story, and Ferdinand listens in Naples. The king complains that his granddaughter should be duchess by now."

Ludovico looked up from his wine to catch Ercole's impatient stare. This subject came up every time they talked of late. He would not stand by and see his daughter dispossessed.

"I know, but Gian Galeazzo is my dead brother's son, and I cannot have him killed. Confinement with his Isabella will have to do."

"Well." Ercole placed his empty glass on the table. "It is your business. You will live with the consequences. On another front,

Maximilian can aid in your legitimization. You would do well to seek the emperor's endorsement."

Ludovico kept his plans for Bianca, Gian Galleazo's sister, to himself. The widowed emperor needed a wife, and Ludovico's young niece had no husband. Ludovico drained the glass and set it down. "I will think about it."

Chapter Seven

Michael propped his hands on the broom and surveyed the warehouse. He had forgotten how gratifying physical work could be. The disorder after a long day of trading had become orderly rows and stacks of merchandise on clean floors. It reminded him of his custodial job in college, not glamorous work, but it paid the bills and got him through school. It beat begging, and it was more fruitful than his search for a way home.

The questions he had for traders and merchants who came through Rizzo's business failed to turn up anything useful. Most ignored him, dismissed him as a menial laborer who spoke a country dialect, not the language of commerce.

He worked on that problem when he could, and practiced the words and the accent from conversations around him. He had done the same years before when he tried to lose the southern drawl of his childhood home in North Carolina. He still tended to lapse into country bumpkinese on occasion, then and now.

What was that line from Sherlock Holmes? When you reject the impossible, what's left, however outrageous, must be the solution? *Something like that.* He wasn't dreaming, and he wouldn't accept being crazy. That left one thing: he had wound up in 1492 somehow, and he would just have to live with it until a better explanation came along.

Michael put up his cleaning tools and walked back to the front. Rizzo sat bent over a set of books in his cubbyhole office built into the corner of the back wall.

"All finished, sir. Do you need anything else?"

Rizzo didn't look up. "Hmm? Oh, no. Not now. That's good enough for today." He occupied himself with a column of numbers and twisted a strand of beard around his index finger, a nervous habit Michael had observed.

"Is everything all right?"

"Yes. No, there's a mistake somewhere."

He must be preoccupied if he gave me that much.

Michael peeked at the books once when alone in the office. Rizzo's attempts at accounting had turned them into a spaghetti mess.

"I don't mean to intrude, sir, but I could help you with that."

Rizzo turned from his papers, the scowl now focused on Michael. "How much could you know about this bookkeeping?"

"I trained under a master." *Actually a Ph. D.* "I can show you an easier way."

"An easier way? I speak with merchants from over the world. They all do it the same." He looked back down at the books and twirled more whiskers.

"Yes, sir." Michael knew when not to push. "It works for lots of people. Good night, sir." He left for his room in the back and grinned to himself.

Rizzo would give in sooner or later.

* * * *

"Michael, come in here." Rizzo sat at his desk with papers scattered about, just like they had been for the last several days.

Michael set down a sack of beans at the door. "Yes, sir?"

"You say you can't read, but you can change my bookkeeping system?" Rizzo growled, but he had the appearance of a man forced to admit defeat.

An opportunity. "I would need help spelling account names and things like that. But numbers are the same in any language."

Rizzo narrowed his eyebrows. "How do I know that I can trust you to see this information?"

Michael's raised hands indicated his lack of power. "I'm kind of at your mercy."

"Hmm," Rizzo grunted. He paused for a moment. "All right. Tell me about this new way of keeping records."

Good. Finally, something Michael knew about. He took the liberty and scooted a chair up to the desk.

"The thing about this double-entry bookkeeping is that you always can see how your business is doing. All you have to do is add up the numbers. When you post a transaction, you make at least two entries. For example, if you spend some money you'll deduct that amount from your cash account. But there is a reason you took out the cash, so you make an offsetting entry somewhere. Maybe you bought some goods to resell, so you add the amount to the account called 'inventory.' Or, maybe you pay an employee and add that to the expense account. The system keeps itself in balance. Does this make sense so far?"

Rizzo stared at Michael for a moment and then looked down at his books before raising his eyes again. "What?"

Michael bowed his head in a chagrined apology. "I'm sorry. I started you off in the middle. It's really not that hard, but it needs an introduction. Do you mind if I begin again with the basics?"

"I guess."

Michael spent the next couple of hours guiding Rizzo through the highlights of introductory bookkeeping. At first, Rizzo sat and fidgeted and sometimes nodded as if saying he already knew one thing or another, but by the end, he asked questions and repeated the concepts. Michael found a new appreciation for his boss.

"...so we deduct the *cost* of the spice, say two ducats, from the asset account called 'Spice Inventory' and add the same amount to an expense account called 'Cost of Goods Sold.' The difference between the changes in 'Spice Income' and 'Cost of Goods Sold' is two ducats, your profit.

"If you follow this system, you always can tell how much money you have, how much you owe, and how much profit you've made." That was about enough for a while.

Rizzo stared at his old books. "Are you sure it works?"

Michael nodded and flashed him a confident smile. "Yes sir, it works."

"Hmm. See what you can do with it, then." Rizzo rose from his chair and shifted the responsibility. "We will run both systems for some time, though."

"That's a smart thing to do." Michael looked toward the back door. "I should get to the back and sort the new shipment."

"No." Rizzo pointed to the mess on the table. "I'll get it done. This is your job now. If you do it right, we'll speak about raising your wages."

"Very good, sir." Michael nodded. "Thank you."

Rizzo sighed. "I guess we'll need someone to handle the inventory. If anyone comes in, tell them I'll be right back."

When Rizzo left, Michael moved to Rizzo's chair and spread his arms on the desk.

Step one.

He sighed with relief, free of the physical work, at the prospect of earning more money. Perhaps he could buy some clothes that fit. *Maybe even get a room with a real bed.*

Chapter Eight

Girolamo

Girolamo Savonarola placed his pen in the ink jar and looked up from his sermon notes to the shuttered window on the right. The storm that raged outside mirrored the one in his soul. In each of the other cells, from novices up, a scene from the life of Jesus applied in fresco by Fra Angelico gave the resident a subject on which to focus. But not in this cell. Perhaps they thought the monastery's prior had no need of reflection.

God had rescued him from depravity in the house of Ercole d'Este, where his physician grandfather served until he died. God blessed Girolamo with the call to preach, to rid the people and church of their corruption. And then God cursed him with the burden of administration.

Everyone in this monastery of San Marco had looked to him since he arrived in Florence from Assisi. Of course, some sought his leadership while others watched for any weakness that might disqualify him from the post.

His first months here were smooth enough. Lorenzo de' Medici, himself, put forth Girolamo's name for consideration as prior when the previous occupant of the office died. Why, he would never understand. Lorenzo proved himself as corrupt as any of the rest. When Girolamo preached against the decadence in Florence, the Medici family and their allies began to denounce and plot.

At least Lorenzo wrestled with his conscience. He had called Girolamo to his bedside only last night as he thrashed about and sweated from the fever. Now Florence worried about its commerce and its safety over the impending loss of Lorenzo and his stabilizing influence on the community.

More than at any other time since his arrival, Girolamo felt the need to teach, to guide the people at this time of opportunity.

The duties of running the monastery pressed on his time. What would Jesus have him do?

A knock on the door broke his contemplation. *What do they want now?*

"Come."

The rosy face of Girolamo's friend, Fra Domenico da Pescia, peered in the open door. Domenico caught a deep breath and then blurted, "Just as you prophesied. Lorenzo is dead."

For the first time, Girolamo appreciated the awe in his friend's voice.

It is a short distance from respect to cult.

"No, Domenico, not my prophesy, but God's."

"Yes, of course," the friar conceded. "Perhaps the unbelievers will believe now."

"Much more must happen before they accept the truth, I am afraid. The man who wears the tiara must also die, and Italy must be humiliated by foreigners before the people will turn from their evil deeds."

Domenico's mouth dropped open. "The Pope? Now His Holiness will die?"

Holiness. Had Giovanni Cybo, the man who took the name Innocent VIII, kept the office holy? The one who maintained his wicked sons and daughters with him at the throne of Peter? Girolamo still marveled that men gave respect to those who plundered the church and extorted the masses.

"God will judge and pass his sentence." Girolamo retrieved his pen and went back to work until Domenico took the hint and slipped out. The wind howled its mournful song. Someone had come for poor, dead Lorenzo's soul. He hoped it was God.

Chapter Nine

Agostino

Agostino pushed his chair back from his desk and rose when Toma brought the ambassador into the chamber. "Zohane, thank you for coming." He navigated around the desk and semicircle of chairs to greet him.

Zohane da Parma smiled and clasped the doge in a firm embrace. "Agostino. It has been too long." He stepped back and looked at his friend with mischievous eyes. "You look well for someone of your advanced age."

Agostino found his lowest, gruffest voice. "I am five months younger than you, old man." The doge and his emissary burst out in a shared laugh. Agostino motioned Zohane to sit and pulled a chair around to face him. "How is your family?"

"All is well, I think. My grandson is beginning to tend the business."

Agostino shook his head. "Already! What happened to the time?"

"I don't know, my friend, and I have four great-grandchildren now. Since Besina died, the little ones console me when I get to see them. I have been away in France for months." Zohane stopped short. "Well, you know that. And your family?"

The losses flashed across Agostino's memory: his brothers, his wife, his only son. "My daughters and their families are fine, thank you. Time has a way of taking from a person, but in all, I have no complaints."

Zohane nodded in understanding. "What is so urgent that you have called me back from Paris?"

"I have a mission for you. I want you to go back to France and suggest to Charles that we will not oppose his claim on Naples."

Zohane studied Agostino's face for a moment before responding. "Does the senate approve of this? Does the council?"

"No, they know nothing of it, and they must not. But this is key to our survival and prosperity. Charles has a standing army waiting for something to do and growing impatient. I do not want him tempted to come here. Besides, this action would distract our enemies on the west of the peninsula."

All congeniality disappeared from Zohane's clouded face. "My friend, this is a dangerous game you play. The council will not tolerate your interference in these affairs. This could have serious consequences for you and your family. And mine, by the way."

"Then they must not find out." Agostino emphasized the statement with an unwavering gaze. He watched Zohane wrestle with the ramifications and then went on. "Charles will have little trouble taking Naples, but he will find it difficult to keep. He will have a long supply chain to protect, and we will be happy to rescue the western lands when we are asked, for a price."

"And what will be the price?" Zohane's mouth pursed in an expression that Agostino knew meant anger.

"What we've always wanted, Northern Italy, Milan, and Ferrara. It gives us land routes we need and a buffer from incursions from the west so we can concentrate on the Turks to the east." Agostino paused. "And we can repay the infidels for killing your brother in Otranto."

The diplomat eyed him for a long moment. He shifted in his chair. "I don't understand what you get from this plan, Agostino. You already have everything you can want." Zohane sighed. "Why not enjoy the rest of your life without starting this conflict?"

Agostino leaned forward in his chair and tapped his finger on the arm. "Those great-grandchildren you mentioned? I want mine to enjoy the safety and wealth they have a right to expect. I will not be dissuaded on this."

"What about the *Notaio Ducale*? Toma, do you agree with this scheme?" Zohane turned to look at him.

Agostino had almost forgotten he was there.

Toma straightened and cleared his throat. "I admit to some reservations, but I must agree with my doge. We are at risk if we fail to take action."

Zohane closed his eyes and ran a hand through his hair, then fixed his gaze on Agostino. "I fear for my family if the council discovers my complicity. They have taken heads from more than one 'enemy' in this building. I prefer to keep mine."

"I understand your concern." Agostino leaned back again. "But there is no need for them to discover any of this. In fact, there will be little to discover. When you have an audience with the king, you can merely equivocate on the subject of his rights to the kingdom at Naples. He will do the rest. His keepers will see to it."

"You lay a burden on my heart, Agostino. I pray that the outcome is what you intend. I should go now and see my family before I return to Paris." Zohane waited for permission to rise.

"Of course." The doge smiled for his ambassador. "Give them my regards."

Toma gazed at the closed door for a moment after Zohane left. "Can he be trusted?"

"Yes." Zohane was an old friend, and the success of his family business owed much to Agostino's assistance over the years. Agostino trusted him. "But have him watched anyway."

Chapter Ten

Michael struggled with the quill pen. He wished for the hundredth time for a decent ballpoint. The thing didn't even look like a quill, at least not the long, feathery plume he thought of, but a thin, sharpened stick.

The instrument's business end, though, impressed him. Instead of simply cutting the feather off at an angle as Michael assumed, one carved it into a divided point much like the tip of the old fountain pen he had found in a box of things left by his father, but unlike the steel pen, this one frequently wore down into a rounded mess. While he learned to manage the knife used to sharpen it, Michael cut himself a couple of times. Once, in evil humor, he thought he could at least write the credits in blood red.

Rizzo grumbled, too. How could anyone know about bookkeeping and not be able to use a pen? Michael made excuses and fumbled through. He wrote out the chart of accounts, beginning in a crude handwriting and improved as he went.

The ledgers were almost finished. He would soon start on a financial statement, but the transactions had piled up. He chafed at the need to enter them before he could start on the good stuff.

Rizzo interrupted Michael's work. "Where do you come from, again?"

Michael had readied a story. "I'm from a small town in northern England. My father died when I was young and my mother apprenticed me to a local merchant. I learned to keep books from him." At least they spoke English there. Maybe he could actually understand parts of it if he ran into someone from the area. Shakespeare had been difficult.

"England is a long way from here. A journey of a month or two around the Great Sea at best." Rizzo pointed at Michael's clothes. "Book a cabin in the captain's quarters, did you?"

Michael smiled and nodded his understanding. "I kind of had to leave. My employer died and left a son who didn't like me. He went to the authorities and charged me with theft. I panicked and stole aboard the first ship I found unguarded. I hoped to land again in England and sneak off, but the ship's master found me and clapped a chain around my leg and made me work. I finally escaped here and wandered around until Baldo found me. I'm grateful to you for giving me this chance." Michael hoped Rizzo would overlook the many holes in his tale.

Rizzo looked at Michael with doubt on his face, but only asked, "'Patriate.' What kind of family name is that?"

"It's French. Something about 'homeland.' I'm not sure about the full meaning."

"Hmm." Rizzo seemed content to let the conversation end.

"Sir, if it's all right with you, may I leave early this afternoon? I'd like to buy a coat before the shops close." Winter crept closer and Michael was in need of warmer clothing.

"I suppose. Come in early tomorrow morning." Rizzo turned to meet a customer.

"Thank you, sir." Michael cleaned his pen, put up the books, and went to his room. He pulled his watch from its hiding place under his shirt and checked the time. He could still make it.

The city had grown on Michael. On Sundays, he liked to walk along the beach, past the tied-up fishing boats then turn back toward town and explore the grounds of the church, centuries old even now, where the bell tower stood its solitary watch. Michael found it moving when he heard the bell peal its call to the faithful. But this time he concentrated on his mission.

He located the little store where he had seen a coat he wanted. The thought of spending most of his savings on one piece of clothing made him hesitate, but the temperature pushed him in the door.

"May I help you?"

The proprietor gave Michael a sideways inspection ending on his shoes, the same shoes the farmer had left for him in that little shed, and went back to sorting buttons.

"This coat. How much is it?"

The shopkeeper didn't look up this time. "Thirty *denari.*"

"Thirty! Four more than two weeks ago? That's robbery."

"It's colder now than two weeks ago." He continued his work. "Do you want the coat?"

The coat would only get more expensive if he waited, but if he bought it today there would be just enough left to buy food for the next week. He had to show Rizzo some results so he could ask for that raise. "Yes, I want the coat."

At last, the man put down his buttons.

Michael counted out the coins. "Could you tell me where I might rent a room, cheap?" He might as well scout for a place to live.

"The Red Lion, if you don't mind doing business with a woman. Her husband died and she needs the money." The shopkeeper gave him directions and greeted another customer.

Michael picked up the coat, a long cloak in a style he had seen merchants wearing, and threw it around his shoulders. He welcomed its weight for protection against the wind. As he made more money, he would upgrade his wardrobe, maybe even get the cute little tri-cornered hat and pointy shoes.

When in Serenissima...

Michael rolled it across his thoughts. *La Serenissima Repubblica di Venezia*, The Most Serene Republic of Venice. The name could almost be The Beautiful Woman of Venice, which reminded him. He had to go see a widow about a room.

He turned left out into the street as the sun began to set and looked for the hostel the merchant had described. A few minutes later Michael came to the sign featuring a faded red lion head in profile, and opened the door under it.

He stepped inside and waited for his eyes to adjust to the light thrown by the oil-lamp and fireplace. It reminded Michael of his great aunt's living room. His army colonel great-grandfather had been stationed somewhere in northern Italy after the war and brought back boxes and trunks of antiques, knick-knacks, and art along with an enormous set of ancient furniture that sat in a den nobody ever used. As old as Aunt Rachel's stuff looked, it might have been this very set of furniture.

Michael ran his hand along the tooled leather back of a sturdy armchair. How long would it take a craftsman to make something like this? More than likely, several artisans contributed to its construction and embellishment. No wonder it looked built to last. They couldn't afford to replace them very often.

Someone had set up the large room to accommodate groups and individuals. A couple of arrangements of chairs surrounding a short table dominated the center of the room, but individual chairs sat around against the beige painted plaster walls. A small desk isolated in the back corner under the staircase kept a silent vigil.

Up the far wall and to the left ran the staircase that led to a dark hall. The banister intersected the ceiling, which was cut back for access to the upper floor. So the rooms were overhead, he surmised.

Through a door to the right of the staircase, Michael could make out a couple rows of chairs and tables in the dim light. The spicy aroma from the kitchen area started a rumble in his belly.

A female voice drifted from upstairs. "Just a moment." A door closed.

The movement caught Michael's eye. He spotted a black shoe and hem of a dress on the landing behind the banister. A woman of perhaps thirty made her way down the stairs. Michael watched her take every step. The modest black dress couldn't hide a full form that drew Michael's gaze, but his attention focused on her bearing.

Her long, raven hair blended into the dress to form a...a shroud, almost. The pale skin of her partially obscured face and the hand on the rail appeared ghostly in contrast to the darkness of her hair and clothing. She took each jarring, flatfooted step with an air of resignation. This woman had been attractive. No, she still was attractive, only sad.

In mourning.

The air of melancholy reminded him of his mom until she brushed the jet-black hair from her face and spoke. "Hello. May I help you?"

Michael marveled at her large brown eyes, only a shade removed from the color of mahogany, set in the tired beauty of her face. Her question penetrated his distraction, and he abandoned his contemplation of her attributes. "Yes, I hope so. Do you have rooms available for rent? And at what price?"

She responded with a joyless laugh. "Yes, we have rooms. Unfortunately, we have a selection. What do you need?"

"I can't require much now, I'm afraid, but I hope to be in a better financial situation soon." He liked this woman for some reason. She reminded him of someone.

She crossed her arms like she needed a barrier between them. "You're a foreigner. I don't recognize your accent. Will you be here long?"

Michael thought about that for a moment. "I don't know. I don't have any plans to leave right now." Or anywhere to go.

She continued to probe. "Are you employed here?"

Checking references.

"Yes, I work for Rizzo Bernardigio. I'm his bookkeeper."

She winced and nodded. "I know of him. He and my husband were acquainted."

Michael waited anxiously while she considered his credentials.

A log popped in the fireplace. The lady in black looked over her right shoulder and turned to walk back toward the fire. Michael stared at her shapely outline for a moment and then averted his eyes.

She pulled a poker out of a bucket and adjusted the stack of burning wood. "Name?"

"Michael Xavier Patriate."

Michael's grandmother, a fan of the musician Xavier Cugat, had insisted on the name, and his father saw the humor and went along. Had his dad been prescient? Michael X. Patriate had become Michael, *expatriate*.

"But please, just call me Michael."

She trudged back and stood close enough for him to reach out and touch her.

"Well, Michael, ten *denari* per week or forty per month, in advance. Let me know when your situation improves." She moved toward the kitchen in dismissal.

"I will. Thank you."

Michael closed the door behind him and hurried to get back to the warehouse before dark. Halfway there, he realized he hadn't asked her name.

Chapter Eleven

Girolamo

"Fra Savonarola?"

Girolamo looked up from the list of purchase requests on his desk to see a familiar figure at the door to his cell. "Domenico, why do you do that?"

His friend's eyes widened. "Do what?"

"You can call me by my first name."

"Oh." He held onto the doorway and leaned inside. "The brothers," he whispered. "I think it is more respectful when they are present."

Girolamo sighed and nodded. "You are right, Domenico. What is it?"

Domenico straightened and stepped into the room. "Laro Valori is here asking to see you. Shall I send him away?"

"What does he want?"

Domenico shrugged. "He wouldn't say. He only demanded to see you." He frowned. "Quite rudely, too."

Girolamo put a hand to his mouth in thought. He had expected a visit from Piero de' Medici, Lorenzo's idiot son. So the arrogant dandy couldn't be bothered to come in person. At least Lorenzo had made the trip to the monastery himself, if only to be ignored. "Send him in."

Domenico disappeared. "This way," Girolamo heard him say.

The smirk riding on the face of Piero's representative, henchman if the truth be told, befitted someone of Laro's imagined importance. Girolamo kept his seat and folded his hands on the orderly desk.

"Fra Savonarola." Laro nodded his head in greeting, barely.

"How may I help you?" Girolamo asked, but he made no attempt to appear helpful.

Irritation painted itself across Laro's countenance in a frown and a clenched fist. "You don't ask me to sit?"

Girolamo pointed to a chair. "Sit, if you wish."

Laro paused for a moment. A muscle in his jaw twitched. "I will stand."

"Very well, then. You have business to discuss?"

"Yes." Laro stuck out his weak chin. "The Advent sermon was too much."

Girolamo kept his expression neutral. "I see. What did you not like about it?"

"No, not I. Ser de' Medici. He did not like it. Your words of the 'sword of God' about to fall and cut him off, sin, and punishment, and pestilence."

Their eyes are blind, and their ears are deaf to the truth.

"So." Girolamo retrieved his pen from the ink well. "He does not respect the prophecies that foretold the death of his father and of the Pope? Does he not fear God?"

Laro wagged his head. "He fears God, but your message only irritates him. It's depressing and bad for business. He doesn't like your words, and..." He punctuated his words with a pointed finger. "He does not like you."

Girolamo had neither time nor inclination for adversarial banter. "Tell Piero that he flatters himself. The warning is not for him; he is insignificant and will be undone by his own hand. God will not need to cast a stroke in his direction. Good day." He looked back down at his work.

Laro opened his mouth to speak, and instead whirled and stomped out of the room. Girolamo raised his head to watch him go and realized he had pushed too far. Piero would make sure he left Florence soon, one way or another.

Chapter Twelve

Michael rubbed his aching forehead. Accounting hadn't proved quite as easy as he hoped. Because of dual monetary systems, business operated on both gold and silver standards that were loosely related to one another.

Gold served as the basis for commerce in the west, silver in the east. Venice, more or less in the middle, used both types of coin. Silver was for everyday transactions, like wages or overland transportation costs and sales to individuals, and gold for commercial sales. They traded in gold *ducats* and *soldi* and paid expenses in silver *lire* and *denari*.

He remembered reading about this in school, but didn't pay much attention then, since it didn't apply anymore. *It applies now, doesn't it?* At least Venice's system was a world standard. He didn't have to start out with multiple sets of coinage.

Rizzo poked his head in the door. "How's your work going?" He had shown less patience lately.

"Good. Um, well. It's going well. There's work to do yet, but I have a picture of the state of your business. I'll show you if you like."

Rizzo walked in and leaned over Michael's shoulder. "Tell me about profit."

"Yes." Michael began with the good news. "These numbers are for the prior twelve months. Gross profit, the difference between your sales income and cost of goods, returns, damage and so on, is good at forty percent. You drive a hard bargain."

"Go on." Rizzo wasn't immune to flattery, only resistant.

"The operational figures are different. Shipping expense, direct labor costs, overhead, those things are on the high side. They bring the operational profit down to two percent."

"Hmm. Two percent." Rizzo rose up and crossed his arms. "I could put my money in the bank and earn almost that much in interest, and I wouldn't have to work."

"Yes, that's true, although part of the expense is the salary you pay yourself to manage the business. But, the results here will give you an idea of the areas where you can make improvements to make your overall profit bigger." Michael waited to let his employer digest this. "At the end are general and administrative costs of about one-half percent." That included Michael's salary, an amount he hoped to increase.

"Hmm. One and one-half percent profit. Michael, I would not have been able to see this until I spent myself out of business. Make a report on those operating costs. They will have to come down." Rizzo seemed pleased to have something to attack.

"Yes, sir." Michael decided the time was right. "Sir, when I started this work you said you'd think about raising my salary when it started showing results. I'd like to move out of this warehouse and…" He looked down at his garb. "Get some better clothes."

An indulgent smile worked its way across Rizzo's face. "I'll take care of you. Let me consider what this is worth. In the meantime, that report."

"Thank you, sir. I'll have it for you soon." Michael breathed easier when Rizzo left him to his work. He was still lost in this backward place, but he had his feet under him again.

* * * *

The mild December weather and a little money in his pouch put a bounce in Michael's step. Rizzo made good on his promise. Although Michael wouldn't get rich on his new salary, life would be easier. He left when the shop closed to take care of some business.

He recalled something a roommate told him years before when they were both broke. On Friday, his friend cashed a paycheck for a week's worth of washing cars and carried the money around until Monday, even though it was destined to pay bills.

"You know," he told Michael. "There's something about having a hundred dollars in your pocket that just makes you feel better."

Yes there is.

The sun had already hidden behind the buildings when the hostel sign came into view. Michael admitted some excitement as he opened the door. The owner sat at her desk under the staircase. Dressed in black again, something about her looked different. She had pulled her hair away from her face.

"You return," said the woman. She laid her hands on the desk and looked at Michael with eyebrows raised.

Michael couldn't decide if she was she glad to see him or merely surprised. At least she looked alive this time.

He closed the door behind him and took off his cloak and folded it across his arm and then wished he had left it on. He realized, too late, that he still wore the ill-fitting clothes Baldo had given him, the rags that left his ankles and wrists exposed.

"Yes, I return." Michael smiled and gestured upstairs. "I want to rent that room."

"So you have money today."

She made fun of him now. *What's her deal?*

He nodded affirmation. "Yes, it seems my fortunes have improved."

She turned her head until she eyed him from an oblique, skeptical angle. "I asked *Signor* Bernardigio about your character. He couldn't provide much information. Are you a dangerous fugitive?"

Michael shook his head. "No one will be breaking down your door looking for me. I'm a quiet man. You'll hardly know I'm here."

She pushed back her chair and stood, disbelief flashing in her eyes. "I doubt that. Come on, I'll show you to your room." She removed a lighted lamp from the wall behind her.

He followed her up the stairs. To the left and right, the hall ran the length of the building. A window to the right let in the last of the sunlight. His guide turned left.

Another hall, halfway down and left again, separated two blocks of rooms. She produced a key and inserted it into the first door on the right.

"You might as well have a window." She opened the door to a small room, just large enough for a bed, a chair, fireplace in the corner, and a few furnishings. Lamplight shadows on the walls skulked away from her as she entered. Michael followed, aware of the odd feeling of being alone with this lovely, sad, matter-of-fact woman.

She went on. "There is a chest where you can put your clothing, and on the table is a lamp. It's full of oil now, but when that's gone you'll need to supply your own. The window opens onto the square. You can draw water from the well out there."

Michael walked past her to the window and a reflected movement from behind him caught his eye. The combination of a darkening sky and light from her lamp had turned the window into a passable mirror. He turned to face her, but she fixed her gaze on the patterned quilt covering the canopy bed.

"Dinner and supper are provided. You are on your own for anything else. I lock the front door at ten." She faced him again with something in her eyes that hinted at mischief. "I am irritable if you wake me up. Any questions?"

He grinned for the first time in a while. "No, I think get the idea. May I pay you weekly for now and monthly when I can?" He had received a nice raise, but a week's worth of pay hadn't raised him from poverty just yet.

"Either way." She made a move toward the door, but clearly waited on payment. "I have a supper to finish. Do you need anything else?"

"No, not now." Michael took ten *denari* from his purse and handed them to his new landlady. "I never asked your name."

She straightened. "Oh? I'm sorry. It's Cecile. Cecile de Piro."

"Thank you, Cecile." He began to feel a little bit more normal with the exchange of names.

She bowed her head. "You are welcome, Michael. I'll see you downstairs at supper."

"I'll be there." Michael watched her walk to the door. "Oh, Cecile."

She turned about with a question on her pretty face, not drop dead gorgeous like Sheila, but... "Yes?"

Michael drew the moment out just a little. "Could I ask you to light this lamp?"

Cecile smiled. "Of course. I shouldn't leave you in the dark."

He picked up his lamp and angled it to catch the flame from Cecile's. How long had it been since he had been this close to a woman not wearing a conservative business suit and presenting an executive summary?

Too soon, the wick caught. She gave him another quick smile and headed for the door.

"Thanks," he said.

Cecile turned at the door and gave him an amused half-smile. "You're welcome." Then she disappeared, leaving behind only the sound of her delicate footsteps along the hall and down the stairs.

Michael stared out the empty doorway and sighed. Staying here might not be so easy.

He started around the bed and kicked something under it that clanked. He peeked under the bed and recognized a chamber pot. He shoved it farther under the bed.

When he stood, a reflection in the window again attracted his attention, but instead of a beautiful woman, a scruffy vagabond held the flickering lamp. He had trimmed the beard and hair the best he could, but the guy in the window couldn't be only thirty-four. No wonder Cecile had given him a hard time.

He pulled out his purse and counted his meager stash again. Tomorrow, he would find a barber. Better clothing would have to wait until next week. First, he needed a shave and a haircut.

Chapter Thirteen

Luca

Luca resisted the urge to fidget, sitting in the small anteroom. He was in the middle of illustrating a problem when the call came. What had he done to be summoned like this?

The old secretary, here before anyone else could remember, broke the silence with his customary cheerful voice. "Fra Pacioli, you may enter now."

"Thank you." Luca rose and strode into the cozy office of Petrus de Clericis, *commissaris* of the monastery in Sansepolcro.

"Good morning, Luca." Petrus stood behind his desk.

Luca nodded a greeting. "Fra Petrus. I hope you are well today."

"It is a good day to serve the Lord. Please, sit." He motioned Luca to a pair of hard-backed chairs by a window open to an unusually warm February afternoon.

Luca watched the prior squeeze into the chair. He liked food a bit more than Luca found suitable for someone who had renounced worldly pleasures, but on the whole had proved himself a capable administrator.

Petrus folded his hands in his lap and stared at them for a moment before he began. "Luca, I want to ask something of you."

"I am at your service, as always."

"The Lenten sermons. I want you to give them this year."

"Me? The outcast?" Luca shook his head. They had banned him from teaching, disgraced him. "Please do not mock me, Petrus."

Petrus held up his hands in a conciliatory gesture. "I would not mock you Luca. I respect you too much."

"What, then?"

"I want to bring us together and show some of the thick-headed among us my support for you." Petrus crossed his arms across his generous girth. "You have not been well treated here, I know, but you must understand the insidious nature of jealousy. You leave this town a young man and return as a famous teacher and favored by the pope." He tilted his head forward. "Many here believe you think yourself above them."

That again. Luca pointed upward. "My work is dedicated to serving God and man."

"Many wonder how numbers can serve God." Petrus shifted in his seat. "I say this only to tell you the things I hear."

Luca gazed out the window. They would never understand.

"Numbers do not serve God, they serve man, and man serves God." Luca turned back to Petrus. "He created mathematics to benefit us in our service to Him. And yes, I have heard the arguments, but what good does a man do when he only sits and studies upon logic and philosophy and never does anything to help his fellow travelers?"

Petrus nodded. "You do not need to convince me."

Luca regretted the outburst. He bowed his head. "I am sorry if I give offense, it was not my intent. And thank you for the opportunity."

"None taken, and you are welcome."

Luca changed the subject. "I wish to let you know in advance. I will be taking a leave, early next year."

"Oh? For what purpose?" Petrus wore a concerned frown.

Luca held up a hand. "No, it is not because of any conflict here. I am in contact with a man in Venice who will publish the work I have been compiling."

The frown changed to a smile. "Congratulations. So, your ceaseless studies bear fruit. What will you name this book?"

Luca hesitated. He had never said the name out loud. The utterance would make it real. *Why not?*

"*The Collected Knowledge of Arithmetic, Geometry, Proportions, and Proportionality.*"

Petrus raised his eyebrows. "I see. That is an ambitious title. Is the material as extensive as it sounds?"

"It is my life's work." Despite his efforts at self-control, Luca felt frustration and desire continue to animate his words. "I have seen students who want to learn struggle for lack of well-organized study material." He shook his head. "Few teachers themselves possess comprehensive understanding of these subjects. This will be my legacy."

Petrus studied Luca's face, and then drew an understanding breath. "There is passion in your voice that I have not heard before."

"Forgive me, friend." Luca lowered his gaze to the floor between them. "I do not intend to lay my frustration on you. I want only to give students and artists and businessmen access to this information all in one place and in a language they can understand, Italian, not Latin." Scholars could possess all the learning they wanted and still not have any effect on real-life problems.

"Well, good fortune in your endeavor, but back to the reason I called you here. What will your Lenten lessons cover?"

Luca forced a neutral expression. "The practicality of Jesus."

Petrus smiled. "Of course."

Chapter Fourteen

Michael hummed a tune on his way to work. Cecile had responded to his parting smile, and seemed in a good mood for a change. The past week or so, around her husband's birthday she finally admitted, she had been sad and remote. She could change in a flash anyway, pleasant in the morning and testy in the evening. Or vice-versa. He never knew which to expect. Women weren't that different here, but the feeling her smile gave this morning kept him warm against the cold March wind all the way to the warehouse.

He entered Rizzo's office to find his employer studying Michael's current project, a cost analysis. Rizzo tried to stay out of his way, but Michael knew he liked to keep an eye on his progress.

Rizzo looked up from the report. "What are these entries for deferred expenses?"

Michael had been annoyed at first when Rizzo questioned his methods, as if he distrusted Michael. He came to realize, though, that this was personal to Rizzo. Michael had always worked with someone else's money, but Rizzo risked his future in every transaction. Michael became more patient in the explanations, even if his employer never knew the difference.

"Do you remember the discussion about the 'matching concept' where income and expenses are recorded in the period when they are incurred, regardless of whether money actually changes hands at the time?" Rizzo nodded and Michael continued. "You do this, in part, so that you can properly calculate actual profit for the period."

"Yes, I remember." Rizzo furrowed his brow. "You told me then to go ahead and acknowledge that expense in one month, and now you want to put it off."

"Yes, sir." Michael lowered his head, acknowledging the apparent contradiction. "But these are different types of expenses. In the first example, you took delivery of shipping supplies —

boxes—on credit. Here we have a situation where you pay your rent annually, in advance. Do you want all the expense applied in the first month? Or should the expense be spread out through the other eleven months?"

Rizzo studied the papers a moment. "I suppose that monthly profit or loss figures would be more accurate if you broke it up in twelve pieces. It makes sense."

Michael allowed himself an inward smile; Rizzo had actually praised him.

"Michael, when you get the books straight, I want you to help me with these costs. We'll be negotiating with some of our suppliers. Do you have any bargaining experience?"

"Yes sir, some." Did a multi-billion dollar merger count? Yes, he had some bargaining experience.

"Good. Well, let me know when you're ready, and we will get started." Rizzo stood and turned to go.

"Yes sir. I should be caught up by tomorrow." He had a way to go, but he intended to get the accounting buttoned up before he left for the day.

* * * *

Michael opened the door to the hostel. His aching neck and shoulders and his empty belly fought for his attention, but he let out a satisfied sigh, glad to be home. Cecile sat in the common room, sewing on a piece of clothing, a blouse. *Something with color?*

"You missed supper. It was good." She continued to sew.

Michael nodded, then took his coat off and draped it over his arm. "I'm sorry to be so late. I start a new project tomorrow and had to get some work done before then." He put a hand on the back of his neck and worked his head around to relieve the tension.

"You're working your way up." Her hands rested in her lap now.

Michael got the distinct impression he had done something to upset her. "A little at a time. But tonight I'm tired. I believe I'll go on to bed."

Cecile picked up her sewing again and pulled a needle through the fabric. "All right. I kept back a roll in case you were hungry."

"Bless you. I might have starved to death before tomorrow." He grinned and patted the belly that had expanded with Cecile's cooking.

Cecile shook her head and gave him an exasperated grin. "We don't want that."

She stood and laid her sewing on the chair and then walked to the kitchen. With tired eyes, Michael watched her disappear into the dark room and reflected on his good luck.

Glad I didn't rent a room from the old one-legged man down the street.

Cecile came back with a piece of bread and a soft smile.

Michael accepted the roll. "Thank you. It's been a long day."

"You're welcome," she replied. "Now go to bed."

"Yes, ma'am." He grinned and started up the stairs, but stopped partway up and looked down to her.

"Thank you," he repeated. "Good night."

He finished the climb with a lighter step.

She had given him a sweet roll, with bits of dried fruit baked inside. He took a minute to stop and think while he ate.

He had adjusted to an impossible situation, found a way to support himself, and to live a decent life, slower and more relaxed. No running for days on coffee, cigarettes, and adrenaline, trying to beat the next guy out of a nickel.

And in the mix: Cecile. He remembered she reminded him of Annie, dark-haired and confident. They met in college, took some of the same classes, and studied together sometimes. She made it easy to be with her, didn't make demands on him or try to make him hers. Michael noticed one day that he hadn't seen Annie in a while and never found out where she went. School and work and ambition crowded everything else out. The same ambition called him again.

* * * *

Michael woke to the peal of the church bell and groaned. Another early day. He swung his feet onto the floor and felt in a dark drawer. He pulled out a clean *braies*, a piece of linen that sort of served as a pair of boxers, and slid his fingers across the coarse cloth. Funny how a simple pair of soft cotton briefs that didn't ride up or chafe could seem so luxurious and out of reach. He slipped on the *braies* and tied it around his waist.

After dressing, he practiced his ritual of shaving, flossed his teeth with a length of waxed thread and brushed with the hog-bristle toothbrush that had cost half a week's wages to have made. Few old people possessed a full set of teeth, and many suffered. Upon hearing descriptions about the state of dentistry, he resolved to avoid the need and sought out a brush maker.

And the guy had the nerve to market the thing as his own new invention. Michael would have been more upset if Cecile hadn't bought one too. His irritation stuck with him until he hit the bottom of the stairs and saw her.

Cecile busied herself with some other boarders, so he just nodded, smiled, and headed on to the warehouse.

He hummed a tune he couldn't quite identify while he walked. The cold snap had let up a bit, leaving the air cool and brisk. Spring was still some weeks away. The sun hinted at rejuvenation though, rising earlier and higher in the sky each day.

Rizzo had beaten him to work, as usual, and left the warehouse door unlocked. Michael doubted he had a life away from the business.

Kind of like I used to be.

"You've been busy." Rizzo again sat at the desk and leafed through the journal.

"We're caught up for the most part, I think." Michael reached into a drawer for his writing tools. "I'd like to sit in on your shipping contract discussion today, if you don't mind." He thought he caught a cue from Rizzo yesterday.

"All right." Rizzo retrieved a sheet of paper from the desk. "Here's the list of merchandise we've arranged to transport from Venice. Have you looked at our shipping costs yet?"

Michael took the list and scanned it while he talked. "Only from compiling the expense totals for you. But it looks like the price per ton for goods you ship rarely changes for trips from and to the same places, even when different shippers are used. Is there no real competition in this business?" He had puzzled over several of these types of costs.

Rizzo chuckled. "Yes, there is competition, but not in price. Transit times, damages, losses, these things we bargain over. Prices are generally set by the government."

Michael set the paper aside and opened his books to the previous night's stopping place. "But this kind of thinking bloats the expense structure. It makes the system inefficient." Government hardly ever made anything more efficient.

"Perhaps," Rizzo allowed. "But it gives us order and lets us plan better."

Order? For much of the twentieth century, government regulated both land and air freight, making shipping predictable and stable, but also expensive and unimaginative. When the regulations eased in the Reagan years, competition spurred both lower rates and innovation in shipping services, but it also introduced turbulence. Many inefficient companies went out of business. Michael considered how he could use this knowledge to advantage in his current situation.

They still used galleys in Venice's territories, even on long-distance shipping. The galleys, light and mobile in relative terms, worked fine for moving smaller shipments around the coast. They drew less water and could get into shallower ports, but they used manpower to row if the wind didn't cooperate. For hauling larger payloads and going longer distances, the bigger sailing ships like the oarless caravels he saw in port last week cost much less to run, if only because they required about half the crew. Competition would spur the inevitable changeover, anyway.

"Aren't there different seasons when these shippers are more or less busy?" Michael felt the rush of a deal brewing.

Rizzo paused and looked away. "Hmm. Some holidays are slower, and Carnival will start soon. And in advance of the trade fairs, shippers are busy, but they might have excess capacity afterward."

Michael spread out his papers. "I have an idea."

* * * *

Pantaleo de Vercelis walked into the warehouse front.

This is our boy. Michael recognized the weathered face.

"Good morning," Michael said. "Rizzo is in the back. I'll go and let him know you're here."

"No hurry." Pantaleo looked around the shop.

"He'll want to see you. I'll only be a moment."

Their guest browsed through bolts of cloth when Michael followed Rizzo back into the room.

"Pantaleo, my friend. How are you?" Rizzo hurried to shake his hand.

"Fine, Rizzo. And yourself?" Pantaleo released Rizzo's hand and crossed his arms, standing with legs spread wide as if still standing on his ship's deck.

"Good, good," Rizzo answered.

Michael noticed Rizzo start to reach for a whisker to twirl and then force his hands back down by his sides. *He doesn't like this.*

Pantaleo went directly to business. "Where will we be picking up your freight?"

"At Lendenara in Venice. Four tons, cloth and leather."

"All right, four tons at twenty-five *denari* per ton, plus ten *denari* port fees..." Pantaleo stared at something on the ceiling and muttered under his breath while he calculated. "Five *lire*, ten *denari* plus or minus, depending on actual weight. Good. When do you need it picked up?"

Rizzo ducked his head when he answered. "Pantaleo, I've been looking at a list of costs and found that shipping costs are close to the top. They must be reduced if I'm going to stay in business."

Pantaleo glared at Rizzo as he would a rebellious child. "You know shipping costs are fixed. We don't discount. We provide you with a good reliable service."

Rizzo nodded and put up a hand. "Yes, and we appreciate it, but we have a proposal." He pointed to Michael.

Michael cleared his throat. "Sir, I would like to put some ideas in front of you." He took Pantaleo's silence for permission to continue. "We know everyone has been busy getting ready for the holiday period, but during Carnival work slows, as does your freight business. Yes?"

Pantaleo answered, "Yes, so?"

"Your costs may be less while your ship is in port, but the expenses don't stop altogether. You incur fixed costs like loan payments or repairs even when the ship is docked."

Pantaleo nodded. Michael continued.

"What would it be worth to you to keep your operation running during the slower periods? Even at reduced rates, you could cover your fixed costs."

"But the rates are not negotiable."

Michael dipped his head to acknowledge the fact. "Of course not. We wouldn't want you to break the rules. But would you consider booking the goods at regular rates and then letting us ship some amount extra, maybe ten percent, at no charge?"

The seaman made no comment and Michael continued.

"Certainly, we wouldn't ask for these concessions during your busy periods, only those where you would experience longer periods of down time."

Pantaleo took a thoughtful breath. "I suppose we could come to some agreement if you're able to provide us with enough work to stay busy."

"Good," Michael said. "We've spoken with some of the other merchants. We're ready to designate you as our preferred shipper in return for your generous cooperation. With some planning on our part, you can look for more and steady shipments during the usual slow times. Obviously, your normal rates would apply the rest of the year, and we wouldn't advertise our agreement."

Pantaleo turned to Rizzo. "Where did you find this fellow? I thought he cleaned your warehouse."

Rizzo's face creased in a rare smile. "He has other talents."

After the shipper left, Rizzo complimented Michael. "You handled that well. Did you learn that from your old employer?"

"Yes, sir." Arnie had taught him a lot of things, among them, some things not to do. He went off to serve fifteen years and left his pampered wife living a humble existence.

Rizzo pointed at his manifest. "I guess you're aware this is only a small part of the cost we need to reduce."

Rizzo had hopes of enlarging his profit potential, and Michael intended to help. "I don't know how many items we can reduce this much, but there's room to cut an amount that you'll notice."

"Well, I have something for you to consider." Rizzo leaned toward him. "For each increase in the profit margin, I'll give you a bonus of some percentage. What do you think is fair?"

This isn't the time to get greedy. Michael bowed his head in a humble gesture. "Sir, you've treated me well since I came here, and I trust your judgment. When the time comes, pay me what you think I'm worth."

"All right." Rizzo appraised him for a moment, apparently pleased with a good answer. "Well then. Cost reduction is the start, but we need to look at the sales side, too."

"Yes, sir. That's where the real opportunities are." Michael had more work to do and still possessed an incomplete understanding of the ways this world worked. "I'll have to ask questions. Some of them will sound odd, but there are a lot of pieces to this puzzle."

Rizzo nodded. "I understand. Let me know what you need."

I need to go home.

But it felt good to be back in business.

* * * *

His good mood persisted that evening when he walked into the hostel.

"Good evening," he called to Cecile. Silence. "Hello..." A chair creaked in the kitchen and slow footsteps made their way to the door.

She stood in the doorway with a towel in her hand, "sad Cecile" again. No, she looked beaten, sort of the way Sheila did when she found that she couldn't compete with Michael's work.

Cecile took a lifeless breath. "Hello."

Michael felt a compassion that rarely made it to the surface. "What's wrong?" He took off his cloak and draped it over the back of a chair.

"I'm a woman." Her absent eyes rested somewhere around his shoulder.

"I've noticed." He left out the leering undertones he might have used another time.

She snapped her eyes up to meet his. "I own this property. My husband willed it to me. It is mine. They don't have any right to it." The words began to come faster and louder. "You men think you own everything, including us women. It's not right."

Michael declined to take offense. He took a deep breath before he spoke. "What happened?"

"I went to pay my taxes. The pig of an official wouldn't take my payment, because I am a woman, he says. If they go unpaid then others can make claim on this property." Cecile waved her arms about in agitation. "I can't pay because they won't take my money.

"Paganinus is a friend to my husband's brother. My brother-in-law thought this place should go to him instead of me. So, they work together." She threw down the towel and turned her back to Michael, shoulders heaving in silent sobs.

Michael sighed. *That's the problem with women*, he thought. They tended to let their emotions take over when they should be trying to solve the problem. He spoke to her back. "When's the payment due?"

"In a week, but what does it matter?" She sniffed and wiped at her face with the back of her hand. "I should just sell out to him and go back to my parents."

He put his hands on Cecile's shoulders and gently turned her to face him. "Hold on. Let me see what I can do tomorrow."

Michael flinched when Cecile looked up at him with fire in her eyes. Had he committed some taboo by touching her? He couldn't tell whether she might throw herself into his arms or slap his face. Instead, she broke free and ran up the stairs, using one hand to pull the long dress away from her feet and the other to touch the wall every few steps. He followed the sound of footsteps down the hall and winced when the door slammed.

The towel Cecile had held lay at the door to the kitchen. Michael picked it up and leaned in the door to toss it on the counter. *No supper tonight.*

* * * *

On his way to work, a disturbing thought occurred to Michael. What if he had been dropped here as a woman? How would he survive? The options for females in this culture seemed limited: marriage, domestic service, the convent, and prostitution. Nothing else came to mind. He couldn't see much room for advancement.

He walked along the narrow streets and looked at the people making their way around town. What choices did any of them have, really? If a man was fortunate enough to find a trade as a tailor or baker could he ever change? But as limited as the man might be, the woman's fortune depended on his.

Cecile had been put in limbo with her husband's death. Michael felt himself drawn to her and wanted to help, but he didn't know the law here. He did learn in school that most of Europe used civil law instead of English common law which the U.S. system evolved from. Civil law covered only situations expressed in the code, and not much could be decided on principle.

Cecile said her husband willed her the hostel. Did she have a right to keep it? Maybe she needed to get married or sell out. Michael puzzled over the problem until he reached the warehouse and walked back to the office. Rizzo looked up and stopped twisting his beard for a moment.

"Good morning," Michael said.

"Hmm." Rizzo returned to his manifest.

Michael stood at the door. "May I ask you something?"

Rizzo looked up again and gave Michael a look that said, "I hope this is about business."

"Cecile de Piro. She rents me a room. Are you acquainted with her?"

Rizzo's expression softened. "Yes. Her husband Johannes was my friend. I used to do business in his place, but I haven't seen her since he died."

So Rizzo had a heart after all, but something didn't make sense. "She asked you about me once."

"Well, not directly. She sent a note with another merchant who stayed there. One of the few now." Rizzo shook his head and looked at the floor. "It wouldn't do for either of us to visit the other. People would talk. My wife would be discomforted. The 'scheming widow,' you know."

Michael saw an image of his mother after his father died, bitter about being shunned by her married friends because of their fear that she might go after their husbands. She spent several lonely years with her only female companions, other widows, until she remarried and moved back into the land of the living.

"Yes, I do," Michael said. A question occurred to him, and he wrinkled his brow. "What did she ask?"

"You were quite the sight. You looked like a runaway from some noble's estate or maybe an escaped prisoner. I had the thought myself." Rizzo shrugged. "Maybe you are, but I don't want to know."

"You told her I was reliable?"

Rizzo gave Michael an impatient stare. "I told her you had a job."

"That must have been enough." Michael frowned. "She's afraid of losing the hostel." He recounted the story she told him.

Rizzo nodded. "Paganinus. He *is* a 'pig of an official,' but he's not on good ground here. She is entitled to run her dead husband's estate. I'll go see him today and take care of this, but she might do well to hire some man to make these kinds of transactions in the future." He smoothed his beard. "Perhaps you?"

"Me? Why?" The suggestion surprised Michael, but not as much as he thought it should.

"Why not? Everyone else in town has one agenda or another. They're kin to someone or know someone." Rizzo pointed a thick finger. "Except for you."

"Maybe. I'll think about it." He moved around to his side of the desk. "She might not even want me to do it."

"Only an observation, do what you wish. Can we get to work now?"

"Yes, sir," Michael said, glad to leave the subject behind. "I want to get to work on those brokerage costs. You know, if we bought direct from the Levant, we could bypass the houses in Venice? There are enough merchants here in Caorle to pool resources and contract ships on occasion."

Rizzo gave him a sober look. "Be careful. The power lies in Venice. We don't want to be accused of smuggling."

"No, that wouldn't be good. We'll see what can be wrung out of current operations first."

At the end of the day, Michael had come up with several ideas which showed promise. One involved making larger volume deals by forming a purchasing association among the area merchants. At a good stopping place, Michael decided to go home and beat the cold that would come as the sun went down.

On the way, Michael perused several vendor carts still out. One drew his eye. The owner hawked trinkets, decorative combs, necklaces, rings, all inexpensive adornments.

Sheila had liked receiving little, random gifts. Once, when he brought her some silk roses he found at an old mom and pop store...

Michael spotted a bracelet and, on impulse, bought it for Cecile. He hurried home.

He eased the door closed and tiptoed to the kitchen, then peeked around the corner to see Cecile busy chopping a pile of bright yellow carrots.

"Good evening," he whispered.

Cecile's head snapped up and then her surprise turned to a smile. "We're almost ready to eat," she said. Last night's strained face had given way to happy eyes, and something else had changed. She wasn't wearing black.

The dark hair that had blended into Cecile's mourning clothes now emphasized the light brown dress, which featured a low neckline that drew his gaze.

Don't stare.

She laughed at him, and he worked to keep an embarrassed grin off his face.

"My husband always liked this dress. It's been a year. I thought I should wear it again." A ray of late afternoon sunshine from the rear window illuminated motes of dust around her head like a halo.

"It looks good on you. I brought you a present." He held out the bracelet on an open palm.

Cecile laid the knife on the counter and took Michael's gift. For a moment, he thought she might refuse it. With a shy smile, she slipped the ornament on her wrist and looked it over. "Very sweet. Thank you." She paused and drew a breath. "I received a note from Rizzo today. He says I can pay my taxes and keep my home." She turned her dark eyes on him again. "Do I have you to thank for that?"

Having her smile at him that way reminded him of silk flowers. He looked away at the thought, but only for a moment. "Thank Rizzo. He made the arrangements."

"Well, I doubt he thought of it himself." Even her dark eyes smiled now. "But tomorrow tell him I am grateful."

"I will, but he was glad to help. He's sorry he couldn't bring you the news himself."

Cecile's look turned serious as she studied her hands. "Michael, my life changed in many ways when Johannes died. My family told me I should go to a convent. The people I thought were my friends turned their backs on me."

Michael nodded. "I've seen that happen before."

"So have I." She sighed and shook her head. "And I'm no better than them. I think we don't appreciate someone else's troubles until we have them ourselves. But many of the men who have come in here since Johannes died have expected…" She frowned. "A house of prostitution. You didn't. You respected me, and I'm grateful."

Good thing she can't read minds. "I'm not a saint. I'm alone, too. You took me in when I looked like a…" He searched for the word.

Cecile grinned. "A fugitive?"

They shared a laugh at the memory, but the moment slid away in silence. Michael thought he should say something, but could only look into her lovely eyes. Then the front door opened and let in another boarder.

"I should finish your supper." Cecile smiled at him again and turned to her business.

Michael watched her slender hands at work and listened to the boarder stomp up the stairs behind him. "Yes, I ought to go and get ready, myself." He started out of the kitchen, but halted when she spoke again.

"Go to Mass with me on Sunday."

He paused and looked at Cecile, who continued to chop carrots. "Church? Except for a few weddings and funerals I haven't been to church since I was a boy."

She turned to face him. "It's time, then, for both of us. I have avoided going since Johannes's funeral. I didn't want the people to pity me. Of course, if I go with you, they will see me in another way." She raised her chin. "But I don't care."

Michael had to admire the bravery of this woman who fought the odds and dismissed the conventions of society, besides he liked her company. A lot. "Of course I'll go with you. What should I wear?"

"You don't need any fancy clothes." She motioned him away with the back of her hand. "Now leave me alone and let me work."

Michael gave her a grin and backed out of the kitchen.

He lay thinking that night. Something important had happened, some connection made, and it left him ambivalent. On one hand, he felt an attraction to Cecile, and he believed she liked him, too.

The other hand told him being involved with a woman brought complication, and his life was complicated enough. Unless he somehow got back to New York, he would remain stuck in this place and be forced to make up his mind about what he wanted. But he would go to church with Cecile this Sunday, even if that situation brought more problems.

He grew up in a Baptist church, at least until his dad died, and they didn't go anymore. A couple of funerals were his only first-hand experience with Catholic services. The priest had said something and the congregation answered, and then everyone knelt on cue. Michael hadn't recognized the cues and didn't know even if he should join in, so he just mostly sat and watched.

Sheila tried. The sudden thought made him take a sharp breath. She asked and then begged him to go with her. Why didn't he, if only to please her Boston-Irish family? Things might have been so different. He pushed away the painful thought.

How could he explain his ignorance? He decided to make up some story and ask Cecile to teach him what to do.

* * * *

Cecile laughed as they left the church. "Well, that wasn't too bad, but a few heads certainly turned, didn't they?"

Michael smiled and appreciated the change. She glowed today, despite being wrapped up against the cold. It occurred to him she had started to live again. He spoke as they walked.

"Rizzo suggested something." Cecile looked up to him, and he continued. "He said it might be easier for you to have a man take care of some of your business, like paying your taxes."

She stopped short. "What do you mean?"

He immediately saw the ambiguity of his statement. "Well, as a sort of manager." That didn't seem the right thing to say, either.

"So you want to run the Red Lion? Or take it over?" Her eyes narrowed, and she snapped her words. "I have enough people trying to do that."

Michael held up his hands. "No, I'm sorry. I haven't said this well." He stared at the ground for a couple of seconds before going on. "I would only do what you asked. Maybe I could pay your bills, or be there when you're making some purchases, only so people wouldn't try to take advantage of you. You could fire me any time."

She seemed to consider his words for a moment. "And you would do this for free?"

He gave her a stern look. "Absolutely not. One *denarius* per year." He leaned toward her. "In advance."

A mutual laugh erupted, and the tension disappeared. "All right, maybe."

They walked the cobblestone street, while ahead a mother chided her son for taking off his coat.

It reminded Michael of a day from his childhood. He and his parents went to the car after the church service, headed to a restaurant for lunch. Michael had stopped to pick up a rock or flower or something, he couldn't remember. But his dad had said, 'Hurry now, we gotta beat the Methodists.' Michael smiled at the memory. He and Cecile weren't going to a restaurant, but she had a meal waiting at home.

Home.

Chapter Fifteen

Ludovico

Ludovico savored a last glass of wine and walked out the front door to the nearly empty hall, when a familiar voice behind him interrupted his moment.

"Beautiful wedding."

He didn't turn to greet his father-in-law. "Hello Ercole."

The event was a grand success, everyone agreed. With Bianca, his niece, now married to Holy Roman Emperor Maximilian, Ludovico would soon be viewed as the equal of his counterparts in Venice and Florence, and especially in Ferrara.

"How much did it cost you?" The Duke of Ferrara sidled up beside him.

"For the wedding?" Ludovico knew what he meant.

"No, for Maximilian."

"Four hundred."

Ercole gasped and spun around to face him. "Four hundred thousand ducats? I know this was necessary, but..." He shook his head, and let his wide eyes wander back and forth. "Four hundred thousand."

Just how much was Ercole worth, anyway? Four hundred was a steep price, but the price of doing business, nonetheless. Maybe he overestimated this man. Ludovico shrugged. "The investment will pay for itself."

He admired the clay model placed on the lawn for this occasion. Leonardo's giant stallion, a tribute to Ludovico's father, would soon immortalize the late *condottiero* in bronze.

Ercole snapped back into his usual superior stance. "Well, I suppose then that the emperor now recognizes you as the legitimate duke."

"Soon." Ludovico took another sip. "We travel to Innsbruck in a few weeks for the consummation." He smiled and relived the experience of acting as the emperor's proxy for this wedding.

Soon.

Chapter Sixteen

Michael bounced down the stairs. The old cliché, *The sun is shining, and the birds are singing*, rang true today, despite the dark clouds outside and the sound of rain dripping off the roof. Spring had returned to northern Italy. It helped that things were going well here at the hostel and at work.

Not all the rooms stayed full, but only one or two went empty most days. Merchants and other travelers who had stayed away from a woman-operated establishment came back to a place where a *man* ran the place. Michael operated as manager in name only. Cecile made all the decisions, relying on his help on the few occasions when she needed it. She was a smart, capable woman, and they both knew it.

Cecile looked up at Michael when he made the bottom step and gave him a smile, but one that only he could see. It wouldn't do, they agreed, for the townsfolk to think they were lovers. And they were not. In another place, Michael might not have objected, but here it didn't seem right. A conscience seemed to have afflicted itself upon him. Besides, a serious relationship could be a distraction, and he had plans.

Cecile carried an empty water pitcher back toward the kitchen and stopped to wait on him. She wore her hair up in ebony ringlets today. "Good morning," she said.

"It is, isn't it? You're facilitating quite a bit of business these days." He motioned to a clump of merchants talking shop and making deals.

"Careful, you will give this place a bad name." She propped a hand on her hip.

He grinned. "Too late—it already has a reputation."

Cecile arched her eyebrows. "I may have to get rid of a bad influence or two."

"Just let me know which ones." Michael scanned the room with a fake scowl. "I'll do it for you."

She shook her head and loosed a curl that he longed to put back in its place. "You amuse yourself, I see."

"On occasion." He gave her his best rascal smile and then grew serious. "Do you have any chores for me today?"

Cecile looked around as if remembering where she was. "No, we only need vegetables from the market. I may be able to handle that myself."

"All right. I need to catch the books up before I leave."

She shooed him away. "Go on about it then. I have work to do."

He sat at Cecile's desk in the corner and watched her glide about the room. Quite a change in the, what, seven or eight months since he came to town? Lots of things had changed, here and at Rizzo's place too. He forced his eyes back to business. His thoughts wandered as he jotted down his entries.

Rizzo's distribution costs had started to come in line, even if Michael couldn't make all the changes he wanted at once. He had tinkered with the operations side, making it more efficient. A good objective, but they could cut only so much fat before they got to muscle.

Rizzo ran a wholesale distributorship. He purchased goods in bulk from larger merchants, mostly based in Venice, repackaged the goods into smaller units and resold them. But the big risks and big profits were borne and reaped by players in the larger cities like Venice or Genoa. Michael intended to help Rizzo select a strategy that gave him an advantage over the other merchants beating each other up for a ducat.

Michael finished his entries. No need to bother Cecile while she tended to customers. He grabbed his hat and cloak and paused at the door for one last glance before he headed out into the light rain.

He stepped up off the cobblestone street onto Rizzo's porch and stomped the water off his shoes. By the sound of the voices coming from inside the store, Rizzo had company. He removed his hat and shook the moisture from it before he went inside.

A couple of local merchants sat with Rizzo in front of the cold fireplace. They looked up; then they ignored Michael and went back to the news. It seemed the crazy Genoan, *Cristoforo Colombo*, had returned to Spain from his voyage west with claims of finding a shorter route to Asia.

"Columbus can't have gotten there and back in seven months," said Leonhard Krantz an importer from Lienz, Austria. "And he didn't bring much back, a handful of gold and a few slaves, I heard. No spices or anything valuable."

Michael eased to a spot in the aisle closest to the group and absently smoothed his hand across a bolt of Rizzo's prize silk, barely noticing the luxurious texture.

He had expected this day. These fellows couldn't imagine how disruptive the discoveries would prove. They had built their system on predictable trade routes and familiar products. The balance of power would shift west as Spain and Portugal and then England claimed new lands. Venice would fade in importance.

A more immediate threat to Venice loomed over the horizon in the forms of Portugal and Vasco da Gama. When Vasco opened the direct route to India around the south of Africa, goods like the spices, currently requiring multiple overland and sea journeys to reach Venice, would go straight to Lisbon, fresher and cheaper. Michael couldn't pin down the year it would happen. U.S. grade schools had no handy mnemonic song for da Gama like they did for Columbus, but it would come soon.

The visitors finally tired of the talk about Columbus and sea journeys and finished their business. Michael had Rizzo alone, still seated by the fireplace.

"How long do you plan on being in the business, Rizzo?" Gone was the "sir."

Rizzo blinked at the question. "I don't know, why do you ask?"

"What are your long-term objectives?"

"I suppose..." Rizzo stared out the gray window for a moment. "I should want to make a profit, live to an old age, and leave this business to my sons-in-law when my daughters marry, God willing on all accounts."

Michael eased into a chair in front of Rizzo. "You're still a young man. Chances are you'll be in this business for another twenty years or more. So you're still in a position to think in longer periods of time."

"I don't understand what you're saying."

Michael swept his arm in a wide arc. "The world is changing. You saw that today. It'll change for you and your business in one way or another. You have the opportunity to be swept along with these changes or use them to your advantage."

Rizzo frowned. "You want me to be a fortune teller now?"

"No, let's just step back and look for a minute. We can't see the future, but we can make a good guess by following the flow of goods and money. First, what's your most valuable trade?"

Rizzo pointed around the warehouse. "We make money from many items."

"I know, but what group of products has the highest profit?"

"Hmm. Spices, I guess."

Michael jabbed a finger in his palm. "Right, because the prices are high and the margins are good. Why are the prices so high? They come from places like India and China and have to be freighted into Venice. But they make several journeys on sea and over land and everybody gets a cut along the way. In another way of saying it, everyone adds cost at each point, but what happens when someone opens a direct route to India or China?"

Rizzo pulled on a whisker and then put his hands in his lap. "Someone will make a lot of money."

"And who will that be?" Michael wanted Rizzo to come up with the answer himself.

"Not Venice." He stared past Michael. "They're happy to keep things the way they are. They already control the trade in spices. If the Spanish have found this route with Columbus..."

"And not Spain." Michael looked down at a knee and back at Rizzo. "In northern England, we heard stories of explorers who found a land to the west. It was rich in natural resources, but there were no civilized people there." Okay, he had revised history a bit. Leif Ericson landed very far north of where Columbus had been, but he had to have some reason for seeming clairvoyant.

Rizzo turned his face up with revelation written across it. "The Portuguese."

Good boy. "Yes. The Portuguese. I know you've heard rumors that they're trying to find a route around Africa. The news of Columbus's discovery will push them to beat the Spanish to India, and they'll succeed because Spain is preoccupied with this new world."

Rizzo sat, silent, and focused on a display.

"These things might not happen this year, or the next, but they will happen." Michael picked up a peppercorn from the display Rizzo had put out the day before. "And what will that do to the price of pepper?" *Keep him thinking.*

Rizzo's face went slack. "It will be gutted. Venice will be ruined."

"Maybe. They still have lots of resources, but more importantly, what does this mean for the people of Caorle and for you, yourself?"

Rizzo shrugged. "I don't know. Spices are an important part of our trade, but not the major part. This isn't a rich area like Venice. Not many people can afford to buy large quantities of luxury goods."

"But what if they could?" Michael put the peppercorn back in its sack. "Remember that the price will drop, maybe to a third or less of its current value. Then, the demand for spices will rise. People want to be rich, don't they?"

Rizzo frowned. "Of course they do, but this won't make them all rich."

Michael leaned forward and spoke in a low voice. "No, but think about it." He pointed a finger to make sure he had Rizzo's attention. "More people will eat like the wealthy. They'll scramble to buy these products that used to be out of their reach."

"Perhaps. But, with prices reduced so much, where will the profits come from?"

Almost there. "Your costs will be reduced as well. And, with the increased volume, you'll get efficiency in shipping and distribution."

Rizzo leaned back in his chair. He folded his thick arms across his chest. "Hmm. Much speculation, with little information to base it on." After another moment, "You have something in mind. What is it?"

Michael had him now. "I wouldn't forget about the Spanish. There will be new products coming from the new world, and we should be ready to take advantage, but the better opportunity will be in Lisbon. We'd be smart to make contacts, pay bribes, whatever we need to be ready when the time comes. Lots of people here, and in Venice, will be slow to react. If we're prepared, we can put ourselves in position to make a lot of money."

Rizzo hopped up and paced the aisle, twirling a strand of whiskers. Michael stood to watch, feeling a bit like an *inside trader*, using knowledge that the general business community couldn't access. It wasn't unfair, he reasoned, others should be able to interpret the signs available to them, just as he had laid them out for Rizzo. But people didn't really want to acknowledge disruptions to the system. Just like the bursting of the housing bubble in the U.S. Everyone knew it would come, but were surprised when it did. No, he wasn't cheating. Not much, anyway.

Rizzo halted and turned to face Michael. "You have a plan, I suppose?"

Michael smiled inside and nodded. "I'll have something for you tomorrow." In the back of his mind, he noted how odd it was to accept this was really 1493.

Chapter Seventeen

Luca

Luca carried his bowl and cup from the kitchen into the subdued atmosphere of the monastery's refectory. Only the sounds of eating broke the silence. The prior dined alone at a table to the side. Luca made his way across the room and stopped next to the table. He waited until Petrus looked up.

Petrus smiled and motioned to the opposite bench with an open hand. Luca nodded his thanks, placed his food and drink on the table, and sat. Petrus returned to his meal. Luca mouthed a silent prayer and picked up his spoon. This would be the last time he ate with the brothers for a while, and the conflict he felt would be no different than all the suppers past.

They had never really accepted him here. Luca found success in the academic world before he heard God's call. Connections he made over the years gave him access to sources and funding for his studies, but created friction with his jealous peers, who questioned his devotion and credited his achievements to patrons. All but Petrus, it seemed. The prior had befriended Luca and tried to make everyone happy, with limited success. The Lenten sermons had been sparsely attended.

And Luca had contributed to the problem, he admitted to himself. His abrupt, logical manner put many people off and made him seem condescending and rude, but he supposed he was too old to change that now. Perhaps he would fit better in Venice.

Petrus stayed seated until Luca finished his meal. Luca followed him back to the kitchen where they left their dishes and strolled out into the courtyard. A cool evening breeze caressed Luca's face and stirred the loose sleeves of his robe. Petrus spoke as they walked across paving stones laid out in a cross-hatch pattern.

"So you leave us."

"Yes, early tomorrow. I want to be in Venice before cold weather sets in. The publisher will not begin work for several months yet, but this gives me a chance to go over the bookkeeping section again with some practitioners there."

Petrus smiled. "Always the perfectionist."

"It does not help those who need the information to supply them with errors. Besides, if one undertakes a project, he should finish with the same fervor with which he begins."

Petrus peered off into the last glow of a summer sunset. "You're right, of course, but sometimes I fear you will wear yourself out in study." He stopped at a stone bench, corners rounded with use, and motioned Luca to sit.

"God puts me where I am useful." Luca eased onto the seat. "I can only do his will to the extent of my abilities."

"A good example for us all. Where will you stay while in Venice?"

"Steffano de Rompiasi has invited me to stay at his estate."

Petrus pursed his lips. "Rompiasi...do I know the name?"

"His father, Antonio, commissioned a painting from Piero della Francesca when I worked in his studio many years ago."

"Yes, the merchant. I remember now," Petrus said.

"He later hired me to teach his three sons. I saw Steffano, the oldest, at Piero's funeral last year." Luca bowed his head. "I miss him. Piero, I mean."

"A good man."

Luca nodded. "He gave me the love of mathematics, you know. It was all he had after his sight failed him, and he could no longer paint."

"Friend, you cultivate the reputation of a cold man, but I see in you a warm heart."

Luca looked up at Petrus and then straightened himself. "In any event, Steffano is expecting me. It will be good to see him and his brothers."

Petrus sighed and gave Luca a sad smile. "You are welcome here any time. Good fortune."

"Thank you Petrus." Luca turned his gaze to the east where a faint haze of light hovered over the buildings of Sansepolcro.

They sat in silence and watched the moon rise.

Chapter Eighteen

Fall again. Still warm, but the wind took on a different character. The sun sat at a lower angle. Michael gazed at the green foliage of a tree as he passed on his way to work and imagined it still springtime. The end of summer always made him a little sad.

Had he really been in Caorle for a year? Quite different circumstances now, but he remained lost, without hope of finding a way back home. He had always adapted in changing situations and adjusted to new realities, the way one must act in business. Stay the same and die, sometimes slowly, sometimes quickly. He intended to survive.

He worked on Rizzo, helping him see the value of incorporating. The law didn't yet allow for the legal limitation of personal liability available in modern corporate law. Still, he pushed for a long-term joint venture involving Rizzo and some of his nominal competitors.

"Why should I help them any more than I already do?" Rizzo had asked.

Businessmen here often formed partnerships, buying shares in a ship's load of merchandise to spread the risk. The merchants might have dozens of them going at the same time, but when the ship came in they split the goods, took the profits, and dissolved the partnership. The scenario repeated in constantly changing relationships.

"Because," Michael told him. "If we expect to profit when the Portuguese make their spice run, we need contacts in their trading centers."

"Well let's go make them."

Michael nodded. "We will, but it's too big a gamble if we go it alone. If the local merchants band together..." He clasped his hands in illustration. "Each one can put in what he can afford. And we'll all make lots of money."

They needed a separate entity with all contributing resources and supporting the effort. When it paid off, the merchants would take shares in the profits, but it wouldn't end at that point. The corporation would continue to carry out strategic and tactical operations. The merchant owners would be the board of directors, and after today, Michael would be the CEO.

* * * *

Michael leaned against a stack of sacked barley in the back storage room of the warehouse. Rizzo's other goods had been pushed aside too, in order to clear a central space for the meeting of a couple dozen local merchants. From his inconspicuous spot to the side, he watched the show start.

Before the last couple of stragglers found a seat, Jacobus Marzarius from down the street bellowed his dissatisfaction. "Rizzo, why are we meeting in your warehouse and not somewhere more accommodating?"

Michael looked the old fellow over. His dress and affectations were on the extravagant side, especially for a man in his sixties. The way he scanned the crowd around him, wearing a pompous smile, foreshadowed a rocky meeting.

Rizzo stood up and faced the group and Jacobus in particular. "I think you will want no other ears hearing what we discuss today. We plan our futures here."

"We are all aware of your theories about changes in this new world of yours," Jacobus said. "Columbus this and Columbus that. You wear us out and still we listen."

Rizzo nodded an admission. "I was skeptical too, when the news first came about this discovery, but they must have found something of value there. We have reports from Spain that Columbus is going back with seventeen ships this time. He may be gone already."

Across the room, Enrico de Rippa rose from his seat on a wooden box and addressed Rizzo. "So you have spies in Spain, now."

Younger than Jacobus, in his late twenties, Enrico stood taller than average and dressed in the latest fashion. *Ladies' man.*

"No spies," Rizzo said. "But we should all pay attention to the news brought to our door and sift fact from fiction."

He and Michael had agreed not to concentrate on Portugal yet, but go with the news fresh on the minds of these men.

"What do you want from us, Rizzo? It seems you have this all figured out." Jacobus spoke again.

Michael searched faces for signs of opposition. Not so much opposed to the proposals they would bring today, as to Rizzo himself. Who wanted the power here? So far, Jacobus put himself up as prime candidate.

"I want us to cooperate," Rizzo said. "There are things we can do as a group that no individual can afford."

Enrico piped up. "And you would lead us, Rizzo?"

Michael saw a pattern developing: a challenge from Jacobus, echoed by Enrico. Captain and lieutenant?

"We will all participate. My colleague…" Rizzo looked at Michael. "Has proposed we form a body, a trade association, that will perform functions we all share."

With the attention on him momentarily, Michael straightened and folded his arms across his chest.

Jacobus made a show of turning in his seat and examining Michael, as if he were an amusing curiosity. His smile held ridicule. "He does, now? Isn't this your warehouse laborer? Or is it bookkeeper?" He looked back to Rizzo, but pointed to Michael. "He will now explain how to run our businesses? Perhaps next he will give us advice on pursuing women as well."

Several of the other merchants laughed, Enrico the loudest.

Rizzo nodded as the noise died down. "You can mock if you want, Jacobus, but Michael has proved himself a good businessman. And he is right about this. That's my judgment based on evidence we've all seen."

"Your judgment, your experience," said Jacobus. "But we haven't heard from this mysterious man, himself." He turned back to Michael. "Convince us. Why should we submit to your plan?"

Michael looked to Jacobus, then around the room. This reminded him of his first pitch to a bunch of disaffected shareholders in a hostile takeover scheme. His old mentor, Arnie Blackshire, had pushed him out on the floor. 'Go get 'em kid,' he said. He had missed Arnie, but never visited him, God rest his soul in federal prison.

Back to work. He moved to the front of the assembly and faced the audience.

"Sirs. Thank you for the opportunity to speak. I'm not offended by your questions. You're right to show caution; this is a serious matter. It seems you want to know two things from me. If you will bear with me, I'll try to answer your questions."

"We listen," Jacobus said.

"You want to know who I am." Michael got to the hard question first with the speech he had polished and rehearsed. "My home is in Norwich, England. A merchant there, a dealer in cloth and wool, took me as apprentice when my father died. He kept me in his employment after my apprenticeship ended, and I learned much under his able and visionary leadership."

Jacobus interrupted. "Yes, yes, we've heard the story." He looked at Michael, but spoke to the rest of the group. "It does not tell us why we should entrust our fortunes to this runaway."

Anger colored Michael's vision, and he opened his mouth to respond, but Rizzo broke in and snapped at Jacobus.

"You and the others here have already profited from his ideas. When we banded together to reduce shipping costs, his ideas and execution made it possible."

Jacobus faced Rizzo. "My friend, this is no matter of negotiating minor concessions with a second tier shipper. You ask us to wager our futures on speculation that this Columbus fellow has discovered a shortcut to riches. We have done well in our association with Venice. She has proven a reliable partner for hundreds of years."

Michael took a deep breath. For all of his posturing, Jacobus had a valid point. Heads turned back in his direction.

"Yes, Venice has been a reliable partner, but please, indulge me while I tell you a story." He hurried on before anyone could raise an objection.

"It concerns the city of Bruges." Michael called upon his knowledge of the city in Flanders, part of modern Belgium from his perspective. "You older men may have done business with their merchants, or perhaps your fathers did. When last did you have the occasion to even hear the name?" Some of the men looked to one another. None spoke.

"Years ago, the river flowed freely, boats moved inland and ships went to sea with all kinds of cargo. Spinners and weavers added value to raw materials from around the world. City leaders controlled movement of commerce. Everyone profited, but they became complacent and the river silted up. What happened when those responsible for the well-being of the city failed to act and clear the channel to the sea?" Several heads nodded.

"Trade moved from Bruges up the coast to Antwerp. Their artisans are leaving. It now controls only a minor part of commerce in the region. Who mourns the old, great Bruges? Who will mourn Venice? Or Caorle?"

Michael let the story sink in for a moment and observed the reactions. Some paused in thought. Others, including Enrico, looked to Jacobus and waited for his response. Michael wouldn't let him have it just yet.

"Friends, I have seen what happens to those who live on past success and fail to act upon challenges forced on them by a changing environment. I have an involvement in this situation, thanks to Rizzo, but your survival is at stake. Today you have a choice that will determine how your children and their children live. Will you meet the world's changes with a plan to profit by them, or will you face a long decline?"

Michael resisted the temptation to break the silence. He left the pressure on Jacobus, who looked about in an apparent effort to gauge support for his leadership.

At last Jacobus spoke. "You may be right. Perhaps. But we cannot spend ourselves into poverty on a gamble that may never pay off. How can you assure us our contributions will be well spent?"

"With a transparent accounting of all transactions. The books will be open to all partners, investors, if you will."

This might just work.

"Books can be manipulated," Jacobus retorted. "I need more reassurance. Speaking only for myself, of course. Would someone volunteer to help Michael in his noble quest?"

Enrico, Michael thought, even before the old merchant's mouthpiece moved to speak.

"I would be honored to do what I am able." Enrico bowed his head.

"Well, Rizzo," Jacobus said. "It looks like your team is in place. Are you ready to take responsibility for the consequences your plan may bring?"

Rizzo seemed unprepared for the question. He shot a questioning look at Michael before his face snapped back to its characteristic scowl. "Yes."

After the meeting, Michael watched them go. He had work to do. It would be harder now with Enrico stuck on his hip, but he had dealt with worse. At least he knew the guy was hostile. He went to Rizzo's office to set up a charter for the association.

Chapter Nineteen

Girolamo

With every step Girolamo's body complained, shooting pains from sore feet through an aching back. Dust from the road coated his skin; then the skin, burned by the sun, sloughed off. His cracked lips left small bloody spots on the back of his hand when he wiped away the dirt, but he relished each pain, each discomfort.

God had sent Girolamo to Bologna after Piero banished him from Florence. There, God had given him mighty words which drew believers and assassins. God had delivered him from harm and then sent him on his way again. Girolamo had even announced the hour of his departure and left on foot to walk the daunting trail over the Apennines, daring his enemies to attack and reveal God's power and protection.

Now he strode once more through Florence, across the *Piazza della Signoria* staring past the gawking crowds, ignoring the buzz that preceded and followed his passing. Let Piero try anything—he would feel God's swift hand. Onward Girolamo went to the monastery, where loyal friars waited. The time had come to begin the redemption of Florence. At San Marco, he marched in and faced the faithful who assembled at the news of his return.

"There will be a change."

Chapter Twenty

Michael cut the last piece of lamb. He tried the meat once before, on his honeymoon with Sheila.

'Leg of lamb,' he ordered like a big shot, the way he had seen in the movies. When it arrived, the smell made him gag and he sent it back. Sheila laughed and then so did he. But he liked the way Cecile prepared this dish.

He took a bite and smiled at Cecile, who had only picked at her food and now watched him across the kitchen table. She made the two of them a supper separate from the other boarders, for some purpose he didn't yet know. He waited.

As he chewed, he looked idly at the fork, an instrument which did not yet enjoy wide usage. Places like this didn't provide them, usually only a spoon. If a man wanted a fork, he carried it with him. Knife, too. Most men carried a dagger with them for eating and other purposes. It made for an exciting after dinner debate on occasion.

Cecile broke the silence. "What was her name?"

Here we go. "Whose name?"

"The one who hurt you."

He put down the knife and fork and met Cecile's dark eyes. They became more beautiful every time he looked into them. "It might be described the other way around. Why do you ask?"

"I see it when you look at me. You are reserved, cautious."

He took the napkin from his lap and wiped his mouth, then set the plate aside. "Sheila. Her name was Sheila."

Cecile's gaze dropped. "Sheila."

Michael hadn't noticed the similarities in their names, at least on a conscious level.

"Did you love her?" She continued to look away.

Did I? "She loved me, but I'm not sure I knew what love was. We got along pretty well the first few years, and it was good for business to have an attractive wife."

She met his gaze. "It's hard for you to admit that."

He shrugged. "I've had a while to think about it."

"What happened?"

This conversation troubled Michael, but he could see what drove her questions. She wanted some assurance that a relationship with him would be safe.

"Many things, but I guess my priorities were out of order. My work came first, and she was second."

Cecile raised her eyebrows. "And she couldn't accept it? Many women I know live with the same arrangement."

Michael nodded in understanding of a sad situation. "Many do. Sheila couldn't. She said she wanted me and not the things I bought her."

She hesitated and lowered her eyes. "When did she die?"

The question hit him from nowhere. "What?" He realized his mouth gaped and shut it. "No, no. She divorced me."

"Divorce?" Cecile made a couple of fish-out-of-water tries before she managed another word. "How?"

How could he have missed this? The church said "no" to divorce, and he had used the word so casually. He should have just told her Sheila died, but Cecile was one person he didn't want to tell a lie. He held up his hands to ease Cecile's distress and looked in her disbelieving eyes.

"No, it was a... What do you call it when you say you were never really married?"

"Annulment?" A little understanding crept across her face.

"An annulment. When you have enough money and lawyers, you can do about anything, I guess. I haven't heard from her for several years." He hated stretching the truth, but she couldn't accept the reality.

Cecile nodded and looked away. "Would she change her mind if you asked?"

Michael did give her a smile now, a sad one. "Even if I could go back, I don't think she would listen to me again." He let his gaze drift down to the tablecloth, but he saw only Sheila's empty closet. Pain he thought he had locked away reared its head.

She sat up straight with new conviction in her voice. "You can be forgiven, Michael. Go see the priest."

Where did that come from? He paused. "I have my doubts, but I'll go."

"Tomorrow."

She reminded him so much of a teacher assigning math homework that a chuckle escaped before he could think. "Did your husband take this kind of abuse from you?"

She nodded. "He was terrified of me, of course." Only the hint of a grin belied the solemn look on Cecile's face.

"I think I might believe you." Michael breathed a satisfied breath. "Cecile, thank you for cooking this meal for me. It's nice to eat away from the others."

Cecile rose and started to clear their places. "You're welcome. I enjoyed it, too. We could do this more often."

She moved with a different rhythm, purpose, something familiar Michael couldn't quite identify. But it drew him. He pushed back his chair and hopped to his feet. "I'd like that. Here, let me help."

He gathered the cups and utensils and followed her to the counter where a pair of small copper tubs waited for the dishes. "I'll rinse," he said. He caught a questioning look, but set the dishes down beside the wash tub and eased around her to the rinse side.

Cecile paused a second, then immersed a plate in soapy water and washed it with deliberate motions. She probably never had a man volunteer to wash dishes before. He watched her hands. Smooth white skin, slender fingers, but the short nails told the story of a woman who worked hard running her business.

She slid the plate into his rinse water and sneaked a glance up at him before getting another.

Michael grasped the plate with two fingers, letting the water drip back into the pan before setting the dish into the wooden drainer already full from the earlier crowd's supper. But from his peripheral senses, he was aware of her. She only came up to his collarbone; her dress hugged her shoulders and left her arms bare.

Tendrils of silky hair stirred restlessly with her short, nervous breaths. The scent of her seductive perfume aroused his male instincts. It was a good thing she didn't wear it every day.

He hadn't heard any of the other guests stir for a long time. Michael wanted to take her in his arms and kiss this lovely creature. He opened his mouth to speak and came out with the news he had been putting off for a week.

"I'll be gone for a while. My shadow and I are traveling to Venice in a few days."

She sagged and let out a barely audible sigh. After a few seconds she spoke in a flat tone. "How long is a while?"

Smooth move. He shook his head. "A week or so. We're meeting with a businessman there." The fellow had contacts in Spain and Portugal, but he wouldn't mention that yet.

"Oh." She washed the inside of a cup a little longer than necessary. "How are you traveling?"

"The canal. Rizzo arranged for us to accompany freight on a barge." He smiled. "I'll be back before you realize I'm gone."

Cecile gave him a sober look. "Be careful. There are serious people in Venice."

He nodded. "We'll be fine."

After he helped a quiet Cecile put away the dishes, Michael climbed the stairs and reflected on a confusing evening. He could have kissed her, and maybe more. He pushed open the door to his room and tried to shake it off.

When he lit the lamp beside his bed, he noticed the toiletry items laid out on the chest were arranged differently than usual. He always put them in the order used in his morning and evening routines. Had someone been snooping? No, he must have hurried this morning. *Don't be paranoid.*

Undressed and in his night gown, he climbed under the heavy covers and reached for the lamp, but stopped and left it lit. From the sash he wore around his neck, he took his watch. He knew he should get rid of it. The thing would cause him no end of trouble if someone discovered it, but he had lost everything else.

Monday, the twenty-second. Thank goodness it didn't display the full date. Seeing January 1494 would have been too much.

He turned it over and ran his thumb across the inscription he couldn't read in the dim lamplight. *To my dearest Michael. Love, Sheila.*

Their last night came flooding back.

* * * *

Michael walked into the apartment with the grand view of Central Park to find Sheila sitting on the couch wearing a long green jacket and holding a matching purse in her lap. His face must have asked a question, because she spoke first.

"I didn't want to leave a note." She nervously tucked a strand of long blond hair behind her ear.

"What do you mean?" He already knew.

"We've been through it too many times. I'm not going there again." Sheila stood and faced him with an aura of resignation. "You have what's important to you. And I hope it's enough, I really do.

"Sheila, just hang on. We're almost there." He pointed in the direction of his office. "After this deal goes through we'll have lots of time."

Sheila turned her ice blue eyes to the ceiling and gave him a mirthless laugh before looking at him again. "It never changes with you, does it?" Tears welled and threatened to escape. "No, there will always be a next time, just not for us."

For a moment, he could only look at the stunning woman surrounded by the city lights in the window behind her. "I can change."

She shook her head as if to convince herself. "Goodbye, Michael." She walked around him and opened the door.

He continued to stare out the window.

"Take care of yourself," she said before the door closed.

He never heard her voice again. The lawyers did their business and Michael poured his life into his work.

* * * *

What's she doing now?

He took a last look at the etching and put out the lamp. As he drifted to sleep, Michael heard a piece of the song popular on the radio when he received the final divorce decree in the mail.

He sought for words to hold her,
that would make her want to stay,
but instead...
Goodbye was all he said.

Chapter Twenty-One

Ludovico

Ludovico stood by the mirror and watched Beatrice prepare for bed on her first night back in Milan from Venice.

If she weren't so beautiful.

Ercole had been working on his daughter, meddling, Ludovico thought. She returned this afternoon from visiting her father on the way home from Venice. As she brushed her hair, Beatrice delivered another message from the Duke of Ferrara.

"My father says you should seek help from Charles."

Ludovico watched the hairbrush ride a waterfall of golden brown hair over a white, delicate left shoulder.

"I know, but we have no need of more complications. Naples is far away." He gathered himself from his preoccupation and turned to his own routine. "Besides, Florence would hardly allow Ferdinand's troops to pass through her territory to get here." He pulled the tunic over his head and stood in his white undershirt. A movement drew his attention back to his wife.

Beatrice switched the brush to the right side and pulled with long strokes. She graced him with a glance from those soft brown eyes.

"Yes, but Ferdinand can go around. Genoa will allow his ships access, and Aragon herself is not far away."

Ludovico nodded in reluctant agreement. Ferdinand's cousin of the same name, serving as ruler of Aragon and co-ruler with Isabella of the United Crown of Spain, would support his kin.

"What did you learn about Venice's intentions? I don't want to have to fight her, too." Ludovico understood how much Beatrice enjoyed the role of ambassador when a dreamy, calculating smile crossed her face.

"The doge was noncommittal in the presence of his advisors, but he secretly sent me a message of encouragement." Beatrice looked up from her mirror. "Agostino wants this action against his enemy."

Ludovico, swayed by her confidence and beauty, buoyed by the support, or at least noninterference, of Venice, capitulated. Although troubled by the decision, he would invite Charles VIII, King of France, to invade Italy.

Chapter Twenty-Two

Slow as the progress seemed, Michael had to admire Enrico's grasp of the new bookkeeping system. Impatient, he itched to get to the real work of this joint venture, but he admitted the validity of the association's demand for transparency. They had all put up their share of money. Except for Michael, of course.

They worked from a table in the back room, next to Michael's old "bedroom," where their efforts were out of public view. Michael gave Enrico the balance sheet and waited while he ran down the list.

Enrico straightened up and stretched his back, then leaned against a crate.

"I see what we've contributed and I can guess what we'll spend, but where are the profits from this adventure going to come from?"

"It's a consulting business," Michael said. He rose from his seat and walked to a bench where a water jug and a pair of cups waited. "It charges fees to its customers, who are also its owners." He poured himself a drink and took a sip.

"So, it won't generate income on its own."

Michael swallowed and shook his head. "Not from sales, anyway. It won't compete with anyone, at least within its membership."

Enrico looked Michael in the eye. "What do you get out of this?"

"I'm paid a salary out of the consulting receipts. It's here in the books." Michael knew Enrico asked a different question.

Enrico rose and walked around the table to face Michael. "No, I've seen people like you before. You don't work for a salary. There is always something more. You make contacts in the right places, maybe? Make a deal with somebody, secure a part in the ownership, move people out, wind up in power?"

Smarter than I gave him credit for. Michael set the cup back in its place. "I work for you and the rest of the association members. It's true that opportunities sometimes pop up and people who are prepared can take advantage, but I'm happy with my job here. And you're here to make sure I do it."

Enrico stood a little closer than Michael found comfortable. "We understand each other, then."

"I'm sure we do."

Enrico studied Michael's face for a moment then turned and ambled back to the desk. He sat with his arms folded in front, leg propped up on a brace. "It seems odd to go to Venice when we plan to bypass her merchants."

He had something to say about everything Michael planned.

"Do any of us have contacts in Spain or Portugal?"

"No."

He knows that. He just likes to needle. Michael held out his hands, fingers splayed wide. "Then we have to find someone who does."

* * * *

Michael shifted his position on the box he used for a chair. The lean-to that served as the barge's dry storage compartment blocked most of the wind at their backs, but the distant winter sun in their faces did little to warm him and his traveling companion. Down in the canal, they could see little beyond its steep banks.

"We could have hired a carriage and saved a day," Enrico said. It wasn't his first complaint this morning.

"Yes, but then we wouldn't have a good excuse to be in Venice. We don't want to attract any more attention than we have to." *I hope he doesn't do this the whole way.*

"It's cold."

Michael didn't answer him. He and Enrico were in better shape than the barge operator steering in the back and the driver, a man walking alongside the tow horse up on the right bank. Those men weren't protected from the wind. Enrico huddled with his arms pressed across his torso. Michael felt the cold, too, but he had dressed better. Besides, he wouldn't let Enrico see him shiver.

Early in the afternoon, the wind died down and the temperature rose a little. Michael left Enrico asleep and ducked out to sit on some covered containers of grain. He nodded a greeting to the man now seated on the horse. The sharp sound of hooves on hardened dirt contrasted with the hush of the country gliding by them. He hadn't ventured out of town since he arrived in Caorle.

A movement attracted Michael's attention forward. Another barge floated toward them, hugging the left bank. Operators on both sides exchanged greetings. Michael waved. The barge soon left them in their own world again.

They passed a stand of trees, whose bare lofted branches prayed for the return of spring. It reminded him of a day in the woods outside his childhood hometown in North Carolina. He must have been nine or so then. Before his dad died. Why did that day stand out in his memory over twenty-some years later? Nothing out of the ordinary happened. He had ambled alone in the quiet woods with no past chasing him and no future to dread. *If I could only go back to that day.*

The sound of running water brought Michael out of his reverie. Up ahead, the canal opened into a river that flowed right to left, crossed by an arched wooden bridge of a hundred feet or so to the right side of the canal. A smaller bridge crossed the canal at a right angle to the larger. He could make out an open walkway along the main structure to the outside of its framework.

The driver slowed his horse and guided it onto the walkway. The helmsman, as Michael thought of him, moved the barge to the center of the canal to take up the slack in the rope, while the driver got settled. Soon the rope tightened, and they were on their way across the river, driver and horse on the bridge walkway, and the helmsman steering the barge against the river current.

"That doesn't look very safe." He watched the driver lead the horse across the narrow walk.

"It's not too bad," the helmsman said. "But I lost a friend here one time, after a rain up the river. The horse went off with my friend, and the barge got loose. A ship found it later out in the sea. The barge, anyway. Don't know about the horse."

That's reassuring. He didn't care to be swept out to sea. To his relief, they made it across without incident.

The air grew colder again as they chased the sun toward the western horizon before them. Michael stood to rejoin Enrico, and the driver called down to him. "We'll be at Jesolo soon. Maybe your friend will be happier there."

Michael waved and nodded. "Good, thanks."

Jesolo. Midway between Caorle and Venice, it sat at the northeast end of the lagoon that protected Venice and its many islands. They could get a hot meal and a bed, and transfer, along with the cargo, to a galley and head across the lagoon on their way to Venice in the morning. Michael hoped they would get there before dark.

He reclaimed his seat in the storage compartment. Enrico leaned against a box, mouth agape. Michael let him sleep.

* * * *

The dock sat at the edge of a harbor where the canal terminated. Michael held onto the roof of the barge's shelter while he watched the horse's driver unfasten the harness in the dying sunlight.

"The water's rougher here," said the helmsman. "You probably want to wait there until they get you tied up." He jumped from the barge to the grassy bank and stepped up to the path.

"Thanks for the ride," Michael called. "I hope we see you on the way back." The helmsman waved without turning around.

Several barges floated ahead along the mooring in the shadows of the sunset. Theirs joined the line as the dockworkers pulled the ropes tight. Michael followed Enrico off the boat to the landing and a welcome firm footing. They might hire a carriage back to Caorle.

One of the workers gestured to a two-story building. "You can get lodging there. This cargo will all be loaded in the morning."

Michael nodded. "Thanks."

He let Enrico lead the way to the inn. Since he had only rented the one room back at the hostel, he might as well let Enrico show him what to do.

Enrico spoke to the first man inside the door. "Can you point me to the proprietor?"

Michael closed the worn door and scanned the room. Light from the fireplace gave more illumination than the dim lamps set up at various positions about the place. Half a dozen crude tables sat in the middle of the dingy room, two of them occupied. A girl served food and a beverage at one; a story generated laughter at the other.

"This way." Enrico led them toward a dark corner, glancing over at the serving girl. At a small table that Michael hadn't immediately seen, sat a man with supper in front of him.

"Do you have a room for the night?" Enrico asked.

The man continued to cut a piece of meat. "One room or two?"

Michael and Enrico answered in unison. "Two." Michael had seen about enough of Enrico today. He assumed it was mutual.

"Four *denari* each. Five if you want supper."

Michael counted ten *denari* out of his purse and held them out. The man raised the bite to his mouth before he took the coins and, still chewing, rose as if he'd rather not. He left his table without speaking.

He led them up the stairs, then right down a narrow hall where he pointed toward adjoining rooms. "You can leave your things here. No one will bother them. We have mutton stew tonight. Do you need anything else?"

Michael liked directness as an attribute. "No. This is good."

He swung the door open while the proprietor padded away down the hall, and reached inside for the light switch. Michael sighed when he found only smooth wall. After more than a year in this backward place, he still missed the things he used to take for granted.

Just enough light from the window filtered in to make out the furnishings. Not much different from the one he called home, but worn. In better light it might look dirty.

Good enough for tonight.

He dropped his bag on the wood frame bed. All the important items like his money and letter of introduction were with him anyway. He left the door open when he went back out into the hall.

"Enrico, are you going down to eat?" Michael preferred to be alone, but he didn't want to go into unfamiliar territory by himself.

"Yes." Enrico walked out into the hall and closed the door.

Michael pointed behind him. "Leave it open, and it'll be warmer when you get back."

Enrico paused and then opened the door again.

Michael let Enrico lead the way downstairs. Another bunch of guests had claimed a spot. Enrico took them to a vacant table. They sat on opposite benches.

The story, or one like it, continued at the next table, where a young man with long, greasy hair enthralled the occupants with an obscenity filled tale involving alcohol and a fight over a woman. The serving girl broke away from the show and shuffled over, dragging a stiff leg, to the table where Michael and Enrico waited.

"Eating tonight?" A big laugh from the other table drew her attention again until Michael answered.

"Yes, please," he said.

The girl glanced toward the storyteller and hurried to a back room. She came back in a moment with a platter holding two bowls of steaming stew, bread and two mugs. "I'll be back if you need more." She limped away again.

"Must be interesting," Enrico said.

Michael nodded and looked over the party, then turned back to his meal. Cecile's lamb took away his prejudice against sheep, and the rank smell of this mutton stew gave it back. But he could eat this or do without. The hunger after only the midday snack of biscuits and dried meat Cecile had packed for him helped his appetite. He used the fork he had remembered to bring to stab the big pieces, while he scooped the liquid up with folded bread, and washed the stew down with cheap wine, eager to finish eating and get to bed.

Enrico had turned quiet. Michael appreciated the relative silence. Before he could finish his stew, a young woman came down the stairs, dressed in a way that made Michael wonder what looked different. He figured it out when she surveyed the room and settled on him.

"Lonely?" She seated herself beside him and rested a hand on his arm. How old was she, twenty, thirty? Her years sat heavy on her.

"Thank you, but I'm very tired after my trip." He turned back to his supper.

"I can help you rest." She slipped her arm around his and snuggled close.

Michael fought the urge to edge away, but only shook his head. "Thank you again, but no."

"How about you?" She raised her head to Enrico, who looked at Michael, then at the girl. He shrugged, and then nodded. She got up and slid onto the seat next to him.

Michael tried not to make too many judgments of people. They made their choices and took the consequences. He was never tempted to go to a prostitute, but he had visited a strip club in his younger days. How did the term 'gentlemen's club' become attached to that kind of place? Once past the initial titillation, he saw only sadness, customer and dancer using and being used. Just like Enrico and this woman. They left for the stairs, arm-in-arm.

You've used people, too.

Michael scraped up another bread crust's worth of the cooling gray concoction that suddenly reminded him of congealed gravy. He dropped the fragment, pushed the bowl away, and went upstairs before something else happened.

He retrieved the lamp from his dark room and lit it from one in the hall, latched the door, and started a fire in the small fireplace. He turned to the bed and, partly out of curiosity, pulled back the covers. The linens might not have been washed recently, but tonight his tired body overrode the objections in his mind. Maybe the bedbugs wouldn't carry him off.

Bedclothes on, he slid under the covers and eased back on the thin pillow with a sigh. Clean or not, the bed felt good after a long day. A woman's soft voice floated from the next room, then a door opened and closed, and light footsteps receded.

Good night, Enrico.

Even exhausted, Michael didn't sleep well. It had always been that way the first night in a strange bed, even when his home had largely become a series of hotel rooms. Through the long night, he dozed and woke, several times in confusion or relief from a disturbing dream. Sharp reports from someone beating on the door jolted him awake.

"Michael. Are you up?"

No. But he tried to sound as if he were. "Yes. I'll be right down."

Michael jumped out of bed and hurried, further encouraged by the cold, to dress. If he ever made it back home, he would remember to be thankful for carpeting.

Downstairs, Enrico met him with a frown. "They are waiting on us."

"I'm ready" Michael nodded at the owner and walked to the door. A sliver of sun over the horizon greeted them as they went down the steps, dreading another long day on the water. He hoped it would be warmer than the one before.

Chapter Twenty-Three

Steffano

Steffano de Rompiasi closed the door to his residence and started down the stairs to the first floor, the warehouse level. He enjoyed the quiet of early morning, the time of day he could get work done before everybody started wanting things from him. Footsteps above told him someone else had also started early. He looked up a flight to see Luca walking down the steps and stopped to wait on him. He felt odd having the teacher here again.

Luca had come to this house to tutor Steffano and his two brothers some thirty years earlier and for six years until Steffano's father died, lived in the room he again occupied upstairs. Steffano had kept in touch for a few years afterward, occasionally feeling the need for advice, since he took over the family holdings at only eighteen. But Luca's focused tutelage and utilitarian, almost ruthless rules of conduct, had served Steffano well. As he succeeded in commerce, Steffano lost track of Luca. But now he returned, a man of God, a Franciscan brother.

I wonder if his principles have changed? Steffano bowed his head in greeting. "Good morning, Master Luca."

Luca reached the landing and returned Steffano's gesture. "Please," he said. "It has been half a lifetime since I was your instructor. You may dispense with the formality." He motioned to the stairs and took a step downward with Steffano. "Besides, you are a master in your own right. Your father would take pride in the things you have accomplished." He slid a hand along the railing.

Steffano slowed his descent when Luca winced at bending a knee. "Thank you. I hope so. I only wish he could be here to see them."

Luca nodded. "Yes, it was a sad time for me when he died. I thought of you and your brothers often over the years. It warmed my heart to see you again in Sansepolcro."

"Mine as well. Your publication? The project goes well, I suppose?"

Luca looked up from the steps and spoke with a lighter tone. "Yes, it does, thank you. The publisher has scheduled the printing for later in the year and recommended an artist to help me with the illustrations. I am on my way to see him now. I have also contracted a woodcut maker who will engrave the illustrations and the paragraph capitals I designed. We begin the work on those things next week."

They reached ground level and the door to the warehouse. Steffano paused with his hand on the latch. "Good. Is there anything you need?"

Luca pursed his lips. "There is one favor I would ask of you in connection with the book."

"Of course."

"It would be beneficial for many eyes to proofread the text for inconsistencies or errors. Would it be possible to impose on any of your employees to read over the section on bookkeeping?"

Steffano took his hand from the latch and faced his mentor. "More than possible. I will see my bookkeeper tomorrow. You are welcome to bring your work if you like."

Luca bowed and spread his hands in a grateful gesture. "You are very gracious. I will try not to waste his time."

"It is not a waste," Steffano said. "In fact, I am sure the finished product will be useful to us. Some of my associates may also wish to contribute."

"I am grateful at any rate, but now I should go and see this artist. The illustrations should not be left up to his imagination." He reached for the outside door.

Steffano lifted his hand. "Master Luca." He paused at the rare good-natured frown and smiled at the silent admonition. "Luca. Pardon me, but I must ask a question. Why do you insist on teaching and living in that monastery? You know I would gladly take you into my organization and pay you handsomely." He raised a finger to forestall Luca's objection. "And I would gain the better end of the bargain."

Luca shook his head and pulled up the gray hood to leave only his craggy face exposed. "No. Thank you, but I have found my calling. Money is not my primary concern."

"Then I suppose you will refuse payment for your books?" Steffano had always enjoyed tweaking his teacher, just a bit.

Luca gave Steffano the closest thing to a smile he had ever seen. "Even a teacher must prepare for the day he can no longer stand in front of his pupils."

Steffano chortled. "Well said, professor. Let me know if I can help." He dipped his head and opened the door into the warehouse.

Chapter Twenty-Four

Michael welcomed the warmer air in the lagoon and was pleasantly surprised at the delightful complexity of the *laguna* system. He had imagined a dank, brackish liquid concealing a 1950's Hollywood monster lurking beneath the boat. Instead, he passed marshes teeming with birds, isolated islands hosting fishing boats, and rode on blue-green water in a lane marked for traffic by pieces of floating wood tethered to the bottom. The engineers of Venice must have dredged out this path to facilitate shipping and commercial activity.

He stood on the deck of the galley, hands flat on the smooth railing, his heavy coat open and fluttering in the crisp breeze. The creak and surge at each stroke of the twenty-four rowers' oars made for a calming rhythm. Enrico stood beside him while a dozen or more birds flew around the ship. A chain of islands varying in size passed to the left, structures and evidence of human activity on some of the larger ones.

"You've never been to Venice," Enrico said.

"No."

"You can't imagine." A look of rapture had taken over Enrico's face; his eyes didn't seem to see the water anymore. "It is rich beyond measure, and the things you can do there, if you have money."

"Too bad we don't." *Forget any ideas about padding the expense report.*

"Sadly." Enrico looked for a moment at an isolated cloud. "My father took me as a boy. I was in wonder of it all: the markets, and the churches, and the *palazzi*. The doge's palace especially. A marvel. Then I went back as a guest of my cousin some years ago. I saw a different Venice, then." He gave Michael a lewd smile.

Michael turned back to the water and tasted salt-laden mist on his lips. "You'll need to show me around. But remember, this is a business trip."

"Certainly. All business." The mischief in Enrico's voice belied his words.

Michael tried to keep Enrico focused. "This is the first step. We need contacts here. We need them to get to the right men in Iberia. That's where the trading potential is."

Enrico stared at the water. His eyes narrowed and opened again. Remembering past escapades or planning new ones?

"I understand," he said at last.

Michael watched a pelican skim over the water alongside the galley, waiting for its next meal to be scared up by the boat's passing. He felt a kinship with the bird. They, the merchants, nobles, and kings, were all pelicans, predators that would take advantage of any situation to bring trade and riches their way. Columbus would now be back in the New World, taking, enslaving, killing and converting so Spain could enrich its treasury. The Portuguese, English, and Dutch would follow this path in the East and West. And Michael Patriate would be there to grab his part of the spoils.

The pelican skimmed ahead of the galley and dived into the water, only to bob back to the surface and float. As the boat slid by, the stationary bird consolidated its catch, a wriggling fin still protruding from its mouth.

They continued on their south-westerly course into the early afternoon. The widening passageway became more crowded with fishing boats and transport ships as they passed between two larger land masses. On the left, an opening appeared. Michael assumed from memory of his maps it represented the main inlet to the lagoon, leading out to the Adriatic Sea. Venice shouldn't be too much farther ahead. He hoped so. The steeper waves affected his disposition. The boat soon passed inside land once again, where the water calmed. Better, but he still felt queasy.

Another half-hour or so later, they turned northwest and followed the coast of an island. Densely packed housing gave way to palaces growing in stature, countless examples of medieval architecture locked in a jarring tangle of competing styles. Michael studied the elaborate arched windows of one residence when Enrico grabbed his arm and pointed ahead.

The object of his excitement stood out, given prominence in part by the space it occupied. Surrounding houses crowded shoulder-to-shoulder and competed for a place to stand. But carved out of their midst, several structures lounged around a spacious plaza.

A red brick bell tower rose behind a massive monolith made of pink and white stone. As they neared the front of the imposing building he tried to gauge its deceptive size. The third floor featured only seven windows, but each provided enough room for perhaps a dozen or more spectators to watch the water traffic. Tiny people strolling around columns on the first level rendered perspective for its imposing presence.

"What place is that?" Michael asked Enrico.

"The *Palazzo Ducale*, where the doge lives and the senate meets. The Campanille there." He pointed at the bell tower to the left. "The Basilica of Saint Mark behind." Golden domes revealed themselves behind the palace as the boat passed by.

If the Venetians had built the doge's palace to awe visitors, they succeeded. It slipped out of sight, but more wonders took its place. The coastline became a canal, the *Grand Canal,* Enrico said, and opulence surrounded them. Michael awakened to the temerity of their plan. Great wealth and power lined this canal, Manhattan and The Hamptons crowded together. And his little band of merchants would thumb their noses at these giants? His grave reservations turned to thoughts of abandoning the quest. *It's too much.*

Enrico seemed to catch his mood. "Impressive?" He grinned. "Are you ready for this?"

"Ready or not." The phrase sounded childish when it left his mouth. "This is all going to change, whatever we do." He said it as much for his own confidence as for Enrico.

What's that smell? An odor tinged with sewage thrust itself on Michael's consciousness. The water carried the smell, he realized.

When you confine a bunch of people to a small area, the waste has to go somewhere.

Enrico again pointed ahead. Commercial activity now bristled along the canal. Workers loaded and unloaded ships and boats tied up alongside docks. "We should be stopping here soon."

Michael's attention moved to the flow around him in the canal. Ships and boats moved among each other in some pattern he couldn't perceive. He had heard Venice described as a city of love and romantic gondola rides, but this place meant *business*. Commerce went on everywhere he looked. Markets displayed food and goods across the canal from ships unloading bulk freight in late afternoon shadows. Men bought and sold, lifted and moved, sat and talked.

The rowing stopped. Motion and sound that had been their companions since they left Jesolo vanished. The sound of oars being stored came from behind. Michael turned from his sightseeing to watch the crew operate.

Momentum carried them forward while the pilot steered toward a dock, swerved side-to-side several times to cut their speed, then eased them to the side. The crew threw ropes to the dock workers, who pulled them tight and tied them off. Michael admired the skill in their choreographed activity. He might not have even felt the boat stop if he had closed his eyes.

"Welcome to the Rialto," Enrico said.

Michael only nodded.

With everything secured, two crewmen put out a ramp and one gestured to Michael. He and Enrico picked up their bags and walked to the stone landing, looking for the hotel.

They walked toward a group of men carrying goods off a ship tied up in front of the combination of home and warehouse. Something intruded on Michael's consciousness, the noise. In a city this congested, he was used to whistles, car horns, and truck motors. Plenty of sounds attracted his attention, a worker stomping across the deck of the boat, calls among coworkers, laughter from down the way. But nothing remotely like New York, not even a creaky horse cart in this water-bound city.

"Can you direct us to the Sturgeon?" Michael asked a sinewy young stevedore who wore only a long-sleeve shirt and short pants in the cool air.

The man nodded and pointed across the canal behind them.

Michael followed his direction and spotted the sign. "Thank you," he told the worker, who had already turned away. *Now to get across.*

A bridge spanned the canal only a couple hundred yards ahead. They set off for it, weaving between men working, walking, laughing, and making serious talk. Commercial mixed with residential, with warehouses built right into the first floors of some homes.

Michael looked up at the houses while he tried not to appear a tourist. More impressive from the ground, the homes towered over the walk and made it seem narrower than it really was. Houses came in three, four, or even five-story affairs. Wide arches and thick, ribbed columns and beautiful artwork decorated them in incredible colors and diverse detail.

The wooden bridge pitched up to the center at a steep angle. Tall, planked sides hid crossing pedestrians except at the center section made up of two ramps that could be raised, Michael assumed, to allow masted ships to pass. Rows of square posts butted together formed columns that supported the structure. Michael and Enrico joined the crowd that crossed both ways at once. Soon they were on the far side and headed back down a path similar to the one they had just left.

There weren't many women on the street. Michael looked around when he realized it. Several ladies appeared at windows or on balconies, wearing elaborate dresses. The few walking were all accompanied by one or more men. A couple of gondolas out on the canal sported finely dressed females and their masculine escorts.

More boats, commanded by gondoliers outfitted in variations of a sort of costume or uniform, floated at the edge of the walk. Some evidently waited for their owners. Other operators announced their availability for hire like taxi drivers at an airport arrivals gate.

Laughter attracted his attention to some kind of gathering in progress on a second-floor terrace above. Michael forced his attention and his progress forward. He didn't want to gawk any more than he already had.

They passed a sparsely patronized market area. Pictures on signs hung over stalls indicated the items sold there.

"In the morning you will hardly be able to squeeze in here," Enrico said. "Delicious food."

"We'll have to make a stop then." Michael nodded toward a doorway marked with a round sign that hung from a pair of chains. "There's our place." As they grew closer, he noticed the fish painted on the sign looked a lot like the one on the brand of caviar that was Sheila's one indulgence.

He stepped up and opened the stone-framed door of the Sturgeon. But for the Middle Age dress of the staff and customers, it could have passed for many of the expensive hotels he had visited in Europe.

The gleaming beige marble floor inlaid with darker brown panels plus high ceilings gave the lobby a spacious air. To the right, a long staircase set at a leisurely angle led away from them up to second floor rooms set behind intricate wood banisters. On the left, marble columns and arches, each crowned with an inset Greek cross, gave entrance to a sitting room, where men sat on beautifully carved and upholstered couches and chairs, discussing business. To one side, several men gave their attention to a woman, gushing about the artist who had just completed her portrait.

Michael made his way toward the counter set inside the reception area to the right of the staircase. Almost there, he stopped at the sight. The ceiling at the center of the room opened up to reveal a glassed-in roof, lighting three floors of gleaming balcony railings and staircases.

"Enrico, did Alvisio book these rooms?" Michael stared up at the workmanship.

"I think so. He said he could get us a bargain."

Michael shook his head and looked back down at Enrico. "Well, I hope he did. This may blow our whole budget."

Enrico continued to gape. "I thought you said we have to spend money to make money."

"I guess I did."

"May I help you?" A man appeared from a door behind the shining white marble counter.

Michael set down his bags and flexed his stiff shoulders. "Yes. You should have two rooms reserved for us. *Signor* Patriate and *signor* de Rippa from Caorle." He changed the pronunciation of his name to the *Pahtriahtay* used by the clerk back in New York.

Enrico turned to Michael with a curious expression.

Michael gave him a sheepish look and shrugged. "Sounds better."

Enrico grinned and shook his head.

The clerk consulted a book filled with elegant script. "Yes, sir. We have two rooms waiting for you for three days. The charges for the rooms are two *lire* and ten *denari* per day each for a total of fifteen *lire*." He waited for the payment.

Michael took out his purse and counted out the coins onto the polished stone. "That should be it." He pushed the pile to the clerk. It did seem a bargain at only ten times the rate for that dump in Jesolo.

The man handed Michael two keys. "Your rooms are number seven and eight on the fourth floor. We serve two meals per day here in the dining room, or in your room if you like, for an additional charge, of course."

"Thank you," Michael said. "Oh. Where is the dining room?"

"Right behind you." The clerk pointed to a swinging door, now closed, between the sitting room and stairs.

"Please let me know if you need extra services."

Michael wasn't sure he wanted to know what "extra services" meant. "Thank you, we'll be fine." He picked up his bags and headed for the stairs.

"Sir," the clerk called. Michael stopped and turned to face him. "We will carry your things up for you."

"Oh. Thanks." He set the bags back down on the floor.

The clerk struck a bell on the counter. A boy dressed in the same red and white uniform of tunic and tights as the clerk hurried out the door and picked up Michael's and then Enrico's bags. Michael followed the young man up the stairs with Enrico in tow.

Thick, red carpet padded the stone steps. While he climbed, Michael skimmed his hand along the polished, carved railing on the left and viewed the passing collection of paintings of landscapes, mercantile, and religious themes on the right. The fourth floor hall boasted similar luxuries.

The bellhop, he didn't know the term here, took Michael's key, unlocked the door, set the bags inside and waited. Michael, unsure of a customary tip amount, looked back out in the hall to Enrico, who held up two fingers. Michael guessed that meant two *denari* and took the coins from his purse. The young man smiled his thanks and went to let Enrico in his room.

Michael paused in the doorway and called to Enrico. "We have a few hours before meeting our friend downstairs. I'd like to get some rest before then."

Enrico nodded. "No argument from me. See you in a while."

The elaborate room furnishings held no interest for Michael. He had use for only one thing at the moment. After he placed his bags on a chest and looked out at the canal for a moment, he went to the bed, pulled back the canopy drapes, and plopped on the soft mattress. Sleep came quickly.

* * * *

The tolling of bells roused Michael. Through the window, he spied a patch of sky that held a faint glow left over from the day. It must be six o'clock, an hour yet until their meeting. He turned over and reached to switch on the lamp on the bedside table.

They don't switch on here, either, he reminded himself.

Past the problem of being lost in a strange place, the thing that irritated and wore on him was the time consumed in doing the little chores. Light the lamp; draw the water; start the fire; empty the waste pot, all primitive tasks that drained time from the day. He longed to go into the bathroom and start a hot shower or set the thermostat on a level that would keep his feet warm. The idea occurred to him, and he looked over at the lamp. He could invent electricity.

Why not? He knew the basics. Put a copper wire in motion relative to a magnet and you get a flow of electrons through the wire. The paper he wrote one time in college covered the invention and marketing of electricity. He should be able to construct a generator. Materials for the components existed in this time. Columbus employed a compass with a small magnet and, of course, copper found many uses.

But lodestone magnets and copper weren't available in the large quantities needed for production of generators and transmission facilities. Copper production in this time depended on finding relatively pure veins of the stuff that could be melted down. Mining and separation of copper ores wouldn't begin in earnest until the end of the nineteenth century, and they didn't yet know about aluminum for cheap transmission lines. Maybe that wasn't a short-term project, but what other things could be developed?

The steam engine. It could be used to drive all kinds of machinery of which, obviously, most had yet to be invented. He would have to find people here with some engineering talent who could wrap their imaginations around foreign concepts.

Leonardo da Vinci lived sometime during this time period. He was the archetype of a man ahead of his time. His concept drawings were little understood, if even seen by others of his generation. Michael would ask about him. With a general knowledge of how things worked, and people like Leonardo working for him, Michael could become the Westinghouse or Edison of his day, with a shop pouring out inventions and making him rich in the process. For that matter, he could just invest in the coal mining operations these inventions would cause to boom.

Slow down. You don't have resources or connections yet.

He pushed these thoughts to the side for later consideration and rose to get ready for their appointment. He washed from the basin, changed into fresh clothes, and headed out to get Enrico. They made the long trip back down the stairs.

Michael peered into the full dining room and pointed back to the lobby. "Let's wait in here." Lively guests crowded the room.

I am underdressed.

Enrico scanned the room. "I need something to drink. Do you want something?"

Michael shook his head. "No, thanks."

Enrico wandered off, leaving Michael to survey the men in the lobby. He had been to more than a few gatherings like this, networking, making contacts, staying in the loop. It was kind of like dating, he realized. One needed to build trust in a relationship before becoming vulnerable to another, then keep working at the relationship to prevent your partners from drifting off, as in the marriage he hadn't worked at hard enough.

The front door opened to admit a man in his forties, and one younger, twenty-five or thirty. Both dressed in heavy coats. They looked about the room, and the older man went to the counter and spoke to the clerk, who pointed at Michael. *Two, not one.* Uneasy at the change, he started toward them as they came in his direction.

"Enrico?" the older asked.

"Michael. Enrico will be here in a moment. There he is." Michael waved him over and then remembered to smile at his new acquaintance.

The older man spoke again. "Anzolo Contarini." He shook hands with Michael, then Enrico. "My associate, Mora Vitturi."

Mora offered his hand. "It is good to meet you."

Michael returned the greeting. "You as well. Would you eat with us?" He waved to the dining room.

"Yes, thank you," Anzolo said. "Mora, check our coats, please?"

When Mora returned from the front desk, Michael led the way to the dining room. The staff had cleared several spaces at a table. After the four took seats, a waiter appeared and brought wine. On the menu tonight, baked fish. When the attendant left, Michael took a cue from Enrico.

Time to start the show. Michael stood and gave his guests across the table a gracious smile. "While we have a moment, I would like to discuss the purpose of our visit."

Enrico glared at him in warning.

Michael nodded. *Eyes watch; ears listen.* He continued.

"Our little band of merchants wishes to improve relations with our trading partners here in Venice. We hope to meet with several of you over the next couple of days. But tonight, please enjoy our hospitality and the meal."

Anzolo and Mora bowed in apparent appreciation. Enrico merely looked relieved. Michael intended to be taken for an ordinary trade representative out wining and dining prospects. He smiled and took a seat.

The waiter brought out the main course, eel, tender and flaky, if blandly spiced. Enrico took over the conversation, going on about his previous trips to the big city. Michael listened and watched, content to observe and size up these men.

The *desserte* arrived, a pear pie seasoned with something he couldn't quite make out, but delicious. Michael wished for coffee to go with it, but alas, the beverage hadn't made it to this part of the world yet. Then with dinner out of the way, it was time for serious talk. He stood, pushing back his chair.

"Gentlemen. Would you care to retire for a quiet drink with us?"

Anzolo looked to his friend for confirmation. "Yes we would, thank you,"

He signaled the waiter. "A bottle of wine and glasses, please."

At the room, Michael opened the door and motioned for his guests to enter. Once inside, the pretense stopped.

"What do you have in mind?" Anzolo went straight to business.

Michael set the wine bottle on the table where Enrico had placed the glasses. "We didn't know you would have a partner." He looked to Mora, who settled against a bedpost, then back at Anzolo.

Anzolo walked over to the window and stared down at something interesting before he turned back. "In business, one learns to share risk. Will it be a problem?"

Michael considered the situation. Maybe they should have just gone to Portugal and asked around instead of coming here. It was a gamble in either case. "No...No, it won't be a problem."

Michael gathered his hands behind him and walked over to Anzolo. "Your cousin, Alvisio, one of our group of merchants, may have told you something about us. We've banded together for our common good and to share our risks, as you said. We want to make contacts with merchants in other areas so we can spread our base of trading partners."

"So why come here?" Anzolo asked. "You already trade with us."

"Yes, and it is good trade." Michael held out his hands as he talked. "But I'll tell you what we're looking for. You maintain relationships with people in countries where we want to establish points of trade. A letter of introduction from you would give us credibility with businessmen in those places. Your identification of those people alone would help us a great deal."

Anzolo looked at Michael for a moment before he grimaced. "What does that profit me? It seems you want me to help you bypass us here in Venice. My popularity would not be enhanced with my fellow merchants, or with the council." He pointed toward the canal, back the way Michael and Enrico came in earlier. "You saw the *Palazzo Ducale* when you arrived, I assume."

"Yes, it's big." What did that have to do with anything?

"The Council of Ten meets in a room there. I hear..." Anzolo tapped an ear. "That outside the room, there is slot in which one can secretly place a note about an enemy of the Republic, a dishonest businessman, perhaps a man who has seduced one's wife. The council takes its responsibility to meet threats seriously. Sometimes offenders are not seen again. In the least, I stand to lose business, perhaps more."

Michael nodded. "I hear you. We're not anyone's enemy, and we're happy to cut you in on these new partnerships."

"Are you? To which areas do you wish to expand your trade? You are aware that virtually all of the routes to the Levant and eastern lands are split between Venice and Genoa? There is no room for a small band of Caorle merchants who own no warships."

"We understand that," Michael said. "We're looking more to the west with Spain and Portugal." When would Enrico jump in here? He and Mora stood still, observing.

Anzolo laughed. "So you chase the treasures of Columbus. He babbled for years in Genoa and then Portugal until at last he could get a hearing in Spain. Ferdinand and Isabella would have dismissed him, then, if they were not desperate. And now he thinks he has discovered a western route to the Indies. We do not know what he found, but it is not India. A few trinkets returned and Ferdinand sends him back. I do not need a partnership in that dream."

Michael nodded. "I understand your position, but we'd like to make contact with merchants there, anyway."

Anzolo took several quick steps toward the door and turned back to emphasize his point with a stern look. "You should go back to Caorle and concentrate on buying and selling what you have. There is no future in antagonizing those who help you."

"I see." Michael tried not to let the disappointment show. "Thank you for your time anyway."

Anzolo's expression softened. "It is always good to make new friends. Let us put this subject aside and start over. We can come again tomorrow and discuss more profitable transactions. I owe cousin Alvisio at least that much."

"We appreciate anything you can do for us." Michael felt little enthusiasm now.

"You've never been to Venice," Anzolo said.

Michael sighed and glanced out the window. "No. This is the first time."

"Well. Then we can show you around the Rialto tomorrow. There are many people that you will benefit from meeting. And you can buy yourself a mask. You realize it is Carnival time."

It wasn't what Michael had in mind, but he would make the rounds. "Yes, thanks. When would you like to start?"

"Nine o'clock?" Anzolo gave Mora a grin.

"We may be detained this evening," Mora agreed.

"Nine o'clock, then." Michael shook hands with the businessmen as they left.

"That was a waste of time." Michael listened to their visitors' footsteps fade behind the closed door. He pulled out a chair and plopped on it.

"Maybe." Enrico mulled over something. "We can still get some valuable information here. They see something, or they wouldn't come back tomorrow."

"I suppose. We never got to the wine." It was just a prop anyway, an excuse to talk in private.

"Well, it shouldn't go to waste. Like a glass?" Enrico moved to help himself.

"No, thanks." Michael wanted to think. "I'm tired."

Enrico took the bottle and a glass. "All right, I should get some rest, too. We may have a lot to do tomorrow." He flashed that mischievous look Michael had learned to hate. "Good night."

After Enrico left, Michael went to the window to look out on the city. Pinpoints of light testified that boats still moved on the canal, ferrying people across its length and width. The crowd seemed different than it did in the afternoon. From his third-floor vantage, he saw in dim lamp light many wore masks and more women walked below. *Carnival time.*

Across the canal, he could see into lit apartments. Apparently no one bothered with curtains here. Life went on everywhere around him, and he sat alone in a hotel room stewing about his problems, when he could be at home talking with...

Maybe Anzolo was right. He should go back to Caorle and become another merchant and make a decent living, probably for the rest of his life. He had dramatized the bit about Spain and Portugal taking over the world to stir his new partners to action. Yes, radical change would happen, but likely over a long period of time from their point of view. Inertia counted for a lot. Even when the focus moved from one part of the world to another, it took everyone a long time to notice.

Focus on the present.

Why not go back to Caorle and work, maybe marry Cecile and have kids? It would be a good life, yet...

The ambition that had driven him in his past intruded again. He could do nothing tonight, he decided, but get ready for bed.

He lay in the dark, thinking, hearing occasional laughter from the street and activity in the hall. A party raged through the city.

* * * *

Michael assumed from Enrico's droopy, red eyes that he'd had a big night. He didn't bother to ask. He turned from Enrico's door and huffed down the stairs, then waited at the bottom for Enrico to catch up.

The dining room door was closed. They didn't eat breakfast here. The church had added an early morning meal to the things it frowned upon for some reason. When he ate at a late hour, like last night, his belly always claimed to be empty the next morning. *What I wouldn't pay for some bacon and eggs.*

Slow, plodding steps announced Enrico's descent. Michael looked up at the sorry sight and then turned away in disgust. He took a seat in the lobby and leaned his head against the high back. While he examined the elaborate chandelier overhead, he assessed his own attitude. It stunk. He didn't get what he wanted last night and had decided to give up. He knew better. They were still in the game.

Enrico occupied the seat across from him and went back to sleep, with his face turned to the chair's back. For lack of anything better to do, Michael watched for a minute until a line of drool started to work its way down Enrico's chin. Michael shook his head and got up to walk around. He could still make his plan work.

A church bell rang nearby and then another. Soon, a cacophony like a neighborhood of barking dogs marked the hour. Anzolo and Mora came through the door as the last sounded, nine o'clock sharp. Anzolo barked a laugh at some unheard comment from his companion. Their banter stood in sharp contrast with Enrico's lethargy. Michael banged on the back of Enrico's chair and turned to meet the Venetian merchants.

"Good morning, Michael," Anzolo said.

The cheerfulness of Anzolo's greeting was more than he wanted to deal with this morning, but he managed a response.

"Yes, it is. I hear it's misty out, though." Cold, still air over warmer water made for a soupy mixture.

Anzolo's smile persisted. "Yes, but not bad. Sometimes the fog is thick enough that one can hardly see anything. Now, where shall we go first?"

"I'd like to visit the market, if you don't mind." Michael looked back for Enrico, who had made it to his feet, at least.

"Yes. It is marvelous. We shall go there first." Anzolo turned to leave, then stopped. "It is cold this morning. Do you have a heavier coat?"

Michael noticed the fur lining in Anzolo's cloak. "No, but this will do. I'm wearing layers."

Anzolo shrugged. "Very well, let us take you out to see the city."

Michael let the others pass and made up the rear of their group. He wondered at the difference in Anzolo's demeanor since last night. At dinner he was quiet, then direct and abrupt in private, today, ebullient. Anzolo and Mora led the way out the door with Enrico following them. Michael had the feeling he might step on Enrico's dragging tail. *Hope it was worth it.*

The hum of activity from the previous day had turned to a curious quiet punctuated by calls from gondoliers announcing their movements, murmurs of passing conversations, an occasional slap of a wave in the canal. The fog seemed to soak up light and stifle sound.

The walkway became more crowded with people who carried packages and bags. Sounds of vendors hawking wares began to make their way through, and then a wonderful, confusing medley of aromas led them to the market. The open square bristled with carts and bins full of fresh and salted fish, dried fruits and vegetables, breads, spices, other food and goods. Rows of fish silently accused Michael with staring eyes. A sheep bleated somewhere. Judging from carcasses hung in a line, this didn't figure to be a good day for the animal.

Anzolo led them through the crowd to a cart toward the back of the market. Small loaves of bread covered it a couple of rows deep. "You must try this, Michael."

Michael handed the man behind the cart a coin and picked up a loaf the size of his fist. He tore off a piece and filled his nostrils with the full bouquet before taking a bite. "Mmm, this is good."

It was moist and dense, very sweet and lightly spiced, like something Big Rich would have served back in New York. Pity they didn't serve coffee, too.

"One more." He paid the man again, wrapped the extra in a scarf, and stored it for later. Enrico stared at the food like a starving, sick dog. Michael felt sympathy, but not much.

While they wandered, Anzolo and Mora greeted the market merchants as colleagues. Michael felt better and even warmer after eating the bread. Since his scarf wrapped the other loaf, Michael wiped his hands on his coat and brushed out the crumbs.

When they reached the other side of the market, Anzolo asked, "Do you need anything else here?"

"No, not now, thank you."

Anzolo looked over at Enrico and gave him an amused smile. "Come this way. We will meet some people who may be of use to you some day."

The fog had lightened while they were in the market, making it easier to see the activity going on around them. Two men sat at a bench and looked over some kind of document. "The bankers are at work already," Anzolo said.

He used the Italian word for bench, *banca*, to describe the banker. Was it the origin of the term? Lots of business practices began in this part of the world. Michael marveled to see them in their infancy.

Anzolo led the party along the walk, greeting passers-by. He introduced Michael and Enrico to several, explaining they were businessmen from Caorle looking for contacts and so on. Michael tried to remember their names, but Anzolo didn't dwell long on any of them. Then Michael saw Anzolo's gaze light on a pair of men approaching and noticed his attitude change.

Anzolo whispered. "One of the richest merchants in the city. You should pay attention now."

They were an odd looking couple. The younger one, forty or so, dressed in the style of obvious wealth and bore himself with an air of superiority. The sharp eyes above a narrow nose and chin reminded Michael of a fox. The older man wore a gray hooded cloak that seemed to blend into the mist. Intense eyes peered from an otherwise bleak face.

Anzolo began in a hearty voice. "Steffano. It is good to see you this morning."

"Good morning to yourself." The gentleman made no move to shake hands.

"I would like to introduce my friends to you, but I am not acquainted with your companion." Anzolo looked to the man in gray.

"Luca Pacioli," the stranger answered. He held on to a leather bag.

Michael's attention sharpened at the name he recognized, but couldn't place.

Steffano gave his companion a deferential nod. "Master Pacioli is here from Sansepolcro to publish a book."

Anzolo offered Luca a short bow. "Impressive." He turned to Michael. "Steffano de Rompiasi, these are friends from Caorle, Michael Patriate and Enrico de Rippa. They are here on business."

"Patriate. That is a French name?" Steffano asked.

"Yes, sir, but I'm from England."

"Unpleasant place, London."

"So I've heard." Michael returned a deprecating smile. "I grew up in Norwich, some distance from London."

Steffano's eyes narrowed. "You seem to have misplaced your English accent."

The direction the conversation took troubled Michael, but he tried to maintain an air of confidence. In the periphery, he could see the others looking at him with some attention. "I've worked on it lately. It seemed to make me sound..." he hesitated. "Unsophisticated."

Steffano paused a moment, then let the topic go with a raised eyebrow. "I suppose it would. Does business bring you here?"

"Yes, it does." Michael said, glad to be on a different subject. "We're here on a sort of mission. The businessmen of Caorle have formed an association to promote trade in the area. We hope to visit with merchants like you to get some exposure for the opportunities there."

"What kind of opportunities would those be?" Steffano looked down the walkway. He probably heard this pitch every day.

"We have access to grain, timber and other resources, and transportation inland to get them to Caorle and on to you here in Venice. We can transport by ship in the Adriatic and through the lagoon and canal. We supply food and raw material for your industry, and you have ready markets for the goods you make and distribute." Michael noticed that Luca, standing to the side fidgeted with his bag.

Steffano shifted to a foot in the direction he and Luca had been headed. "We already do business in Caorle. What is new in your proposals?"

"There are opportunities to expand trade, but they require investments. Digging a deeper harbor is one," Michael explained. "We're looking for partners with resources to take on those kinds of projects."

Understanding straightened the frown on Steffano's face. "Ah, you want our money. Yes, I see your intentions. I am afraid, though, that my money is tied up in current investments. Perhaps another time."

"I understand." Michael eased back a step to allow Steffano an easy exit. "Thank you for stopping to talk to us. Other opportunities may come along."

"There are always opportunities. Perhaps we will speak again." Steffano glanced at Luca. "But now, we must be off to see a bookkeeper."

Michael nodded. "Of course. Thank you for your time."

"Good day gentlemen." Steffano and Luca took their leave.

Michael watched the pair go with a nagging thought he couldn't quite bring to the surface. He tapped Anzolo's arm. "Who was that with Steffano?"

Anzolo followed his gaze. "He is a teacher of some note. I believe Steffano's father employed him years ago as a tutor for his sons." He looked at Michael with a question on his face. "Do you know him?"

"No," Michael said. "I've only heard the name somewhere." It bothered him when he couldn't remember.

"Your interview went well in any case," Anzolo said.

"Oh?" Michael turned his attention back to business. "I thought he wasn't interested."

"Steffano is interested in many things, but be careful if you come to be associated with him. He ends up owning outright many of his 'partnerships.'"

Michael nodded. "Warning taken."

"Are you ready for more?"

"Lead the way."

It wasn't what he came here for, but if he had the opportunity to meet with some of the most powerful men in the world, he would take advantage of it. Enrico and Mora stood to the side in conversation, Enrico finally engaged in their expedition. "Come on," Michael called.

* * * *

Steffano looked back over his shoulder. "What did you think of our new friend from Caorle?"

"His speech and dress mark him as a simple country trader." Luca shook his head. "But he seems something more."

Steffano nodded. "I do not know what he is, yet."

* * * *

Michael came back from a relaxing bath to catch Enrico locking his door on the way out. He could only shake his head. "Don't get into trouble."

Enrico held up the grotesque white and gold mask he purchased that afternoon and grinned. "I'll be all right."

"We have another day of this tomorrow."

Enrico shrugged. "You seem to be handling it just fine. The chance to be here during Carnival doesn't come often."

"I'll see you in the morning." Michael sighed as he opened the door to his room. He had seen this behavior many times. Get a person away from home on a business trip, and he acts like a child out of sight of his parents. It always mystified him. On a mission like this, one needed to be at his best. *Not tired and hung over.*

Something in the room felt odd. He closed the door and looked about. The bags seemed to be in their places. His clothes lay where he left them. But there on the dresser, his toiletry items rested almost the way he placed them that morning. Since the day he thought his things were disturbed at home, he had been arranging them in a particular way, out of misplaced anxiety, he thought. He always left the razor folded and at an angle to his comb with the blade side of the razor just touching its corner. It now lay at the same angle, but the blade faced away from the comb.

Someone had searched his things. They wouldn't find anything of interest, of course. Anything valuable to him was on his person or in his head. But how had he become the object of someone's attention in the short time he had been in Venice? Or did the concentrated wealth in this place generate paranoia, a suspicion of any outsider? *Standard operating procedure?*

Cecile had been right. There were, indeed, serious people here. It was different than where he learned business. There, everyone played hardball, but you generally didn't have to worry about your enemies making you disappear. This was a different time and different rules applied. Not completely, but different enough. He had to watch his step while learning the nuances. The day had been good education, and business school was open for one more time in the morning.

* * * *

Michael read the note on the ship back to Jesolo.

"This is all I can do for you. Remember me when you find success," Anzolo had whispered, and palmed the paper to him as they shook hands goodbye.

In it, he found the names of contacts in Barcelona, Valencia, Porto, and Lisbon. Michael refolded the list and put it in a breast pocket sewn inside his cloak. The rowers' steady cadence seemed to inch the galley toward home. He chafed at the delay, eager to get back to Caorle and prepare for his target. Portugal.

Chapter Twenty-Five

Girolamo

The people were turning to him. As Girolamo scanned the throng packed into the cathedral, he saw it in their faces as they waited to hear his message.

He had effected many changes here in Florence over the last few months. He declared the monastery independent of the Lombard League vicars who tried to keep him muzzled, and now he answered, grudgingly, only to Rome. He expected objections from the new pope, Alexander VI, but heard nothing.

Girolamo had sent the less capable brothers and those unwilling to work from San Marco to more rural settings. A new school teaching arts, languages, and philosophy generated income and brought in many petitioners eager to take the vows. Most satisfying were the thousands who attended his sermons, hoping to witness a vision given to him by God.

Girolamo wasn't pleased for himself, of course, but for the enthusiasm with which these people accepted the Word given to him. In a long Noah's Ark series, he included in his sermons prophesies and warnings to the people about the consequences of vanity. Only a few more lessons and he would reveal their full meaning.

He let them settle in until every eye looked to him in urgent petition for his revelation and then raised his hands.

"This is the time, oh Florence! God is preparing the crucible, and it is Italy. A new Cyrus comes from the north to destroy the grip of this present Babylon that multiplies its perversion hour by hour. Pray! Pray for the day of trial God has prepared to prove the faith of His children. Pray for the cleansing fire that purifies the soul. The Medici oppressor will be swept away. The Whore will be thrown down. You, Florence, will be spared from God's wrath on that day if you turn from the evil that is Babylon. For you will become the New Jerusalem and be transformed into a beacon of light for the world!"

Girolamo looked about at the men and women pressed into the nave, hanging on his words. These people belonged to him. Not even the Borgia pretender to Saint Peter's legacy could stop him now.

Chapter Twenty-Six

With nervous anticipation, Michael held onto the gift through supper. He waited until all the boarders had gone to bed, until he and Cecile had the common room to themselves. Cecile rested in her favorite chair at the end of a long day.

"Hey," he said, trying not to grin. "I brought you something." He handed her the gift and then took a step back leaning against the chair across from her.

Cecile wore a puzzled expression as she stared at the folded piece of cloth in her hand. Her face lit up in recognition, and she squealed.

"Oh, it's lovely. Thank you!" The hands that, moments before, had rested motionless on the armrests, found the edge of the lace doily and shook it open. A dreamy look spread over her face. "You spent too much."

Michael hadn't prepared himself for the pleasure her smile gave him. "Not that much," he confessed. "I know a fellow in Venice."

"You are sweet, anyway." She glanced at him with sparkling eyes that made him grateful he had listened to Enrico's advice and bought her the gift.

He returned her smile. "I'm glad someone thinks so. It'll look good on your night table."

She narrowed her eyes in mock warning. "Don't start thinking about anything in my bedroom."

Michael sucked in an innocent breath. "Me? I wouldn't dare."

Cecile laughed and spread the doily in her lap. "What was *La Serenissima* like?"

"Beautiful." *Like you.* He pushed himself away from the chair and moved around to sit in it.

Cecile looked through the doily with a suddenly vacant expression. "I have never been there. Johannes went once. He went on for weeks about it."

"Well, then." Michael dipped his head. "You should go sometime."

She brightened. "Is that an invitation?"

Michael smiled and shrugged. "Maybe."

"Be careful what you promise." She gave him a mischievous grin.

And now the bad news. "When I get back." He sighed. "I have to leave again, probably for several months."

Cecile's forehead wrinkled. She paused. "Go? Where?"

Michael wished for the smile to return. "Portugal. For the association, to trade there, we hope."

She looked back to the doily in her lap. "When will you leave? I thought...This is so sudden."

"In a month or so. There's a lot of planning to do."

Cecile remained silent and slowly smoothed the pretty cloth with slender fingers.

"But I'll come back, and we will go to Venice, even if people talk."

"We can give them reason not to talk." She looked up with something akin to terror across her face. "No, I didn't mean to say that. I'm sorry."

Michael wished he could reach for her hand. "It's all right. We can see about that when I get back from Portugal."

She nodded and folded her arms across her body before she looked away. "It's late. You must be tired."

"Yes, it was a long trip." He suddenly dreaded the long journey to Portugal. "I should get to bed."

Later, lying awake, he wondered. What had he promised her?

Chapter Twenty-Seven

Agostino

Agostino looked up from the report as Toma entered the doge's chamber. He placed his cup on the silver platter and pushed the remains of the noon meal aside. "It seems we have an unlikely ally in France."

"Yes? Who?" Toma took a seat in the chair to the doge's right. He folded his slender hands in his lap and assumed the familiar, yet respectful attitude that had marked their years of friendship.

Agostino held up the sheaf of papers. "Zohane sent us these notes. Our friend, Cardinal della Rovere is in Paris after hiding at Ostia from the pope." Hardly a friend, though. Giuliano had long complained of Venetian independence, insolence even, toward the church's authority.

Toma nodded. "I suppose he continues to have designs on the papacy. Can't he wait his turn?"

"Impatient, no doubt. He has urged Charles to invade Italy. It only makes sense if Giuliano intends to take Rome. I suspect that Milan is also friendly to the idea. Giuliano and Ludovico Sforza have been in contact. Beatrice let that piece of information slip during her visit here."

Toma paused a moment. "Then that puts Ludovico's brother, Ascanio, in an uncomfortable position."

Agostino leaned his head back on his chair and thought about the ramifications. Without Cardinal Sforza's bloc of votes, Rodrigo Borgia, now known as Alexander the Sixth, might have lost the papacy to Cardinal della Rovere. *How delightfully complicated.* He sat up and grinned.

"The exiled cardinal wants Rome; the French king wants Naples. Toma, this might be interesting."

Chapter Twenty-Eight

"You need to learn Portuguese." Enrico sat across their makeshift desk in the warehouse, nagging Michael like his mom did when his room was dirty. "It is important if you still insist on going to Porto."

Michael frowned. "I don't have time to learn a new language." He pointed to the stack of papers in front of them. "We only have a month, and I have to get these cost estimates done so we can make good deals. We can hire an interpreter when we get there."

Enrico nodded. "Yes, we can. But how do you know we can trust him to speak for us? Besides, it isn't a whole new language. Much, if not most of it, is the same or very similar to what you're speaking now. And now that we're talking about it, you don't always speak very well."

Michael stood and walked away a few steps. They might come to blows if they didn't get out of this warehouse and on their way soon. "If they're so similar, why do I need to learn it?"

Enrico shook his head. "It's in the nuances and the words that sound alike but mean something much different. We don't have time for you to become an expert, but you at least need to understand most of what an interpreter is saying for you."

Michael lowered his head and tapped his foot a couple of times. As much as he hated to admit it, Enrico was right. And he surely didn't want Enrico to be the only one who understood. "All right. I'll find someone to teach me the basics."

"Great," Enrico said. "I know a man, if you're interested."

* * * *

Michael neared Paolo's house and realized he would miss these sessions with his language teacher. He had gone looking for an education and stumbled upon a unique character and something of a friend.

Paolo Camazarin worked as a ship's master for Venetian merchants for thirty-some years, traveling and dealing with counterparts along Mediterranean and Atlantic coasts. He spent considerable time in the port cities of Portugal and knew the language of business. He moved to Caorle when he was forcibly retired after an incident he never discussed. Michael paid him for his services, but judging from his villa, he didn't need the money.

"Good morning, *signor* Paolo," Michael said when the portly maid showed him in. He corrected himself when Paolo shook his head and frowned. "Oh, I'm sorry. *Bom dia, senhor Paolo*."

The teacher motioned Michael in. "That is better. Speak only in Portuguese now. Correctly, please." He smiled and motioned behind. "Come in."

Michael followed him into the living area decorated in the eclectic style of a world traveler. "Yes, sir. That is why I am here, but it is not the only reason. I have enjoyed our visits."

"I, also. An old man like me has few visitors. Please, sit. What would you like to talk about today?" Paolo eased into a soft leather-upholstered chair and leaned back.

Michael sat at an angle to him on the end of a matching couch. "We have gone over Porto well enough, I think. What about Lisbon? I will need to go there sometime."

"A beautiful city." The old traveler smiled and then shook his head. "But too much intrigue for me. I was there ten years ago when King John killed his brother-in-law. The nobles were panicked, and for good reason. A number of them died. It made everyone nervous, wondering what would happen next. I left when business dried up for a while, and I never made it back."

"It sounds dangerous."

Paolo laughed. "Life is dangerous. I have seen more men killed by merely losing their footing on a ladder or catching an unlucky wave than by the hand of another man."

"I have noticed that," Michael said. "This world supports abundant life generally, but doesn't care." He noticed a stern look pop up again. "Sorry, *does not* care much for the individual."

"And yet, we each expect it to cater to us." Paolo shrugged. "Even at the expense of others."

This statement struck Michael, although he had thought about it at different times. When he read about people dying in wars or storms or famines, he realized he thought about these people as *others* who had less value than himself, that their misfortunes were less important than his. Even when calamities happened close to him, his friends killed and injured in the car accident he had come upon, and his father's sudden death, he dwelt primarily upon the impact it had on him personally. "Is that so wrong?"

The old man breathed deeply, and his focus went to another place or time. "I prospered by looking out for myself. I worked hard for my employers, yes, but in the end it was for me and my own good. I am comfortable here today with the wealth I accrued during that service. But I enjoy it alone, if enjoy is the right word."

"You describe me, Paolo."

"Ah, but you are a young man yet. There is time for you to change your life, if you want something different."

Michael picked up a carved ivory hunting horn from the table between them and fingered the intricate scene of man's conquest over nature. "That is the difficult thing. I have always wanted only to be successful."

"There are many kinds of success." Paolo rested his elbows on the chair's arms and touched his fingertips together to form a pyramid. "And not all mutually exclusive either, by the way."

"Balance is important, I suppose." Michael set the horn back in its cradle. This was beginning to feel like a counseling session.

The old seaman looked directly in Michael's eyes. "There will always be balance. You are on one end of a board placed across a beam. What is on the other end keeping you up? Is it money? Power? Love? What will comfort you in your old age?"

Michael thought of his empty apartment back in New York. "Now you convict me."

Paolo laughed again. "I do not need to convict anyone. We do that to ourselves, though sometimes we understand it in hindsight."

Michael nodded his agreement.

"Look, we were talking about Lisbon and ended with philosophy. What about your trip? When do you leave?"

"There is a merchant convoy departing Venice in a few days. I will leave tomorrow.

"So soon on the water." Paolo shook his head. "Not that many years ago, we would not dare move before the first of March, if then. Things change, I suppose."

"Yes, I understand the larger ships are more stable."

"Still, there is time for bad weather." Paolo caught himself. "Oh forgive me, the old grow cautious." He sighed. "Or perhaps the cautious grow old." He straightened and placed his hands on his knees. "So you are off to Venice. A city of marvels."

His time was up. Michael sat forward in his seat. "You should go with me and visit. I should have a day or two before the ship leaves. I would like the company."

Paolo waved off the suggestion. "No, it would not be prudent. Tell me about it when you get back."

"All right," Michael conceded. "I will, and perhaps with exciting stories of other places as well."

Paolo smiled. "I wish you a tranquil, uneventful journey."

* * * *

"Here we are again," Enrico said, hefting his bags onto the barge.

"It's not too late to back out." Michael didn't relish traveling with him again. "You know, I'm not sure if I'd want Jacobus running his fingers through my business while I was gone."

"He'll take good care of me." Enrico grinned. "I wouldn't miss this for a whole month in Venice."

Part Two

Chapter Twenty-Nine

That Enrico was late didn't surprise Michael. He waited at the pier, watching the crew prepare their ship. Maybe his partner had been detained somewhere and wouldn't make it before they left. *Come on, Enrico.* Headed into an unknown situation, Michael needed someone's help, even if that someone was sent to keep an eye on him.

Out of the fog some distance down the canal walkway, a disturbance parted the crowd. Enrico ran with his bags, open coat flapping behind him. He gasped for air when he arrived. "Sorry."

"Don't worry about it. They haven't called us yet." Michael leaned closer. "Are you all right?"

Enrico bent over and sucked in deep breaths. He held up a hand for Michael to wait. Despite the cold, sweat ran down his red face.

Michael shook his head at the pathetic scene. That's what he got for staying out all night.

After a minute or two Enrico straightened. Some of the red in his face had faded, but he clipped his words. "I was afraid you might be gone when I saw your note."

"I knocked on your door." Michael shrugged. "It was all I knew to do."

Enrico managed a nod. "You know…" He drew another lung full. "Your spelling needs some help."

Michael winced. He had learned to write enough to keep books, but hadn't practiced much else. "I'm working on it. Where's your hat?"

"Back there." Enrico pointed over his shoulder.

"We won't be leaving for a bit. You can go find it if you want."

"All right." Enrico blew out a breath. He went off and left Michael in peace again.

Again Michael examined the ship waiting for them, *La Donna Maria*, floating in front of him like a giant sixty-legged water bug with its idle oars in their upright, parked positions.

Belonging to the class Great Galley, it enjoyed a state of the art reputation among the Venetian merchant ships. Back in New York, the word galley would have brought up visions of a big rowboat. But seeing this ship up close, he knew why the Venetians were masters of the Mediterranean.

According to his research, the vessel could carry two hundred and fifty tons of cargo along with one hundred and twenty passengers and, if necessary, could be outfitted for war. The ship sat one hundred and eighty oarsmen, who rowed when entering or leaving port, in battle, or in the extended absence of favorable winds.

From the front and rear of the ship flew the red and gold Venetian flag that featured a winged lion resting its paw on a book displaying a Latin phrase. The lion represented Saint Mark the Evangelist, the patron saint of the city.

Michael could still hardly believe the city would steal a body, put it in a church decorated with stolen artwork, and adopt the body's former owner as its patron saint, but that's what they claimed here. Someone's remains lay in the church next to the doge's palace, surrounded by booty taken during the sack of Constantinople in the thirteenth century. Maybe it did belong to the writer of the New Testament gospel. Michael didn't argue with anyone about it.

He looked into the mist for the other ships of the Flanders Fleet, a fleet with only five ships named for a place it didn't go anymore. He hadn't exaggerated to the merchants in Caorle about the troubles in that duchy's city of Bruges. Business there had almost died. The fleet now made its last stop in England instead before heading home.

Their itinerary read like a pleasure cruise, listing ports down the eastern coast of the Adriatic in Dalmatia and points south, areas Michael recognized as Croatia, Serbia and Albania. They would hit Messina and Palermo in Sicily, the Balearic Island port of Palma de Majorca off the coast of Spain, Lisbon and Porto in Portugal and Winchester in England. Michael and Enrico planned to stay in Porto and wait for the return trip in a month or so. They hoped to be back home in August or maybe September.

A shout from aboard the ship drew Michael's attention. A burly man stood atop the side railing and gestured for them to board.

Michael looked for Enrico and caught him walking up, still adjusting his brimless felt hat. "Hey, it's time," he called. He hoisted his canvas bags and stepped up on the boarding planks.

Enrico caught up with him on deck and cut in front of several other passengers as the line snaked around the deck. No one seemed to mind.

Michael, dwarfed by the main mast and rigging that towered overhead, followed the line to a flight of steps and found a single large cabin where most of the passengers would room together. Michael's stomach turned at the stench.

"What is that smell?" he asked Enrico.

Enrico only wrinkled his nose and shrugged.

The line stalled ahead at a registration table. While Michael waited his turn, he studied the single long room formed by curved planks and timbers on either side, the deck overhead, and a plank floor. Oil lamps suspended from hooks jutting from the timbers revealed sooty spots on the low ceiling. Down each wall, registered passengers stowed gear against the hull and settled into quiet conversation. Soon, he came to the registration table and a man he heard called "the scribe."

The clerk wrote each man's name in a book, took his passage fare, and then pointed him to a spot along one side or another of the room. The registered guests hung their bedrolls on nails driven into the walls and placed their properties underneath. The scribe appointed each guest a "berth," a space on the floor the width of his bedding.

Michael wondered whether, jammed into this small area for the next several months, the passengers might either learn to like or despise one another on the way.

"Name?" asked the clerk.

"Michael Patriate."

"Destination?" He never looked up.

"Porto."

"Forty five *ducats*." Upon receipt of the fare, the scribe wrote Michael's name with a flourish. He then pointed to the next empty spot on the far side.

Michael hung up his bedroll as Enrico signed in. He finished as the pen flew across the paper again and the clerk pointed to the vacant place on the near side.

"I'm with him," Enrico said.

The clerk merely shrugged with raised eyebrows and waved him in beside Michael.

Michael sighed at the prospect of sleeping next to Enrico for this entire trip.

Enrico plopped his bags on the floor and looked around. "Cozy."

Michael had taken Sheila on a cruise once. That was a fun trip, but this would take some getting used to.

Toward the center of the ship, something that looked like a small well caught Michael's attention. He left Enrico unpacking and walked over to look down into the foul looking source of the odor.

"Bilge water," said someone with a quiet voice and distinctive German accent.

Michael turned to see a short, thin older man in the black habit of some religious order. A vestige of pepper gray hair contrasted with the dark outfit. With his shiny head and hooked nose, he looked like a bird. *A bald eagle.*

He gave Michael a kind smile. "You'll get used to the smell. *Guten morgen,* good morning. *Frater* Felix Fabri." He offered his hand.

"Michael Patriate, Brother Felix." Michael shook hands with the monk. "And good morning to you, too."

Felix bowed. "Where are you bound, *herr*, no, *signor* Michael?"

Michael caught Felix's infectious good mood. "Porto in Portugal. And yourself?"

"Rome, thank our Lord, but I will depart this ship at Messina. I saw you came with a companion."

Enrico approached Felix from behind on the walkway. Michael gestured with an open hand to him. "Frater Felix Fabri, my associate, Enrico de Rippa."

Felix spun about and offered a hand. "I am delighted to meet you, *signor* de Rippa."

Enrico shook his hand. "And I to meet you."

He can act civilized when he wants.

"What kind of business do you have in Portugal?" Felix asked Michael.

"Nothing exciting, I'm afraid. Buying and selling." Michael didn't want to get into specifics with someone he didn't know. "And you? What takes you to Rome?"

Felix's smile turned to rapture. "I travel to see the Holy Father, Pope Alexander the Sixth. My wish for an audience with him before I die was granted, and I have just now received the opportunity."

Michael congratulated him with a nod. "Well, then, I'm happy for you."

"Thank you. Oh, I must introduce you to an acquaintance." He waved to get the attention of someone across the cabin. An elderly man rose from his seat on a piece of furniture placed under his hanging bedroll. "This is my friend Konrad Albrecht, Knight of Rhodes."

The gentleman wore a gray cloak similar to Felix's, though cut in a less severe style. His white hair, combed back, reached his shoulders and complemented a short white beard. He walked erect and moved gracefully, but with deliberation, as if the old joints took their own time. His amiable eyes almost level with Michael's, Konrad spoke in a low, sincere voice, also accented in German. "Good day gentlemen."

Michael and Enrico introduced themselves again.

"Where are you bound?" Michael asked.

"I travel to gather support from knights in England, for the building of the fortifications at Halicarnassus."

He spoke as if Michael would know what this meant. The name did sound familiar.

"Ah. I wish you good fortune." Maybe the story would come out in conversation. He knew he had much to learn. *Be quiet and listen.*

"Konrad and I have been acquainted for a number of years. We met in Rhodes," Felix said.

"How interesting," Michael responded. "You'll have to tell us about your travels."

"There will be time for that, I assure you." Felix obviously appreciated a good audience. "Please excuse me, I should meet the others."

Michael watched Felix go and turned back to Konrad. "Your friend enjoys being with people."

Konrad's laugh accented the lines in his face, several scars among the wrinkles. "That he does. Of course, he can be stern with those who stray from teaching, but his heart is good." He glanced at Felix, busy greeting another passenger. "Do you have merchandise aboard the ship?"

"No, on this trip we only talk."

The old eyes sparkled with a touch of humor. "I see. After being confined to this ship for some time, you may find your words are used up."

"Let's hope not." Michael found himself liking this gentle knight.

* * * *

After half an hour or so, the additions to their group dwindled, then stopped. The scribe looked around, climbed the steps to the deck, and disappeared.

Michael started for the hatch with Enrico close behind. He stopped at the spaces where Felix and Konrad bunked. "Would you like to go up and watch the departure with us?"

Konrad looked up from his padded seat on the chest. "No. I have seen enough of them. I think I will rest for a while, but Felix, you go."

Felix, spry for a man of his years, jumped to his feet.

Leaving the dim lamplight in the hold, Michael squinted in the sunlight. The fog of morning had lifted, revealing Venice in crisp detail. A westerly breeze rustled the flags and coaxed an occasional lazy snap from their fringes.

Felix led Michael and Enrico to the left rail, dockside. "We'll be able to see from here," he said.

The three ships in line ahead of them already glided toward the sea, oars at work, sails still furled. Arrivals and departures were surely common, yet people stood along the canal and in windows and on balconies above watching their fleet leave.

In a movie, Michael decided, this would be the scene where the navy sailed away to engage the enemy, urged on by a grateful nation. Perhaps that observation wasn't far off the mark.

The great ships paraded past magnificent buildings, parting the crowd of smaller ships and boats.

Crewmen released the mooring ropes and hurried aboard, then pushed the *Donna Maria* away from the dock. The right-side rowers dug their oars in the water as soon as they were clear and the ship began to turn about. Palaces soon slid by again. Their opulence impressed Michael more each time he saw them.

"This is always the good part," Felix said. "Everyone is excited and the journey is full of promise, but too soon the traveler loses sight of the people at home, and the daily routine begins to wear. At the end, one is merely relieved to return. I try to savor each part for what it is, but this is the most enjoyable."

Michael peered once more at the ducal palace across the way. "I heard someone say once we rejoice when a baby's born, and mourn an old man when he dies, but those things and everything in between are necessary to complete a journey." Where did that come from?

Felix's eyes lost some of their focus. "Yes, that becomes clearer as I move toward the end." He took a deep breath and glanced up at Michael. "The important thing is what we do with the time in the middle."

Michael had no response for Felix, and they settled into silence. Soon they were out in the lagoon. The unfurled sails filled with the wind and rowers locked their oars.

When they passed the barrier islands and headed out to sea, Enrico spoke up. "It's cold up here. I'm going below."

"All right." Michael glanced over. "I'll be here for a while."

Enrico left Michael and Felix alone at the rail.

"Have you sailed on a ship like this before?" Felix asked.

"No, this is the first time. I've gone between Jesolo and Venice on a smaller vessel, but never on a long journey like this." Michael chided himself. Not an hour on the ship, and he'd already blown his cover story about coming from England, but he didn't feel any danger from this man. He found it difficult to stay on guard.

Felix ran his eyes over Michael's face and turned back to the sea. "You are uneasy."

"A little. I'm unsure about traveling this far for the first time."

Felix tracked a gull in its circling flight, his upturned eyes windows into a soul that had let go of fear. "I have known many in my travels. Men may wrestle with nature and enemies and circumstance, but they wrestle most fiercely with themselves." He turned his gaze to Michael.

Is this fellow a mind reader? Or only fishing? Michael studied him for a moment, trying to take his measure. Felix wouldn't accuse him; neither would he flinch from telling him the truth. "I wrestle with a lot of things, Father, Brother. What should I call you?"

The genuine smile disarmed him. "Call me Felix."

They talked the rest of the afternoon.

Sunset began as a yellow ball of fire among scattered purple clouds on the horizon. As it eased into the sea, golden rays radiated up into the moisture-laden air, creating an enchanting halo that took Michael to a different reality. *It was her favorite part.*

That night on the cruise was "formal night," where everyone dined dressed in their finest. Michael had tried to hurry Sheila back to the room so they could get ready.

"It'll only take a little while." She smiled at him and pulled a pair of deck chairs together.

They held hands and watched as the sun dwindled to a small yellow spot on the water.

Trumpets startled Michael and shredded the memory.

Felix jumped up from the deck and motioned Michael to follow.

"We need to hurry if we want a good seat."

Michael took a last look at the glow on the watery horizon and pulled up from his seat at the rail.

Enrico must have been waiting for the call. He caught up with them before they moved very far.

They moved rearward, passing the uncovered kitchen and an empty stable where, after Lent ended, a mix of livestock would stand penned and wait for slaughter.

The captain's table, actually three tables set in a horseshoe shape, waited in the poop, a structure rising above the main deck at the rear of the ship. Supper seemed to be a first-come, first-served affair.

The three of them made it to the head table before seats filled up around them and toward the ends of the other two tables. Felix scanned the room for a few moments and then announced, "Konrad isn't here yet. He moves more slowly these days. I will eat with him below." He rose from his seat.

Michael jumped to his feet. "No, Felix. Please, I'll let him have my place when he gets here."

"It is all right, Michael. He often doesn't feel like eating with a crowd. Enjoy your meal." A latecomer rushed to claim the empty chair as Felix left.

Michael sat again.

"Did you enjoy your time with the monk?" Enrico asked.

"He's a friar. Dominican." Michael looked for the servers. With Felix gone, he didn't have anyone to explain the rules.

"I could tell. The black cloak gives him away."

Michael shrugged. "He seems like a good man."

Enrico looked over Michael's face with a grin. "He must have been preaching hell fire. You have a sunburn."

His face did feel warm to the touch. *Probably need a floppy hat.* Tomorrow he would ask among the oarsmen.

Felix had told him that on a ship of any other nation, the men who rowed the vessel in and out of port would be slaves. Venice paid its oarsmen, although they might still be commonly referred to as "galley slaves." Some also performed personal services like laundry or brought wares with them to sell and trade aboard ship and in whatever port they might visit.

The first wine arrived, a *malvoisie*, someone across the room exclaimed. Michael had never been much of a wine drinker, but his new life had given him some amount of discrimination. *Not bad.* Maybe the food would taste better than he'd heard.

A salad arrived, one that Michael would not have been surprised to see at home. He retrieved his fork and began, pushing the vegetables with a piece of fresh bread. "This is good," he said to no one in particular.

Michael's neighbor, occupying Felix's seat, spoke up. "Wait until we are away from port a few days. You'll be lucky to get a hard biscuit. That shouldn't be for a while, though. We'll be not far away from port until we leave Palermo."

Palermo was the last stop on Sicily after rounding the boot of Italy. The ports after that point would stretch farther apart.

"Let's enjoy it while we can, then." Michael looked around at the guests. "I thought this was the captain's table. I don't see him." Although they had not been introduced to the captain, Michael had seen him on the deck during the day.

"No, the captain and officers eat later, after we are finished," said the man on his left. "And you may want to eat quickly. They will rush us off so they can get to their meal."

Michael nodded his understanding. "Thanks. By the way, I didn't get your name. I'm Michael Patriate." He extended his hand.

"Uberto Zerbus." Uberto shook Michael's hand briefly and returned to his meal. "Veneto?" He referred to the region controlled by Venice.

"I'm sorry?" Michael asked.

Uberto swallowed a mouthful of salad. "Veneto. Your accent."

"Oh." Michael nodded. "Caorle, and yourself?"

"Milan."

This surprised Michael. Milan and Venice were rivals and sometimes outright enemies. "Ah."

The server placed a dish of fresh fish in front of him. Six weeks until Easter, there would be many more meals of fish.

"What business are you in?" Uberto reached for his glass.

Michael chewed a bite and swallowed. "We buy and sell general merchandise. I work for a man called Rizzo Bernardigio. My friend Enrico operates his own business there." Introductions went around again.

"I would assume that you trade primarily with Venice."

"We do," Michael said. "But we intend to visit merchants on our route to explore a possible expansion."

"That might not be popular in *La Serenissima*."

Uberto sounded as if he had some experience there. Michael decided to skirt the subject. "I doubt that our little operations make much difference one way or the other in Venice. What brings you with us on this voyage?"

"Much the same." Uberto scraped flesh away, baring a row of white fish bones.

"I thought Milan trafficked more through Genoa."

"Things always change." Uberto frowned. "Conditions are strained at the moment."

Michael understood that Uberto didn't want to discuss details of his business. Neither did he. They ate in silence for a while.

The servers brought dessert, a pudding, which Michael enjoyed. Soon the trumpets sounded again. Men began to drain their cups and leave, the servers moved in to begin clearing tables.

They had stripped the tablecloths from one before Michael and Enrico followed Uberto out the door.

Uberto said his goodnight and walked off toward the side railings.

"More time on the deck?" Enrico asked.

"No, I'm tired. Think I'll hit the bed." Michael shrugged against the wind, which had turned colder while they ate. Darkness surrounded them, with only a glow coming from the stairwell leading to the hold below. He relaxed in the warmer cabin.

Travelers, sixty or seventy he thought, sat about individually in their berths and in pairs or small groups talking shop or nonsense. Down by Felix's berth, four Greeks with shoulder-length hair played a card game. Felix watched, shook his head, and frowned. A rotund man folded his bed to one side and lifted a plank out of the floor. He scooped out a place from the underlying sand and put a wine bottle there before covering it and replacing the plank. A crude cooler of sorts.

Michael's eyes tracked the ship's beams down the rounded wall to the plank flooring. They had poured sand over the keel, probably for ballast, and fit boards on top to make a floor. It might also let any water coming in seep down toward the bilge well. A random thought crossed his mind. *Do they ever change the sand?*

While Enrico set up his own nest, Michael moved his bags to the end of his space and took down his bed, unfastened the ropes that bound it for carrying and rolled the bed into its place. Some of the others had hung their bags on the long nails in the beams where their beds had hung out of the way during the day. He heeded Paolo's warning against that practice. A sudden wind in the night could cause the ship to shift and drop the bags on one's head.

With his pillow and a bag for support, Michael sat and leaned against the wall. All in all it hadn't been a bad day. The wind blew steady but not rough, he had met new friends, enjoyed the supper. Now he'd see what nights were like.

A piercing shout shattered the quiet buzz of conversation. "You're in my place."

Michael rose up and watched. One traveler, a slender young man with bulging eyes, had come back to his berth and found a neighbor had lapped his bed over onto his space, or so he claimed. The alleged offender denied the incursion. Michael couldn't tell that one had any more or less room than the other. The first man cried out to the men around him for support, but the ones who paid attention remained silent. Others just ignored the whole incident. Felix and Konrad huddled in uninterrupted conversation. The complainant, seeing no help coming his way, ceased his arguing and smoothed out his bed, pausing at intervals to glare at the other.

"I hope he doesn't do that for the whole trip," Enrico said.

"Me too." But he probably would. He looked the type.

Enrico lay down on his bed with his fingers laced behind his head and elbows splayed out. "What did you and the friar talk about all day?"

"Not much, as a matter of fact. He read to himself most of the time."

"Sounds pretty exciting."

"Relaxing."

"Well, you will have a lot of time for it."

Michael scooted down from his sitting position and tried the bed out. It was hard, but not bad. He sat up and slipped off his coat and shoes, then crawled under his covers, clothed, as he saw others doing. Even this simple bed felt good after a long first day.

An hour or so later, the lamps started going out. Conversations continued for a while in the dark, but soon dropped off and quiet settled in. Michael could hear the sound of the water rushing against the hull and an occasional footstep from one of the crew above, until a neighbor started snoring. Rather than disturbing him, the noise reminded Michael of Jim, a good-hearted guy and roommate in college for two years. He turned over and pulled his covers close. *Good night Cecile.*

* * * *

Roused by the morning bell, the travelers rose and rolled up their beds. Michael joined the crowd leaving the cabin. Up on deck, the barely risen sun cast the crew in a brilliant golden light. Crew members scrubbed decks and performed various necessary chores during the shift change in progress. The sails hung limp and waves no longer sped past the ship. Presently, a whistle sounded back from the castle.

The crewman who had blown the whistle held up a board painted with a picture of the Virgin Mary cradling her child. The crew, oarsmen and guests all kneeled. Michael followed their example.

"*Ave Maria, gratia plena Dominus tecum,*" or "Hail Mary, full of grace, the Lord is with thee," began the chant. Michael joined in. *Thanks Cecile, for dragging me to church.*

After the short prayer, many stayed in the kneeling position for some time. Michael stood after others began doing so.

Morning prayer time over, the crew returned to work. Most of the travelers went back to the cabin out of the way of the busy crew.

Michael spotted Felix and Konrad standing at the rail and headed their way with Enrico behind. He followed Felix's gaze ahead to the other ships sitting in the calm water, sails slack, oars parked. "This is a galley. Why aren't we rowing?"

"The men are good for shorter distances on a heavy ship like this," Felix said. "It would wear them out for no good reason to attempt rowing the distance we have to go." He looked up. "Did you rest well?"

Michael sighed. "Mostly. Yesterday was tiring."

"I couldn't sleep," Enrico said. He had slept most of the day before.

Felix scanned the clear sky. "On a ship, one never knows what the weather will do. It can be wise to take rest when one can. Pardon me if I sit." He sat at the railing with his legs around a post. Konrad followed suit.

Michael leaned against the rail, thighs pressed to the top timber, and peered into the deep blue water undulating against the side of the ship. Out toward any horizon, more blue water met the pale sky. Only the other four ships in their convoy broke up the relaxing scenery.

Felix interrupted his sightseeing. "Has anyone given you instruction on the dangers of ship travel?"

"My friend Paolo is an old ship's master. He warned me about a lot of things." Michael laughed. "I did think twice about coming."

"And you, Enrico?" Felix turned to look behind Michael.

"A little."

"Well, then, permit me to 'preach' a bit, and indulge an old man if you have heard this before.

"First, when on the deck, watch for crewmen doing their work. When they move they can be like lightning, for certain things must be done instantly. They will run through you in their haste. Many unsuspecting passengers have been knocked overboard and lost. Also, never trust a rope. A slack rope can be suddenly pulled by a change of wind in the sail and pull you into the water or take off a finger. And a firmly stretched rope that you pull on for support can go slack and leave you lurching. Never sit or stand under pulleys or blocks used in the riggings. I saw an officer of a ship killed by one swinging loose. A terrible loss." He dropped his head for a silent moment.

Michael looked around the structure that couldn't be more than a few years old. "Bad things can happen at sea, but this seems like a safe ship."

Felix wore a grim smile as he looked up at Michael. "A philosopher named Anacharsis was asked which ships were the safest. He replied, 'Those which lie on dry ground and not in the sea.' He also said men on the sea were not counted among the living or the dead on account of the sudden perils that may occur."

"Well, at least nothing bad can happen in calm weather like this," Enrico said.

Konrad spoke up from his spot beside Felix. "If this calm lasts for a number of days, you will see your bread eaten by maggots, and your water turn foul and stink before we get to port.

I believe that storms are better. At least the men are busy and the storm blows the ship one way or the other."

Enrico raised an eyebrow. "That's encouraging."

"A voyage like this can be a rewarding experience." Felix rose from his position and turned to face the deck. He made a gathering motion with outstretched hands. "The friends you make on board will be your friends forever, even if you never have the good fortune to see them again. And the trials will teach you what is important in life, if you learn the lessons."

"What's important?" Enrico asked.

Felix gestured again. "Look about you at all these men. The captain and his officers command men and are obeyed. The sailors prepare the sails to harness the wind. The galley slaves are powerful men, but here we sit and wait, and for what?"

"The wind?" Enrico made a disrespectful face.

Felix ignored the insult and raised his arms to the sky. "A gift from God. He gives us the wind as He sees fit. He rescues us from the storm. It is He that brings us to our destination. What is important is that we learn to trust not in our own importance, but in Providence."

Enrico shook his head. "You make it sound like men aren't worth anything."

"Men are valuable because God values them, but not of themselves." Felix pointed toward the bag tied at Enrico's waist. "The coin in your purse, what worth does it have? Its only value is that men want it and will give up something in exchange. The value of a man is that God loves him and wants to have a relationship with him. When a man refuses that relationship, he is worth only what he himself can produce. But when he accepts God, he becomes a tool in a powerful hand, capable of far more."

"I was unprepared for a sermon this morning," Enrico said.

Felix cocked his head to one side and gave Enrico a sheepish smile. "It is what I do."

Enrico pivoted on a foot. "I failed to bring any wine with me. I believe I'll see what our traders have to offer."

Felix looked as if he wanted to say something else to Enrico, but held his tongue and only gave him a slight bow of his head and watched him walk away. "I have seen many men drink their way through a voyage. It usually does not turn out well."

"It doesn't help your thinking." Michael turned his back to Enrico's exit. He didn't want to talk about his partner today. "You mentioned you two met in Rhodes. I'd like to hear the story."

Felix looked down at Konrad, still seated, who gestured for him to start the account. "All right. Well, in 1480, only fourteen years ago, I traveled on a pilgrimage to the Holy Land aboard a Venetian ship. That was the year Mahomet the Great, Emperor of the Turks, besieged Rhodes with intent to dislodge the knights there. We were warned against making the trip because of the danger of Turkish ships, but we went nevertheless, and by the grace of our Lord evaded the Turks on our way to the Holy Land.

"On our return trip, we heard how the Turks had given up their quest at Rhodes and abandoned the fight. After being stranded at sea for some days in a calm not unlike this one, our provisions were almost gone when at last the wind stirred again.

"We decided to head for Rhodes. The wind drove us to the far side of the island where, with the help of God, we found fresh water that restored us in body and spirit. By the time we made it round to the harbor it was dark."

Konrad slapped his hands on his thighs and broke in with an uncharacteristic guffaw. "Then we tried to shoot them."

"Yes, they tried to shoot us." Felix grinned. "They reasoned ours must be a Turkish ship returning to continue the fight, since they had been gone only a few days. So, they fired their cannon at us. We lit lamps and made the sign of the cross while calling to them that we were friends. Ours was the first Christian ship to have sailed into the harbor for some months." He laughed and held up a skinny finger.

"One of our crew cried out 'We are Venetian, and the galley belongs to Saint Mark.' I will never forget. He could not speak again for a week after the captain's servant struck him in the mouth. The inhabitants were unhappy with Venetians and their business arrangements with the Turks. They might have sunk us anyway. Instead, the captain had another sailor explain that we were returning pilgrims."

Konrad interrupted again. "We must have been a sorry sight to the pilgrims when they entered the city. At the end, there were only six hundred knights left against fifteen thousand Turks, and many of us wounded. We could scarcely be good hosts, but were overjoyed to see them."

"Yes, we were happy to see them as well." Felix's face turned serious. "But the city was devastated. Cannonballs littered the street. The walls were ruined and food was scarce after the Turks plundered the island, but they, and we, were alive. Konrad helped me secure two fowls for one of our men who had fallen very ill. If not for his help, the man might have died."

"Felix was a great help as well," Konrad said. "He tended our wounded and sick. God delivered us in our time of need and sent us angels to care for us."

"You exaggerate, Konrad. You were doing nicely when we arrived."

Michael interrupted the combination love-fest and argument. "So, Konrad, did you travel back to Germany with Felix?" He sat on the deck and leaned against the rail.

Felix reclaimed his place.

Konrad shook his head. "No, my work was in Rhodes with my brothers. We are tasked with caring for the sick and ailing among the pilgrims as well as protecting them from pirates and Turks." He looked out on the sea. "It has taken these many years to recover from the siege."

"Then how do you come to both be aboard the *Donna Maria*?"

Felix piped up. "God willed it."

"It must be," Konrad affirmed. "The *Bailli* of the German Tongue in Rhodes sent me to the Grand Prior in Germany to request assistance in fortifying the castle at Halicarnassus."

The name found a place for Michael. "The Mausoleum."

"I beg your pardon?" asked Konrad.

"I'm sorry to interrupt. I only remembered the Mausoleum at Halicarnassus. One of the Seven Wonders."

Konrad's face drooped. "Ah, yes. It is sad to see, now. I remember the stories, but the earthquakes have laid it low. We have used some of the broken stones in building fortifications. It is our prayer that with help we will not be forced to use the great stones."

Michael sat in amazement. He read about the final destruction of this ancient marvel in a high school history class, when pieces of the monument could still be seen embedded in the castle walls. And here on this smooth wooden deck sat one of the architects of its undoing.

Konrad continued. "But as I said, I went to the Grand Prior in Germany. He sent me on this mission to go to the brothers of the Castilian and English Tongues to gather assistance in our endeavor. When I saw Felix in Venice, such joy came into my heart!" He gestured to Felix, but spoke to Michael. "It has been good to see my friend again."

Michael nodded. "I wish Enrico had heard this story."

"Your friend pretends he does not care." Felix gave him a confident smile. "But I believe there may be more to him than you think."

* * * *

The ship creaked with a sound Michael recognized as the mast transferring stress from full sails. He hoped the crew would be less irritable with the wind blowing again. After an incident between the Neapolitan businessman and Albanian crewman had forced them downstairs, he wondered what would happen if the calm had lasted much longer.

He leaned back on his makeshift chair in the cabin and glanced up toward the deck. "Sounds like we're moving."

Enrico fiddled with an oversized deck of cards. "Maybe we'll make it to Zara tomorrow if the wind doesn't die again."

Michael stared at the ceiling. "We can hope."

"What do you want to do when we get there?"

"We might as well get some work done." Michael sat up and, hands behind his head, he tried to stretch some of the stiffness from his neck. "Some of the merchants may be interested in direct trade, and it'll get us off this boat for a while."

"They say the food is good in Zara," Enrico said, always ready for a meal.

"That's what I hear." They had to eat in the city, anyway. The captain didn't provide them with food while the ship sat in port, part of the contract. "You might want to go easy on the wine there."

Enrico pitched the cards in his bag and gave Michael a sour look. "What's the matter with you?"

Michael looked away. "Nothing."

"There is something. You've been in a bad mood all day."

Michael sighed. "It's my father's birthday. He was born on February twenty fifth."

"Oh." Enrico's expression changed to confusion. "I'm sorry. I never paid much attention to birthdays. How old is he?"

"He died when I was eleven."

Enrico nodded. "That's young to lose a parent."

Michael waited, silent for a while before he spoke. "Are your parents still living?"

"My father died several years ago." Enrico looked at the floor. "I don't know about my mother."

"That's a shame. What happened to your mother? If you don't mind me asking."

Enrico waited while an intoxicated passenger lumbered down the aisle. "No, it's all right. She disappeared when I was twelve or thirteen, I don't remember. My father said she died, but we never had a funeral. I think she ran away."

Now his self-destructive actions made a little more sense. "I'm sorry."

Enrico shrugged. "She was probably better off. My father could be unpleasant."

"Who took care of you after she left?" Michael began to feel like some kind of counselor.

"My older sister took the job. She cleaned and cooked and watched the other three of us. My father stayed away much of the time until he brought home a new wife. My sister married and left as soon as she could."

"It sounds like a hard way to grow up." The empathy Michael felt for Enrico's situation surprised him.

"You get used to it, but it wasn't all bad. I learned the business with my father when I was old enough. When he died, his friend Jacobus helped me along the rest of the way."

"Ah, I wondered about your attachment to him."

Enrico nodded.

"And you have never married."

Enrico chuckled and shook his head. "No. Never tempted. Did you?"

Michael shrugged. "I was married once, but she was jealous."

"Of your mistress?"

"Of my work. Much the same thing."

Enrico laughed and then grew serious. "How did your father die?"

There it came again. "His heart. It stopped one day while he was working." The shock of that day was still fresh. So much had happened since then, but Michael still found it hard to believe his dad was gone.

"Look at the two of us," Enrico said. "Feeling sorry for ourselves. I should go up and buy two more bottles of wine. We could drink to your father's birthday."

"I could almost let you do that." Michael didn't want to start that habit.

"Suit yourself. It'll be time for supper soon anyway."

"Yes it will. We can go up on deck now and get a good spot at the table."

The cold made Michael shiver when he stepped up into the wind. The bright sunlight of the morning had given way to overcast skies. He turned up the collar of his cloak and looked out at the sea. Distant mountains sat on the horizon. Michael and Enrico joined half a dozen men standing around the main mast.

"Where is that?" Michael pointed landward.

"Dalmatia," answered one man. "They say we may be in Zara tonight if the wind holds."

Good. Although the seas hadn't been rough, he already wished for firm ground, and it was rougher now that he noticed. The ship rolled more than it had so far on this trip and it made him take a wider stance to keep his balance.

"Looks like a storm," said one of his companions, an extra coat pulled up around his neck like a shawl.

"Maybe," another commented. "Perhaps only a wind tonight."

The trumpets blew after a while. Michael and Enrico joined the rush to the dining tables. Michael ate a light meal. He'd rather not have much to lose if the sea continued its churning.

Felix and Konrad made it to supper, and Michael watched them with interest. Felix's exuberance contrasted with Konrad's quiet charm. They were good friends after having spent little time together.

Did he have any friends he could count on like that? He hadn't seen his high school buddies in years. Their lives had grown so different that the ten-year reunion he attended was awkward. He concentrated too much on his work in college to cultivate deep friendships; later, he made only business associates.

"Time to go," Enrico said. Michael hadn't noticed the trumpets sounding an end to supper.

The furled main sail above made an eerie cross against the gray sky. It seemed odd since they were so close to port. He asked a crewman why they had stopped.

"You want to swim?"

"No. Why?"

"If it were a clear night, we might see our way, but the clouds and the wind would cause us to be wrecked on the rocks. Better to stay at anchor tonight."

"I don't see the other ships," Enrico said.

The crewman nodded. "They're with us."

Michael looked around. "Why don't they have lights so each one knows where the others are?"

"Because we don't want an enemy to know where we are and sneak up on us."

"That makes sense. Think we'll be at the port in the morning?"

"If the wind doesn't turn into a storm. We'll have to wait and see." The crewman looked over his shoulder and took off at a mate's call.

* * * *

Michael escaped the dank confines of the passenger compartment and made his way across the deck to the railing. After the rough night, he exulted in the simple act of filling his nostrils with fresh air. The memories of hugging a stinking waste pot while those around him lost their supper drove away his usual morning hunger.

The gray morning sky merged with the choppy water off in the distance to the left and surrounded the mountains to the right and behind the ship. The swaying deck didn't help his nausea, but the crew seemed unaffected. Men scampered up the rigging and ran about the deck making ready to go.

"Morning." Enrico's voice.

Michael turned his head. He hoped he didn't look as bad as Enrico. "Thankfully." He looked back toward the coast, praying his associate would keep quiet this once.

The two lead ships had already weighed anchor and turned their backs on the wind toward land. The third ship followed, then the *Donna Maria*. Soon all five vessels sailed in formation.

They passed behind a cluster of barrier islands that formed a lagoon similar to the one protecting Venice. One by one, the ships turned to the right and passed into a channel where the water was smoother than on the open sea. Michael looked at the sky for a hint of direction. The overcast skies yielded no information. The crew waved as several merchant vessels leaving Zara met them. Fishing boats bobbed off one island or another.

"There's the port." Enrico pointed ahead.

"Looks busy," Michael said. Boats and small ships were tied up alongside the docks. Larger vessels sat anchored farther away. "A shallow port?"

"It is an old one." Felix's voice came from behind.

Michael turned to greet him. "Good morning. Have you been here before?"

Felix stepped up to the rail. "No, I missed it on my pilgrimages, but I have heard much. The churches are said to be very impressive."

"Then you should see them while we're here."

Felix raised his eyebrows in an expectant smile and a golden glow lit his face. A break in the clouds let in a ray of sun. "Oh, I intend to. Several men from my hometown have given me jewelry to venerate by touching it to the relics. They might never have another chance."

Venerating jewelry. Michael had never heard of the practice. "What kind of relics?"

"Oh, there are several martyrs entombed here, but I look forward especially to seeing the body of Saint Simeon, the holder of our Lord."

"The holder?"

"You don't know? The old Jew who held the infant Jesus in the Temple?"

"Yes, only I didn't know that his body was here."

"How could you not know that?" Felix frowned.

Michael searched for a good excuse. "I'm from England." It was true that many thought of the English as a bit backward.

"Oh." Felix seemed to accept the answer. "Well, then. The legend says a merchant stopped here during a storm, carrying the body of Saint Simeon back to Venice. No one knows how he came by it. He fell ill, but told his caretakers before he died." Felix's face took on a look of rapture. "Priests of the town saw visions and knew his story was true. Saint Simeon rests at the

Church of Saint Mary the Great, lying in the silver ark made for him more than one hundred years ago. Imagine seeing the hands that held the Lord!" Felix cradled an imaginary baby.

Michael's incomplete knowledge of this time and culture confronted him again, but he was learning.

Crewmen furled the sails and the oarsmen positioned their ships in a line several hundred yards from the port, where they turned into the wind and dropped anchor.

Each ship carried a pair of boats strapped to its sides. A smaller skiff ferried a few people at a time, while the larger boat facilitated transferring combinations of people and cargo. As soon as crewmen lowered them to the water, captain and officers claimed the first vacancies and left for the city. The boats would return and carry others who wanted to go in. Michael, Enrico, Felix, Konrad and several others waited their turn together.

Felix started off for the right side of the ship. "Let me show you something."

Michael followed him.

"Watch as that man moves to the skiff." Felix pointed down to a fellow descending the steps to one of the boats. "Keep your grip firm on the rail and make your step sure when you reach the bottom."

Michael nodded. "Looks cold."

Felix shook his head. "You don't understand. You would die."

"I know how to swim." As he said the words, Michael felt his dad's hands holding him afloat in the warm swimming pool water.

Felix pointed at Michael's chest. "Not in those clothes. You would sink. I have seen it happen."

"Oh. Thank you for the warning. I'll be careful." Michael wouldn't let go of that last step until he was securely in the boat.

At last their turn arrived. Michael called Enrico from a conversation on the other side of the deck and made his way down, one rung at a time. Under clearing skies, the craft carried them through a congestion of fishing boats and skiffs from the bigger ships anchored in the harbor. Another ladder took them to the dock and *terra firma*.

Michael welcomed the solid ground, but he still experienced a sensation of swaying while walking on the stone-paved path to town. They passed a market, where Michael bought some bread to ease his nausea. A familiar aroma of waste to which he had become accustomed in Caorle reminded him of home and Cecile.

They headed toward the city center with Felix in the lead like a three year-old drawn to a candy counter. He turned to their group and urged them on with his eyes. "Shall we go to the church first?"

Michael couldn't work up any excitement over seeing a mummified corpse, even a bona fide saint. "Enrico and I have some business to do, but I hope you enjoy your visit there."

Felix stopped and blinked. "All right, but you may never have the opportunity again."

"I know, maybe later." Michael hated to disappoint him.

Felix's face drooped. "Very well." He brightened. "Shall we meet for dinner?"

What time was it? Michael looked at the sky and guessed they had a couple of hours before noon meals were served. "I would enjoy it. Where?"

"One of the other merchants told us about an inn, the Adria, on the east side of the city. You can ask someone for directions when you are ready."

"Good. We'll see you there."

Enrico watched Felix and Konrad amble down the narrow cobblestone street. "I didn't want to see the dead man, either."

Michael pointed the other direction. "I saw warehouses back the way we came. Why don't we go there?"

"Always business with you." He shrugged. "It's early in the day."

On the way they passed an inn with a group of sailors gathered outside. A young woman smiled as she watched them from the doorway. When she saw Enrico, she ignored the scruffy mob and began to run her gaze over him instead. Enrico grinned at her as they went by.

"We're at work," Michael reminded him.

"A shame." He turned his head back to their path.

Michael chose the largest of the lot, a white building with a red tile roof.

"Kind of a fancy place for us country traders," Enrico said.

"Might as well start at the top."

Michael climbed the five steps and called out a greeting as he walked through the door. "Good morning."

A head, bald on top, appeared from behind a stack of packaged goods. "What can I do for you?" the man asked in a Slavic-accented Venetian.

Michael glanced around the place and saw no one else. "We're looking for the owner."

"I am the owner. Frederik Dragisic." He looked back to his work as if annoyed at the interruption; then he put something down and walked around the display.

Michael held out a hand and shook Frederik's reluctant offering. "Good morning. I'm Michael Patriate from Caorle. This is my associate Enrico de Rippa. Could we ask for some of your time? We won't take long."

"What are you selling?" Frederik asked.

"No, it's not what you think. We represent a group of merchants from Caorle. We're interested in promoting direct trade with others here in the region."

Frederik nodded his head in understanding. "You want to reduce your dependence on Venice."

Michael held up his hands. "No, no. We don't wish to cut anyone out of trade, only to make ours more profitable."

"I see." Frederik appeared unconvinced. "What do you have to offer?" He looked beside him at a slumping sack of grain and took a step while watching Michael. He bent down and jerked at the corners of the heavy bag in an effort to straighten it.

Michael hopped over to help and grabbed one side. He pulled with Frederick and then gave the bag a shake to make it stand up, the way he had learned from Rizzo.

"Thanks," Frederick said. He stood and waited for Michael to continue.

"Our first objective is to gather information." Michael gestured to Enrico. "We hope you will give us some of your valuable time so we might discover ways to help each other."

Frederik looked at Enrico and back. "I suppose talk won't hurt, but I won't do anything to jeopardize my relations with Venice."

"Neither will we," Michael said.

Frederik motioned with his head to the back of the store. "I'll show you around. Come on, you can see the goods we deal in."

Frederik led the way down a neat row of empty ceramic jars with Michael and then Enrico following. They talked for a few minutes before Frederik stopped in mid-sentence. "Where's your friend?"

Michael looked about. "Enrico," he called. Nothing. "He must have stepped outside for a moment."

Frederik shook his head. "This is a dangerous area for strangers like you to be walking alone."

"I guess I ought to go find him. I think I know where he went."

Michael hurried toward the inn where they had seen the girl in the door, checking down side streets and alleys. He cursed Enrico for putting him in this position.

I should just leave him here.

Almost at the inn, he crossed a narrow alley. There, a noise. He stopped to listen.

From the alley behind him came a cry followed by a muffled blow. He peered back around the corner of the building to see a person partly exposed behind a cart on the other side of the aisle, only fifteen feet away, looking at something on the ground. Michael knelt down and looked under the cart. Enrico.

"Shut him up," the man said.

Two of them. Michael froze for a moment. He had never been faced with something like this. A bully or two in school, sure, but never a situation where he feared for his life. But he couldn't

184

leave Enrico there. Would anyone come if he shouted? After Frederik's warning, Michael thought not. It was up to him. The sound of another thump spurred him into action.

Michael took off his bulky cloak to free his arms and untied the scabbard holding his small dagger. He tiptoed down the near side of the building, away from the assailants for a better view of the action. The two were concerned with rifling through Enrico's clothes. He had to act before one of them looked up. Michael ran as quietly as he could and threw his shoulder into the back of the robber he had seen first, slamming the man into a rough-cut stone block wall, where he dropped next to Enrico. Michael pulled out his dagger and faced the second man, who had gained his feet and held his own knife.

"I will kill you." The man spoke in an uncertain voice. He stole a glance down at his motionless companion.

Michael nodded toward the two on the ground. "We're even now. Why don't you take your friend, and I will take mine." He hoped he looked imposing to the shorter man.

They stood in crouched, defensive positions for a moment when the thug acceded. "All right, but don't try to stop me."

"I won't." Michael backed away.

Enrico's assailant bent over his accomplice while he kept an eye on Michael. "Get up." He kept his knife ready while he rolled his friend over. The injured man moved a bit and then released a moan. He managed to get to his feet with assistance and held a hand to his bloodied forehead. The two crept down the alley and disappeared around the corner.

Michael stretched Enrico out where he could get a look at the damage. The attack had opened several cuts on Enrico's head. Blood ran from his nose and mouth. He tried to think. Where could he go for help? He couldn't carry Enrico all the way back to the docks, and the only person he knew in this place was the merchant, Frederik. Back to the warehouse.

He pulled Enrico into a sitting position; then he hoisted him over his shoulder and tottered off under the load.

Back on the main street, Michael paused to pick up his cloak. Enrico's extra weight hurt his knees when he bent to retrieve it. He almost fell before he snagged the collar and straightened to hold onto Enrico with both hands. He staggered under his load back to the warehouse. The cloak slapped against his legs with every step. People turned to watch them pass, but no one offered to help. At least no one interfered.

Just when Michael thought his legs or lungs might give out, Frederik's place came into view around a bend in the street. *Just a few more steps.*

"That doesn't look good." Frederik stood by while Michael laid Enrico out on the floor.

Michael knelt on one knee and tried to catch his breath. "Can we get a doctor for him?" He looked up at the merchant.

"I sent for one when I saw you coming, but you need to put pressure on those wounds so he won't bleed so much." Frederik motioned to the trail of red spots that led back to the door.

Enrico stirred and cried out. "Don't." His eyes remained closed.

Michael put his hand on Enrico's shoulder. "It's all right, you're safe now. Be still." He took out his scarf and concentrated on stopping the blood from his head cuts. Enrico went slack again.

Frederik looked out toward the door. "The barber is here."

"Barber? Oh, yes. Good." The barber-surgeon. It seemed an odd combination. Michael preferred to think of him as a doctor at the moment. A man with a bag parted the crowd that gawked through the door.

"Move, please." The surgeon moved in to examine Enrico. "Most of the bleeding has stopped. He will recover. Here." He handed a small jug to Michael. "Get someone to boil this."

Michael pulled out the wood plug and sniffed. It smelled like salad dressing. "What is it?"

The doctor knelt down and spoke without looking up. "Oil, of course. To sear the wounds."

"Sear the wounds?"

"Yes." The doctor paused and scowled up at him. "It will help the skin to bind back together. May I get to work now?"

Pouring hot liquid on a wound would only further damage the tissues that had already suffered enough abuse. What else would they do to him?

"He can't pay you," Michael blurted.

The barber, Michael didn't think of him as a surgeon now, stopped.

Michael felt the eyes of all in the warehouse. "He was robbed."

The doctor looked up at Michael. "What about you?"

"All of my money I lost in a card game last night. He was helping me."

"Then he is an unlucky man, too. I can't work on him for free."

Michael pushed the stopper into the jug and handed it back. "I understand. I will get him to the *Donna Maria*. Someone on board will help him."

"There is still a charge for my visit." The doctor's eyes were hard.

Michael didn't want to cause a disturbance and risk unknown penalties in a strange city. "I'll arrange for one of his friends to pay it this afternoon."

The doctor looked over to Frederik, who nodded. He relented. "All right. Frederik knows where I can be found." He left and took the crowd along.

Michael waited until they were gone. He was uncertain what to do for Enrico. There were no handy bottles of antiseptic or boxes of Band Aids sitting on the shelves.

"Frederik, do you have any vinegar?"

Frederik turned from looking out the door at the departing crowd. "Yes, I have some full bottles."

"Good." Michael smoothed back Enrico's hair and examined a cut. "Can I buy one from you?"

"I thought you were penniless."

Michael shook his head. "No, that was just to get the doctor to go away." He turned to Frederick. "Some white cloth, also?"

Frederik looked doubtful, but nodded and went away. He came back in a minute with a bottle of vinegar and a small bolt of cloth. Michael tore the cloth into strips, poured vinegar over them and applied them folded on the head wounds as bandages, tying them with longer strips.

Frederik stood over Enrico and observed Michael's procedures. "Why are you using the vinegar?"

They didn't know about germs here. What story would Frederik buy? "It will kill any worms in the cloth that might get into the wounds."

"Oh." He looked impressed. "Where did you learn that?"

"My mother. She was a healer." She worked as a clerk in a doctor's clinic, close enough.

Enrico roused and tried to pull a bandage from his head. "What you doing?" Enrico said. Or something like that. His swelling lips didn't work very well.

"Patching you up. Be still." Michael pushed Enrico's arm back to his side.

"Happened?" His closed eyes compressed further.

"Someone hit you on the head."

He took a couple of shallow breaths. "A few...other place...too."

"Well, you aren't bleeding from them. Let me look at your head." Michael ran his hands over Enrico's scalp and found another cut and a couple of lumps. "We need to shave your head so we can dress these wounds."

"Don't want be bald." He winced at Michael's touch.

Michael stood and spoke down to Enrico. "Your hair will grow back, and the women will love you again. We can do it back on the ship if we can get you there."

Frederik interrupted. "I will arrange for someone to help you take him." He pointed to Michael's clothing. "But you probably want to clean up first."

Michael glanced down to see his shirt and pants smeared and spotted with Enrico's blood. His hands were sticky with it. "Let me finish here, and I'll wash as best I can." He could get his clothes cleaned on the ship.

Frederik's assistant and a man borrowed from another merchant worked on a makeshift stretcher to carry Enrico back to the dock. Michael rinsed the blood off his hands and put his cloak on over the blood-stained clothing. He pulled coins from his purse. "Here, this is for the supplies and some for the barber if you don't mind seeing that he gets it."

Frederik held up his hands. "You don't owe me anything."

"Yes, I need to pay you." Michael pointed out the door. "You helped when I didn't know anyone else in town."

"You are a good friend." Frederik took the money.

Michael looked over at Enrico and his new helpers placing him on the stretcher and shivered as the danger he had put himself in dawned on him. "You never know what you'll do until the time comes."

"We're ready," said Frederik's assistant.

Michael walked over and stood over his new ward. "All right, Ladies' Man, let's get you back to the ship."

* * * *

Michael leaned back on his bedroll propped against the hull and watched Enrico sleep. Patches of shaved scalp shone through gaps in his bandages. Blue and black welts ran from his swollen left eye to the cut in the corner of his puffy upper lip. The sound of Felix laughing and talking in German drifted down the steps, followed by Felix and Konrad in person.

Felix's jovial countenance vanished when he saw Enrico. "What happened?" He knelt and examined Enrico's injuries.

Michael stared at the sad sight. "Someone used him for a human *piñata*."

"I beg your pardon?" Felix asked.

Michael looked up and shook his head. "Sorry. He went off by himself and met the wrong fellows." He stood despite his exhaustion from the ordeal.

Felix nodded understanding. "Konrad and I were concerned when we didn't see you again. Will he be all right?"

"I think so. He took some blows to his ribs, but I don't think any are broken." Michael shook his head. "I didn't realize head wounds bled so much."

Konrad bent over Enrico and inspected Michael's work. "They usually look worse than they really are. Heads are hard things. You did a good job of bandaging his wounds, if unorthodox." He sniffed. "Is that vinegar?"

Michael laughed. "You're not the first to comment. The cook thought it was unorthodox, too, when I asked him to boil the bandages."

"Well, what matters," Felix said, "is his recovery. I will pray for him."

Konrad nodded. "I will, too."

"Thank you both. Enrico will be glad for your help."

Felix stood and put his hand on Michael's shoulder. "It is good to have a friend on a journey like this one. I am sure he will return the favor if misfortune finds you."

Michael looked down at his vulnerable companion. "I don't doubt it." But he did.

* * * *

Michael saw Enrico watching him when he stepped onto the cabin's flooring. He set a tall mug the cook lent him beside Enrico. "I brought you some soup."

Enrico nodded and struggled to speak clearly. "Thanks for saving my life." He shifted and closed his eyes. "Mmm... Dizzy." He looked at Michael again. "And thanks for not leaving me there."

The swollen mouth still made Enrico's words slow and indistinct, but Michael saw some light in his eyes for the first time in a couple of days. The relief he felt to see Enrico coherent surprised him.

"You're welcome. What do you remember?"

"Not much. Felix told me what happened while you were gone. This eye doesn't work very well." Enrico winced as he tried to push himself up on his bed.

Michael stooped over and helped prop him on a cushion made from some blankets and sat down on his own bedroll. "The swelling is going down. It should be all right in a few days."

"I suppose I'm lucky to have everything else work. Do I remember you saying that all my money was stolen?"

"No. You still have your money."

"That's good. I was afraid I might have to put myself further in debt to you."

"Well, there are the supplies from Frederik and the cost of the boat ride back to the ship." Michael grinned. "We'll call it a business expense."

Enrico laughed, then groaned. "I must remember not to do that. I owe you an apology."

Michael waved a hand. "No, you don't owe me anything."

"Yes I do. You know I came to keep you in line, to spy on you, really."

Michael nodded. "I know."

"Well, I won't do that anymore."

Michael pulled a long spoon out of his pocket and picked up the mug. "Why don't we just work together? Here, you need to eat something."

"All right. Where are we?" Enrico turned his head and looked up the stairs. "What time is it?"

Michael followed his gaze to the open hatch and the blackness there. "It's night. We sailed from Zara yesterday. They say we should be in Ragusa in two or three days if the weather holds, but I think they expect a storm."

He filled the spoon with the thin liquid. "Open up."

* * * *

The storm approached late the next afternoon after a calm, unusually warm day. Michael watched from the deck as a line of dark clouds slowly advanced from the northeast.

"Fascinating, isn't it?"

Michael turned to see Uberto, the man they had dined with the first night on the ship.

Uberto gazed at the clouds. "Today the sun shines warm, but the cold wind seeks us out. Have you been through a storm on the sea?"

"No, it's the first time for me, if you don't count the one before Zara." Michael pointed to the rear. "I can see the coastline behind us. Why don't we go look for shelter there?"

"It would take too long to row there without wind. Then the rocks would break us open when the storm arrives." Uberto looked back to the open hatch. "You should go below before it gets here and tie down your belongings."

"I will, thanks." Michael watched crews of five ships drop anchors and begin their wait; then he went below.

Enrico reclined on his bedroll.

"A storm's coming." Michael said.

"I gathered that." Enrico pointed down the line of berths. Many of the others were in the process of packing loose items in their bags and tying them to nails driven in the planking.

Michael watched for a moment, and turned back to Enrico. "Can you move if you need to?"

"I think so." In slow motions, he pushed his clasped hands in front of his chest, moved them behind his head, and stretched. "Everything's still sore, but I'll manage."

"All right. I better get our things tied down." He reached in his bag for the rope.

"I feel kind of useless sitting here while you do all the work."

Michael laughed. "It *is* interrupting my busy schedule. You ought to get some rest while you can."

"That's all I've been doing." Enrico leaned back his head and closed his eyes.

After Michael tied the last knots, he walked down to see Felix and Konrad. "Any advice for the inexperienced traveler?"

"Keep your chamber pot handy," Felix said. The way he smiled made Michael understand that he meant it. "Otherwise, we will be fine. It shouldn't be too difficult since we have already anchored and taken up the sails."

"How is your friend?" Konrad asked.

"He's still weak and sore, but getting better. He appreciates your kindness, even if he doesn't show it."

"It is hard for us to let someone else care for us." Felix looked toward Enrico and sighed. "It forces us to admit that we aren't in control as we think we should be."

Michael knew it true for himself. He would rather help someone else than be indebted for accepting assistance.

Felix looked up at the ceiling. "Another lesson in control has arrived." Lamp flames danced as the ship rocked with the rising wind. "Pray to God for our safety."

"I will, Felix. Pardon me, but I should get back." The movement of the ship grew more exaggerated as Michael walked back to his berth. The ship tugged against the anchor and pointed into the wind. As it rode the waves, the floor alternately rose to meet Michael and then fell away from him. He sat on one of his bags beside Enrico and put his hand to the floor to steady himself. "Are you all right?"

"If this keeps up, I'm going to be sick." Enrico closed his eyes and clenched his jaws.

Michael swallowed that ominous taste again. "I think we all will."

The wind made an eerie howling noise across the open hatch to the deck until a crewman fastened a cover over it. Michael sat and endured the pounding of the rising and falling ship, and put another hand on the floor. Judging from the looks on faces around him he wasn't the only one ill. The sharp, acid smell of vomit attacked his control. The contents of his stomach wanted out and would not be denied. As he reached for his waste pot, Enrico did the same.

Michael thought vomiting would make him feel better, but the nausea only worsened, and it didn't stop when his stomach emptied. He wanted a quiet, still place to lie down, but quiet and still fled before the storm.

As the wind and waves rose in intensity, the length of travel between high and low increased until the anchor's chain stopped them at each peak with a jar that seemed to pull the floor from beneath them and a groaning noise which surely meant the ship was coming apart. Stress on the hull created tiny spaces in between the planks, and beads of water turned to rivulets that sped toward the floor before disappearing underneath it. Whatever discomfort Michael experienced, Enrico's had to be worse; he flinched at the impact of each wave. Michael could do nothing for him.

The hatch opened and a crewman shut it behind him and ran to the bilge pump. With both hands he worked the short wooden handle up and down in even strokes. The foul smell from the rotten water magnified the stench already permeating the cabin.

Michael squeezed his eyes shut and braced himself again for the sharp pull at the top of the wave and opened his eyes in surprise when it did not come. Heads popped up round the cabin.

"The anchor!" someone cried above the noise. It must have slipped its hold on the bottom of the sea. Wind pushed them uncontrolled across the water.

Forces restricted to two dimensions found themselves free to toss the ship in random motions that sent men and belongings crashing.

Enrico rolled against the hull. Michael got him to his feet and found a support pillar in the middle of the cabin, where he sat Enrico with his arms and legs hugging the beam. "Hang on," he called above the din.

Michael stood above him and held on. Men cried out in prayer and terror. Even Enrico called to God. Michael thought it couldn't get any worse, but as happened with irritating frequency, he was wrong.

The *Donna Maria* rolled on its side. Men, bags, and chests flew to the new bottom of the ship. The crash of breaking goods and the creaking of tortured timbers cloaked the angry sound of the winds and waves outside. Then screams of terrified men pierced even that veil. Michael couldn't be sure some weren't his. Something slammed into him, but he managed to hang on. He looked for Enrico and barely made him out. Only a few lamps remained lit. Enrico must have summoned hidden strength. His arms and legs remained locked tight onto the pillar.

The ship righted, then went over the other way, throwing the contents of the room to the opposite side. Michael became aware of being cold and wet. Water sprayed through an open hatch cover.

God, I don't want to die this way.

Michael saw Cecile at home, sitting and sewing, waiting. He yearned to call out to her, to...

Another jolt tore him away from the post, and he landed hard on the floor. But now the floor oriented itself down and stayed that way, even though it still rose and fell away. The anchor had found some other purchase on the sea floor. The motion which moments earlier seemed like torture felt like blessed salvation. Someone close prayed for the anchor to hold. Moans drifted throughout the near darkness.

Enrico, still held tight.

Michael took a deep breath to clear his head. "Are you all right?"

"I didn't know Hell was so wet." Enrico's head hung low.

"Just stay where you are in case the anchor lets go again."

Michael looked for Felix and found his familiar outline. He and Konrad still gripped their own post. They had been through this before. Up and down the cabin, belongings littered the berth areas that had been clear a short time before. Some men knelt, giving thanks. Others tended to several injured. Michael could only sit.

He waited until the storm eased enough to let him get around and began to retrieve as much of their property as he could find. *Never could tie a good knot.*

Enrico's bedding, like everything else, was soaked with seawater. Michael squeezed out what he could and laid it in the general vicinity of Enrico's berth. He pried loose his friend's grip on the pole and helped him to the bed.

Enrico groaned. "My head hurts."

"You hit it and opened one of your cuts, but the bleeding isn't too bad. We'll get you fresh bandages when I can find them."

"This isn't fun anymore." Enrico's eyes stayed closed.

"It'll get better. Try to sleep."

Enrico passed out before Michael could complete the sentence. Michael leaned back against the side of the ship, exhausted. His weary mind entertained delirious thoughts of plastic bags. He could get his asking price for a box of those large locking bags that would have kept everyone's clothing dry. Maybe he could find an oilcloth sack in the next port. He dozed intermittently for a while and then woke with his head on a wet pillow. The storm had passed.

Michael stirred and looked over at Enrico. Asleep. He rose and stepped over debris to make his way above. Low clouds still obscured the sky, but a favorable wind filled the sails. The smell of fresh salt air refreshed him after breathing the wretched fumes below. He stayed on the deck until the chill of cold wind through his damp clothes drove him back below. Michael checked on Enrico, who still slept, and went to Felix's berth, where he and Konrad sat on Konrad's trunk.

"Good morning. Is everything all right here?"

Felix wore an uncharacteristic solemn face. "We are well enough, but our friend Uberto was badly injured and died." He pointed across and down the narrow aisle where Uberto lay covered. His legs projected from the blanket.

"How?" Michael held onto a pillar for support against rubbery legs.

"Uberto struck his side violently when the anchor caught. He coughed up blood. We could not help him." Felix stood and stretched his back. "He barely had time to confess to me and receive absolution."

Most likely a broken rib and collapsed lung, Michael figured. He wondered if the man had family. They might not find out about his death for months. He stared at the soles of Uberto's exposed black shoes, at the hole in the left one. "So what happens to his body?"

Felix took another glance at Uberto and shook his head. "Sometimes the dead are carried to the next port and buried in a proper cemetery, but no one on board speaks for him, so the captain will probably bury him at sea."

Konrad looked up from his seat. "We will give him a proper service."

Michael placed his hand on Felix's shoulder before he realized it. He didn't usually like to touch or be touched, but he felt the need. "It's good that you're here, Felix. You too, Konrad."

"The Lord puts us where he will," Felix answered.

Michael gave him a grim smile. "Please let me know how I can help."

"I will, when we know the method of his burial."

As Michael left them, an odd feeling settled over him. He had barely known Uberto. They only spoke on a few occasions. But then, one of those times was just before the storm. What had he said about the wind seeking them? Michael wasn't superstitious, but it was just spooky. Could he see the future?

Enrico leaned on an elbow. "What's happening over there?"

Michael glanced down at the covered form. "Uberto died last night, injured in the storm."

Enrico's face contorted. "Oh. That's terrible."

"Yes, it is." Michael looked back at Enrico. "How are you this morning?"

"Better than Uberto."

Michael nodded. He pointed up at the hatch. "I'll see if I can get some fresh water to wash bandages and get someone to rinse the salt out of our beds."

"I'll be right here." Enrico lay back on his pillow.

Michael took an empty jug and the small pot Baldo had given him and headed in search of water. Several of the oarsmen who washed clothing for passengers were doing a brisk business.

Michael wondered how much fresh water they could carry on a trip like this. He made arrangements to have some of his and Enrico's things cleaned and then trudged to the railing and stared out at the gray sea.

* * * *

Enrico jerked his head back from Michael's touch. "That hurts."

"I know the vinegar stings, but it'll help your cuts heal faster. When the rest of these bandages dry they won't hurt you as much." Michael tied up the last of the dressings. "You're healing well enough. Only that one cut broke open last night."

"That's good." Enrico settled back. "I'd take another drink of water."

"Not too much at once." Michael handed him the jug.

Enrico turned his head. "Here comes Felix." He held the container to his lips.

"Is it time?" Michael rose to meet the old friar.

"It is." Felix looked old. "Can you help us bear his body?"

How many times had Felix assisted a poor unfortunate along like this? Michael nodded. "Any way I can help."

"Thank you, Michael. Pardon me, I must speak with the captain." Felix headed for the steps.

Enrico took a swig and handed Michael the water jug. "I want to go."

"You sure?"

Enrico nodded and propped himself up on his hands. "I need out of this place for a while."

"I can understand that. Let's get some more clothes on you."

* * * *

The rush of water against the hull ceased. Felix had talked to the captain, and the little fleet of ships stopped in respect for the burial service. Michael and the five other bearers worked in the silent cabin. A few injured passengers lay in their berths. The others waited above to witness the ceremony.

Michael grasped a corner of the blanket they used to carry Uberto's body and headed up the steps. On the deck, a somber crowd waited under an overcast sky and leaned into a stiff wind. Men stood in rows, silent, on either side of a path guiding the pallbearers to a spot near the aft railing.

A bed sheet turned shroud lay spread on the deck, partly covered with sand dug from under the flooring, exposed edges flapping in the wind. Michael grabbed Uberto's ankles and helped heave his body onto the sand, a bag of rocks at his feet. Already the dead flesh felt stiff and cold. They wrapped the shroud around Uberto and tied it with ropes, then lifted the body and carried it, feet first, to the side of the ship. At the head of the bearing party, Michael waited by the rail. *Don't drop him yet.*

Felix and Konrad began a Latin chant, *Libera me, Domine*, which Michael had asked Felix to translate for him:

Deliver me, O Lord,
from eternal death,
on that fearful day
when the heavens are moved and the earth
when thou shalt come to judge
the world through fire.
I am made to tremble, and I fear,
when the desolation shall come,
and also the coming wrath.
That day, the day of wrath,
calamity, and misery,
that terrible and exceedingly bitter day.
Rest eternal grant them, O Lord,
and let perpetual light shine on them.

Felix nodded. Michael leaned over the rail and, along with his partners, gave their package a push out away from the ship. A second later, a splash ended their mission.

As Uberto's body disappeared into the water, Felix raised his hands and eyes toward the leaden sky. "The body sinks to the depths, but the soul climbs to Heaven."

Michael lingered, staring at the choppy grave. Soon the travelers dispersed, the crew went back to work, and the ships sailed again on a heading to Ragusa.

Chapter Thirty

Ludovico

Ludovico sat in an outer room, anxious to see the king after his long journey to Paris. Charles kept him waiting, demonstrating his greater relative importance. Ludovico accepted this effrontery without resentment. He routinely did the same with a visitor of lower standing.

At last his turn came. An assistant showed Ludovico through the door. Charles VIII, King of France, sat in the midst of a richly decorated room on a massive oak chair, surrounded by advisors of one sort or another. On his right stood a noble, who was notable for his imitation of the king's elaborate dress, from the fur-trimmed jacket to the soft black silk hat over shoulder-length, albeit gray, hair.

"Welcome, Ludovico." Charles remained seated.

"Thank you, your Majesty." Ludovico bowed to the young king. "I am grateful you can see me."

"It is curious to me you came all the way from Milan yourself, instead of sending an ambassador. Could you persuade no one to make the trip?"

Ludovico looked at Charles with some fascination. *Barely more than a boy.* His head seemed too big for his body, his limbs small in comparison, hardly regal. His pointed question, notwithstanding, Charles seemed uninterested in the meeting. It fit the rumor of a king unconcerned with the responsibilities of governing. But some of his keepers relished their positions. Ludovico spoke to those men as well.

"Your Majesty, I am here to beg a favor, one I believe might benefit us both. Its sensitive nature compelled me to bring it personally."

"Go on." Charles's posture radiated indifference, as if trifling proposals from fawning courtiers burdened him on a regular basis. He studied the back of his hand.

"It is my understanding, Majesty, you wish to undertake the valiant task of liberating the Holy Land in Crusade."

Charles's eyes snapped up, but he remained silent.

"Naples offers an advantageous staging area and the wealth to fund such a Crusade."

Charles looked away. "This is not news to me."

"Of course not." Ludovico bowed his head. "I know you have rightful claim to the crown there through your grandmother's line."

Charles turned back to Ludovico with some appreciation in his eyes.

Ludovico gave him a short nod. "I wish to aid your quest."

The king glanced up to the man on his right and back to Ludovico. "Just what kind of aid can you give me?"

"The long journey from France to Naples is a deterrent to such an undertaking." Ludovico stole his own glance at the watchman, who showed no reaction to his proposal or his glance. "I can offer your troops free passage and opportunity to rest. They will need provisions after the difficult passage through the Alps."

Charles sharpened his voice. "And no interference?"

Ludovico bowed again and spread his arms. "My men and I are at your disposal, your Majesty."

The king paused, apparently in thought. His attendant bent to the king's ear and whispered. Charles's gaze drifted to the floor.

"Yes, Étienne." Charles turned his attention back to Ludovico. "What do you gain?"

Ludovico stared at the attendant for as long as was politic. *Étienne de Vesc.* The king's tutor during his childhood and regency while Charles lived under his sister's control. This courtier had taken full advantage of his position during the reign of Charles's father, Louis XI. He wielded power and prestige. No doubt the *Sénéchal* of Carcassonne wanted more. Ludovico forced his attention back to the king.

"I gain your protection, Majesty, from Venice and from Ferdinand of Naples, who threaten me."

"Your nephew's father-in-law. Why should I not deal with the rightful duke of Milan– what is his name, Jean?"

So the sénéchal keeps him abreast of a few things. He cleared his throat.

"My nephew's name is Gian Galeazzo. But Emperor Maximilian recognizes me as duke, unofficially as yet. He has married my niece and will disclose his approval shortly."

"Good for you." Charles took in an indifferent breath. "So Milan welcomes France. What about the others?"

Ludovico paused. Did Charles not know where he stood with the duchies of Italy?

"Sir, Lucca and Siena do not possess the resources to stand in your way. They will be neutral. Venice and Rome have some interest in seeing Naples weakened. Rome cannot marshal the strength to resist, at any rate. Florence is the only power that might challenge your passing, but she is led by Piero de' Medici, who vainly thinks himself equal to his father, Lorenzo. He is weak. Florence will give way." Ludovico swept his arm in a path southward, toward Naples. "The path is open to your glory."

"A Crusade," Charles said. He briefly turned to de Vesc. "Perhaps Fra Savonarola is right about me." Charles smiled when he looked back. "I will give you my answer tomorrow."

Savanarola. They listened to that crazy priest in Florence. *They were already planning this.*

All the way home Ludovico wondered if he had made a mistake.

Chapter Thirty-One

Michael stepped down into the cabin to find Enrico going through one of his bags. He stopped at the end of his berth and frowned. "Can I help you?"

Enrico didn't look up. "Where's your mirror?"

"Why?"

"I want to see what you've done to me." Enrico kept digging.

Michael shook his head and grinned. "Here, let me look." He took the bag and dug under some shirts. He handed Enrico a small mirror he bought in Venice.

Enrico swiveled his head back and forth. "Not bad, considering the alternatives."

"Your hat will cover most of it." Michael took the mirror. "Sure you feel like to going into town?"

"For a step on hard ground and a good meal, you bet. I'll rest when I need to. Are Felix and Konrad going with us?"

"No, they're off visiting more relics." Michael tied his bag closed. "I intend to make some contacts here. We'll need to find someone to carry our cargo if things work out. Will you stay with me this time?"

"I won't leave your side."

"Good. It's been an eventful journey. Let's keep it nice and boring from here on out."

* * * *

Stops at Ragusa and Durazzo and the island of Corfu were pleasant and productive after the assault at Zara and the storm that followed. Michael and Enrico met with merchants and made their pitch for increased trade with Caorle as if it were their primary mission. They practiced for Portugal, but Michael reasoned they needed a fall-back position anyway. Enrico continued to recover from the beating, pleased his hair would cover most of the scars. He refrained from wine except at meals and hardly gave women in the city second looks. Third looks, anyway. Michael wondered how long that would last.

After Corfu, they turned west around the southern tip of Italy for the longer voyage to Messina, on the northeast shore of Sicily. Michael enjoyed the warmer climate, but several days of calm slowed the voyage. He sat with Felix in their customary place by the rail, legs dangling over the side.

Felix watched a piece of wood float by. "I had hoped to spend Easter in Rome."

"Maybe you'll get there in time."

"No, I do not think so." Felix shook his head and sighed. "I have yet to make arrangements at Messina for passage. Unless God blesses us with a favorable wind soon, there will not be enough time. No matter. I was only thinking of myself. The Lord will be praised no matter where I am." He sat in silence for a while, then breathed deeply and turned up suddenly intense eyes. "I must ask you something."

"Of course." This promised to be uncomfortable.

"How will you praise God?"

Michael wasn't sure why Felix's question surprised him. He tended to be painfully direct. "What do you mean?"

"I have watched you on this journey. You have been a help to those around you, especially Enrico." He tapped Michael on the chest. "I believe your heart is good."

Michael shrugged. "I try to be a good man."

"Is that enough? I have not seen you curse or drink too much wine or gamble or run after women." He raised a hand in supplication. "But is a man defined by what he does not do?"

Felix had turned into a good friend, but why couldn't he just leave things alone? Michael found a cloud to focus on so he didn't have to look at him. "I avoid those things, mostly I think, because they strike me as unprofessional and distractions. But what would you have me do?"

"Praise God. Praise Him with your life. Praise Him with your words. Praise Him with your actions."

"I don't think God knows who I am, Felix." He waited to see what Felix would do with that.

Felix sucked in a breath. His face contorted into a pained mask. "What do you mean? He knows everyone."

Michael pulled his legs up and swiveled to lean back on the railing. "One evening when I was a boy I came in from play. My mother sat on the divan with her sister. Some others, I don't even remember who, stood around her. They looked at me with this terrible, tragic look. I'll never forget it. My mother was crying. I asked her what was wrong, but she didn't answer, just sat there. Finally, her brother, my uncle, took me outside and told me my father had died. No warning, he just fell over and died while he worked."

Felix frowned and leaned back, looking out toward the horizon. "That can be a hard thing for a young man to bear."

He doesn't understand. And why should he? It happened all the time here. Michael had no answer for him.

"What did your mother do afterward?"

"She went inside herself for a long time. She took care of me, but wouldn't talk about my father or what had happened. She eventually married again." Michael realized he had pulled his knees up under his chin and made himself straighten his legs on the deck.

"And how did that affect you?"

Now he's a shrink. "Oh, her husband was good enough to me, I guess." Michael tried to push away the memories. "But I wasn't his son, and he wasn't my father. They had another baby just before I left home."

Felix kept it up. "And you were forgotten?"

"I guess. I was good and did all the right things so she would notice me."

Straight A's, football, basketball, boxing, chess, debate. A full merit scholarship to Duke. *Duke.* He could still hear her stock response. *"That's nice, dear."*

Michael felt his eyes moisten. He blinked and forced down the old hurt.

Felix nodded and looked out over the ocean for a moment. "How long has it been since you have seen her?"

How could he answer that question? Did five hundred years count when they went in reverse?

"Several years. I used to send her a birthday card, I mean, a letter on her birthday."

"And you thought success would prove your worth?"

"I don't know. I guess so."

Felix leaned in close and spoke in a gentle voice. "Don't you know you are valuable to God no matter how much or little material success you have in this life?"

The anger that was never far away flashed and thickened his voice. "If I'm valuable to him, where was he when my father died?"

Felix's face sagged in a sad, understanding smile. "Michael, that is a question asked many times through the ages. Job asked it when his children and possessions were taken from him. Naomi despaired when her husband and sons died and left her in a strange land. God stood by them and used them to illustrate his concern for us. He stayed with you and gave you the things you needed when your mother could not. He will use you, too, if you let him."

Michael clenched his jaws before he snapped, "What about Job's children? And Naomi's husband? They stayed dead. Why wasn't God looking out for them?"

Felix's eyes turned hard, but softened after a few seconds. He cleared his throat and spoke gently. "There are things we will not understand in this life. We can put our trust in God or hold on to the hurt and resentment."

Well, I'm tired of trying to understand.

Felix sighed and turned his eyes toward the water. "*I hope you find your peace, Michael.*"

Michael spent more time with Felix, but avoided subjects of any depth. At Messina he waved to the monk, who returned the salute from a ship leaving port. He might see Rome by Easter, after all.

Good luck, friend.

Chapter Thirty-Two

They sailed west toward Palma, making good time for a change. With Lent at an end, the captain had brought animals aboard at Palermo for fresh meat at meals.

Michael settled into a routine and, except for infestations of fleas and lice, found it an enjoyable experience. He and Konrad struck up a friendship, both missing Felix. On deck late one afternoon, Konrad spotted the storm clouds rolling toward them.

Michael followed his eyes to the gathering darkness. "I suppose we'll stop soon."

"Probably not." Konrad motioned with his arm. "If the wind comes at a good direction, this storm can push us much faster than we have gone so far."

"Why did we anchor at Zara, then?"

"The waves are much worse in the shallow waters, and the wind would have pushed us ashore, but in the deep waters, the storm can be a blessing and speed us along."

"I don't like the looks of it anyway."

Konrad gave him a reassuring smile that reminded him of his dad. "Don't worry Michael, these men are good at what they do."

* * * *

The cooks had been unable to operate in the rough waters. Supper that night consisted of salted fish and cold biscuits. Michael didn't have much of either, remembering the last storm. Later, in his bunk, he heard the rush of the water against the hull, even over the sound of wind whistling across the hatch. They traveled at a fast clip.

Wind and waves rattled raw nerves much of the night, but failed to live up to the storm that had killed Uberto. A steady breeze pushed them along the next morning when Michael went on deck, but something seemed different when he stopped at the railing.

"Where are the other ships?" he asked another passenger.

"We lost them during the storm."

They should keep a light on. "That's great. I wonder how we find them."

The man shrugged. "We'll meet them at Palma, I guess."

Michael didn't like it. They traveled together for a variety of reasons, safety in numbers being a big one. A vague unease bothered him for the rest of the day.

* * * *

Routine set in again. Michael spent much of the time below. He borrowed a copy of Dante's *Divine Comedy* and struggled through the Tuscan dialect while Enrico made other friends.

Dante and his guide stepped onto a ferry to Hell, when a passenger stuck his head in the hatch and announced, "Sails in the sunset." Michael shut the book and hurried to join the men on deck, all trying to get a glimpse of the ship on the horizon.

The captain and his men gathered at the bow to look, shading eyes against the sun. No one spoke as time stopped. One of the officers turned and shouted.

"Corsair!"

Michael looked around for Konrad and found him alone at the rear railing, arms folded across his chest. Michael ran to his side.

"What does that mean?"

Konrad wore a grim expression. "Pirates."

Chapter Thirty-Three

The captain shouted orders in quick succession. Men who previously stood still, scarcely breathing, scrambled in sudden motion. The crew ran to their stations, disregarding anyone standing in their way, and they knocked aside several passengers who occupied the wrong spot. One of the Greeks went partway over the side rail before his friend pulled him back.

Many passengers ran in panic to hide in the cabin. Michael rushed with Konrad to a spot on deck out of the way. The *Donna Maria* turned right, much too slowly to suit Michael, and began its escape from the menace to the west. Oarsmen churned the water in choreographed unison to an unseen drummer.

The new heading, almost due north, put a light wind at their back for maximum pressure on the sails. The pirate vessel ran at an angle to the wind, but already at full speed, it crept toward the Venetian ship.

The master-at-arms came forward with assistants close behind, hauling crates filled with weapons of various sizes, shapes and uses. Michael looked at Konrad.

The knight motioned over his shoulder. "We may need to fight."

The master of arms pointed at Michael. "You. What can you use?"

Michael stared at the bewildering array of weapons in the cache. His experience in combat came with a wooden sword in mock battle against his childhood friends. They spent most of the time clacking the sticks together and shouting insults at one another. He'd never tried to kill anyone, even during the incident at Zara.

Konrad looked over the assortment and pulled out a short spear, small sword and a wooden shield for Michael. "Use the javelin first and try to keep them away from you."

The master-at-arms went on to other customers.

Michael bundled the items in his arms. *What am I supposed to do with these?* He turned to Konrad. "Didn't you get a weapon?"

"I have my own." Konrad gazed back at the pirate ship.

An icy blast of terror washed over Michael. He was a businessman, not a soldier. *This cannot be real.*

Konrad stood calm in the fading light, with an almost expectant look on his face. "I believe they will not catch us before dark." Indeed, the sun had almost completed its daily disappearance into the sea.

Sunset on the water often provided spectacular displays. Rays from the hidden sun lit the bottoms of clouds in gorgeous oranges and reds and, finally, purple as it gave up on the day. Michael prayed for it to hurry.

The captain maintained the course until darkness cloaked their position. Michael noted with gratitude that the moon hadn't risen. With oars stored, only the sound of wind against sail and water against hull broke the silence. A whisper nearby was rewarded with a thump and a soft cry of pain. The ship turned to the left, but not sharply.

Michael fidgeted, crossing his arms, pulling at a stray hair, turning to look for a glimpse of Konrad, standing beside him in the faint starlight.

When a thin moon rose an hour or so later, they could see no enemy sail and still Konrad watched. Finally he broke his stance.

"We should go below. We may need rest for tomorrow."

"I thought we lost them." Michael looked once more.

"We can hope." He turned toward the hatch. "But there may be others."

Michael followed Konrad down the steps. A quiet buzz greeted them. Men huddled together in worried groups. Wine bottles made the rounds. Konrad moved through the crowd to his berth, where he sat on his chest, alone, and lowered his head in prayer.

Michael watched for a moment. *Give him his privacy.* He hurried to his berth.

Enrico sat up on his bed and grinned. "Well, aren't you the fighting man." He had his own sword propped against the hull.

Michael looked down at himself. Sword tied to his waist, spear and shield in hand, the tension came out as laughter at the incongruity. "They will be afraid." He thumped the blunt end of the spear on the floor in a childish show of bravado.

Enrico laughed. "Careful, you'll hurt yourself."

Reality intruded. "You're probably right." Michael took off the sword belt and sat at his berth. He stared down at the weapons that he might have to use and shook his head. *It's too much.* He picked them up and walked down to Konrad's space.

The old knight had gone to bed. He looked dead. Michael stood for a moment before Konrad spoke.

"Yes, Michael." Konrad opened his eyes.

Michael held out his sword. "Konrad, I need some help. I don't know how to use these things."

"You have been sheltered." Konrad sighed and sat up.

"I've been lucky, you're right, but I think you've been through a fight or two."

Konrad nodded. "It is part of our mission."

"I hate to admit it, but I'm not that familiar with your organization." He had never heard of it until he boarded this ship.

Konrad's weathered face wrinkled in a frown. "How can you not know about us? We have been taking care of pilgrims for three hundred years."

"Like you say," Michael's head drooped, "I've been sheltered."

"Yes. Well, what would you like to know?"

"A general history, maybe?"

"All right. Come here and sit. I seem to have time." Konrad leaned against the hull.

"The order to which I belong is known by several names. Knights of Rhodes, Knights Hospitaller, the Order of Saint John. The full name is The Order of Saint John of Jerusalem and Rhodes. It was founded in the year of our Lord eleven hundred and thirteen, by members of the Benedictine order to maintain the hospital in Jerusalem for the treatment of sick pilgrims."

"So, the name of Hospitaller." Michael dropped the shield, sat on it, and propped his arms across his raised knees.

"Yes. And we cared for the ill there until the fall of Jerusalem in 1187. The pilgrims also needed protection, so the prior created a military division. After Acre fell a hundred years or so later, the order moved to Cyprus and then made their way to the island of Rhodes. We have been there since."

"I didn't know that." *What else did I miss in school?* "And you still provide medical treatment for pilgrims?"

"Well, yes. That is our primary mission. Everything else we do is of necessity." Konrad's face brightened. "You know, I was interested in your method of treatment for Enrico's wounds. Rarely have I seen injuries of that sort heal so cleanly, often patients are disfigured by the doctors' efforts."

Like the boiling oil the quack in Zara wanted to use. Although Michael commanded a limited knowledge of biology and medicine, he realized he could put what he knew to good use. "There is more I could share with you if you want."

"I would like that, but later. There is more story to tell."

Was that a twinkle in his eye? Michael grinned and listened.

"Since our move to Rhodes, we have been a thorn in the foot of the sultans. They laid siege to us in 1444 and again fourteen years ago when Felix came to visit. We were almost done in this last time. Only their own terrible losses led them to retreat before we succumbed. It has taken us many years to recover."

Michael frowned at a thought. "The knights are an order of the church. So, you are a monk and a soldier?"

"Something like that, yes."

"But, isn't that a contradiction?"

Konrad gave him a stern look. "No. We fight for Christ and the protection of his children against the aggression of the infidel. There is no contradiction, only survival."

Michael thought for a moment. "I'm glad to be on your side."

A smile creased the old warrior's face. "And I yours. We should see about suitable weapons for you."

"Suitable for me?" Michael snorted. "I don't think I'm suitable for any weapons."

"The ones you have, I believe, would not help you much. Wait here. I will return in a moment." Konrad took off for the stairs and nodded to Enrico on the way by. Enrico got up and watched him climb the stairs, then ambled down the aisle to see Michael.

"Where did Konrad go in such a hurry?"

"To see the master-at-arms, I think." Michael stood and stretched his legs. "Have you ever used a sword?"

"I hacked the bark off a tree once with one my father bought somewhere. I'm not sure if he was angrier about the dead tree or the bent sword."

Michael laughed. He remembered some of his own boneheaded stunts.

Konrad returned after a few minutes with a leather bag slung across his shoulder and carried a device Michael recognized as a crossbow. With a familiarity that must have come from experience, he hefted the weapon for Michael to inspect.

"Have you used one of these?"

Enrico shook his head.

Michael looked the weapon over. "No, but I've seen them." *In a museum.*

"I think this will be better for you if you have no skills with the sword or spear. It requires little training to use for shorter ranges, and it allows you to engage your enemy at a distance, unlike the sword. Here, hold this and get a feel for it."

Michael took the weapon by the handle on its back end. It was fashioned from a piece of wood about three feet long and more or less two inches square, with a short metal bow mounted forward on the top and a lever on the bottom. A curious piece of metal, shaped into some kind of strap, jutted out from the front end.

"This long piece," Konrad began, "is the stock. The end you grasp is the tiller. It works by locking the bowstring in place in the nut here to create tension." He pointed to a notched wheel rising out the top of the stock. "The trigger on the bottom slides into the notch on the bottom side of the nut and holds it in place until you release it by pulling up on the trigger. Do you follow me so far?"

Michael remembered the blank look on Rizzo's face when he started talking about double-entry accounting. Now it was his turn. "I think so."

"Good. To span, or stretch the bow, put your foot in the stirrup—that piece on the end—and pull back on the bowstring with both hands until you can set it in place on the nut. Go ahead and try."

Michael slipped his foot in the stirrup and began to pull.

"Be careful," Felix said. "That can give you a bad bruise or take skin off your fingers if you let go of it before it is set."

"All right." Michael had to strain, but managed to set the bowstring into the nut.

"Now you are ready to lay the bolt in place." Konrad took a short, heavy arrow from the leather bag. "Point this away from anyone and do not touch the trigger unless you intend to shoot."

Michael pointed the weapon at the wall and dropped the bolt into the slot on top of the weapon.

"Now you are ready," Konrad said. He pointed a finger. "Be careful even when you are sure there is no bolt loaded in the bow."

Michael nodded his understanding. While Konrad reached for the bag, Michael removed the bolt and again pointed the bow away at a clear spot. He held the stock with his left hand, the tiller with his right, grasped the trigger with four fingers and...

"No!"

Michael recoiled from Konrad's shout. He looked up at him, afraid of the anger in his friend's face. Several faces around him stared in alarm.

Konrad took a breath and relaxed. "Never shoot an unloaded bow. The recoil can break it apart."

How was I supposed to know? He'd never even held one.

Konrad smiled. "Sorry, but I have seen the damage when they shatter."

"No, it's my fault." Michael shook his head. "I just don't know about these things."

Konrad only nodded. "Perhaps you can practice in the morning." He continued as if nothing had happened. "You can expect perhaps three or four shots off in a minute. In this kind of conflict, you may not get more time than that, anyway. Keep the sword in case you can't reload in time. Oh, and don't get the bow wet. If you do, the string will stretch, and you won't get enough tension on it. Now, gently, unspan it."

Michael placed his foot in the stirrup and pulled back the bowstring. "Thank you, Konrad. I think I can do it."

"You can operate the bow, but will you be able to shoot a man if necessary?"

Michael sighed. He rested his hand on the stock. "I don't know. I didn't think I would be able to take on two men like I did in Zara. It just happened."

"Well, consider this. If they take us, you may be killed. If you survive, then likely they will chain you to a galley slave's seat where you will probably die in the service of their Allah. Unless someone ransoms you. Is there someone who would pay one thousand *ducats* to gain your release? Or even one hundred?"

Worse and worse. Michael looked at Enrico, who only shrugged. "That's some motivation."

"Motivate yourself however you like, but try to stay alive and free."

"I will."

Enrico piped up. "Does the master-at-arms have another of those?"

"He did when I left with this one."

"I'll be right back." Enrico disappeared up the steps.

Konrad slipped the strap from his shoulder and handed the bag to Michael. "This training may be unnecessary. It is a big sea."

Michael accepted the bag and slung it over his arm. "I hope so. Thanks for the help, Konrad."

As he turned toward his bunk Skender, the Albanian wool merchant, jumped up from his bed a few feet away and ran toward the hatch screaming nonsense, brandishing a half-empty wine bottle. He tripped over someone's outstretched legs, vaulted headfirst into the steps, and fell at the base as though shot dead.

Michael ran and knelt at Skender's side. He felt the man's neck and found a pulse. When he checked his head his hand came away streaked with blood. Skender moaned.

"Drunk fool just knocked himself silly."

Michael looked up, but didn't see who said it. He turned his eyes back to Skender. Drunk and scared. He hoped this wasn't an omen.

* * * *

The sunrise greeted interested observers gathered in clumps about the deck, all alert for signs of the enemy. Anxiety seemed contagious as men murmured to their neighbors. Some joked and displayed false bravado, but mostly Michael heard the quiet sound of fear. Then someone behind him exclaimed, "There!"

Michael turned and looked back across the deck. A few degrees south of the sun, distant sails filled with wind. The oarsmen matched the drum's quick cadence.

Michael sought out Konrad. Enrico tagged along. They found him standing with his knees against the rail, staring into the distance.

"Is it them?" Michael asked.

Konrad squinted. "It is too far away to tell." He paused. "But they seem headed for us."

Michael strained his eyes, trying to focus on the ship. "What do you think they'll do?"

Konrad looked at Michael for a moment as if reluctant to think about what might come. He turned back to the sea. "They will try to disable us. They can fire their cannon at the rigging or at the oars. We are no good to them if we sink. If they can, they will ram us and break the outriggers."

Michael frowned. "What good would that do?"

"Come over here." Konrad pointed down, over the side. "If you look here, you will see the outriggers keep the three rows of oars separated from each other. If they are broken, the oars will strike each other and impair their effectiveness. We will not be as mobile."

Michael looked over at the thin wooden beams he had seen but not really noticed. "But that would damage them, too, wouldn't it?"

Konrad nodded and pointed again. "Look to the front of this ship. Do you see the heavy 'beak' on its point? That tip is made for use as a weapon, a ram of sorts. We would do the same to the other ship if we were able, but it is smaller and faster than this one and not loaded with cargo."

Doesn't look good for the home team. Michael gestured toward the seaborne threat. "What are our options?"

"The captain will use as much wind as possible to delay their arrival." He smoothed back a long, gray strand of hair blown into his face by a gust. "One never knows when a strong wind or storm may come along. We would have the advantage then, especially in a rough sea, because it would be harder for them to board. If they do catch us, he might turn and try to ram them or use the cannon mounted on the prow, but that entails some risk because they are probably more maneuverable."

Michael nodded. "All right, say they catch us. What then?"

Konrad tapped the railing. "When they are able, they will throw their hooks and try to tie the ships together so their men can come aboard. Success will hinge on which group can fight best, and we stand a good chance there. The crew is experienced and each oarsman can fight. The pirates must believe this vessel a prize to pursue it alone."

Enrico looked at the ship, now visibly closer. "How long?"

Konrad peered over the water. "Two hours. Three, perhaps."

Why didn't they just stay home? Michael chewed on his lip. "What do we do?"

Konrad looked about the deck. "First, stay out of the way of the crew. Find shelter from the pirates' arrows where you can shoot your own. On the far side of the poop, perhaps, whichever that becomes, or behind the kitchen, but they will swarm around the back if they are able. Watch for that. Until then, pray."

Michael watched the activity on the deck and tried to stay out of the way. Enrico went below. To think, he said.

The pirate ship drew nearer each minute. Men placed weapons and built defenses. The crew nailed planks along the side rails to protect the crew and passengers who would be throwing stones and darts, shooting arrows, a handful of men held an *arquebus*, forerunner of the musket. At the front of the ship, a small stack of round-hewn stones waited for the cannon mounted there. Michael looked out over the water. It wouldn't be long. He went below to fetch his weapons.

Enrico sat on his bedroll facing away. Michael bent over his own bed and picked up his bow. He hoped to be able to sleep there come night.

"Hey. It'll happen soon."

"I'm ready." Enrico hopped to his feet. "Or, at least, I may as well be. Look." He pointed down the row of berths.

Konrad readied himself. He had replaced the gray habit with a magnificent black tunic featuring a white eight-point cross emblazoned across the breast.

A Maltese cross?

From under the tunic, a shirt of mail rose partway up Konrad's neck. The white hair and beard that earlier marked Konrad as an older man now gave him an ageless look. He fastened a belt holding a long knife on the right side and slid his sword across his body into the scabbard on the left; then he pulled on and buckled a shining helmet. He looked every bit the warrior.

Konrad walked through the center of the cabin with a dignified gait, looking ahead as he passed men on either side. All stopped their activities and murmured as they watched him pass.

"A knight of Saint John," Michael heard.

Men followed Konrad up the steps. Michael hurried to sling the bag of ammunition over his shoulder. He and Enrico joined the parade up the stairs. When they arrived on deck, Konrad had the same effect on those assembled there. The crew and passengers watched him face the pirate ship, draw his long sword out, place the point on the deck, fold his hands on the pommel, and wait.

There is a leader.

The pirate ship closed. Michael wondered what the *Donna Maria's* captain would do, turn and attack or run and make it hard for the *corsairs* to board.

The captain decided to run. Crewmen gathered at the rear of the ship with weapons ready. Then a puff of smoke issued from the front of the pirate vessel. "Down!" yelled one of the crew. Michael dropped to the deck, clutching the bow in his right hand. The boom preceded a pop overhead.

Enrico looked around with wide eyes. "What was that?"

"There." Michael pointed up at a hole in the main sail. At least the cannonball hadn't hit the rigging or the mast. He got up on a knee to see the action.

At the captain's shouted orders, the port side oarsmen stopped their rowing and sank oars into the water. Michael put a hand on the smooth deck to maintain balance as the ship slowed. Crewmen turned the sails out of the wind and furled them.

Michael cried out to no one in particular. "What is he doing?"

"He is forcing the fight before they can reload that cannon," someone close said.

"Paah!" Michael jumped at the soft report of a black powder weapon from behind. He turned and sucked in gun smoke as the thick cloud swept by. Coughing, he looked for the source. A second shot drew his attention. Up on the poop deck, a pair of *arquebusiers* fired at the pirate ship. Their helpers took the empty firearms and handed them freshly loaded ones. A round of shots returned. One whistled overhead; a couple of others whacked the ship's hull with a sound like hailstones on a wooden roof.

Across the deck on the right side, Konrad crouched behind the temporary fortifications. Michael punched Enrico and pointed, then scurried for safety.

The corsair moved to come alongside the right. The captain of the Venetian ship ordered the helmsman to cut hard to the left. Michael put a hand to the inclined deck to steady himself. The corsair copied their tack and moved to intercept.

"Come on; lose them," Michael muttered. He began to catch snatches of men shouting from the other vessel. *Arabic?*

The pirate ship had matched every move of its bigger target and gained each time. As it approached, the Venetian captain ordered the ship to cut harder left, toward the corsair. The timing cadence of the galley bull set the right-side oarsmen to a furious pace. The *Donna Maria* veered toward the pirates in an attempt to ram their ship.

"We're not going to make it." Enrico's face had lost its color.

Some of the men ran for the cover of planking on the left. Feeling exposed, Michael ran and ducked. Enrico slid in beside him; both crouched behind a half-inch of rough-cut wood. Michael glanced back at the spot he had just vacated and shivered. An arrow embedded itself on the inside of the temporary shielding.

"I don't think they're kidding about this, Enrico."

"You may be right." Enrico closed his eyes and moved his lips in silent recitation.

The hail of arrows, darts, and other missiles grew to a crescendo. Then silence. Acrid gunpowder smoke from the *arquebuses* tinged the quiet air. Men up and down the ship grasped fixtures or braced themselves on the deck. Michael raised his head above the planking for a quick look. The scene unfolded in slow motion.

The corsair's elongated bow struck the taller galley's outriggers. A crack of splintering wood preceded the impact of bow against hull. The collision slammed Michael against the railing and onto his back. His crossbow rattled on the deck. He rolled over on his hands and knees and grabbed for the weapon. Someone screamed, then someone else.

Michael looked back at Enrico. "Are you all right?"

Enrico pointed. "You're bleeding."

Michael brought up his right hand. A two-inch diagonal gash ran across the back. He took out his scarf and wrapped the hand. A thump turned his attention forward.

A hook landed on the deck. Its tether jerked taught and embedded the hook in the planking and rail timber behind it. Another hook appeared, and another. A man tried to cut one loose and received an arrow in his chest for the effort. He fell back on the deck in a futile attempt to pull out the shaft, his cries adding to the din. Crew and passengers gathered at the joining of the ships, hurled stones, shot arrows, yelled threats of victory.

Michael was overcome with a strange sense of detachment, separated from the reality in front of him. He sat with his back against the planks and, strangely, recalled, a hunting trip from his junior year in high school.

* * * *

One October Saturday afternoon Uncle Frank dropped by for coffee. He spoke to Michael's tight-lipped mother across the kitchen table. "You know it's time, Frances."

Mom just turned and stared blankly out the window.

Frank snorted and got to his feet. "Come on Mike. You're a man now."

Mike followed Frank to his pickup and waited while his uncle pulled a long black case from behind the seat and laid it on the hood.

Frank made a show of unlatching the case before he finally folded it open. Mike gasped at the beautiful object.

"Eight-millimeter bolt-action Mauser, made in 1937. My grandfather's brother brought it back from the war." Frank covered his mouth with his fingers and paused with a far-off look. "I had the stock cut down and put the scope on it. It's yours now." He stood back and motioned Michael to pick it up.

"Thanks, Uncle Frank. It's great." Mike stared and shook his head at the luck. Mom had told him "no" again just last week. He stroked the cool gray rifle barrel and ran his fingers across the smooth round knob on the bolt. "Can we go shoot it?" He glanced up into teary, smiling eyes.

"Yes sir, we can. Go tell your mom."

He had great fun. The noise, the recoil, his ability to hit a target made Mike feel powerful and in control. The big day arrived at last.

On a crisp fall evening, they drove to a hunting camp and met with other hunters, drank coffee, with whiskey for the adults, and swapped stories that he suspected weren't entirely true. In the morning, they tramped out into the woods where Frank pointed him to a good spot, he said, and left. Mike waited in the cold, squatted against a tall tree, alone with the smell of damp oak leaves and the swish of a winter breeze in the bare treetops. He drew back the bolt and chambered a round with a satisfying click.

In only a few minutes, crackling brush announced the arrival of a visitor. Mike readied his weapon. From behind a patch of brush, a young four-point buck appeared and froze twenty feet away when he spotted Mike. Mike's pulse raced while he wrestled with what he wanted and what Frank expected. Finally, unable to shoot, he spat a whisper: "Get." The deer leaped over a bush and vanished.

Michael never told his uncle about his failure and never went hunting again. He couldn't shoot that day. *But that buck wasn't trying to kill me.*

* * * *

The pirates had set up boarding planks while Michael relived the past. They would be on this side soon enough.

Michael sat next to a gap between two boards, through which he might be able to shoot. He couldn't stand up to span the bow without exposing himself to pirate arrows and guns, so he sat with legs flat, and pushed his foot in the stirrup while he leaned back, almost to the deck, to stretch the bowstring into place. Huddled on his knees, he took a bolt out of the bag hung from his shoulder and laid it in the notch on the stock of the crossbow. He scooted closer to the gap where he could see the boarding planks and waited.

From the enemy ship the frightening cry of "Allah!" signaled the attack. A pair of invaders, protected head to foot by two large shields, led the charge. A line of corsair sailors intent on taking the *Donna Maria* followed. Michael aimed at one in the middle, took a deep breath, and squeezed the trigger.

The man he intended as the target appeared untouched, but the one behind him clutched his knee and fell sideways off the plank. Michael moved closer to his portal to see his man holding to a broken outrigger. An oar battered him until he fell in the water and disappeared. *So that's what it's like.*

The feeling was curiously neutral, no victory or regret. There would be time for them later.

Michael cocked the bow again. He sat up and repositioned it, selected another target, and aimed higher and to the right. The bolt found the enemy's rib cage, but that face...only a boy.

The young man jerked to a halt and looked straight at Michael's peephole in accusation. Then the comrade behind pushed by him, and the boy fell in a slow, awkward arc to meet the dark blue water.

Michael stared at the sea that had just swallowed his victim.

Killer. Murderer. The reality of death paralyzed Michael. *But he would have killed me.*

Michael struggled for sanity until the roars and screams and gunshots and clashing of steel broke through, and he could move again. The front line crashed through defenders and onto the deck. The stream of angry faces on the boarding planks seemed endless.

Michael hurried to reload his crossbow, and caught a movement of gray and black. Across the way, Konrad jerked his sword from the slumping body of a pirate and engaged another with an agility that belied his age. Michael latched the string and moved back into position. He loosed another bolt into the line on the plank. No effect. He stared at the uninjured target, unable to comprehend how he could miss at this range.

Oarsmen streamed from below to join the fight. Some logical part of Michael's mind appreciated the extra labor in running a galley. Several attackers swung over from ropes they had attached to the galley's rigging and climbed up the ship's ladder.

Michael shouted to Enrico over the gunfire and battle yells and cries of pain. "Too crowded." He pointed behind. "Over there."

They ran toward the poop, crouched low. Michael swung around the cover of the structure, expecting any moment to feel an arrow in his back. They spanned their bows again.

"Whose idea was this trip?" Enrico yelled over the din.

"I remember you volunteering."

"That won't happen again."

On a knee, Michael peered around the corner, while Enrico stood over him and took aim. Again, they released their darts and retreated to arm the weapons. Michael stood in the stirrup and pulled up on the bowstring, but his hands grew tired and clumsy. He missed the notch and the string slipped. *Konrad was right.* It would take the skin off.

Michael reached again for the bowstring with raw fingers when a shadow moved across his feet. A pirate stood and brandished his curved cutlass. Time seemed to stop. Michael would remember the man forever. A long, twirled mustache and white turban framed the black eyes that drilled into him with devilish ferocity.

The pirate drew his sword arm across his body in a move that slashed back toward Michael's neck. Michael jerked his weapon up in a desperate defensive motion and felt the muscles in his face contort into a mask of horror. The bow cracked and splintered, but somehow denied the sword its target. It wouldn't hold again, and he wouldn't have time to draw his sword. Michael tensed in anticipation of the next blow when he heard the familiar snap.

The pirate halted his swing at its apex and looked down with unbelieving eyes at the red stain spreading across his chest. The corsair dropped his sword behind him and crumpled back to the deck, staring skyward.

Enrico stood over Michael's shoulder. "We're even."

Michael could only stare at the twitching, dying pirate. "Thanks."

Enrico rushed to load again, but the fight was almost over. The pirate captain had made a serious error in attacking the galley alone. His boarding planks were in use again, but in reverse as Christians rushed aboard the corsair ship, where the remaining Muslim crew surrendered.

Numb, Michael trudged across the deck to the rail and watched as the victors lowered the pirates' flag. Reality hit him; he had killed men. The ruined bow fell from his hand and clattered on the deck.

Bodies lay scattered about. Some still, others writhed in pain or jerked in lifeless reflex. Men cried out in pain and in exultation. A group surrounded one form close to the point where the two ships joined. A glimpse of gray hair horrified Michael.

Konrad.

He shoved men out of his way to reach Konrad's side. An arrow had found its way between the helmet and mail at his neck. Bright red blood stained the white cross on Konrad's chest and pooled under him. He lay blinking against the sun. Michael held out a hand to shade Konrad's face and knelt at his side.

Konrad struggled to move his mouth. "Michael," he whispered.

"Yes, Konrad."

"We won."

"Yes, we did."

"Praise God."

Michael's tears mixed with the blood on Konrad's tunic. Konrad struggled for another breath. His eyes lost their focus.

"Michael."

"I'm here, Konrad."

"Tell...Felix."

A sob wracked Michael's body. *Why?* Anguish twisted his voice. "I will." But Konrad could no longer hear him.

* * * *

The toll was grievous, although not as bad as it could have been. Seven lay dead–four crew and three passengers, including Konrad and poor doomed Skender. A dozen more suffered various injuries, and one or two might die yet. Michael helped tend to them as well as he could.

They gathered again for burials. The dead Muslim attackers had already been thrown overboard. Michael never knew how many. He helped prepare Konrad's body, laying him out in full dress, and bore him to the funeral.

Several new passengers came aboard. Christians among the corsair's galley slaves were freed and Muslims chained in their places. The corsair captain sat in the Venetian ship's temporary prison.

It took the carpenter most of the next day to repair the outriggers, but soon they sailed again. The former pirate ship ran alongside, flying the flag of Saint Mark.

Chapter Thirty-Four

Girolamo

The monastery breathed a cool draft through its winding halls. Girolamo strolled the upper corridor near his cell and savored the early morning, still buoyed by last night's news. He broke the silence with the friar at his side.

"Charles prepares his army, Domenico. It will not be long now." Girolamo had remained steadfast these last few years and now God answered his prayers.

Domenico peered into the open cell of an initiate as they passed by. "Piero says that Italy will unite against Charles. He has allied himself with Naples. Can Charles fight his way through Milan and Florence?"

Domenico had doubts, like many, but he would see the glory of God's hand soon. "He will not need to fight, my friend. God will open the path before him. Piero will capitulate. The pope will grovel. Naples will welcome him. Soon the whole of Italy will serve the Lord again. I have seen it."

Girolamo allowed a rare satisfied smile to spread across his face.

Chapter Thirty-Five

Michael peered over the rail across the water at the nothingness that had become his life.

"Cheer up," Enrico said.

"I'm all right." But he didn't feel all right. He didn't feel much of anything except an inescapable numbness.

"We should be in Palma by the evening. No more wormy biscuits."

Palma de Majorca. A port city in an island paradise, recently made part of the new Kingdom of Spain. Michael hoped he could find a bath there. A hot bath. Hot enough to burn through this dead shell that enveloped him since the battle. Those events oppressed him night and day. Snapshots of horror—the dying boy's astonished expression, a man clutching his chest, gun smoke, the narrow escape, Konrad's dead eyes staring into the sky. The images overlaid everything he did. They pressed him when he laughed at a joke, took a bite of supper, or when he closed his eyes and dreamed. He stood for hours on the deck where he had talked with Felix and Konrad just to feel the wind and sun on his skin, to feel *something*. Where was Felix when he needed to talk?

"Palma," he said to Enrico. "It should be nice."

* * * *

The rest of the Flanders Fleet sat anchored in the harbor, waiting. The *Donna Maria's* captain departed in the corsair ship rowed by its human cargo. He would, so went the rumor, come back with an impressive sum of money in gold coin in exchange for the ship and its Muslim slaves and share it in unequal amounts among the crew. Michael and Enrico went into town and didn't even pretend to be there on business.

They found a hot bath and then a meal with lots of fresh vegetables at an inn where Michael slept in a room to himself, able to stretch out his arms without touching someone on either side, in a soft bed that didn't move. It seemed the most luxurious night of his life.

* * * *

"Feeling better?" Enrico asked.

"Much." Michael pushed back the empty dish and wished for coffee and a cigarette, wondering if he would ever quit missing them.

Finished with the meal, he gazed around the plaza. A church bell tower rose behind a row of shops. Lovers held hands, businessmen haggled, children played. The table sat among several scattered outside the inn's front door. A tree shaded them from the noon sun, clad in leaves of a color green which can exist only in the spring, the kind of day Michael remembered from his youth when, with the gray of winter a memory, the earth lived again.

Sheila—Cecile would like this. Michael leaned back in his chair. "It'll be hard to get back on the ship."

Enrico drained his cup. "I don't want to think about it yet. You know, some people sail for a living."

Michael chuckled. "I'm glad somebody wants the job."

"What do you want to do this afternoon?"

Michael shook his head. "I'm going to walk around on solid ground until it's time to eat again."

"Well, enjoy it while you can."

"I intend to." Michael had been wondering something. "You know, you've hardly looked at a woman since we've been here."

Enrico grinned. "Oh, I've looked."

"You know what I mean. You haven't offered to follow one since we were at Zara."

"I seem to have made a rash promise." Enrico's grin faded.

"A promise?"

"When we were in the storm, I swore to God I wouldn't run after wine or women until I returned to Caorle if He would only save me."

Michael stood and dropped a coin on the table. "And so he did."

"Apparently." Enrico got up and strolled with Michael into the street.

"What if he was just answering someone else's prayer?"

The grin returned. "I'm not taking any chances."

* * * *

The respite in Palma ended. Trumpets from the fleet's ships called the travelers. Michael and Enrico waited at the docks for the skiff back to the *Donna Maria* and watched the activity in the harbor while a warm breeze flapped their clothes and drove lazy waves against the piers.

A middle-aged man with salt-and-pepper hair and short goatee joined them and deposited a pair of light leather bags. Michael nodded a greeting to the man who looked like someone's grandfather.

"*Bom dia, senhores*," the man said.

"Good morning," Michael returned in his best Portuguese. "Are you from Portugal?"

"Yes, sir. From Lisbon." He extended a hand. "Pero Guomez."

Michael shook Pero's hand. "Michael Patriate, and Enrico de Rippa, from Caorle." He received a puzzled look. "Near Venice." Caorle wasn't internationally famous yet.

"Ah, I see." Pero inspected Michael's clothing. "You are merchants, then."

"Yes, we're on our way to Porto. Are you on business here?"

Pero nodded. "My employer's family holds property here in the islands."

"Interesting," Michael said. "I suppose you are headed home."

"At last." Pero sighed. "I spent the winter here." He smiled. "I will be glad to sleep in my own bed again."

"We have a long voyage before we can go home." Michael longed for his room back in Caorle and for Cecile. "Which ship are you taking?"

"I do not know yet." He grinned. "For all my rush, I put this off until the last moment."

"Then we invite you to travel with us on the *Donna Maria*." Michael looked out into the harbor. "Here comes the skiff now.

Pero gave Michael a short bow. "Thank you. I will. The trip is shorter when one has company."

And I'll have some more practice in Portuguese.

* * * *

Without looking, Michael sensed the concern painted on the few faces on deck. The Strait of Gibraltar loomed ahead. At a width of only about nine miles at its narrowest point, the strait limited a ship's ability to escape detection and attack by pirates, but the five ships, when not separated, made a formidable presence. He watched the cliffs slide by as the convoy sailed through unmolested.

"What do you think?"

Michael turned his head to catch Enrico standing beside him and looked back toward the mountains behind. "I try not to do much of that anymore."

"I understand," Enrico said. He stood silent for a while. "We have to decide, you know."

"Mmm hmm."

"If we don't, we'll wind up in Porto anyway."

Michael cut his eyes toward Enrico and grinned. "Yes, *Mamma*."

Enrico returned his smile. "You know how to hurt a fellow. I'm the irresponsible one."

"Sorry." Michael chuckled. "I guess now's the time. So, Porto or Lisbon."

"Your call."

Michael balanced his hands on each side. "Well, Porto's probably safer, but if Pero's telling the truth, we know someone in Lisbon with connections."

"Do you think he really works for the king's family?"

Michael shrugged. "I don't know. Talks a good game."

Enrico only nodded.

"Well," Michael said. "Life's a gamble. Let's go to Lisbon."

* * * *

The "scribe," the ship's clerk who had signed them onto the ship, now checked them out. "I thought you were going to Porto."

"We were," Michael answered. "But we changed our minds."

"There is no refund for the unused portion of your trip."

"None needed." Michael slung the strap of a bag over his shoulder. "But we'll still want to be on the return trip to Venice when you get back from England."

"All right," the clerk said. "But make sure you check for our arrival in port. We should be back in four or five weeks, but we won't stay long this time."

"Understood. Thanks for your help."

A short time later Michael, Enrico, and Pero climbed out of the boat and stood on the dock. Michael shook Pero's hand. "Enrico and I have enjoyed your company."

Pero displayed a gentle smile that Michael had grown to appreciate. "And I yours."

"And we are grateful for your offer of help while we are here. We were lucky to meet you."

Pero shrugged. "It is part of the job. Good business benefits both parties."

"I hope this is good business, then." Michael turned toward the city. "Can you suggest an inn, perhaps?"

Pero surveyed the pair for a moment. "I can do better than that. You will stay with me. I have room now that the children are gone."

How much better can this get? "We couldn't impose on you."

"It is no imposition." Pero turned and waved them to follow. "Come with me. I will introduce you to my wife."

Chapter Thirty-Six

Pero produced an impressive list of contacts, much better than those Anzolo gave him in Venice. As assistant to the next king of Portugal, he had access to the heads of the most powerful merchant organizations. Pero suggested that Michael and Enrico see Duarte Vargas, owner of a business of respectable size, but less conspicuous than some of the larger concerns. They waited in an outer office under the watchful eye of Duarte's ancient secretary.

"He'll be out soon," the old man droned in the same tone he'd used every ten minutes for the last hour.

The assistant turned when the door opened behind him. He nodded at someone and looked back at Michael. "All right." He motioned them in.

Blades of all sorts, great swords, long knives, daggers, hung on the walls and sat on shelves, displayed singly and in groups. Michael flinched when he walked through the open door. What had they gotten into? Their host sat behind a massive desk, ringed by a collection of weapons. On the back wall, a long, curved single-edged knife gleamed, carved from what looked like a single piece of polished ivory. Pero could have warned them.

Duarte spoke in a soft, almost effeminate voice and broke Michael's distraction. "So you are the Venetians."

The soft-spoken man was a sharp contrast to the display of weaponry around him. The slender, middle-aged gentleman sported a short, neat beard and wore a chocolate brown silk shirt with ruffles at the wrists and shoulders. But the eyes weren't so soft.

"We are from Caorle, near Venice, sir. My name is Michael Patriate. This is my associate, Enrico de Rippa."

"It might as well be Venice as far as I am concerned, but you don't sound Venetian."

I ought to have a sign made. "No, sir. I am originally from Norwich, in England."

"English." Duarte grimaced and shook his head.

"Yes, sir." Michael bowed to Duarte's attitude. "I was born in England, but Caorle is my home now."

"Well sit, then. What can I do for you?"

"Thank you." They took seats in front of the desk. "We, the association of merchants in Caorle, wish to trade directly with your company."

Duarte held his head higher. "Oh? What do you have to trade? This is a long way to transport goods."

"Textiles, Asiago cheese..."

"Cheese?" Duarte interrupted. "We have cheese here."

Enrico joined the conversation. "Yes, but this is a delicacy that will be popular here. We brought samples."

Duarte waved a hand in front of his face. "No, no. From Venice I want silk, glass. Not cheese. Can you get me those things?"

"Ah, no, sir," Michael said. "I mean we can, but they will be more expensive than when you get them directly from Venice."

Duarte made a curious side-to-side shake of his head and rolled his eyes. "No silk, no glass. You waste my time."

Michael glanced at Enrico, who displayed an incredulous look that must have matched his own. Pero recommended Duarte. Surely they were missing something.

"Sir, I apologize for..." *What's the saying for beating around the bush?* "...for not being more direct. We want your trade. We'll load our ships with ordinary goods, but we'll bring coin, too. You'll be dealing in much more valuable items before long."

Duarte's eyes snapped back to attention. "What kind of valuable goods are you talking about?"

"*Senhor* Vargas, we think Portuguese ships will soon find their way around the south of Africa and sail directly to India."

"Why do you believe this?" Duarte asked.

Michael didn't like his expression.

The truth wouldn't work, so common sense would have to do. "We all know that Bartholomew Diaz returned from the Cape of Good Hope six years ago, and a route in that direction is possible, even probable. The lands the Spanish discovered, I think you know, aren't India as Columbus claims, but the knowledge of their existence will spur further exploration by them and other countries. This, we think, will push Portugal to pursue the goal of reaching India and its spices. That is our bet, at least."

Duarte paused for a long while. "Since you are fortune-tellers; who will lead this voyage?"

"Sir, we are strangers here. We know only what we have gathered from travelers at home and on the way here, but we have heard the name of Estevão da Gama or one of his sons."

"This will be disruptive," Duarte said. "If it comes true, of course."

Michael nodded. "Disruption generates profit, if we prepare for it."

"Perhaps." Duarte shrugged and looked down at his desk, then up again. "How do you propose to transfer this cargo of yours? I doubt Venice sanctions this plan."

"The ships of Ragusa are for hire."

"Selling spice in the Venetians' own territory. That would be a stick in their eye." Duarte rubbed a sleek bone-handled throwing knife mounted in a display box. "Come back tomorrow," he said. "I must think about this."

"Whatever your decision," Enrico said, "we appreciate your patience and your valuable time."

"Yes." Duarte stood in dismissal. "Tomorrow."

* * * *

Supper at Pero's house that evening consisted of a spicy beef hash poured over a large round piece of bread. Only two days off the ship, Michael relished every meal.

Pero set down his wineglass. "So, how did your meeting go today?"

238

Michael caught Enrico's quizzical expression across the table. "Successful, I think. We have another appointment tomorrow."

"Good. I hope you work out a satisfactory relationship."

Michael sliced off another piece of bread. "I am sure we will. We are grateful to you for your assistance here. You have saved us a lot of time and given us a better chance of success."

Pero nodded. "So, you think Portuguese ships will make their way to India."

He had spoken to Duarte. Was that a good thing?

"We do. It seems an obvious progression of Portuguese exploration."

"And you have spoken of this development to others here?" Pero's grandfatherly eyes rested on his cup.

"Only to *Senhor* Vargas and to you." Michael's appetite waned.

"Well, I hope you are correct. More wine?"

* * * *

Michael brooded as they walked the cobblestones toward Duarte's warehouse. A trickle of sweat ran down his back. Only early May, the weather already turned hot.

Enrico looked back over his shoulder. "I don't like this."

"Me either." Michael stepped around an elderly couple hobbling down the street. "Feels like we've stumbled on someone's big secret, but it's so obvious. Maybe it's only my imagination."

"Maybe. I would feel better if the ship was still here."

"I know, but it's not." He gave Enrico a stern look. "We're committed now. Let's just get our business wrapped up, and then we can enjoy the scenery for a while."

When they turned the last corner, Michael looked up and down the street. "That's odd." The streets had been crowded with pedestrians, but this stretch appeared curiously empty. Only a few milled about, including four soldiers that loitered outside Duarte's place.

Enrico slowed his pace and muttered, "Are they waiting for us?"

"Maybe." Michael walked a few paces and turned around to Enrico. "Come on."

Enrico hesitated. "Let's go back to Pero's house."

Michael moved close and spoke in a half-whisper. "I don't think that will do us any good. Just walk naturally and see if we can get inside."

"I don't like it," Enrico repeated, but he took a step.

Michael nodded a greeting to one man who looked up as they passed. Before they could get inside the door, hands grabbed Michael's arms, and a voice in his ear said, "Move."

Michael struggled to keep his feet under him as the men rushed him across the street to a waiting coach. The scrape of shoes on stone behind told him Enrico followed. Michael's abductors shoved him through the open door.

Two men, dressed in uniform waited inside. One pointed to the opposite bench. "Sit."

Enrico followed and eased into the seat on Michael's right. "What do you want with us?"

Michael touched his arm. "Wait."

Enrico settled back in his seat.

I knew better. Michael cursed himself. They should have stuck to the plan.

The coach rocked as someone outside climbed the ladder with quick steps. Something clicked and the vehicle lurched forward, cracking Michael's head against the wood panel behind him. The driver yelled out, and the coach made a sudden sharp turn.

Enrico slammed into Michael and drove him into the wall. As he pushed him off and back onto his own side, Michael noticed the amused looks on their captors' faces. And their grips on the support rails. *How could you be ready for any of this?*

The men watched them, now unwavering, dispassionate. Staccato drumbeats of hooves from the pair of horses announced their quick pace through the streets. Shouts of warning from the driver declared the coach owned right of way. They turned uphill and bounced around narrow streets.

Through the window slits, Michael caught an occasional view of the city from an increasing altitude. They passed through a tall archway, and Michael glimpsed a heavy wooden door closing behind them before the coach lurched to a halt. One of their keepers grunted another command. "Out."

The coach door sprang open, and a uniformed man peered back at them. When Enrico balked, the soldier grabbed his arm and dragged him out and down. Michael tried to hurry, but a blow to his back impelled him out and onto the paving stones beside Enrico.

Michael cried out in Venetian, unthinking. "We're not resisting."

Guards, Michael didn't know how else to think of them, yanked them to their feet and searched them. Michael's heart sank even farther when he realized that they would find his watch, but the guard's fingers skipped over the slender package hanging from the sash around his neck. Gone, however, was the belt where he fastened his eating utensils and money pouch.

Enrico looked like a scared six-year-old.

"It'll be all right." Michael wished he believed it himself.

They stood in a passageway that ran under a large building, judging from the thick columns holding the place up. Guards pushed them toward a gate in one wall and onto steps that led down into a cramped hallway. All traces of sunlight disappeared as dim yellow lanterns took over. A musty stench attacked his nose. After two or three turns, they came to a row of small rooms with barred doors. Michael beheld a dungeon that could have come out of an old "B" movie. The guards shoved them inside a cell, locked them in, and then turned and left without a word.

The events of the last few minutes had disoriented Michael. Enrico looked bewildered. The guards' footsteps faded to silence. The mildewed stone walls soaked up all sound.

"What happened?" Enrico asked.

"I don't know, but let's not panic yet."

"What good would panic do? We're lost down here." Enrico sat on a hard cot and rested his head in his hands.

Michael inspected their cell as if there might be a way out. The nightmare only worsened. Crumbling stone-block walls bore the scars of what had to be many, maybe hundreds, of years of graffiti. The pervading reek of urine and feces made him gag.

Chains and manacles hung from the back wall. Michael walked back and yanked on one with no purpose in mind. An inscription to one side chilled him. From Dante's book he had just read, the words filled him with dread.

Abandon hope, all you who enter here.

"Who's there?" The call seemed to come from a cell down the hall.

Michael walked to the door and pressed his head to the flat bars, but could see only the opposing wall for a few feet in either direction. "My name is Michael."

"What did you do, Michael?"

"Nothing."

The man laughed for a long time.

* * * *

A crunching sound like someone eating chips pulled Michael from a fitful sleep.

He raised up from his cot and rested on an elbow to clear his head. In the corner a rat munched on a cockroach the size of a fifty-cent piece. Michael didn't even bother trying to run him off. The vermin were impossible to scare. He lay back down and stared at Cecile's name he had inscribed on the ceiling. *This is crazy.*

Michael had pulled himself out of poverty after finding himself dumped in a strange place, five hundred years before he was born. Then he survived an encounter with robbers, storms, and a pirate attack. Now he had landed in jail, for what reason he wasn't exactly sure. What else could happen?

Enrico lay on the other bed. He hadn't moved in hours.

A meal arrived. Supper, Michael remembered from sneaking a look at his watch before the nap. The guard slid a tray with water, bread and some kind of gruel under the door. Michael roused Enrico, and they ate while the guard refilled the earthenware lamp bases with oil. The bread was dry, and the cold porridge tasted terrible. But they ate it, not knowing when they would have another chance. The guard returned and pointed to their dishes. Michael drained the last of his water and slid the tray out into the hall. Then they were alone again.

The routine repeated twice a day, but they varied the times, to disorient the prisoners, perhaps. Or maybe they made the effort only when they felt like it.

The man down the hall talked to them for a while, but he asked questions Michael wouldn't answer and finally shut up. Then guards shackled his wrists and took him away. They heard screams that night.

Michael and Enrico passed the time with talk, what to do first if they were released, business principles, childhood, religion, women. They grew tired of it eventually and became quiet. Michael wondered when the men with the chains would come for him. A week went by, then two and three. The ship home would be back soon, and they wouldn't board it. *And no one will tell Cecile.*

* * * *

Shuffling footsteps roused Michael from his slumber. He shook his head. It seemed too early for lunch. He reached for his watch but remembered where he was and ran his hands through his hair instead.

He rose and went to the door to retrieve the meal tray, but this time several sets of footsteps echoed around the corner instead of the usual one. A guard came into view and motioned him back. Michael complied.

Behind the guard stood a well-dressed gentleman of obvious authority. "Leave us," he told the guard and then looked them over. "Well, it seems we have a pair of Venetian spies."

Enrico had stirred with the break in routine and stood as the newcomer spoke. "No," he began in an unsteady voice.

"Enrico, it's all right." Michael held up a hand and turned to his visitor. "Sir, I am sure there has been a mistake. We are merchants from Caorle, near Venice to be sure, but we conduct business only for ourselves. We have no interest in spying."

"So you say." Their visitor widened his stance and crossed the arms hidden by billowing sleeves. "But we do not trust any of you. Our interests are not mutual. Why were you asking about a route to India?"

Michael drew himself up with as much aplomb as he could muster. "Sir, may I have a name so I might properly address you?"

The dark eyes narrowed. "No, you may not. Answer the question."

Michael dipped his head. "Yes, sir. I apologize. For a long time, we have worked in the shadow of Venice, buying and selling at their prices. The relationship has been profitable, but we can see how the world is changing."

"Changing. How?"

"Venice's position of leadership is threatened by developments coming from here in Iberia, namely Columbus's discoveries, and the ones we think you will make soon." Michael gestured with an open hand. "Even your current relationships in Africa are upsetting things. I do not believe Venice appreciates the situation yet. We in Caorle would take advantage of these changes to avoid the damage to our businesses her losses will bring."

An amused smile raised the gentleman's eyebrows. "So, you think yourselves smarter than the masters of the Serenissima?"

"No, the men who rule Venice have been very successful. There is much to admire about what they have done, but now they are holding on to the old ways that have made them rich. We think we must adapt to changing conditions in order to survive and profit."

The stranger laughed and stepped forward to face Michael at the door. "Do you think they will let you do these things?" he mocked.

Michael shrugged. "I have studied a bit of history. Outright revolution rarely works; it is usually met with fierce opposition. The trick is to know how much you can push without making the other side push back," he held out open palms, "until the balance of power has shifted. We will start slowly and gradually increase our outside trade without drawing attention to ourselves."

"And then what?"

"By the time they notice, we will have made substantial profits and firmed relationships with other merchants in the area. You will be selling spice and other Eastern goods in the region and need to protect your new interests." Michael inched forward. "Dalmatian cities resent Venetian dominance and would welcome a Portuguese presence in the Adriatic to balance their power. This will give you direct access to markets eager to buy cheaper goods, from Greece to Austria."

"An ambitious plan." The man gave him a condescending smile. "Have you given thought to the consequences of failure?"

"Yes, sir." Michael nodded. "At worst, we are wiped out, but we doubt the Venetians will go that far. They are..." Michael hoped he used the right Portuguese word, "pragmatic businessmen. And for Portugal, the loss of a few ships should be an acceptable risk."

"What if I say that I can take your plan and leave you here in this prison?" asked the visitor.

"Yes, you could do so." Now Michael smiled. "But you would lose the contacts we have up and down the Dalmatian coast. We have been to each port and never heard a Portuguese accent."

Again, laughter. "You amuse me. You seem to have thought of everything."

"We have put a lot of work into our plans, sir."

The official crossed his arms and looked at Enrico, then back to Michael. "I will consider these things. I am still unconvinced that you are not spies, but perhaps we will speak again."

Michael inclined his head to indicate the prison cell. "We will wait here for your word."

"'We will wait here,' he says," the man howled. He turned and walked back down the corridor, head back, still laughing. "We will wait here." The footsteps receded.

Enrico joined Michael at the barred door. "What do you think?"

"I don't know, but it's something."

"The ship will be here and gone soon."

"I know." Michael crossed the tiny cell and turned back, suddenly hopeful. "And I'm sure he does, too. We'll either get out of here in a few days or not at all."

Enrico stared at the barred door. "Maybe. It's a better prospect than we had yesterday." He turned and gave Michael a scolding look. "By the way, I didn't know we had all those contacts in Dalmatia."

Michael grinned at his friend for the first time in weeks. "I guess we should get busy on the way back, shouldn't we?"

* * * *

Michael smiled at the back of the official he and Enrico followed down the hall. It wasn't so much the slender build or extravagant goatee that reminded him of Don Quixote, but probably the exaggerated flourish with which the functionary flouted his low-level position. *Donnie, that's your name.*

Donnie led them through a door, which opened into a large room with a window.

Enrico strode past and looked out the opening. "Beautiful," he said. He took a cleansing breath and stared at something outside.

"What?" Michael asked.

Enrico spoke without turning around. "Sunshine."

Donnie pointed Michael to the front side of a counter and slid in behind it.

"Where are we?" Michael asked him. Since their release from the dank cell, everyone they met had shown them restrained courtesy.

The man set a bag on the counter. "*Castelo São Jorge*, of course." He untied the linen bag and let it drape to reveal Michael's personal effects including, he noticed, his money pouch.

"The Castle of Saint George," Michael repeated. "I don't suppose Saint George still lives here."

The official peeked up through bushy black eyebrows. "No. This is the residence of King John." He focused his attention on a list and checked off the contents of the bag.

No sense of humor.

Their *concierge* retrieved another bag and spilled out Enrico's possessions.

"Enrico," Michael called. "Come make sure all your things are here."

Donnie glanced up again, but remained silent.

Enrico ambled over and watched him go over another list. "I guess we'll have to go to Pero's house for our bags."

The man looked up from his inventory and motioned to the door. Their baggage sat to one side.

Enrico looked at Michael and flashed him an impressed look. "I'll have to send my compliments to King John for his excellent service."

Michael suppressed the urge to elbow him in the ribs.

The official inverted the two papers and pushed them in front of Michael and Enrico. "Mark here and here."

Outside the gates, Michael looked back at the castle they hadn't seen on the way in. Parts of it were very old, built in a style he associated with Dark Age English castles. The stranger who visited them in the castle's dungeon was a powerful individual.

"What now?" Enrico asked.

Michael turned his attention back to the road and shrugged. "Hire a ride back to town, I guess. I need a bath and clean clothes." He ran his tongue across teeth coated with pasty residue from weeks of prison food. "And a toothbrush. We'll see who we can talk to tomorrow." He turned to Enrico. "Do you want to go back to Duarte's?"

Enrico shook his head. "He scares me."

"Me too." He patted the pocket sewn inside his tunic. They still had Anzolo's list.

* * * *

Michael and Enrico sat down with Dioguo Bernaldez, a merchant whose tastes in office décor ran to the utilitarian side. He reminded Michael of a rich Rizzo.

Michael skipped the pretense of his previous experience and laid out their position. Dioguo took it all in before he responded.

"All right, I understand what you are trying to do. But goods from this new route you claim will materialize do not exist yet, and may not for some time. What will you trade until then?"

"Simply engage us in normal commerce, as you would with Venice," Michael said. "Send us products like wool and dried fruit. Purchase from us goods like grains, cloth, and cheeses. Probably not spices. Since we will have to buy many of these things from Venice, we will be selling them to you at a reduced margin. We can afford to do this for the short term until your own spice trade comes into being."

Dioguo glanced at a folded letter on his desk. "You have convinced the king. I suppose you do not need to convince me." He nodded. "Send your ships here next spring, and we will have your goods."

Michael felt hope of success for the first time since they left Pero's house. "Thank you, sir."

Dioguo's cold stare brought back an edge. "Understand clearly our agreement. You will operate at a reduced margin. I will not. You will pay the same prices as any other customer."

"I understand." Michael stood and offered his hand. "We will see you next spring."

* * * *

While he dreaded another sea voyage, Michael couldn't wait to leave Lisbon. The feeling they might be arrested again didn't abate until they sailed back through the Strait of Gibraltar and away from Portuguese waters. He expected the trip home to be calmer, at least in terms of weather. Spring had given way to summer, and storms were fewer and less intense.

They rested for two days at Palma, a day too many for Michael. He was tired of this trip, this job, this world. He longed for home. Either the old or new one would do.

Approaching Messina, Michael found himself hoping Felix would be waiting there to return home. The bond he felt with Felix and Konrad surprised him. Konrad's loss to the pirates left an empty space that he couldn't fill, but Felix wasn't waiting in Messina. The ship headed back around the boot heel of Italy, into the Adriatic where they still had much work to do.

Chapter Thirty-Seven

Girolamo

In spite of the hot, humid stillness inside the church, Girolamo reveled in the congregation that packed it. The people, squeezed into their pews, suffered through the liturgy in anticipation of the sermon. Piero de' Medici and his corrupt allies boycotted the services, but these faithful chose their own path.

As the time drew near, he could feel the quiet tension mount. He knew every eye followed him when he rose from his seat and climbed the pulpit steps. His series on Noah and the Ark paralleled the decadence of life in Florence and the folly of its leaders. He had heard the rumors, the whispers in the street, and the questions. When would he announce the calamity to befall Florence's leaders? When would he come to the point?

Girolamo faced the congregation. Today, he would bring the story together for them. It would indeed come to the point, the turning point. He began in a monotone.

"Then Noah and his family entered the Ark, and God brought all the animals two by two onto it. After seven days, the flood waters came upon the Earth. The Holy Scripture says:

"'And in the same day were all the fountains of the great deep broken up, and the windows of heaven were opened. And the rain was upon the earth forty days and forty nights. And all flesh died that moved upon the earth, both of fowl, and of cattle, and of beast, and of every creeping thing that creeps upon the earth, and every man: all in whose nostrils was the breath of life, of all that was in the dry land, died.'"

He ceased speaking and for a moment remained silent. He gazed back and forth over his flock and allowed the suspense to build. Then he raised his hands, and the words thundered forth.

"My children! Judgment is upon us! God's justice is being carried out! Charles the Eighth, King of France is bringing his army toward us. *He* is the sword of God. *He* is the Flood, sent by God to destroy the wicked!"

At this, the crowd stood, turning to one another in their fright. "What can we do?" someone cried.

"Call out to God." Girolamo turned his face heavenward. "Join me on His new Ark, in the haven of the new Florence. We will build a righteous world from this wretched remnant!"

Chapter Thirty-Eight

Michael and Enrico talked with merchants in Corfu and Durazzo, where they pitched the relative merits of trade with Caorle and Portugal. In Ragusa, they arranged for ships to Lisbon. At Zara, where Felix had been so excited about the relics of Simeon and where Enrico almost got himself killed, Michael and Enrico went ashore to repay a debt.

"Well, don't tell me this is the fellow you brought to me with his head split open."

Michael grinned and placed his bag on a counter. "Hello, Frederik." He shook his hand. "Yes, the same."

"I wanted to thank you myself." Enrico stepped forward. "I owe my life to you and Michael."

"He returned the favor on the way." Michael looked from Enrico to Frederik. "Pirates, you know."

"Great adventure from the sound of it." Frederik pointed behind the counter. "Come in and sit where you can tell me about it."

"Thank you." Michael reached in his bag. "I brought you something." He pulled out a brown ceramic jar of about a quart size. A thick layer of wax on top protected the contents. "Quince *marmelada* from Portugal. It's very good, sweet and tart."

Frederick accepted the jar and examined it. "I've heard of this, but never had the chance to try any. Thank you."

"You're welcome. This product is popular in England, and we believe will be here, also. But, we can talk business later."

"Yes, I want to hear about your travels."

Michael sat in a chair and made himself comfortable. "Our journey, after we left you, began with a storm."

Part Three

Chapter Thirty-Nine

After months at sea on the galley, the barge seemed like a toy boat. Not that Michael minded. No storms or rats or pirates plagued this vessel. He enjoyed the beautiful early September day, much like the one that first brought him to Caorle two years before. Enrico stood with him and watched the countryside pass by.

Enrico had changed since their first barge trip. He shed the petulance and pleasure-seeking insecurities, and replaced them with confidence and purpose. He even worked at becoming a good negotiator, taking more responsibility as they went up the coast of Dalmatia. Michael realized he had turned into something of a mentor for Enrico, more than he had ever been to Bernie, a talented young man who Michael relegated to the role of gopher. It was an odd feeling.

The barge finally docked in late afternoon. Michael hefted his bags and took several steps toward home when the thought occurred to him that this was the first night in six months he and Enrico wouldn't spend the night together, or at least in the next room. He swung his load around and faced his friend.

"Enrico, it's been an experience."

Enrico answered with a chuckle. "That it has. I don't want to repeat all of it, but I wouldn't trade it away."

"I know." Michael paused a moment. "Let's go home. I'll see you tomorrow."

The bags were heavy and Michael was tired, but the thought of Cecile and home quickened his step. The hostel neared, and he walked through familiar doors. He saw no one, but heard sounds from the kitchen.

"Is anyone here to serve a customer?"

Cecile appeared in the doorway, and her busy expression flashed to excitement.

"Michael," she shouted.

She ran to him and threw her arms around his neck; he dropped his bags and held her.

Oh, she feels good. He hadn't been near anyone like this since Sheila left him. He wanted to pull her tight and bury his face in the softness of her neck, but she drew back, still radiant in her happiness. Michael returned the smile and tried not to let her see the wave of desire that broke over him.

A tear sneaked down her smiling face. "I thought you might not come back."

"That was never an option." Her infectious happiness gave him a feeling like winning a high-stakes bidding war, only...

She looked him over. "You look thin. Are you hungry?"

"Now that you mention it, I'm starving." How he missed someone caring for him.

"Then, go put your bags away. I'll have supper on the table in a few minutes." She broke the precious contact.

"All right." Michael picked up his bags and watched her as she almost skipped back to the kitchen. She paused at the door and smiled at him again.

I have to do something about that.

* * * *

They talked until late in the night. Her business prospered during his absence. She had done her best with the books, but asked him to go over them when he had the chance. Michael told the story of his trip and the dangers he faced.

"I've never felt so alone. Out on that sea, I became aware that life was out of my control. I had little say in whether I even survived. And when I was in prison...I almost gave up hope."

Cecile reached for his hand and paused when she saw the scar. "You've been hurt."

Michael smiled. "Only a scratch."

She ran a finger across the ragged line. "God brought you back to me."

God again. Michael hid his irritation. "Then I'm grateful to him."

She squeezed his hand and looked up at him. "I am, too." Her eyes sparkled in the lamplight.

Michael almost proposed then.

Wait. Better not make a decision of this magnitude emotional and fatigued. He patted her arm and smiled.

* * * *

When Michael came home from his first year in college, he went to see a teacher at his old high school. The place he knew intimately for four years seemed strange and small. He carried a similar feeling into the warehouse, but a grinning Rizzo, always early to work, jumped up to greet him.

Rizzo's voice boomed. "You're back! Tell me about your trip. How are you?" All while threatening to break Michael's hand with a punishing grip.

"Good, Rizzo. Good." Michael extricated his aching hand and flexed it. "We have a lot to talk about. Are things all right?"

"You know nothing changes much here. Yes, all is fine." He looked Michael over. "You spent some time in the sun."

Michael laughed. "I guess I did." He grew serious. "Well, things may change soon." He pulled out a chair and motioned for Rizzo to sit in another. Even a hard backed chair felt good after six months of sitting on a bedroll and leaning against a hull.

"We've arranged to bring in Portuguese goods starting next year and spices when they become available. We probably need to gather the others and talk about this in detail."

Rizzo nodded. "I'll have them here this afternoon. How did you fare with Enrico?"

"You know, he was a big help." Michael visualized snapshots of their time together. "It started slowly enough, but he came around. I guess we both did."

* * * *

Michael took his place in front of the assembled merchants. He nodded to Enrico and Rizzo, positioned to one side.

"Thank you for coming, gentlemen," he began. "I know you've been waiting a long time for the results of our trip. We're bringing good news today. Come springtime next year, we'll take a shipment of goods to Portugal that will be the beginning of lucrative trade there."

Heads nodded among the merchants standing around Rizzo's warehouse. Michael soaked up the buzz for a moment.

"What will we be trading?" one man asked.

"The same things we do now. General goods. We won't have the spice trade for a year or two until they open up their new route to the East, but they do offer us quality merchandise that will give us a reasonable profit until then."

Jacobus erupted from the back of the room. "Reasonable profit? You promised us riches, not 'reasonable' profits." He stalked to the front and pointed with a ringed finger. "You have taken our money and given us nothing in return."

Michael kept his voice even. "We all knew this would take time." He had anticipated this reaction from Jacobus.

The old merchant wagged his head. "Everything takes time, but we need something more definite than 'a year or two.' A year or two becomes five or ten or never."

"There is an amount of risk in anything we do." Michael took a step to close the distance. "I'll admit, the chance our plans will fail is a fact. That's the price you pay for a shot at big money."

"You know what I think?" Jacobus spoke more to the group than to Michael. "I think you are out to take our money and move in on our businesses. Tell them Enrico. Tell them what you saw."

Michael's instinctive guard snapped up. Had he misjudged his friend? He turned to find out.

Enrico paused a moment and looked at Michael, then Jacobus. "Michael saved my life. He rescued me from attackers when he knew my purpose on the journey. He put himself at risk of harm when he could have turned away and rid himself of an antagonist. No, Jacobus, don't interrupt me; he took care of me when I was helpless. Michael is my friend. This man represents us well."

Jacobus seemed stunned by this turn of events. He stared open-mouthed at Enrico for a moment before gathering himself. "The two of you have conspired to take control of our affairs. I think the rest of us should do this ourselves. What would keep us from going and making our own deals?"

Michael made a show of looking over his accuser's generous girth. "I hope you like Portuguese prison food." Titters escaped from several in the audience.

Jacobus's face colored. "I call for a vote right now," he shouted. "We should terminate the services of this charlatan and take back control of this operation."

The sound of children playing drifted in the windows as silent men looked at Michael for his response. He remained composed. Experience taught him a quiet voice and a neutral expression could be much more threatening than a shout and a red face.

"The deal on the table was made among Portuguese royalty, rich merchants, Enrico, and me. The two of us could leave right now and find the financing we need in Zara. That probably makes more sense, anyway." He stepped closer to Jacobus to emphasize the height differential between them. "If you don't want us to do it, that's fine, but you don't even know who to approach."

The two men stared at each other for a time and then Jacobus blinked.

"Well?" With a slow scan the old merchant polled his peers. When no one spoke his eyes turned to slits. He shot Michael a malevolent glance and hurried toward the door.

Enrico called to the man who had stepped into his father's shoes. "Jacobus, don't..."

The older merchant stopped and stared down his former protégé. "Traitor." He huffed out the door.

Enrico stared at the doorway for a moment and then lowered his head.

Michael felt sorry for Enrico, but not enough to go and call Jacobus back. *Good riddance.* He broke the silence. "Does anyone else have an objection?"

No one did.

"All right, then. Let's get to work."

* * * *

If there were a top of this world, Michael stood on it. He had landed in this place with nothing but the knowledge in his head and worked himself up to a position, which, if not yet powerful and prestigious, was a step in the right direction. He faced danger and beat it back, and now he planned one more change.

He sat through supper and watched Cecile while she served the other guests, eager to get her alone. He helped her with the dishes. Then he led her to the common room, sat her in a chair, and knelt before her.

"I have a gift for you."

Cecile's lovely brown eyes searched his face. "I like gifts."

"This isn't nearly as nice as you deserve, but I hope it'll do until I can afford a proper one." He opened his hand to expose the silver garnet ring and watched confusion cross her face. "Will you marry me, Cecile?"

The beautiful eyes filled with tears. She looked down to his open hand and back into his eyes. And then she moved.

Michael straightened as a hundred pounds or so of sweetness launched itself at him. Her momentum drove him back into the chair behind. Stunned, he found Cecile in his lap and her arms wrapped around his neck.

"Yes, yes," she sobbed.

He held her by her shoulders, not knowing what he should do or what the other guests would say if they saw the two of them like this.

Cecile stiffened and pulled back to a half-kneeling, half-sitting position, hands in her lap, and stared down at the floor. "I'm sorry," she whispered.

He sat for a second and then giggled. "You'd make a good *linebacker*."

She met his gaze with a puzzled look. "A what?"

Michael shook his head and grinned. "Oh, nothing, but you pack a good punch." He made a show of rubbing his chin where her shoulder had hit him.

Now Cecile laughed, and she took a peek at the top of the stairs. "We better get up before we cause a scandal."

"You're probably right. Here, let me help." He hopped up and offered her a hand.

When she was seated again he resumed his position. "Cecile, I'd like to do this by the book. I love you. Will you marry me?"

This time she smiled and nodded. "Yes, Michael. I will marry you." She paused and her voice quivered. "When?"

"We can work out a date, but I want this done properly. Tonight I just need to know you'll be mine." He wiped a stream of tears from her face.

"Yes, I will. I've been yours for a long time." She inhaled a big breath. Her rosy cheeks bulged when she blew it back out.

He offered the gift again. "Then please take this ring."

She held out her trembling hand.

Michael prayed he guessed the right size. He gently supported her slender, pale hand in his tanned palm and slipped the ring over her finger. Grasping for words, he found none and instead kissed her hand, wishing the moment would never end.

* * * *

Michael enjoyed the cool breeze on his way to work. Cecile had spent the last week in a flurry of wedding arrangements. They set the date for November 15, before Advent. About two months away, he wished it sooner. But she was happy. *Good enough.*

Work on the spring Portugal trip had gone well, without interference from Jacobus. The group decided it could live with the terms he set in Lisbon. They scraped together enough orders to fill one ship contracted out of Ragusa. Several merchants in Dalmatian cities had indicated interest in joining their group. Two ships would be better than one, especially if he intended to ride along.

Michael and Enrico planned a return trip down the Dalmatian coast in the next couple of weeks to firm up their orders before winter. He didn't relish getting back on the water, but it was part of the deal.

Freight rates and maximum tonnage tumbled through his mind when he heard the scuff of a shoe on stone pavement behind. Michael turned to see who followed him, but felt a hand on his arm and a sharp object in his ribs.

"Just do what you're told," a man whispered. The man guided him off the street and into a small garden, where a brick wall shielded them from view. His assailant turned him around and, pressing a stiletto to Michael's throat, pushed him against the wall.

Michael found himself staring down into the face of a stout middle-aged man, whose grin revealed several missing teeth and issued a stench reminiscent of bilge water. *When is this going to stop?*

"What do you want? I don't have much money with me."

"I don't want your money, troublemaker, although I will take it." He worked the knife handle back and forth enough to sting Michael's skin. "You are an irritant, and I'm here to make you go away."

Michael stretched his neck away from the point of the knife. "Whatever you're being paid, I'll double it."

"No, I'm a professional." The man shook his head. "I don't go back on my word. Besides, I like my job. I like seeing fellows like you squirm before they die. And I might just pay a visit to that lady-friend of yours for good measure." The gapped smile widened.

He only had a few seconds to act. He looked back at the entrance to the courtyard as if someone had come in. When the assassin turned his head in reflex, Michael danced to his left and, using his high school boxing training, delivered an upper-cut to the man's chin as his head turned back. The attacker's eyes lost their focus. He collapsed and fell back, and his head struck the brick floor.

"Ow, crap," Michael exclaimed in English.

The pain shooting up from his hand made Michael dance and shake his arm. That never hurt so much when he wore a boxing glove. He settled down and stared at the man laid out on the ground. Who would want to get rid of him enough to send an assassin, Jacobus? The guy was nuts, but Michael wasn't sure he wanted control of their association enough to do something like this.

Michael flexed his arm again. *Sort it out later.* This fellow had mentioned Cecile. He had to see about her, but he couldn't let this guy run free.

He looked about for something to tie the goon up with and remembered the sash he kept his watch on under his shirt. He untied it and stuffed the watch in a pocket inside his coat, then picked up the stiletto and cut the sash into two lengths. He rolled the unconscious man over face down and tied his hands and feet as well as he could; then he tossed the knife behind a bush and ran out to the street.

He took a step toward the hostel when he spotted a pair of boys on their knees, playing some kind of game. He sauntered over and tried to keep the shakiness he felt out of his voice.

"Gentlemen."

The boys jumped and looked up with apprehension.

Michael reached in his purse and pulled out two silver *denari*. "Could you men do me a big favor?"

The boys kept silent, but stared at the coins.

Michael pointed toward the waterfront. "You know where Rizzo's warehouse is?"

One of the boys nodded.

"Good. I'd like you to go there and give him a message for me. Could you do that?"

Another nod. Michael knelt beside them.

"Listen, this is important. Tell him a man tried to kill me; my name is Michael, and Rizzo needs to come and get him from that garden." He held up a coin in each hand. "I'll give you each a coin now and another when I get back if you speak only to Rizzo and no one else. Will you be here?"

"Yes, sir," one boy said, wide-eyed.

"Good. Here, take these. Now hurry."

The boys took the coins and rushed off in the direction of Rizzo's place. Michael dashed back to the hostel, barely noticing the open stares of people along the way. He hadn't run this far or this fast in a long time. By the time he reached home, stabbing pains jabbed at his lungs.

"Cecile," he shouted in between gasps. She came out of the kitchen, wiping her hands on a towel, and rushed to his side.

"What's wrong?" The concern on her face grew as Michael struggled to get his breathing under control.

"Nothing now. A man attacked me." He took a controlled deep breath. "Rizzo should be taking care of him now. I wanted to make sure...you were all right."

Cecile came close and put her hand on his face. "I'm fine, and I'm glad you are, too." She wrapped her arms around him and laid her head on his chest. He stroked her hair and relished the closeness while his breathing returned to normal.

"I have to go see about this man." Michael pulled back and looked into her eyes. "I'll be back as soon as I can."

Cecile nodded. "Be careful."

He lurched off on rubbery legs.

Rizzo waited for him in the street outside the garden. "Inside the house. I know the owners. And I paid those boys."

"Good." Michael started for the door.

"They said you gave them two *denari* each?"

Michael stopped and grinned. "Don't believe everything you hear." He motioned inside. "What's this fellow saying?"

"He hasn't come around yet." Rizzo gave him an odd look. "What did you do to him?"

Michael worked his sore arm again. "Just got lucky."

He followed Rizzo through the garden. They stepped into the house and found Rizzo's helper guarding the man who was now awake and sitting in a kitchen chair worse for the encounter, hands still tied. A bloody clump of hair showed where his head struck the paved ground. Swelling distorted his jaw.

Rizzo bent over and glared in the man's face. "What's your name?"

"Gino," he mumbled.

"Gino what?"

Gino stared ahead.

"Who hired you?" Rizzo asked.

The man remained silent.

"Look," Rizzo said. "We want to know who you work for. If we're satisfied with your answers, we won't turn you over to the authorities."

The man looked at Rizzo for a moment, then spat, "Jacobus."

"The merchant?" Michael asked. "Why?"

Gino shrugged and closed his eyes. "I think he's crazy."

Rizzo turned to Michael. "We need to get over to his place."

"He's gone," Gino said. "Left for Venice yesterday."

Michael and Rizzo stared at each other. This could mean disaster if the powerful rulers of the Adriatic learned of their plans too soon.

"Hey, what about me?" Gino asked. "You said you'd let me go."

Rizzo's eyes turned hard. "No. I said we wouldn't turn you over to the authorities. What would you do with us if our fortunes were reversed?"

Gino paled.

Michael interrupted. "You said you were a professional out there, when you had a knife at my throat. Are you that professional still?"

Gino drew himself straight as he could with his hands tied behind his back. "Of course."

"Can you give me your word you will leave and not come back?" Michael didn't want this to become public. He didn't want to be involved in a murder, either.

"I give you my word."

Michael looked to Rizzo, who nodded. He retrieved his knife and cut Gino's restraints.

"I'd like my stiletto," Gino said. "It was my father's. Family business, you know."

Michael pointed. "It's behind the bush in the corner."

"Thank you." Gino stood, still a bit unsteady, and placed a hand on the chair. "By the way, that was a good move. You taught me something today."

Michael rolled his eyes. "Glad I could help."

"Gentlemen." Gino fetched his hat from a counter and made his way out the door.

"What do we do now?" Rizzo asked.

"Wait, I guess."

A fly buzzed over Michael's head in a loud, lazy arc. In the fall, the insects headed inside to escape the coming cold. Michael began to wonder where could he hide from the wrath of Venice.

"It's my fault. They may focus on me. I'm the one Jacobus thinks stole his position." He looked down at Rizzo. "Maybe I should leave."

"You would abandon us?" Rizzo frowned.

Michael waved his hands. "No, no, but depending on what Jacobus is telling them, it might be better for you if I'm not here if they come."

Rizzo nodded in understanding. "We all made the same deal. We'll stay together for whatever comes."

They would stand behind him, then. For what that was worth. "Thanks. I guess we should get the others together and talk."

Chapter Forty

Steffano

Steffano stared at the wild-eyed merchant shifting from foot to foot opposite the desk. Most people who came in here showed proper respect, awe even, after passing through the show of power and wealth that filled the rooms leading to his study. But not this one. Still full of venom, he raged against those who had mistreated him and supposedly threatened Venice.

His lieutenant, Vitaliano, snickered off to the side a couple of times. The merchant never noticed him during his tale of lies and betrayal.

Interesting. "Well, Jacobus. I appreciate your concern for our position here." He gave the lunatic a reassuring nod. "Your loyalty will not go unrewarded."

A look of hope buoyed Jacobus's countenance, and he opened his mouth to speak.

Steffano stopped him with raised palms. "I will consider your...account. Until then, please go back to your inn." He looked at Vitaliano and back. "We will contact you soon.

He kept his quiet until Jacobus closed the door behind him and then turned to Vitaliano. "What do you make of him?"

Vitaliano, his assistant, paused for a moment. "Unstable, I think, but there may be something to his story."

Steffano stood and retrieved a pitcher of water from a shelf. "I have met this fellow he mentioned, Michael Patriate, earlier this year. He was a guest of Anzolo Contarini, who introduced us." He filled a glass from the pitcher. "I even inquired about him at the time."

Vitaliano nodded. "The man with no history."

"The one. We should go to Caorle and meet this mysterious deal maker."

"I'll make arrangements." Vitaliano jumped up and headed for the door.

Steffano sipped the cool liquid. "First, make sure our friend Jacobus stays quiet about this."

Vitaliano sighed. "Yes sir. I understand."

"No," Steffano said. "Have him stay as our guest. Somewhere out of the city. He may still be of use to us."

Chapter Forty-One

The kitchen buzzed with talk and laughter. After a long day, Michael sat alone at a table and reflected.

He dreaded leaving again. After the association meeting, Michael went ahead with arrangements to visit his contacts in Dalmatia. Since Jacobus hadn't returned from Venice, they couldn't be sure he had told anyone, and winter would make traveling difficult if they waited too long. Cecile expressed her displeasure that he would go away before their wedding. Michael smiled to himself. *Like being married already without the benefits.*

A guest at the next table caught Michael's eye. The man was a bit overdressed for this part of the world, and he was sure he had he seen him before. The man looked up to meet his gaze, then went back to his meal. A sick dread took Michael's appetite. Steffano de Rompiasi. Anzolo had introduced them that day in the Venetian fog, him and the gray monk. Was it coincidence? He couldn't get that lucky. *Might as well get this over with.*

Michael stood and went to the Venetian's table.

"Pardon me, *signor* Rompiasi?" He waited until the man made eye contact. "Michael Patriate. We met in Venice."

Steffano smiled as if greeting a long-lost acquaintance. "Ah yes, Michael." He pointed to his left. "This is my associate, Vitaliano Barozzi."

The man beside Steffano rose and offered his hand. A little shorter than average, but stout with a no-nonsense expression. Steffano's muscle.

"Good to meet you *signor* Barozzi." Michael completed the handshake.

"You as well." Vitaliano gestured to an empty chair. "Please join us."

The two men sat, Michael opposite his visitors.

Michael fought the urge to rush. "We don't often receive guests of your distinction here in Caorle."

Steffano smiled with a hint of condescension. "Yes, it has been some time since my last visit. Too bad, it is a pleasant little town." He wasn't giving anything away.

I hope I don't know why you're here. Michael played the small-talk game. "I agree with you on that point. The pace is certainly slower here."

Michael remembered thinking in Venice that Steffano resembled a fox. The smile he wore when he spoke might have been reserved for a big fat hen backed into a corner.

"It is relaxing for a change. I especially like the quaint little place you have here."

Michael shook his head and smiled in spite of the insult. "No, this isn't mine. I'm only a guest here."

"Oh? I was under the impression that you and the lady were engaged to be married." The simple statement said: "We know about you."

Michael tried to laugh off the growing alarm. "Yes, that's true, but for the next few months I pay my own way."

Steffano's face grew serious. "Michael, it should not surprise you that we came here for you."

Michael's stomach tightened. *Time to be honest.*

"No, sir. It would not surprise me."

"Good. Is there some place we can speak? It is somewhat," he looked around the room and back, "public here."

You could just go back to Venice and stay there. "My room, upstairs." Michael inclined his head toward the ceiling. "If you don't mind the close quarters."

"That will do." Steffano picked up his knife. "Let's finish our meals now. We'll follow you when you are done."

"Yes, sir." Michael stood, and they shook hands as if parting friends. He went back and pushed his food around for a few minutes, dreading the coming meeting. What had he started?

"What's wrong?" Cecile stood over his shoulder with pitcher in hand.

Michael smiled up at her, his calm demeanor a lie. "Nothing. My friends over there are here on business. I'm letting them finish their supper."

"All right. Can I get you anything?"

"No, we'll go upstairs. Thanks, though."

He took her hand and squeezed it. She smiled at him and went back to her customers.

Soon the visitors drained their cups. Steffano flashed an executioner's smile. He and Vitaliano got up and headed for the stairs. Michael drew a deep breath and followed.

He closed the door to his room and faced the men from Venice. Vitaliano entered first and stood by the chest at the window. Steffano took up residence at the fireplace. Whatever they knew, whatever they wanted, he was about to find out.

"I'm sorry there's not much space in here," Michael said.

Steffano shrugged. "It is good enough."

Vitaliano studied Michael's personal items, laid out in order as usual. "You are a man of routine, *signore*."

Him. "You searched my things."

"Did we?" Steffano's expression conveyed more dispassion than innocence.

"At least once, in Venice."

"We were curious, I admit. But…" Steffano glanced at his assistant. "Vitaliano should be more careful in the future."

"Is that why you are here? You are curious?"

"My dear Michael. You do invite curiosity. You are not who you claim to be. Your accent told me that when we met, but I checked anyway. I know several men from Norwich, and none of them recognized your name or your story."

"I guess there are many men who leave a past behind." But not many left a past ahead.

"Yes, I suppose." Steffano picked up a decoration from the mantel, a gift from Cecile. He examined it absently then replaced it. "Do you remember the gentleman with me when we met in Venice?"

"The monk?" *What does he have to do with anything?*

Steffano laughed. "Yes, the monk. Only there is more to him than you see. For the last ten years, he has compiled bookkeeping practices from all around Italy and guarded them while he readied a book. It will be published before year's end." His face narrowed. "And now I find his concepts suddenly at work here in this quiet little town. Even before Luca's book is printed."

That's it. Michael knew the name had sounded familiar. This man received at least an obligatory mention in almost every beginning and intermediate accounting textbook. Luca Pacioli, the "father of accounting." The guidelines he laid out were still in use more than five hundred years later. Some argued that the economic expansion of the Renaissance was made possible in part by the efficiencies he introduced into the world's businesses.

"Michael, are you all right?"

Michael shook his head to refocus his thoughts. "I'm sorry. I have heard of him, but couldn't place his name at the time."

"I see." Steffano drew a breath and cocked his head. "The question remains; who are you? Where do you come from?"

"*Signore*, my name is Michael Patriate. I am a businessman, but I can't tell you from where or how I came to be here. You wouldn't believe me." Michael had tired of telling the made-up story anyway. He had based his whole life here on a lie.

"I have seen and heard many things. You can tell me."

Michael crossed his arms, turned and walked the few steps to the door. He stood there a moment before facing Steffano again. "Respectfully, if I did you would call me either crazy or a liar. The things I remember can't be possible. It's better for both of us if I don't try."

Steffano raised an eyebrow. "Well, I suppose this is better than the untruth you told me in Venice, but Michael, I must insist. Tell me no more lies."

"I don't understand."

"Come to work for me," Steffano said. "You have a rare quality. I know you came here penniless and now you control this association of businesses. You've crafted deals with leading merchants in Portugal and major points in the Adriatic Sea, all in what, two years? My operations are expanding, and I need men like you to see that the expansion continues."

"What about the merchants here?" Michael pointed at the floor. "What will you do to them?"

Steffano waved his hand. "They, and you, are fortunate Jacobus did not go to the senate or the council with his story. He knew me from past transactions. I am not worried about this group and its foreign deals, mostly because it will not have you at its head."

Michael paused. "And if I decline your offer?"

Steffano raised an eyebrow. "Then this information might find its way into unfriendly hands, but that is not the important thing here. Think of the opportunity in front of you."

Michael had a responsibility to the merchants he had put in this position. But he stood with them on a leaky, sinking boat, while a seaworthy ship floated alongside. Michael did what any self-serving rat would. He jumped.

* * * *

One last time Michael went to the warehouse. He found Enrico sitting in Rizzo's office. Good, Michael didn't want to explain this more than once. He laid the situation out for them.

Rizzo stared out the window for a moment. "It's all right, Michael," he said. "We'll survive here. You've given us something to build on."

"I wish it were different." Michael looked at his hands. "I just don't see a way around doing what Steffano wants. Jacobus's story would ruin everybody."

"Don't beat yourself up," Enrico said. "This was a risk we all took together."

"I know." The books Michael set up for Rizzo sat on the desk between them. That period already seemed a long time ago. "What are you going to do now?"

Rizzo spoke. "Enrico can handle negotiations with some help, I think. We'll all meet and talk soon."

Enrico cleared his throat and stared at the floor. "Do one thing if you can. I think Steffano has detained Jacobus somewhere." He looked up at Michael. "Please make sure he comes home."

Michael held his opinion of what ought to happen to Jacobus for Enrico's sake. "That may be dangerous for you," he said instead.

"Even so, he is one of us, and he..." Enrico looked away. "I'll take responsibility for him."

Michael nodded. "All right. I'll speak to Steffano, but I suspect he'll be guarded closely until you get him back."

"I hope so. Thank you Michael, for all you've done."

Michael walked back to the hostel with tightness gripping his throat. Gone. All of the hard work, the friendships, gone. Nearing home, he forced his head up. Rizzo and Enrico had accepted the new reality. He hoped Cecile would understand.

* * * *

She sat in the chair where he had proposed to her. This time she wasn't happy. Cecile straightened against the backrest. "You're leaving me before we're even married?" Tears welled again in her eyes, but this time fire flashed behind them.

"No, I'm not leaving you." Michael walked around behind the facing chair and looked off into the kitchen for a moment. He rubbed his hands back through his hair. He needed her to understand. He turned back to Cecile and pleaded. "I don't have much of a choice about taking this job, but I still want to marry you. Come with me to Venice."

She clutched her crossed arms tight against her chest. "I can't abandon my home. What would happen to it if I left it with someone else?"

This can't be happening again. He put his hands on the chair back and leaned over. "You won't need it. I'll be making enough money to support us nicely. You won't need to work." He took a breath. "Please."

Cecile stuck out a trembling jaw. The words snapped out. "No. I don't want to move. If you want to leave, go ahead. Just go." As she turned her head away, he glimpsed a wild, unreasoning look in her eyes.

Michael realized hurt and fear prompted her reaction. "Cecile, I have to go. I wish I didn't, but I do. Don't shut me out."

She remained silent except for a stifled sob.

"I'll be back in a couple of weeks. Please, let's talk about it then."

Cecile jumped from the chair and stomped past him into the kitchen.

He muttered under his breath. "Fine."

Chapter Forty-Two

Michael scowled as he left with the Venetians. They rode in a carriage to Jesolo instead of the familiar barge. It would save them a day, though, and Steffano's own galley would pick them up at Jesolo. But the scene with Cecile bothered him. She had put this on him, and it wasn't his fault. Everything would have been lost if he refused to go. Why, then, did he feel guilty?

"You look sad, Michael," Steffano said above the road noise. He and Vitaliano shared a seat across from Michael.

Michael tried to wipe the look from his face. He wouldn't broadcast his emotions the first day on a new job. "I'm sorry. The quick departure caused some anxiety for my fiancée. It'll be all right."

Steffano nodded without expressing much sympathy. "Yes, I am sure it will, but if not, she may be happier in Caorle. With her independent spirit, she might find life in Venice confining. Wives there tend to stay home."

Vitaliano grinned and joined the conversation. "Mistresses, on the other hand..."

"One woman is complication enough for me, thanks." Michael watched the fall foliage hurry by the window. As much as he disliked being on the water, the barge made for a smoother ride.

Steffano changed the conversation. "So, Michael, what would you like to know about my business?"

In spite of Michael's resentment toward his new employer, he was curious. He turned from the window to face Steffano. "I don't think I have ever worked for someone without finding out in detail what they do before. Maybe an overview."

"Yes, that is probably the place to start. Where to begin? The obvious, of course, is the spice business. My grandfather's grandfather started it. We buy from the Levant in bulk and resell parts in large amounts to other wholesalers and repackage others for smaller distributors, such as those in Caorle." Steffano paused, and Michael nodded that he understood.

"Of course," Steffano said, "we deal in a range of products. The term 'spice' also includes goods such as dyes and scented materials."

"Yes, sir. We sell...sold those items in Caorle. Only not in the quantities you're used to."

Steffano shrugged. "True. You will see the benefits of scale soon, but we have branched out in other areas as well. I own, or am a partner in, many types of businesses. We make textiles of wool, cotton, and silk, and buy and sell foodstuffs like grain and dried fruits."

Same old stuff.

"We build expensive summer homes on *Terraferma* and, oh…" Steffano leaned forward and grinned like a boy catching his first fish. "Recently I bought into a printing company, a fascinating process." He plopped back in his seat wearing a smug smile and then took on a more pensive look. "The one endeavor that has evaded me is glass production." He sighed. "The glass makers are a strange bunch. I have not given up, though."

"You have a well diversified business." Michael realized the two other men in the carriage were staring. *Oh.* He had used an English word for which he didn't know an Italian equivalent. "I'm sorry. I mean you have spread your risk well."

"Do not…" Steffano paused when the carriage bounced, "…apologize for bringing in new concepts or ideas. That is the reason I hired you. We will let you know when we do not understand."

"Good. I hope we all learn new things from our association." Michael began to feel more at ease with these businessmen.

"I expect we will. Michael, you cannot take in everything at once. You should pick one area first and get some experience in our organization. Does anything intrigue you?"

Michael thought for a moment and shifted his position. Even the padded seats were becoming hard after some time on this rough road. "Silk."

"Silk," Steffano repeated. "Why silk?"

"Because I don't know anything about it."

Steffano laughed in delight. "Vitaliano, I like this man. He wants a job where he can learn. Yes, I think we can find a place for you there."

"There is another reason for my interest," Michael said. Steffano listened.

"I like industries where you can add value. Anyone can buy and sell commodities, but with them, you're captive to all kinds of forces you can't manage. When you add value, though, you make money on the underlying commodity *and* the new item you produced from it."

"So you don't like commodities."

"No, they have their place, especially if you are *diversified*." He had coined a term. "But you run big risks if you depend on a single type."

Vitaliano spoke again. "I understand your argument, but we have done well in the commodity business. All our other businesses have been built on the profits of spice and related goods."

"It's been profitable, all right, but some outside changes are coming that will squeeze your margins."

"The Portuguese connection," Steffano gave him a dismissive nod. "Yes, we have been hearing of this impending doom for years now."

"It'll happen soon, and when it does prices will collapse."

"So, you can tell the future?" Vitaliano asked.

"Call it intuition. It only makes sense. Besides, I've been to Portugal and talked to the men who will make it happen. A year, maybe two or three, it's unavoidable." Michael much preferred this line of conversation, something he could control.

Steffano stroked his chin and looked away. "We will think about this." Again, he looked Michael in the eye. "But in the present, we need to get you involved in the business. Silk it is."

Chapter Forty-Three

Ludovico

Ludovico had never seen an army as vicious as the French and Swiss troops. Italian Rules ignored, they sacked and burned at any resistance and killed all in the towns that did not welcome their presence. While the *condottiere,* contracted mercenaries, had over generations formed gentlemanly ways of warfare that hardly disturbed Italian local populations, the French had learned in the Hundred Years War with England to fight for survival and give no quarter.

And the outsiders were well equipped. Their numerous and deadly *cannoniers*, *arquebusiers*, archers, cavalry, and pikemen gave them tools to face almost any situation. Through village after village and town after town, the French army marched south.

A question occurred. What would happen to him and to Milan when Charles chose to head back to France? After the Swiss killed even the bedridden in Rapallo, Ludovico excused himself. He decided on the way home to send ambassadors to Rome. Maybe the pope could help.

Before Ludovico could reach Milan, messengers brought the news. King Ferdinand I of Naples had died and left his irresolute son, Alphonso in control.

Why didn't Ferdinand have the courtesy to do this six months ago?

Chapter Forty-Four

While the gondolier tied up the boat, Michael stared up at Steffano's *palazzo*. Located a short walk from the Rialto Bridge he and Enrico crossed those months before, the building quietly humbled the houses around it. The late afternoon sun silhouetted a golden cupola at the peak. Wrought iron and gilt decorated the red plaster front, even the double warehouse doors. They were closed, but Michael caught the sounds of labor from within, the opening of a wooden crate, a supervisor's shouted command, the creak of a wheel.

"Welcome to my home." Steffano stepped from the gondola, steadied by his waiting servant's hand.

"It's impressive." Michael continued to gaze up at the structure as he followed Steffano onto the walk.

"You will find it pays to impress, Michael. Pascal, take *Signor* Patriate's things to his room."

The graying attendant nodded and opened a smaller door for them. He never made eye contact, but kept his head lowered.

Michael tagged behind Steffano into a narrow entryway and stopped for his eyes to adjust to the darker interior.

Steffano gestured to another door to his left. "This is where we receive and distribute the higher value goods like spices and silk. I will show you around here later, but first we will get you settled." Steffano walked to a staircase and started the climb. Michael followed.

Ornate carving decorated the stairs leading from the business on the ground floor to the residence on the top three. At a marble landing on the first floor, Steffano pulled open a thick, polished wood slab of a door and gestured for Michael to enter. "This is my domain."

They walked into a large room furnished like a men's club parlor, with overstuffed chairs and couches scattered about. High windows allowed enough indirect light in to remind him of a childhood classroom with the lights turned out for a video.

Steffano cleared his throat and Michael snapped back to the present. Sculptures and carvings stood on the floor and occupied prominent places on shelves. An ancient bust of maybe Greek or Roman origin stared wide-eyed at an unseen horizon. Paintings outlined in thick elaborate frames hung all around the room; most were portraits of distinguished men. He stopped at the likeness displayed over the fireplace. Another fox.

Steffano followed his gaze. "My father, Antonio." He pointed. "And his father there, my forebears and relatives all around. We are an old family."

"It's good to know your history," Michael said while he scanned the portraits. "I don't know as much as I would like about mine."

"A shame. You should look into it sometime."

"Yes, I guess I should."

Steffano continued the tour. "The room behind this wall is the dining room. Through that door is my study, where I work, and library beside it. Beyond that is my bedroom. You can get the full tour later. Come, I will show you upstairs where my wife rules."

Michael followed back to the stairs and up another level.

"This is the family area." Steffano walked into the richly furnished room turned toward an open door before he called out. "Catarina. We have a guest."

Hurried footsteps announced an arrival. A girl of maybe eighteen years came through the doorway and stopped. Michael took her for a daughter or perhaps a servant until he saw the way she looked at Steffano. The young woman dressed in conservative fashion and wore her hair up in the style of a mature lady, but her smile belonged to a teenager in love.

Michael had heard most merchants delayed marriage until their thirties in order to first establish their businesses. The less successful might never wed, and then the first order of business would be to produce an heir. But the difference in their ages, thirty years or better, bothered him somehow.

"Catarina, this is Michael Patriate. He works for me now. Michael will be our guest for a few days until we arrange suitable lodging for him."

Catarina gave Michael a deferential dip of her head. "I am pleased to meet you, *signor* Patriate."

Michael returned her bow. "The pleasure is mine."

"Where is Antonio?" Steffano asked.

"Asleep." Catarina smiled a mother's smile.

Steffano turned to Michael. "Antonio is my son, named after my father."

"I see." What would it be like to grow up in a house like this? The boy would have all the advantages of money and power, but it might turn into a prison of expectations.

"He is two. His nap times seem to be the only quiet we have here." Steffano took a gentle tone with his wife. He did have a tender spot in there somewhere. "We will be going up to let Michael settle in now. He will join us at supper, I hope."

"Of course." Michael bowed again to Catarina. "It has been good meeting you."

As he followed Steffano upstairs, Michael took in the trappings of success. Paintings and tapestries in vivid colors on the left of the staircase, a fresco depicting almost-exposed lovers in a vineyard running up the right. At the top of the stairs, a hall ran the length of the building with rooms to each side. It could have been a five-star hotel. Thick rugs covered hardwood floors; paneled walls boasted yet more artwork.

"I believe we have put you in here." Steffano entered a room that turned out to be a suite. "Yes, there are your things. You can rest and prepare for supper. Pascal will let you know when we are ready."

Michael forced himself to ignore the elaborate decorations for a moment and turned back to Steffano. "Thank you. I would like to rest for a while. What should I wear for supper?"

Steffano laughed. "You need nothing special for tonight, but you should buy more suitable attire for future meetings. Much business is done over meals, you know."

Michael nodded. The act of eating together fueled many a deal. "Good. I'll be there."

Michael sat on the bed after Steffano left. He hadn't been on one this soft since New York. He looked at himself in a full-length, polished metal mirror attached to the wall. No expense spared here. He was playing with the big boys now.

* * * *

The knock came at five minutes before six o'clock according to Michael's watch. He closed it in his hand and went to answer the door.

Pascal waited. This time he looked Michael in the eye. "Supper will be ready in a few minutes, sir. In the family residence."

"Thank you," Michael replied. "I'll be right down." He shut the door and replaced the watch on its new sash.

Pascal ushered Michael into the dining room where his hosts sat at the long table, Steffano at the head and Catarina by his side. "Welcome, Michael," Steffano said.

"Good evening." Michael bowed his head to his hosts. Pascal guided him to a place across from Catarina with one place empty in between him and Steffano.

"Master Pacioli will be along directly." Steffano smiled. The fox had returned.

So he would eat with the man he had read about in school, the man who had been dead for five hundred years by his reckoning. "Good." Supper should be interesting.

"Ah, Luca," Steffano said. "There you are. You may remember Michael Patriate."

Michael jumped up to meet the monk, who dressed again in gray. "I'm glad to see you again."

Luca nodded to Steffano and turned his attention to Michael. "Yes, I remember. I understand that you have some skill in the art of bookkeeping."

While Luca's words were friendly, his dispassionate demeanor reminded Michael of a certain condescending law professor. He bowed his head in humility. "I merely stand on the shoulders of giants, sir."

Luca raised his thin eyebrows. "Ah, you are a philosopher as well."

Michael noticed Steffano's attention on this exchange. "No, I'm sorry to say. I only heard that phrase once and thought it appropriate."

"The theologian, Bernard of Chartres," began Luca, "is reported to have said: *'We are like dwarfs standing upon the shoulders of giants, and so able to see more and see farther than the ancients.'*"

Got me there. "I can't argue the statement. What knowledge I've gathered has been handed down by generations of men greater than me."

Luca studied Michael for a moment and then gave him a thoughtful nod. "That is well said. But now, please sit. We delay our hosts."

"After you, sir. I'm sorry, what may I call you?"

"I am but an ordinary brother. You may call me Fra Luca, or only Luca."

"Thank you, Fra Luca." Michael seated himself at the table. "I've had the privilege to call another man brother, a Frater Felix from the monastery in Ulm."

"This friend of yours is Dominican?"

"Yes. Yes, he is, sir."

"Preachers." Luca frowned. "Obsessed with legalities and short on concern for their fellow man."

Michael chuckled at the thought. "Well, Felix gave his share of sermons, but he was also my friend." And Michael hadn't sent word to Felix of Konrad's death as he had promised. *Tomorrow, Felix.*

"Well, they have their usefulness." Luca turned to Steffano and Catarina. "I apologize. We do not even start the meal, and I monopolize the conversation."

"It is no problem." The fox grinned again. "A lively exchange stirs the appetite. Pascal..." Steffano maintained his gaze on the two. "Tell them to send in the food."

Chapter Forty-Five

Girolamo

Girolamo glanced up at the movement from the watchman. The boy turned from his perch on the wall, his outline in stark relief against the gray November sky. "It's him," he called.

Next to Girolamo, Piero Capponi gazed out the gate and down the road. A former advisor to Lorenzo de' Medici, the deceased first citizen of Florence, Capponi had reluctantly accepted his role as the de facto leader of Florence.

"Piero returns," Girolamo said. "What will you do?" He watched Capponi struggle with the decision.

They awaited the approach of Lorenzo's son, Piero de' Medici, returning from his parley with King Charles VIII. Advance messengers carried the news of the Florentine ruler's capitulation to Charles. He had given the French king the fortified cities of Pisa and Leghorn and promised him large sums of money with no guarantee of safety for Florence. Now Charles's army stood poised to move into the city, and Florence found itself divided. If Piero returned, civil war might result. Or perhaps it would happen if they refused him entrance. It was the same to Girolamo either way. Charles had come to fulfill the prophecy.

"Shut the gates." Capponi threw off his long coat and ran to the ladder leading to the watch position.

The statesman climbed quickly for a man of middle age.

Against a blanket of low-hanging clouds, Capponi shouted down at the head of a powerful family who had just lost his rule. "Piero, you will better serve yourself and Florence if you leave now."

Girolamo could hear only a muffled, angry reply from beyond the gate.

Capponi called back toward the ground. "If you like, I can let this mob have you."

Behind Girolamo milled a group of twenty or more angry men armed with an assortment of weapons. When he heard the horses leaving, Girolamo knew that Capponi had just saved Piero's life. The revolution was complete, and without bloodshed.

Capponi climbed down the ladder, slower now. At the bottom, he turned to Girolamo. "Fra Savonarola. We need to send another delegation. Will you go?"

Girolamo paused. He could represent the people as peacemaker or help pick up the pieces after a massacre. He nodded. "I am here to serve, of course. Will someone volunteer to accompany me?"

Capponi gave him a look of gratitude. "We have plenty of brave citizens in Florence."

* * * *

Rain dripped from Girolamo's nose. He pulled a hand from the protective sleeves of his robe and wiped his face. Any minute Charles would enter the piazza. The announcement that he approached the gate had gone out two hours before. His winding route through the city must have been planned for maximum exposure, but it left those waiting in this square drenched and cold. A minor inconvenience compared to the glory of God when Florence was elevated to lead Italy out of the wilderness.

The echoes of hooves and feet, the clatter of armor and weapons, and the cadence of shouted commands announced the army's impending arrival. Around a corner appeared an advance cavalryman followed by the king.

Girolamo caught his mouth agape and closed it. Why did Charles enter the city with such an aggressive posture? Girolamo's mission to the French camp this morning appeared successful. He praised the king, who, aware of Girolamo's prophesies, respectfully entertained the preacher. And, although Charles had given no pledges, he made no further demands. Girolamo and his entourage returned to Florence hopeful of a peaceful encounter with the French army. Florence had promised Charles its support.

So why this evening did he lead the troops as conqueror, lance level and rested on his thigh?

Charles spoke to an aide, who ordered the procession trumpeted to a halt. The king sat on his horse at the front of an army that snaked out of sight into the city's twisting caverns of narrow roads and towering buildings. Charles's countenance conveyed insolence and contempt. But many of his men cast anxious glances up at the windows around them, with good reason, Girolamo knew. Florentine soldiers hid throughout the city, ready to attack at the ringing of alarm bells if needed. The populace, too, prepared for battle. The high places made excellent points from which to throw stones and pots and other objects that could maim or kill. Charles's men were unable to ignore barricades, which could be quickly put into place to trap soldiers used to operating in the open. Struggling out of a place was different than fighting to get in. Girolamo hoped no conflict would be necessary, but if it were, a French victory would be uncertain, and since he had chosen the peacemaker role, war would interfere with his plans.

He waited with Capponi and other leaders in front of the unoccupied home of the Medici. Charles would, of course, want the finest accommodations in town. A newly-erected arch featuring the *fleur-de-lis* proclaimed Florentine loyalty to France.

"Welcome, Your Highness," Capponi said. "Please accept our offer of this palace as your own while you are here."

Charles looked around at the buildings as if the men waiting on him did not exist. "I do not need your offer. I will take what I want."

"Of course, Your Highness. Please let us know what you desire."

"I desire food and rest." Charles handed his lance to an attendant and dismounted. "See that I get them."

Girolamo searched the front group of riders, but could not find the nobles he had met at the encampment. Étienne de Vesc. That one could be dangerous.

Charles marched to the door, ignoring the line of city representatives. But as he passed Girolamo, Charles looked him in the eye and nodded in greeting. "Fra Savonarola."

"Your Highness." Girolamo bowed his head. He pretended not to notice the stares of those around him.

* * * *

Girolamo left the negotiations to Capponi and the others while they haggled over the terms upon which Charles would quit Florence. Two, three, four days passed and talks dragged. Capponi became more agitated with each outrageous demand from Charles, who, despite his stated mission of Crusade, seemed disinclined to wrap up business and leave.

But French soldiers who had been content with proper food and housing now seemed eager to move on. The residents of Florence were also ready for them to go. The city had seen some minor skirmishes, igniting fears of battle in the streets. Now the new arrogations in the treaty brought by Charles threatened disaster.

"If we could not pay the 200,000 *ducats* that Piero promised you," Capponi said in a loud voice stretched with frustration, "we cannot pay you 400,000. It is too much." He glared down at the king seated on his temporary throne.

Charles returned Capponi's glower. "You seem to be in no position to argue with me. I dictate the terms here. I will have 400,000 *ducats*."

"We will not give it." Capponi looked stretched so tight he might snap.

Charles jumped to his feet and placed himself only a step away from Capponi. "We will sound our trumpets," shouted the king.

"Then we will toll our bells!" Capponi ripped the treaty into shreds and threw them in the air.

The two men stood transfixed in stalemate.

Girolamo spoke before one or the other could move and start the conflagration. "Gentlemen, please. None of us wants conflict here. Your Highness, may I speak with you alone?"

Charles relinquished his glare on Capponi, turned to Girolamo, and then waved the others out of the room. "Leave us."

* * * *

Girolamo stood bareheaded in the warm sun. He watched Charles ride out the *Piazza della Signoria*, on his way to Naples by way of Rome after the two sides had reached a reasonable settlement. The crowd that had armed itself against Charles feted him as the departing hero.

Capponi slipped in beside and nodded toward the king. "God help the pope."

The old anger flared. "The Borgia does not listen to God. Let him not ask for help."

Capponi glanced at him and then looked away again. "What did you say to him? Charles, I mean."

Girolamo breathed and exhaled. "He needed a reminder that he was God's servant and the focus on financial gain interfered with his plans for Crusade, and he required an honorable way out of the situation in which he placed himself."

"Well, Florence owes you its gratitude." Capponi turned to Girolamo. "And I owe you my thanks."

Girolamo shook his head. "Give your thanks to the Lord."

He pulled the hood up and tugged it into place. *Now.* The time had come for Girolamo to begin his work in earnest, time for Domenico to handle the petty details of running the monastery. Florence would belong to him. And to God, of course.

Chapter Forty-Six

Michael glanced across the table at Luca. They ate in Michael's suite since Steffano had gone out for the evening. Luca was a tough one to figure out, a monk formerly in the service of a ruthless bunch like this, currently here as guest. He displayed a hard exterior, but Michael suspected substance lay beneath the surface.

Luca interrupted Michael's musings. "So, how have your first few days gone?"

Michael washed down a bite of bread to answer. "Well enough. Steffano has quite an array of interests here. He's been introducing me to them."

"He is a busy man."

"Yes, he is that. We'll select one area, probably the silk businesses, to concentrate on soon."

Luca nodded, and they ate in silence for a moment.

"Fra Luca, Steffano mentioned you are publishing a book. I'm interested in hearing more about it, if you are inclined."

"Particularly concerning the bookkeeping section, I suppose?" Luca continued to cut the veal on his plate. "There is more to the book than that one part."

"Yes sir, I know, but I'm primarily concerned with practical applications in business."

Luca set down his knife. "Steffano tells me your methods are advanced. What can I add to your impressive knowledge?"

Was Luca testing him? "Well, I know the major concepts, but you seem to be a detail-oriented person. I would compare my procedures against yours and see what improvements I can make in my own practice."

"I am a teacher." Luca's hard shell seemed to soften a bit. "I am always happy to be of use." He looked up at Michael as if a thought had presented itself. "The print is already set. I have the manuscripts in my room. Would you like to see them now?"

Their meal went unfinished.

Chapter Forty-Seven

Agostino

The doge shifted in his chair as the messenger read the alarming report. Charles continued to plow through Italy, stamping out any resistance. He even gained Florence as his ally. Rome, alternatively hostile and friendly with the French, lay next for Charles.

The pope would likely find the meeting uncomfortable, since he had most recently allied himself with Alphonso of Naples. Added to Pope Alexander's discomfort would be the presence of his old enemy, Cardinal Giuliano della Rovere, and his occasional ally, Cardinal Ascanio Sforza, currently aligned with Charles.

Agostino waited until the messenger left the room before he spoke to a grim-faced Toma. "He has no opposition. He should still be in Madena or Lucca with winter upon him."

Toma nodded. "There was always the risk that Charles could conquer all of Italy."

Agostino frowned at Toma's irritating correctness and studied a spot on the wall. His scowl lightened. "We can use this to our advantage."

Chapter Forty-Eight

So much had changed since Michael's first trip into Caorle. He had come into town a beggar, hitching a ride in a wagon. Today the carriage that accompanied him to Jesolo on Steffano's galley gathered envious looks from people on the street. And gone were the rough peasant clothes he had worn that first fall day.

Michael had taken Steffano's advice and bought new clothing from his employer's tailor. In place of the linen shirt he had worn to Venice, a ruffled white silk shirt peeked from beneath a black velveteen doublet. He did make a concession to fashion and wore the popular tight-fitting silk hose, but covered them with breeches that went below the knee. Complete with black woolen cloak and felt beret, Michael looked the part of an aspiring wealthy merchant. How would Cecile see him? He would find out in a moment. The Red Lion came into view.

"Wait here," Michael told the driver. As the sun's rays died in the west, he walked into the run-down little building that he called home only a month before. He took off his hat.

"Hello..."

Cecile walked out of the kitchen, wiping her hands on a towel. Her face went rigid at the sight of him standing at the door. Her voice came in a flat echo from the day he first encountered a mourning, joyless widow.

"So, you come back."

Michael's face refused to wear the smile he wished to give her. "Yes, I come back, for you, Cecile."

"You said you would be here two weeks ago."

Michael nodded and took a breath. "That's what I planned, but sometimes plans don't work out. I sent you a letter."

"Yes, I received it. I'm glad things are going well for you there." She spoke in a controlled voice and twisted the towel into a knot.

"Cecile, you know that's not what I wrote you about. Can we sit down and talk about this?"

Cecile sighed and her shoulders slumped in defeat. "Come into the kitchen." She turned and went back through the door. Michael followed. They pulled out chairs from a table and sat facing each other. Michael looked into the dark brown eyes and saw hurt.

Where to begin? "I'm sorry things haven't gone the way we wanted, but frankly, I'm confused at your reaction." The sudden ache in his throat surprised him. He swallowed and spoke in a hurt voice he hadn't used since childhood. "You said you loved me."

"Love doesn't have much to do with it." She looked down at the floor. "Yes, I do."

"Then what is the problem?" He blinked away the threatening tears. *Get a handle on it.*

Cecile raised her eyes and cocked her head. "When you were a clerk here and then a local merchant, it was acceptable for me to be with you."

"This is a class thing? I'm still the same man I was before this happened."

"Yes, you are." Cecile's voice, stretched with emotion, rose while tears welled in her eyes. "Don't you understand? That's the problem, Michael. You were never the simple man. I wanted to believe we could be together, but this was always bound to happen. Just look at how you're dressed now. You're the kind who will rise to the top."

"I can take you there with me." He knew her decision would not change.

"It wouldn't work!" She stopped and took a deep breath. "It wouldn't work. They would talk about your wife, the innkeeper. I can't go there with you and be an *asset* like Sheila was."

The statement hit Michael in the gut.

He tensed his jaw muscles until the pain passed and drew in a deep breath. "You could stay here after the wedding, then. It's not that far. I could come home often."

Cecile shook her head. A tear started down her cheek. "No, Michael. Please, just let us stop pretending. You need to get back to your business."

It had happened again, first Sheila and now Cecile. Each had chosen self-preservation. "All right," he said at last. "Always remember, I love you."

"I'll remember, and I cherish our time. You helped me get my life back."

The defeated look in Cecile's eyes reminded Michael of Sheila, right before she walked out of his life. "Is it all right if I spend the night in my room?"

She looked at the floor. "I rented it. I'm sorry. We're full tonight."

Michael had to give Cecile a sad smile. "And after I paid my rent in advance."

"Do you want your money back?"

He shook his head. "No. I owe you for taking me in. I'll go see if Rizzo will let me sleep in his warehouse again."

Now she smiled, too. "You'll figure something out."

Michael stood. "Goodbye, Cecile. Take care of yourself."

Cecile remained seated and looked at the floor. "*Addio*, Michael."

He stiffened. Addio. *Goodbye forever.*

The smile slid from his face as he turned and walked out the door for the last time, cursing under his breath. If it weren't for Steffano's threats of reprisal against the merchants of Caorle, he could come back to Cecile and give up his place in Venice. But he knew he couldn't let it go.

Chapter Forty-Nine

Charles

God had blessed his cause. Charles rode in splendor out the gates of Rome, victorious. Pope Alexander VI had confirmed him as king of Naples, albeit with cannon pointed at the Holy Father's residence. The pope's son, Cesare Borgia, now known as Cardinal, rode in the train behind. Also with Charles, traveled the Turkish sultan's brother, Cem, captured years earlier by the Knights of Rhodes and recently prisoner and guest of the pope. The former traveled as his hostage; the latter, he planned to use as a bargaining chip with the sultan in the new Crusade. Next, Naples would bow. Then he could begin his mission. He would immortalize the name of Charles VIII, *The Crusader*.

Chapter Fifty

Pascal let Michael in the door to Steffano's residence. Even this early in the morning, Michael knew he would find him at work. He walked through the club, as he still thought of it, and wondered if he would ever be worth a tenth of the things in this room. Not any time soon.

The door to Steffano's study stood ajar. Michael knocked anyway.

"Come in, Michael."

Steffano already had company. Michael stopped inside the door when he saw Vitaliano and another man he didn't know.

"Good morning sirs."

Vitaliano nodded. The new man simply stared at Michael.

Steffano addressed Michael. "So, you still wish learn the silk business?"

"Yes, sir. If that's all right with you."

"It is probably the most complex part of our organization." Steffano might as well have said, "It's your funeral."

Michael displayed his most confident face. "I look forward to the challenge."

"Well, then." Steffano gestured to the stranger. "I'd like you to meet Benetto Molin."

Benetto was older than anyone in the room, graying on the sides and balding on top. He had the look of a man who had seen hard work and conflict. Michael shook Benetto's callused hand.

"Glad to meet you Benetto."

Michael's polite smile went unreturned. "Good morning," Benetto said.

"Benetto currently oversees our silk operations." Steffano gestured toward the door. "Let him show you how we do things."

Michael nodded. "I'll be honored to learn from an experienced man."

"You have an office prepared in the warehouse downstairs where you can work, but I expect you will not be there much for a while." Steffano had clearly dismissed them.

"Thank you, sir," Michael said to Steffano. To Benetto, "After you."

Michael followed him down the stairs in silence. When they reached the warehouse on the bottom floor, Benetto pointed to a small room in the far front corner.

"There."

Michael walked into his new space and looked about. A modest desk, cabinets and shelves of good material waited to be put to use, but it was the view that caught his attention. The window looked directly out on the Grand Canal. He could see the Rialto district stretch in either direction. Prime real estate, more than a step up from Rizzo's little office.

"Impressive." The irritation in Benetto's voice brought Michael back into focus.

"It should do." Michael turned back to the silk man. "Molin. The name means 'mill,' doesn't it?"

"My family has worked in silk for generations. The name comes from the mill started by my great grandfather."

"I am fortunate, then, to have someone of your capability as my teacher."

"So it seems." Benetto's expression remained flat and guarded.

"You don't like me, do you?" Michael asked.

Benetto started to answer, then paused for a moment. "I don't know you."

"But you resent me coming in here like this."

"It is *Signor* de Rompiasi's right to select his managers."

"Think of me as a consultant," Michael said. "I'm not here to take your job. It's my responsibility to better integrate the business with Steffano's other operations and suggest improvements where I can."

Benetto shrugged.

Michael considered his new partner's recalcitrance for a moment. "I'll make a deal with you. Give me your full cooperation, and we'll share credit for any successes; but I'll take the blame for any failures. When we're finished, I'll move on to something else, and you can take the reins again. Can you live with that?"

"I suppose."

"Good." He dragged out the desk chair and gestured to another for Benetto. "Then why don't we start at the beginning?"

* * * *

Michael learned much about the silk industry over the course of the day. The process started with mulberry trees and moths. The Roman Empire imported silk into Italy from China via the Silk Road, and some of the product still originated there. After a Byzantine emperor had mulberry trees and silk moth cocoons smuggled out of China, Constantinople became an important source. Even in the present era, silk from the Levant, an area Michael recognized as the Middle East, was a major import. Syria, in particular, sent Venice large quantities of fine silks, but increasingly, the industry obtained raw silk at home on the Italian peninsula.

In the thirteenth century, landowners began planting mulberry trees, the only source of food for the domesticated silkworm. Cultivation of the trees had spread from the island of Sicily all the way northward through Lombardy and Veneto.

Workers, mostly women and girls, stripped leaves from the branches and fed them to silkworms, the caterpillar version of the moth. After the caterpillars finished spinning their cocoons, workers collected them and put them in boiling water, saving enough pupae to mature and lay eggs for the next year's crop. The boiling water served to kill the pupae and loosen the glue holding the single silk strand together.

Then the guilds took over. Spinners turned the raw material into threads; dyers sent the colored product to weavers. Mercers took much of it and resold it.

At the top of the commercial heap stood the *setaiolo*, an entrepreneurial silk merchant, *seta* the Italian word for silk. The *setaiolo* measured tastes, anticipated demand, and placed orders for the product along the production chain. He took the risks and assumed much responsibility for smooth operation of the industry. *Setaioli* were members of the Silk Guild that closely regulated operations among its members. The guild was headed by three superintendents and, recently, by a twenty-five member steering committee.

Steffano ranked among the more successful *setaioli* and one of its more ambitious, not only coordinating production of silk items but also going a step further. He invested directly in spinning, dying, and weaving businesses, skirting guild rules in each sector. He maneuvered himself into the steering committee created only this year and kept friendly faces in each of the guilds involved.

Various state offices oversaw aspects of the silk industry and high level bodies such as the senate and the Councils of Forty and Ten wrote or influenced legislation. Even the doge became involved in more contentious issues. It was rumored, Benetto said, that Steffano had political designs and good chances to fulfill them.

"Well." Michael stretched his back. "I guess I should get my feet wet. Tomorrow, we'll go to one of the spinning operations."

Chapter Fifty-One

Charles

The bracing salty breeze almost made Charles forget his frustrations. Alone at last, Charles watched the soft sunset from the terrace of *Castel Nuovo*, the home of Neapolitan kings, now *his* abode. As he watched the sun slide behind a pair of nameless hills across the harbor, he reflected on his conquest.

It had been so easy. Alphonso, son of the dead King Ferdinand I, fled Naples with his treasures before the French advance and left his son to become King Ferdinand II under difficult circumstances. Charles's easy victories on his way, coupled with intrigue in Naples, caused the new young king to withdraw as well.

But bitterness tinged the sweet taste of victory. Two things troubled Charles, and they came from the same source: Borgia. The pope's son, Cesare, escaped from custody and was, he assumed, back in Rome with his father. Cem died a few days after leaving Rome, no doubt poisoned by the Borgias. All assurances, all promises Charles had received from the pope were empty lies. He could still make this plan work, but it would be more difficult.

Chapter Fifty-Two

"What do you mean I can't do that?" Michael demanded.

"Please keep your voice down." Benetto moved Michael to the far side of the shop so the men wouldn't hear their argument. "You can't tell these men how to do their jobs."

"Do they work for us or not?"

The spinners glared at Michael from behind Benetto's back.

Benetto held up his hands and motioned Michael to stop. "Yes, they work for the company, but there are rules. They are all masters of the craft, or they work for the masters. You are not part of their guild, and the guild sets the regulations."

Michael had seen enough foot dragging. "I've read their rules. Nothing in them says they can't cooperate on tasks. It's more efficient than each worker doing the whole job every time."

"Michael, not all of the rules are written. And the men might not otherwise mind being asked to work this way, but they don't like being *told,* and especially not by someone outside the guild."

"I know." Michael sighed. The guilds were similar to modern unions, major impediments to efficiency and profit.

Benetto continued in his imitation of a soothing voice. "I think you can do some of the things you want, but it takes time to get everybody used to new ideas. Michael, we are making profits. We aren't in that much of a hurry."

Maybe you *aren't.* Steffano paid him well to turn things around, even if they *were* making profits.

"You're right." Michael walked back across the shop floor to face several angry men. "I apologize." He held his hands out in a repentant pose. "I'm used to operating in a different situation with different rules. Please forgive me."

He could fake humility when he wanted. The men gradually came off their hard edges and each shook his hand. He would play their game, but some of these laggards might not be working soon if things didn't change.

* * * *

He wasn't out of breath this time. Michael noticed it after the long climb to the top floor of Steffano's house; the four flights of stairs didn't tire him out as it did at first. The exercise must have been good for him. Too bad he didn't live here anymore.

He knocked on the door to Luca's room for what he figured would be the last time. The monk had become a friend, if friendship is what one would call their relationship. Luca could be brusque and even rude at times, but Michael allowed for his personality and liked him anyway. He could almost imagine a smile on his face when Luca answered the door.

"Welcome, Michael. Come in."

Luca motioned him inside, and Michael heard the door click shut behind him. From the looks of the empty bookshelves and bags by the door, Luca would be gone in a day or two.

"Good evening, Fra Luca. Thank you for inviting me this evening. Steffano told me your book is finished."

Luca pointed to a chair. "Please, sit. Yes, praise the Lord. They will be printing for some time, but my involvement is complete for now. I will be leaving for the monastery tomorrow."

Michael appreciated again the soft, smooth leather on the overstuffed chair. "I'll miss you."

Luca nodded as he sat in the chair adjacent to the table between them. "And I you. I have not seen you since you took your own house. Are you enjoying your new home?"

"Yes, sir. I've only rented it. It's not as nice as Steffano's, of course, but it is close to the Grand Canal."

"You do well. Your work must be pleasing to Steffano."

"I suppose. There is a lot to do, though." Michael reached into a bag slung over his shoulder. "Before we leave for supper, I have something for you. A financial statement."

Luca sat forward in his chair. He carried a different look when he was curious. "A financial statement?"

Michael laid the stack of paper out on the table at an angle so he and Luca could both read it. "Yes, at least that's what we called it. It combines elements you have described in your book and puts them in one report. You include two reports in this section: a balance sheet and an income statement. The balance sheet shows all assets and liabilities, while the income statement shows revenues and expenses." Luca, of course, knew all this and did not respond. Michael tapped on the paper.

"Here is a sample format I drew up from Rizzo's books. This financial statement ties the two reports together and adds another concept, owner's equity."

"Owner's equity." A puzzled frown wrinkled Luca's face.

"Right." Michael flipped a couple of sheets to find the spot. "That concept treats the company as property, separate from the owner. Income is the amount left over after expenses are deducted from revenues. This amount is owed to someone—the man who owns the business. Equity can be thought of as the amount due to be paid to the owner or an amount subtracted from the worth of the business."

A light went on. "I see," Luca said, uncharacteristic enthusiasm in his voice. "A purchaser would deduct this amount from the assets of the business."

"That's a way to look at it. So, because it can be considered a liability to the company, it's listed in conjunction with the liabilities section on the balance sheet, and it provides a convenient check. Your assets should always equal liabilities plus owner's equity."

Luca put his hand to his head and gazed for a moment at the sheets of paper spread on the table. "Michael, my friend, you have taught the teacher today. This is obvious when you explain it, but it will be a new concept to anyone I know. I wish I had seen this in time to add it to the book."

Michael smiled. "I hope it helps someone."

Luca jumped from his seat and opened one of the packed bags. He extracted his manuscript and opened it to the end of the section dealing with balance sheets. After inking a quill, he wrote in large letters: "Add Michael's method."

"What's that?" Michael asked.

Luca blew on the ink and closed the manuscript. "For the next printing."

It honored him that Luca would consider adding his financial statement to this groundbreaking work, even if Michael had only carried the knowledge here from his own time. Could he really change history just like that? *What would happen if I did?*

"Michael, I have something for you, too."

Luca retrieved the lone book remaining on a shelf. Michael accepted the large, leather bound tome. *Summa de Arithmetica, Geometria, Proportioni et Proportionalita.* Engraved letters in a thick leather cover proclaimed the name of Luca's ambitious project, now made real. Less than fifty years since Gutenberg printed his first Bible, this was still an expensive proposition.

Michael skimmed his fingers across the engraving. "So it's done. Congratulations. You don't know how important this will be to the future of business. You'll be famous." *Sort of.*

Luca's laugh shocked Michael. "Fame will not help me much. The brothers are jealous enough, but perhaps some good will come of the work."

"Well, thank you for the book, Luca. This is generous of you." He opened the cover and flipped a page. In precise handwriting, Luca had written and signed a note to Michael.

Serious again, Luca rested his hand on the compendium. "It is the third finished copy. The first has gone to my old friend the duke of Urbino, to whom it was dedicated. The second I gave to Steffano for his gracious assistance. This one I give to you because of your interest in the art."

Michael swallowed. "Luca, I'm honored."

"Only make sure to return the honor to God."

Luca's look went right through Michael. *How do all my conversations seem to lead to the same subject?* Before Michael came to this place, he couldn't have imagined striking up a relationship with a religious practitioner. And now he had made friends with Felix and Konrad and Luca in the same year. Michael felt something, someone pushing him in ways he didn't want to go.

I've got my own plans, thank you. He tried not to show his irritation. "I will."

Chapter Fifty-Three

Ludovico

Ludovico fumed as the envoy from Florence lectured him, in his own house.

Matteo Berardi, a merchant serving his newly revived republic, stood before him and clutched a letter composed by the Florentine leadership. "You invited Charles and started this madness. Florence will not help you fight him now. You should be the one to pay for your mistakes. That is the message from Florence, sir."

A rush of anger shot through Ludovico. He jumped from his chair and shouted. "I shall have you hanged."

Matteo stood his ground. He wagged a finger. "I do not think you need another enemy. Florence will live by its word. Good day."

Ludovico clenched his jaws in silent rage as the ambassador turned his back and pranced out the door, but after a moment, reason seeped back into his consciousness.

So Florence would remain faithful to its treaty with France. No matter. As long as Florentine soldiers did not assist him, Charles's army would see defeat before it could return to Milan.

Chapter Fifty-Four

Michael sighed and glanced at the ceiling of the guild hall. He needed another angle. Danielo Carrara, the guild representative, resisted his arguments for increased efficiency in the spinners' shops. Michael took stock of the man seated across from him. *Start on common ground.*

"All right. You say that if we make the shops run more effectively we'll put spinners out of work."

Danielo gave him a blank look. "That only makes sense."

"Consider this, then. What would happen if all spinners in Venice cut their output in half? Would there soon be twice as many spinners working in the city?"

Danielo's forehead wrinkled. "What kind of question is that? We work at the right speed. Too much hurry makes for a bad product."

"It's not a question of working harder." Michael paused to collect his thoughts. "The spinners are a hard-working, conscientious group. But if you assign one element or a few elements of the spinning process to different individuals, they can do those few things better than if they keep switching back and forth among tasks. The shop as a whole will put out more and better product in the same amount of time."

"But, that would put spinners out of work." Danielo brought the conversation around in another circle.

Michael looked down at the table. *This is hopeless.* "Back to my question. What would happen if you cut your output in half?"

"Well," Danielo shrugged. "We would make half as much, since we are paid by the piece."

"And Venetian silk thread would be more expensive, because there wouldn't be enough to satisfy demand. Then the *setaioli* would import more thread from Milan and Florence and Bologna, and their thread would be cheaper than Venetian thread, so the demand for local product would decline. How many spinners would be out of work and forced to leave?"

Danielo shook his head. "But we aren't cutting production in half."

Michael ground his teeth. "On the other side, then, consider raising production through increased efficiency. The spinners in Venice would make more silk thread and more money. The thread would be cheaper, and would increase demand and cause shops in Venice to hire more spinners, who would increase guild membership."

Danielo looked doubtful. "If our men focus on one part of the spinning process, they won't be artisans anymore, just hired men."

"They can switch jobs from time to time. Weekly, monthly, it doesn't matter, but they can remain trained for the entire process. That's better, anyway."

Michael knew anything else he said wouldn't matter and stopped to let the man think.

Danielo remained silent for a long moment. "All right. I'll take this to the guild governors, but I doubt they will agree."

"Do what you can. I appreciate your help." *This is useless*. Michael stood to go. It was time to make Steffano a proposal.

Chapter Fifty-Five

Agostino

How he used to love this seat. Up on the stage in the *Sala del Senato*, twice each week Agostino presided over the Senate. They all looked to him, this select number from the Great Council. In the beginning, he relished praise from the floor and believed he led this group of men who made the laws and determined the direction of Venice. But, each of his nine years had made him feel less...relevant, more aware of his real lack of control.

In reality, the Council of Ten commanded almost total power in the decisions that mattered, and they had missed opportunities to protect and advance his beloved Republic. Perhaps tonight would be the beginning of change. Agostino heard his title announced and stood in front of a hushed crowd. He paused for effect.

"Gentlemen of Venice." He addressed the gathering in a smooth, strong voice calculated to communicate authority and control, tinged with just the right amount of concern.

"There is a threat in the land. As you know, France has invaded Italy and now controls key western areas from north to south. We suspect that Charles may be tempted to continue his conquests, even here in Venice." Agostino noted the anxious chatter among senate members. *Good.* He let this go on for a few seconds and raised his hands for silence.

"Men, in this crisis there is opportunity. The army Charles commands is powerful, but it is also *vulnerable* and can be beaten if we in Italy cooperate. I put before you a proposal for your approval. Together with forces and support provided by His Holiness Alexander VI, Emperor Maximilian, Ferdinand of Spain, and Ludovico of Milan, our army will chase Charles out of Italy." He paused to see delegates nod their heads in consideration.

"In this *Holy League*, Venice will take the lead, providing the most men and command of the army. And," he emphasized, "there may be more opportunity for us, once Charles is gone."

Agostino let the assembly grasp the idea. After they defeated Charles, Venice could find itself in control of all northern Italy. And his voice might be elevated among the powerful.

Chapter Fifty-Six

Michael knocked on the open door to Steffano's study. "May I come in?"

Steffano looked up from his work. "Of course, Michael. What can I do for you today?"

"I'm here to report on my progress and see if you'll approve some changes."

Steffano took a short breath and let it out. "The report first, I suppose. Please sit down."

Michael pulled the chair close to the desk and seated himself, then placed his homemade portfolio in his lap. "We've made some progress. Purchasing is streamlined somewhat, bookkeeping is better. Relations with the spinner's guild are all right, after some rough spots."

Steffano nodded as if he had been following along. Michael went on.

"Profits are better, but I'm not happy with them. I have some suggestions."

"Just as I expect from you," Steffano said.

"Yes, sir. I can go only so far without the spinners revolting. We've implemented changes here and there, but to really overhaul the way we want to operate, it may be necessary to bypass the guild."

Steffano frowned. "You know we must go slowly. The guilds do not necessarily care for one another, but they will not stand for us threatening them."

"I understand. I want to design a new spinning mill where we can build in efficiency from the beginning."

Steffano shook his head. "We have plenty of mills here, and even if you build a new one, you still have the problem of finding someone to work in it."

"Yes, sir." He pointed a thumb behind him. "That's why I want it built outside of Venice. There aren't any regulations

310

against spinning thread in the countryside like there are with weaving, and there is a labor force outside the guilds just waiting for us to exploit."

"Interesting." Steffano sat back in his chair. "Where would you put it?"

"On the Piave River, close to Jesolo, where the canal to Caorle intersects it. The local economy is mainly agriculture, which, of course, is unpredictable. Lots of people in that area would jump at steady employment at a good wage. Plus we would have access to the sea and lagoon from there."

"Why so far away from Venice? Would that not increase our shipping costs?"

"First, we want to build outside Venice to get away from the guild." Michael leaned in. This might be the hard sell. "I have another motive. I want to build a powered mill."

Steffano's eyes widened. "Powered?"

"Yes. We can divert water from the Piave. There are several advantages, including lowered labor costs.

The frown returned. "I heard of something similar at Bologna, but they experienced quality issues."

"That's right." Michael nodded. "I've talked to some spinners who came from Bologna. The problem they have is keeping the spindle speed constant. Water flow varies, which means the feed rates of the spooled fibers into the wheel may not match the wheel's speed. Sometimes you get tighter or looser threads."

"And I take it you have a solution to the problem."

"I think so. Look at a clock. It has a power mechanism that may exert more or less force, but the clock keeps a constant speed. We can adapt that concept to the mill. It'll give us better quality thread than even a master spinner can provide, and with less labor."

Steffano looked unconvinced. "And you are a clockmaker now?"

"No." Now Michael grinned. "But I know one." His grin faded. "You would have to share the patent with him."

"A patent. It would give us exclusive rights for what, ten years?"

"Yes, sir." The patent concept had originated in Venice only twenty-five years or so before, but already provided inventors with lucrative compensation.

Steffano got an unfocused look that told Michael the gears were turning. He took a breath to speak and then paused before continuing. "If I approve your project, how will you make a better quality product with unskilled labor?" He shook his head. "This makes no sense."

"That's the key," Michael said. "We don't need everyone skilled at every job. It's called 'division of labor.' You train managers; maybe take several masters out of your mills here or from other production centers, so you have a set of people who teach specific skills to the employees that do the work. Those employees each learn a part of the whole process, but they learn it well."

"I see." Steffano hesitated. "But you are adding another layer of personnel. I thought the point was to reduce labor costs."

"This method might add a layer of employees, but it reduces the number of employees in relation to the amount of product they put out because it is much more efficient. Your master spinner, on average, is competent at the range of jobs necessary to produce a reel of thread. But individuals, properly trained and motivated, can become very good at a limited number of tasks."

Steffano leaned in. "What kind of motivation are you talking about?"

Michael shrugged his shoulders. *Don't show him how much you want it.*

"In return for higher production, you pay employees more than they can make at a labor job anywhere else, and you show them some appreciation."

Steffano paused for a moment, searching Michael's face. "Where did you learn all this? Or did you just make it up?"

How could Michael tell him about the first time he read Adam Smith's *Wealth of Nations* from 1776? Frederick Taylor's "scientific management method?" Theory X, Y, Z? The concepts made modern industry possible. *Slow down.*

Michael laughed. "I told you I wouldn't lie to you, remember? Besides, they use something similar to these techniques at the Arsenal. I went there one day last week and watched them put together a whole galley. They're organized and produce a good product quickly."

A light came on. "Yes. Yes they do," Steffano said. "Maritime superiority is Venice's power base."

Michael spread his hands to make a point. "Manufacturing superiority can be your power base."

"Hmm. We must be very careful." Steffano drummed his fingers on the desk a few times. "One of the arguments for protection of the mills in Venice is that the poor and widows and nuns can make a living spinning thread in their homes or convents. What about them?"

The final objection—he had his project, and this world wouldn't be the same. Michael contained his elation and nodded. "For one thing, the threads they make are second-choice varieties. We'll be making premium grades. As for the other...are you paying me to care for the poor?"

Steffano blinked. "No."

Michael looked him in the eye and spoke without hesitation. "Then they aren't my concern."

The boss stared for a moment and then laughed. "You are mercenary, aren't you?" The feral grin returned.

"No, not exactly mercenary, just a manager, and the manager's job is maximizing profit for the owner."

"I like your philosophy." Steffano grew serious again. "Prepare a proposal. I want to see the numbers."

Michael flipped open his portfolio. "I thought you might." He handed a stack of paper across the desk.

"Very good. I will look these over. Oh, I meant to ask you. Are you free tonight?"

"I can be."

"There is an event I think will benefit you. The doge is hosting an affair tonight. Would you care to go?"

It wasn't a request. Besides.... Michael gave him a grateful smile. "Yes, it would be a good opportunity. Thanks."

"You are welcome. And, Michael, dress appropriately."

"Yes, sir. I will." *Do I want to go to a party at the palace? You bet.*

* * * *

Michael felt silly. He heeded Steffano's advice and went to see the tailor, where he caved to fashion. Now he sat in Steffano's gondola, costumed in a red silk blouse and a pair of tight black hose he had, until now, resisted. And he sported a fanny pack, only they called it a codpiece and wore it in front. Besides protecting his dignity, the thing also had a pocket.

A fanny pack by any other name. He hoped the tailor lacked a sense of humor.

Saint Mark's Square looked different at night. The lamplight created bright spots and shadows and created an air of splendor and mystery. The gondolier docked in front of the palace. Michael waited until Steffano got out before stepping up to the stone landing.

He had thought the building big before, but its size impressed him more as they neared it. Marble columns boasted reliefs and friezes that relayed stories to which he had no reference. Guards at the entrance recognized Steffano and welcomed him and Michael through the large gilded doors. While he followed Steffano up a flight of marble steps toward a buzz of conversation, he craned his neck at the magnificent paintings in the stairwell on walls that arched into a paneled ceiling. This was only the introduction.

A room opened up at the top of the stairs. Its purpose, it seemed, was to overwhelm. Dozens of paintings, each of which might make a twenty-first century person wealthy beyond his dreams, covered the walls. More adorned the arched ceiling.

Scenes of sea, conquest, and wealth assaulted the poor observer. How would one describe this exhibition of wealth?

Gaudy. The builders intended to intimidate the richest visitor.

Along the far left wall, a staircase impressed with its massive presence, even in the process of its construction. It curved from the level where Michael stood up to the next floor, probably thirty feet above. On the wall, ascending with the steps, hung a sequence of portraits, obviously former occupants of the ducal office. Oddly, one toward the top was blacked out.

Steffano noticed the object of his gaze. "Doge Marino Faliero. He took himself a little too seriously, it seems. Beheaded in the square."

"That's a bit extreme."

"There was a woman involved," Steffano said in explanation.

Michael recalled Anzolo's warning about the council and wondered if someone dropped Faliero's name in the secret slot.

The level of noise dropped as heads turned toward the left of the giant staircase. Through the doors paraded a stout man whose presence set him apart from those around him. The red robe and red silk hat, alone, marked him as special, but his regal bearing identified him as a leader. Even his long white beard was remarkable among this bunch of clean-shaven men. He moved among the crowd, shaking hands and greeting the wealthy and powerful. In his wake followed a taller, slender man dressed in black. Not a bodyguard, but some kind of assistant or confidant.

"The doge." Steffano gestured to the man in red. "Agostino Barbarigo."

Michael watched as the doge turned to his companion and whispered in his ear. The man nodded and left the way he came.

Agostino made his way past the spot where Michael and Steffano stood. "Steffano. Good to see you this evening." Michael recognized the wide smile and booming voice of a politician.

"And good evening to you as well, *Serenissimus.*" Steffano shook his hand.

Agostino's eyes went absently to Michael.

"This is my new associate, Michael Patriate," Steffano said.

"Ah, the Englishman."

"I am pleased to meet you, *Serenissimus.*" Michael blinked at the recognition, but the doge went on to the next handshake.

Steffano leaned close. "You have made some kind of name for yourself."

"Is that good?" Michael watched the red-robed leader recede into the crowd.

"We will see." Steffano looked across the room. "There are some men you should meet."

Michael followed him through the crowd toward a pair talking in a corner.

"Nicolo," Steffano called. A head turned, then another. The duo watched as Steffano and Michael approached.

"Hello, Nicolo." Steffano grasped their hands in turn. "Michael, these are my friends Nicolo Simoneti and Romaso Torta, also in the silk business."

"Michael Patriate. I'm happy to meet you." Michael extended his hand.

"I've heard about you." Nicolo completed the handshake. He held his head tilted back just a bit more than Michael found friendly.

"Good things, I hope." Michael exchanged another handshake with Romaso.

"Interesting things, at least," Nicolo said. "You've been busy in your short time here."

Michael looked toward his boss. "*Signor* Rompiasi doesn't pay me to lounge about, I'm afraid." This repartee didn't seem to be of the good-natured variety.

"Please excuse me, gentlemen." Steffano gave them an abbreviated bow. "I must see a man about some business." The three nodded to him as he departed.

Romaso continued the line. "You have managed to roil the waters in many places the last couple of months. What seems to be your hurry?"

Michael forced a smile for the two *setaioli*. "I believe there's no point in putting things off when you know what you want."

"And sometimes it is better to watch and learn before you leap into the fray," Nicolo said.

"You're probably right." Michael gave him a cold stare. "But everybody works in his own way."

Michael's new acquaintances nodded as if they tolerated an idiot.

Niccolo crossed his arms. The way he canted his head mocked. "Tell us about the new processes you have been trying to install in Steffano's mills. They have the spinners upset with you."

"The spinners should get used to the idea of changes in the way they work." He gestured with his head toward what he hoped was the manufacturing district. "They'll all make more money when they put out more product."

"I am not sure we want them to make either more money or more product," Romaso said. "It upsets the balance, and we like things the way they are."

So that's the way it is. Michael looked him in the eye. "Change will happen whether you like it or not. We're only helping it along for our benefit. Yours, too, by the way. The cloth will be better and your costs will be lower."

Nicolo took a half step into Michael's space. "We do not need your help. I hear you are considering a new mill." It seemed a challenge more than a question.

Michael glanced around for Steffano. "We haven't announced anything yet."

"I should say before you do then, you may find little support for your new operation. Raw silk, personnel, building materials; they may all be in short supply."

"I'll take my chances." Michael looked for an exit.

"Yes, you will take chances. Perhaps even to your person." Nicolo's direct gaze reinforced the threat.

A sudden shot of adrenaline affected Michael's judgment even as he recognized it. He stabbed a finger toward Nicolo's chest. "You want to take us on? Go right ahead. You don't have the nerve to do it yourself, I bet." A bead of sweat rolled down his back.

Nicolo laughed. "I do not soil my hands. That is what *bravos* are for. But you may find there is no 'us,' only you."

"Whatever the case, come after me, and you better watch your back." He looked to Romaso. "Especially when there is no 'us.' I don't mind getting *my* hands dirty." Just ask Gino and the dead pirates.

Nicolo turned toward his companion, but kept his eyes on Michael. "Romaso, he is a feisty one, is he not? We should be very careful. Michael, we will go now, but remember what I said. Pay attention where you step."

He glared at each man in turn and stuck out his chin. "I always do."

"Good. We will be watching. Come, Romaso."

Michael's antagonists melted into the throng of businessmen. He shivered in the suddenly hot hall. This evening of networking wasn't working so well. He set out to find Steffano, now uninterested in the wonders of the room. Startled to feel a hand on his shoulder, Michael turned and found his employer with an amused look on his angular face.

"Are you making new friends?" Steffano asked.

"Sure. I'll fill you in on it later."

"I am ready to go now if you are." He gave the room a quick scan. "I have seen and been seen."

"That suits me." Michael wanted out of this orgy of extravagance.

Back in the gondola, Michael calmed enough to speak. "Nicolo and his friend threatened our project and me personally. Is that the way business is done here?"

Steffano's eyes took on a cunning slant in the darkness. "On the surface, Venice looks like a genteel place, but business is fierce. One must play by its rules."

"All right, but what should we do about their threats?"

"I must be blunt about this, Michael. I fund your projects and pay you for results, but you are responsible for getting them completed. This problem is yours."

The rules became clearer. Steffano reaped the rewards of success while Michael took the risks and would bear the blame for failure. He was on his own again. *Time to play hardball.*

"Yes, sir. I'll take care of it." He reached in vain for a cigarette for the first time in months and issued a silent curse.

Chapter Fifty-Seven

Charles

Charles assembled his lieutenants and gave them orders to ready the army. The League of Venice or Holy League, whatever they wanted to call it, harassed his garrisons and threatened supply lines along the length of Italy. He worried about potential isolation here in Naples and, frankly, had tired of occupying the city. Infatuation for the liberation of Jerusalem left him when Cem died.

He would take the spoils and go home to France where the money and property he confiscated in Naples could repay loans and other debts incurred to fund this journey.

Charles disliked the choice of leaving half his army behind, but with Étienne holding the fortress at Gaeta, and Montpensier installed in Naples as viceroy, he could come back to finish his task later. He would return to France with half his army. *No matter.* It had not taken half his army to conquer Italy. Half would get him home.

Chapter Fifty-Eight

Michael stood in the open area of the wheelhouse and savored the aroma of freshly greased machinery. Although not yet finished, they had made great progress the last couple of weeks. Gears and shafts ran from the water wheel outside to drive the spindle, where counterbalance weights kept the speed constant. Spools mounted on the mill assembly fed in the silk fibers they would spin into thread.

Low-tech by twenty-first century standards, it was Michael's baby. He and clockmaker Carlo Ranieri were birthing a new generation of automated machinery. Soon, they would have a dozen of these mills operating here in this building. With room to grow on this piece of land Michael acquired for a bargain price, the only limitations would be capital and available labor.

The canal under construction would bring enough water from the Piave River to turn eight or ten more wheels. Until the water started to flow, they tested with a horse pulling a rope wound around the wheel shaft. The clattering machinery created a cocoon of noise that allowed Michael to think while he tinkered.

He strolled over to Carlo's seat at the mill on the end and looked over his shoulder, pointed, and shouted over the racket. "That clutch mechanism needs an adjustment. It still shudders a little as you engage it."

Carlo nodded without taking his eyes off the works and raised his voice. "All right. I'll work on it." He peeked up at Michael. "But it's shaping up nicely, eh?" Carlo's pride in his new machine shone through his smile.

Michael ran a hand across a spindle. "Nicely, yes. Carlo, I couldn't have done this without you."

"You have made your own contributions. You never worked with a mill before?"

"No, until four months ago I had never seen one. But maybe fresh eyes like ours are an advantage." Michael looked over the contraption again. "I wish you could stay until we get the whole thing finished." Carlo and his father, Paolo, would soon start on a new commission, a clock in the tower to be built on Saint Mark's Square.

"So do I, but your people are learning. They'll be able to duplicate this one, and you know where I'll be. You can always come by if you have a question."

"Be assured I will." Michael smiled at him and then looked to the door. "I need to go check on the excavators. They're holding things up."

"I'll have the clutch working smoothly when you return."

Michael patted his shoulder and left him at work. He clomped down the wood steps into a country quiet disturbed only by the buzz inside the building.

Gino fell in step as he left the wheelhouse. After his run-in with Nicolo at the doge's palace, Michael felt the need for a bodyguard and searched out the man who had attacked him in Caorle. It made sense to hire a *bravo* who knew who was boss.

"Back to town, *padrone*?" Gino called to Michael's back.

Michael glanced over his shoulder. "No, out to the dig site. They think this is a permanent job."

"Right. Want to ride? The horses are saddled."

"No, I'll walk. It's a nice morning, and I want to check the grade."

They climbed down a ladder into the ten-foot-wide and six-foot-deep dry channel that worked its way up toward the river. Water from the canal would fill a small lake below and spill over into a creek before winding back to the sea. *Oh, for some dynamite.*

A couple minutes later, they encountered a dozen or so men with assorted hand tools standing in front of a wall at the end of the canal, some at work, most with hands by their sides or on their hips. By the looks of their clothes, their boss was keeping most of the money Michael paid him. He headed for the crew leader, a thick weathered man with white beard stubble and a limp.

"Panelo, what's the holdup?"

"The delay is that rock." Anger already charged Panelo's voice. This wouldn't be their first argument about the lack of progress.

"Then get that rock out of the way. You still have a hundred yards to go, and we need water running here in a month. You don't have time for these men to be standing around."

Panelo spoke through clenched teeth. "This is hard work. The men must rest once in a while. I won't work them to death."

"Look." Michael got in Panelo's face. "If you need more men, hire them. If you can't do it, I'll find someone else, but this canal is going to that river in four weeks."

Panelo opened his mouth to speak when Michael felt a hand on his collar jerk him back several feet. As he struggled for balance, a rock the size of a man's head bounced between him and Panelo.

"You all right?" Gino asked in his ear.

Michael ran a few steps away from the wall and looked up to its lip, but if someone had been there, he couldn't see. He pointed at Panelo. "Who did that?"

Panelo stood with his crossed arms resting on his belly. "This is a dangerous place. Things fall all of the time. You should be careful where you stand."

Michael strode back to Panelo and planted himself close enough that the shorter man had to lean his head back to look him in the eye. He spoke in a quiet, dangerous voice. "You have one week to show some progress, or I will replace you and your men. And I know there isn't any other work that pays this well. Are we clear?"

"Clear." Panelo stood his ground.

"Good. You can tell your men to get back to work." He turned and stalked away with Gino beside.

Gino watched back over his shoulder until they were safely away before he spoke. "It's a big rock."

"Yes, it is. Let's go up to the river and check on the new docks." He spotted a rope ladder and set off for it.

Gino caught up and leaned in close. "Do you want me to take care of him?"

Michael glanced at his new security chief. "No, not yet. We need him until I can get someone else to take his place. Maybe they'll get past the rock soon." He clenched his fists to keep Gino from seeing them shake.

Chapter Fifty-Nine

Agostino

Agostino put down the report and leaned back in his chair. His plan was working. Venetian galleys had landed at Genoa and denied Charles an escape by sea. Charles would have to turn inland and fight his way back to France. Now that Ludovico and Milan had allied with Venice, against Charles, that would prove a difficult task.

The League of Venice possessed an army of forty thousand troops and positioned it to confront Charles in Lombardy. Charles had started with a large army, but had left behind parts of it at scattered garrisons, holding on to his conquests. Although his party might number fifteen thousand, perhaps a third or more consisted of servants and women following the main group. Charles could hardly hope to win at those odds, even if Agostino's army was mainly *condottiere,* mercenary.

Agostino had turned to the veteran general, Francesco Gonzaga, Marquis of Mantua, for command of League forces. Emperor Maximilian and Spain's Ferdinand had participated by paying money to raise the army, keeping their men out of Italy and out of Agostino's way.

A smile worked its way across his lips. After they dispatched Charles, Venice would use its army to control northern Italy, from the papal cities of Romagna west to Milan, technically its current ally in the league. And it would include the lands of Ercole d'Este, Duke of Ferrara, the man who had been an irritant to Agostino for far too long.

Chapter Sixty

Michael sat back in his chair for a luxurious moment and watched the gondolas glide by outside his office window. He itched to get back to the mill, but he had to hire men to work there first. Though there were plenty of laborers in the countryside around the mill, he required experienced spinners to teach and manage them. True to form, guild members from Venice refused to go, and Michael sent Benetto to towns on the mainland. He should be back with a half-dozen men any day now. Soon, the thread mill would be operational, and he could start on the real object of his plan for revolutionizing the silk industry.

In many ways, current weaving technologies lagged behind even thread spinning. A typical weaver ran his loom by hand, often out of his home. He manually inserted weft threads through the stretched warp strands in different ways to make assorted types of cloths and different patterns and then pulled a shuttle that packed the newly inserted thread or threads against the previous row. Over and over, the weaver repeated the process until he had a few feet of cloth; then he unfastened the warp threads and moved the cloth, clamped it and started the operation again.

Weaving by hand proved slow and prone to mistakes. The weaver might miss a loop with the weft thread or he might bring the shuttle down with inconsistent force and create a tight or slack space in the cloth that devalued the finished product.

Several men in the eighteenth century, Michael couldn't remember their names, developed techniques for automating the weaving process. One method involved punch cards for creating patterns and piles with the weft threads. Other innovations powered the looms. With something like these technologies in place, Michael could produce cloth of consistent quality at a greatly reduced cost. It might displace thousands of workers, but that wasn't his problem. He would be the king of silk.

Michael even had an engineer picked out to help, although he hadn't contacted him yet. Leonardo da Vinci was alive and well and living in Milan. Leonardo should welcome an outlet for his creative genius once he saw the possibilities.

"*Signor* Patriate?"

Michael left his contemplation to see a young man at his door. "I'm Michael Patriate."

The youth reached in the leather pouch strung over his shoulder. "I have mail for you."

A private mail courier. Michael stood and took a package from him.

"Two *lire*, please." The courier took his money and left.

Michael expected the dispatch to be from Benetto, but the writing looked German. Who could this be from? He extracted a letter from the package. *Felix*. Michael leaned back in his chair, legs crossed, and read the note from his friend.

"*Michael, my joy upon receiving your letter turned to sadness with its message. I will miss my friend Konrad and mourn his passing. But joy returns with the knowledge that he died saving others and he is now at home in the bosom of his Lord Jesus! I am grateful for his life and contributions. Thank you for informing me of his death.*

"*So, you are now in Venice. You must be succeeding in your work to be able to live there. I hope that you are being true to yourself and to the Lord. Always maintain your integrity. It is the only thing you can call yours.*"

The letter went on with happenings at Felix's monastery, but Michael quit reading. Why were they always preaching to him? Between Felix and Luca, Michael had received all of the admonition he could stand. Where had God been when his dad died or when his mother looked through her son with absent eyes? He had been on his own since he was eleven.

I can make it just fine on my own now, thank you.

A gondola pulled in front of the warehouse and disgorged Benetto and several companions. Michael tossed the letter into a desk drawer. *Back to the mill.*

The King of Silk had work to do.

Chapter Sixty-One

Ludovico

Ludovico studied his maps again. So Charles had crossed the Apennines. Why didn't Venice allow Charles to go to Genoa and leave by sea? Should Agostino wish to fight Charles, contrary to the league's stated purpose of forcing the French to leave Italy, they would fight in Lombardy, Ludovico's territory.

Afterward, thousands of troops loyal to Venice would look around for more conquests, and Milan would make an attractive place to start. Now, he could not count on help from his father-in-law. The duke of Ferrara remained a French ally.

Ludovico cursed his bad luck. What had possessed him to get tangled up in this self-destructive scheme?

Chapter Sixty-Two

Charles

Charles cursed the situation that had driven him through the Apennine Mountains. The trip south along Italy's coast had been fun, all conquest and adventure, but Venice had blocked that route, and the return had changed into a march for survival.

Moving the large guns and equipment over the narrow pass proved exhausting work for soldier and officer alike. Still, Charles raced ahead to the encampment at Fornovo, a village at the foot of the mountain, near the Taro River. There he received a dispatch from his last ally in the region, Ercole d'Este, Duke of Ferrara. In accordance with Ercole's message that the Venetian army had not received authorization to fight, Charles sent an envoy to the Venetian commander with a request for free passage and the right to purchase provisions for his troops at a fair price. The emissary returned with a long face. Charles rode back up the trail to a point where he could see and think.

He observed the terrain from his perch on the mountain and sighed. Somewhere across on the right bank of the Taro and hidden by thick woods, Venetian forces waited uphill from the French. A rocky valley separated the two.

Charles's army, tired and hungry from the march over the mountains, would be pitted against a force at least three times its number, the opponent well-rested and fed. His generals, though, showed optimism. "This enemy will flee from your royal name," they said. Charles doubted it. He failed to see a way of avoiding the fight, and this one would not be so easy.

He studied his commanders, who in turn waited for an order. "Send the scouting party."

An hour later Charles watched a group of forty French soldiers move toward the trees. Suddenly, a hundred, maybe two hundred, light cavalry from the Venetian side burst out of the woods and bore down on the reconnaissance party. The *Stradioti*, mercenaries of mostly of Greek-Albanian heritage, overwhelmed the doomed men and, carrying their victims' heads on pikes, disappeared back into the woods. The generals wore grim faces as the day ended.

Charles faced his advisors again. "Suggestions?"

* * * *

In the morning, Charles went to work in preparation for battle, while continuing attempts at diplomacy. He split his forces into three groups. The bulk of the army would be in the second group, which he commanded. Cavalry and light infantry would go in front, led by generals Marshal de Gie and Gian Steffano Trivulzio. The remainder under Louis de la Trimouille would guard the baggage train, which bore the huge plunder from Naples.

All day, the skies threatened rain but held. Charles studied the weather because he had decided to cross the river away from the Venetian army. A rain in the mountains would turn the normally placid stream into a raging torrent. Toward the end of the day, it became clear diplomacy had failed, and they would have to move. Charles ordered his army to rest in preparation for action the next day. That evening he saw lightning in the higher elevations.

It rained all night, and in the morning the Taro ran swiftly. If crossing the river would be hard for the French, so would it be for the League army. Charles mounted his horse and, with the *fleur-de-lis* flying from his raised lance, addressed his troops.

"Brave soldiers of France. Today you will prove yourselves worthy of the trust invested in you. You fight for France; you fight for honor; you fight for God!"

The first group began fording the river, riders in water to their knees and footmen holding onto horses' tails to keep upright. Charles watched for the attack he imagined would come soon. When General Trivulzio's division finished crossing, Charles led his own contingent into the water. After the third group safely crossed, Charles ordered the lightly guarded baggage train placed off to the left side and the troops reunited. Then he heard the noise.

The rear guard came under attack from the League army, under the banner of commander-in-chief, Gonzaga, himself. Already, the sound of sword and lance play, shouts, and trumpets filled the air. Charles ordered the armies to turn right, toward the river, to present a united front against the enemy. *Stradioti* crossed the torrent and moved on the center, while cries from the front section, now on the left, announced the attack there.

The smaller rear guard would not hold against Gonzaga's forces. Charles broke his division into two detachments and gave command of one to the Duke of Bourbon to hold the center, then crossed himself and wheeled his horse right to face Gonzaga.

The Venetian mercenaries, unused to bloody battles, soon retreated in the face of heavy losses and Charles turned back to the center. The battle went badly; the *Stradioti* inflicted heavy losses among the French. Charles called his men to follow and charged back to the fight.

He found a blood-spattered captain mounting a fresh horse. "Where is the duke?" he shouted.

"His horse carried him alone into the battle." Fear strained the captain's face. "We have not seen him since."

"Then follow me." Charles charged to the front of the line. "France, France!"

His lance struck an attacker and broke. He drew his long sword and slashed at the enemy. The *Stradioti* seemed drawn to Charles, but he and his men held their ground.

"My King, your heraldry," called one of his knights.

Of course. Charles tore all the regal markings from his armor and from his horse to deny the Venetian captains easy recognition of their opponent and went back to his grim work.

Suddenly, the enemy fled from him. He found himself alone except for a few knights around his horse; in his bloody hands, he held a crimson-stained battle axe. *What happened to my sword?* He looked after the retreating enemy and let the weapon fall to the ground.

The gory smell of death called for the contents of his stomach, but when Marshal de Gie arrived with a detachment, Charles snapped back to purpose.

"Your Highness, we could not get through to you. Your bravery was exemplary," the marshal said.

Charles looked at the sky. It could be barely more than an hour since the battle started. He reined his horse around. "Regroup."

* * * *

Charles's generals laid out the results of the conflict. The battle had proved the courage of the French army and the ineptitude of the Italian mercenaries. Some of the Venetian-led troops had indeed stood and fought. There were a thousand dead French and two thousand dead of the enemy. But most of the League forces had either fled or broken off the battle to loot the baggage train instead. Charles retained the bulk of his army, but the valuables from Naples with which he hoped to refinance his efforts were gone. Charles cursed the day he started this doomed expedition.

"Send a message to Gonzaga. We propose a truce of one day to bury the dead."

Later in the day, Charles looked over the battlefield with his generals. The men interred many members of noble families, but too many soldiers had perished to bury them all. Two or three thousand corpses lay naked on the field, stripped first by the mercenaries and then by the peasantry.

Charles spoke without moving. "General Trivulzio. Instruct the men to set up their tents and light their fires."

"Majesty, we are staying?" the general asked.

"No." He faced the army's marshal. "After dark, ready for travel, but leave the tents. By the time they see we are gone, they will not have the heart to ford the river."

"Good, Majesty. Brilliant idea." Trivulzio nodded his affirmation.

"Then why do you delay?" Charles turned back to the sea of bodies. Soon he was alone.

He closed his eyes and imagined. A few more weeks and he would be back home in his beloved Amboise. And deep in debt with half an army.

Time to start over.

Chapter Sixty-Three

Michael stared out the coach's window, barely aware of the noise and dust, of his companions, Benetto and Gino, or of the six spinners following in the wagon behind. His mind occupied itself with his last trip to Caorle to see Cecile, when he traveled this road with hope of saving their relationship.

"Are the three mills enough?" Benetto asked.

What else could he have done? *I didn't have a choice.* Just like with Sheila. If only they could understand, be proud of him.

"Michael?"

"Pardon me?" He blinked his eyes to clear the memory. "Oh, yes. They'll do to start. It'll take time to get these men trained so they can instruct the production people. The three machines will let us work out the problems we're sure to have."

Prove the concept this season and go all out next year. Then they'll see.

Benetto shifted in his seat. "I hope you know what you're doing, Michael. I was shut out of a friend's place yesterday. Even my son refuses to talk to me. This situation could become dangerous."

"I know. We may need to hire more security, but when everyone sees how well this works, they'll all want to do it our way, and we'll all make more money." Michael used to consider money the ultimate motivator for people like Benetto, but the man didn't look so motivated today.

"Maybe." He paused. "It sure is a long way out here. I miss being home."

"We'll build you a house here if you want, just keep your priorities straight."

Benetto turned his empty eyes out the window.

Gino grinned and cleaned his fingernails with the stiletto Michael had taken from him that day in Caorle. He straightened in his seat. "Something smells." He slid the knife back in its sheath.

Michael sat up and sniffed. "Smoke. Somebody's fireplace."

"No, it's different," Benetto said with a dark look. "Silk."

Michael leaned his head out the window. A black wisp rose into the air ahead of them. "Hurry," he shouted at the driver.

When they bounced to a stop Michael laid his eyes on the smoldering heap that had been the wheelhouse. Stunned, he sat and stared. The driver opened the door. Gino jumped out and raced to the ruins.

Benetto climbed out next and turned back with a scowl. "Coming?" he snapped.

"What?" When he left this was all...

"Are you coming, I said, to see what you've done to us." Benetto spun away and stomped off toward the blackened mess.

Michael focused on the retreating back. He tried to summon anger to sharpen his senses, but it wouldn't come. Yet. He eased down from the carriage and set off to survey the damage.

Smoking fragments of the structure lay askew among glass shards from the broken windows. Only the wheel remained intact, spinning free with its shaft burned in half. Michael walked on wobbly legs to see still glowing embers on the stumps of support piers. Gino appeared at his side.

"What happened?" Michael whispered.

"Some men came last night after dark. They beat up my men and killed one of them. Then they set fire to the place. Your engineers left this morning." Gino always kept things simple.

Benetto's eyes were hard when he faced Michael. "What now?" He didn't bother to hide his contempt.

Michael counted to five before he spoke. "I guess you can go home to your wife now." He watched the old spinner stalk away.

Gino stood at ease by his side, waiting for orders like always, keeping his thoughts to himself.

Michael forced the anger down and voiced his options, just to have a direction. "We still have the plans, and the canal, and the wheel." He shook his head. "This will take another two or three months, and all the raw material is gone, too. It'll be more expensive now that most people have bought their supplies." He sighed and looked up the canal, toward the river.

"Gino, find a place to lodge these spinners and hire some more men to watch what we have left. We'll go back to Venice and start again."

And hope the boss will give us another round of funding.

The two men started back to the carriage, but Michael pulled up.

"What's the matter?" Gino asked.

"Find out who did this. It's time to play hardball."

Gino gave him a snaggle-toothed grin.

Chapter Sixty-Four

Agostino

Agostino stared out his window at the festival in the plaza. People jammed the square from the palace all the way to the basilica of Saint Mark, celebrating the League's victory over the French army. The crowd exhibited a mood different this morning from the previous evening when they heard news, based on preliminary reports, of defeat.

The chamber doors opened and shut quietly behind him and Agostino heard the familiar breath drawn as a preamble.

"The crowds hail your victory," Toma said.

"It is a wish. A lie." Agostino paused a moment before he turned around. True, the "victors" gained the spoils in Charles's baggage train, but it gave him scant comfort. Though armed with a numerical advantage of more than three-to-one, his army of mercenaries had fled the battle and left a tired French army to rest, regroup, and escape. He faced his aide, weary with the disappointment of his failed dream.

"Gonzaga claimed the Taro was too deep, else they would have finished it." Agostino looked away to his clock. The gilded symbols of power adorning it mocked him. He closed his tired eyes, only to visualize the Venetian army in retreat. "I suspect he thanked God for the rain."

Charles marched across the plains of Lombardy toward France, and Agostino's army would not go after them. Now all Europe would hear of Italy's impotence. The invaders would not stop coming.

"You are *Doge*."

Agostino snapped his eyes open at the shock. Toma had not talked this sternly to him since their childhood. The fists he had not used in anger since Ferrara clenched. "You should choose your words carefully."

Toma took a breath, but stood his ground. "You have the power of the doge. Use it."

"Power?" Agostino shouted. He glanced to the door and lowered his voice. "My power was vested in victory against Charles. What do you think the council will do with this?" He felt the anger drain away to hopelessness. "They will let me stay, but my influence is gone. Our gamble failed."

Toma closed the distance and took Agostino's shoulders, looking him in the eye. "There is a man. He has caused some trouble, but he may be...useful to us. To you."

Agostino took hope in Toma's confident stance. Maybe there was another way.

Chapter Sixty-Five

Michael closed the inn's door behind him and waited for his eyes to adjust to the darkness. Supper was a waste. The businessmen he dined declined his offer to take their money. Steffano had become reluctant to pour more into Michael's venture after the fire, so now he searched for operating funds when he should be rebuilding. Michael needed partners, Steffano said, but partners were hard to find. He might yet resort to borrowing money at a usurious interest rate.

At least a couple of haughty merchants had learned a lesson in crossing Michael Patriate. Gino said he only bruised them, but they were out of circulation for a while.

Gino leaned against the building on this minor canal and hummed a tune. Michael still marveled at the clear conscience this blade-for-hire exhibited. He wondered about his own for a second before he pushed ahead toward the boat. "Let's go."

A disembodied voice called from somewhere nearby. "*Signor* Patriate, may I have a word with you?"

Michael made out a form in the shadow in a recessed doorway. "If you show yourself."

The form moved out into the pale lamplight. A hood shrouded the hidden face.

"I apologize for the secrecy, but it would not do for me to be seen talking to you," the man said. "Might we visit in the garden here, alone?"

"I've been ambushed in one garden, thank you." Michael thought he heard Gino cough.

"Yes, your concern is understandable, but if I wished you harm, you would already be dead. Please, it will be worth your trouble."

Michael thought a moment. Really, it would be easy for anyone to get rid of him. By poison or stiletto, he was vulnerable to anyone who wanted him out of the way badly enough. "All right. Wait here, Gino."

"Good." The hooded man disappeared through the dark doorway.

Michael followed him inside the tiny yard. A rich person owned this place where valuable canal-side real estate was set aside for a few plants. The man removed his hood and turned to reveal his face.

"I've seen you before." Michael studied the familiar outline. "With the doge."

The man acknowledged Michael with a short bow. "Toma Sandeo. You have a good memory, *Signor* Patriate. I try not to attract attention to myself. It limits my usefulness."

"He depends on you. It's apparent in his bearing when he talks to you."

A dim ray of light from a second-story window revealed a stoic face. "You are also perceptive."

"It's my business to watch people. How they move can tell you as much as what they say."

"A key to survival, Michael." Toma pulled a wrought-iron chair back from a small table and gestured to Michael. "Would you care to sit?"

"No, thanks. I'll stand." Michael took an impatient breath. "So what does the doge want with a merchant's assistant?"

Toma gave no sign of irritation with Michael's curt behavior. "I believe you sell yourself short," he said. "Are you familiar with the concept of risk as it applies in a business setting?"

Risk? Of course. Investing was all about risk. "Yes. What's your point?"

"Risk is a two-edged sword. There is the negative side of risk, the possibility of loss. Alternatively, there is the chance of gain. Take our salt industry, for example. It is easy to make. We simply evaporate seawater, then load the salt and ship it out. There is steady demand and little chance of loss. Trading in spices, on the other hand, is filled with danger. Pirates, shipwrecks, and the high cost of money are a few of the obstacles to a successful transaction. Salt is safe and returns a dependable income. Spice is dangerous and tempts with the allure of rich rewards."

"I remember the basics. What does this have to do with me?"

Toma took a step toward him and pointed. "You, sir, are a risk, an unknown quantity."

Michael paused. "A risk. To whom?"

"No one knows where you came from, but since you appeared in Caorle almost three years ago, you have upset things wherever you have been. Sometimes upsetting the order brings profits, at other times it brings ruin. Which will you do?"

Michael shook his head. "It's not my intent to upset anything. I only see ways to increase efficiencies and take advantage of opportunities. I make money for my employer."

"And yourself," Toma said.

"That's the motivation."

Toma shifted to his right in a move that would put him between Michael and the gate. "You also make enemies for yourself and your employer. This society depends on order and control. The successful men you see here have built their businesses over many years, with sacrifice and patience. Your shortcuts threaten them, as you have seen."

Michael moved with the doge's man and Toma stopped.

"So," Michael said, "you're telling me I should quit working so hard for my employer." *Get to the point.*

"No, but there are natural boundaries that, when crossed, may bring negative consequences."

"Well, I appreciate your concern for my welfare."

Toma chuckled. "I must admit it is not my concern for your welfare which brought me here. My purpose is to assess how much danger you might be to the republic. Or what you might offer."

"What do you mean? I'm no threat." What did Toma have in mind?

"Our success is envied across the world, and it is precious to us. We take any threat seriously, intended or otherwise."

Michael shifted his weight as if to leave. "This is all interesting, but I'm due somewhere."

"All right," Toma said. "Just remember we must all operate within the rules."

"I'll keep that in mind." He eased to the gate.

"Or face the consequences."

Michael halted. The night air had turned cool. He pulled his cloak about him, hands hidden inside, as he considered his options. The watch hung on its sash, cold against his chest.

This is it. Michael squared his shoulders. "Thank you for the warning. I'll watch my back."

"I hope so." Toma dipped his head in a parting gesture. "Perhaps we'll speak again. Good night, Michael."

Michael turned and walked out of the garden. He heard a sound and looked over his shoulder to watch Toma bend over into the shadow and retrieve an object from the stone floor. Michael saw a flash like the glint of light on glass. Toma disappeared through a black doorway.

"What was that about?" Gino asked.

Michael stared for a moment then faced forward and headed for the boat. "I don't know yet, but we'll find out soon."

Chapter Sixty-Six

Ludovico

Ludovico leaned back in his favorite chair and smiled at the events of the day–the best possible outcome for him, after all. The French king signed a treaty with him. In exchange for unhindered passage back to the Alps, Charles officially recognized Ludovico as the legitimate duke of Milan, making Ludovico's wait on Maximilian unnecessary, and it capped the good news coming in from other fronts.

A broken Naples posed no threat. Cardinal della Rovere was on his way back to France, Ascanio to Rome. The pope forgave the Sforza brothers. Venice failed in its attempt to grab power in the region. And Ludovico reconciled with his father-in-law, the duke of Ferrara. Beatrice was happy again.

Ludovico intended to redirect his efforts at building his legacy. The seventy tons of bronze Leonardo acquired for casting his horse had, sadly, been appropriated for weapons when he anticipated an attack from Charles. Perhaps he would begin the task of obtaining a replacement.

But first, he wanted a proper family burial place at the convent of *Santa Maria delle Grazie*. Leonardo would paint a fresco there, a depiction of the Last Supper.

The duke lifted his glass in a silent toast to the king of France, his new partner in power.

Chapter Sixty-Seven

Michael stood in the doge's palace again. On his first visit he had entered, fashionably dressed, through the front door. This time in servant's clothing, he used a discreet side entrance, sans Gino. And now he waited in the doge's inner chamber.

Warned by the severe secretary outside against sitting in one of the chairs that formed a semicircle around the gleaming walnut desk dominating the center of the room, he stood in the corner and waited, as ordered.

Gilded grape leaf decorations on the wall behind the desk directed the visitor's gaze to a portrait of the administrator, stern, powerful, and wise. A well-populated bookcase at the end of the room portrayed the doge as a learned man. Only the jeweled, golden clock on the opposite wall failed to direct attention visually to the one who would occupy the seat of power. But its loud "tick, tick, tick" said, "The man in that seat is far richer and more powerful than you can ever hope to be."

Five minutes became ten and then thirty. Michael knew because he watched Doge Agostino Barbarigo's clock count the seconds. Michael's own watch had come up missing, slipping from its hiding place when the sash became untied. He wondered where it was.

At one forty-three in the afternoon, Michael heard a murmur in the anteroom, then sharp words. Two minutes later the heavy oak door opened, and Michael faced the man he had met briefly at the party in the great hall. Agostino dressed in a similar manner this day, clad in a red silk robe and pointed red silk hat trimmed in ermine. *Who's he showing off for?*

Per instructions, Michael remained standing as the doge moved to his chair and sat. An assistant closed the door, and they were alone.

"Michael, please." Agostino gestured to the center seat.

"Thank you, *Serenissimus*." The chairs about the desk were shorter than the doge's, so the powerful man looked down on his guests. Michael's height, though, brought him about even to Agostino's eye level. If it bothered the doge, Michael couldn't tell.

Agostino seemed to study him for a moment before breaking the silence. "You are an odd man."

Michael felt anxiety work its way up his torso and resisted the urge to cross his arms across his chest. He bowed his head slightly. "Yes sir, I suppose I am."

Always agree with a man who can have your head cut off.

"You have a wide range of interests: accounting, finance, business, engineering." Agostino smiled. "Even fighting pirates, it seems."

"I try to be well-rounded." It slipped out before he thought. "Sir."

Agostino glared at Michael for a tense moment, then shook his head and laughed. He removed the hat and laid it to the side on the desk. His face grew serious.

"Everyone wonders where you come from. I have sent my men to investigate you, but it is as if you popped up out of the ground three years ago with nothing to your name, not even speaking the language. Yet here you are in front of me."

Michael shrugged and aimed for an expression of nonchalance. The nominal head of one of the most powerful governments in the world demanded to know his secrets, and those secrets might doom him. Or save him.

"I told my previous employers I was from England. I've been around the world and picked up things here and there; I even learned a bit at a couple of universities." These weren't lies, really.

"So you are no extraordinary person," Agostino's voice held an edge to match his sharp eyes.

"Only one fortunate enough to put pieces of information together and use them, sir." Michael recoiled from the anger that flashed across Agostino's face.

Agostino leaned forward and punctuated his words in a soft voice. "I will not be lied to."

When Michael failed to respond, Agostino reached for a plain wooden box on the desk. He opened the lid and dumped out the contents.

The watch. "I lost it," he whispered.

"And Toma found it." Agostino waited for a long moment before picking up the watch and looking it over. His voice returned to a conversational level. "This timepiece is a masterpiece of engineering. It is more advanced than our clock makers could hope to duplicate. It even seems to wind itself. How is it that you came to possess it?"

"I can't explain." Michael stared at his hands folded in his lap.

Agostino pointed behind Michael. "Did you see my clock? I spent over twenty thousand *ducats* having it built, and every day my secretary sets it forward or back by five or ten minutes to correct its inaccuracy. But this device of yours has been more faithful than we are able to test over the days I have possessed it. I can only think how valuable this would be to our army field commanders or our warship captains if they each had one." Agostino waited for a response.

"As far as I know..." Michael met Agostino's gaze. "That watch is the only one made. I don't know how to reproduce it."

"Regrettable." Agostino laid the watch on the desk and looked at it for a moment before he turned back to Michael. "Even so, I believe you know many things that could help me, help Venice." When Michael did not speak he went on.

"These are dangerous times for us. The Turks harass us on land and sea. We must do business with them, but they have wrested possessions from us in the Levant and threaten to overrun our ports in Dalmatia. France would take us if she could. The Emperor and even the Pope cast eyes upon our riches. I believe our people have become complacent and shallow. We need an advantage to keep what we have built here." He leaned in. "I mean to acquire whatever resources may fall to me to assure that we do."

Michael drew a slow breath through his nostrils and released it. "Sir, have you ever heard about the law of unintended consequences?"

The doge sat back and folded his hands on the desk. "I understand the principle."

"If you will, please bear with me for just a moment." Michael continued at Agostino's nod. He drew upon a documentary he watched when he stayed home sick one day. "Let's say, for example, that you find a way to preserve food for long periods of time. Not only salted beef and fish or dried fruit but all kinds of food like fresh fruits and vegetables and cooked meats. What kind of changes do you think you would see in society?"

Agostino angled his head in consideration. "We would eat better in the winter. Farmers could produce more with less waste. The markets would have more to sell. The ability to preserve food in this manner would be a blessing."

Michael nodded. "Yes, it would, but think what might happen if this process made its way to, say, France."

"They would eat better, as well. So?"

"Right." Michael sat taller in his seat. "The people would have better food to eat, and their army would, too. They could carry fresh food with them on a campaign. This would free them from having to depend on local populations to feed them, and they could bring larger armies through areas that couldn't otherwise support them, at almost any time of year. This is only one example of what might happen with an otherwise beneficial discovery."

An irritated frown settled on Agostino's face. "And you have refrained from introducing new ideas in your silk business?"

"Only improvements on existing ideas." Seeing Agostino's upraised eyebrows, Michael lowered his head again. "I've made some poor choices."

"As have we all, but we learn from the results and go on."

"Yes sir, the innovations we've introduced in the silk thread mill give us only a temporary competitive advantage. We own patents on the equipment, but others will copy or adapt our ideas soon enough. We'll be forced to continue to improve in order to maintain our lead, and the competition will benefit society, but the thread mill doesn't have much military application. The evolution of weapons and tactics has been going on for hundreds or thousands of years. If we suddenly introduce new machines or concepts, well, there's no telling what kind of devastation we'll start." Michael saw Agostino start to respond and hurried to make one more point.

"Suppose again, we come up with some kind of engine that could drive a ship farther and faster than you can imagine. You would own the water, but how long would the advantage last? Five, ten years?"

"Perhaps." Agostino looked at something far away. "But ten years would be enough to clear the Turks from the seas." His eyes snapped back to focus. "Can you build these things?"

Michael sighed again, conceding defeat of his point. "Not by myself. I know generally how things work, but you would need an engineer to make the detailed designs."

"And you know of such a man?"

Michael nodded, head down again. "In Milan. His name is Leonardo."

"The painter?"

"He has many talents, sir." *Westinghouse had his Tesla. I'll have my Leonardo.*

Agostino rose from his chair and paced the room, hands clasped behind his back. At the bookcase, he turned and faced Michael. "You will do this thing for me."

* * * *

Michael could hardly contain himself as he walked out of the square past Saint Mark's Basilica and its stolen artwork. Agostino had ordered him to start on projects to help Venice surpass its competitors in business and war. Over Michael's protests, he had promised full funding and equal rights to the patents of anything he invented.

Michael's decision to drop his watch where Toma would find it had been risky, but it paid off in the form of an audience with the doge. And the part of the presentation in which he took the most delight was his reference to steamships. Michael knew the symbolic husband of the sea wouldn't be able to resist the lure of complete dominance on the water. As a bonus, it turned out the doge was working outside the purview of the Council of Ten and would therefore be easier to control.

It involved danger, but the possibilities were endless. When he sold the Venetian government arms to defeat its enemies, Michael could go through intermediaries and supply the enemies too. It would generate an endless cycle, and he would stand as the beneficiary.

In retrospect, his previous plans were ill conceived and short-sighted. Tomorrow he started his new life. Something or someone had taken the world he knew. He would own his share of this one.

Gino caught up with Michael as he passed the church. "Let's go get packed," Michael said. "We're moving up." He patted the watch, safely back on its sash.

Chapter Sixty-Eight

At twilight Michael climbed out of the boat and paid the gondolier while Gino unlocked the house. Gino held the door when he finished.

"I'm going to change out of these rags. Get your things together." Michael hurried in. The doge had a place waiting for them.

Inside, he hung his hat on the stand and headed to the stairs at the end of the hall.

A sharp voice called out. "Michael."

He stopped short, backed up a couple of steps, and looked into the niche he'd outfitted as a den.

Steffano sat on a couch across the darkening room. "I have been waiting for you."

Not good. Michael stepped through the door onto the Persian rug he found at a market the previous week. "I didn't think you knew where I lived."

The front door closed and Gino's boot heels clicked several times on the terrazzo tiles behind him.

Steffano stared with an emotionless, shadowed expression that shot dread into the pit of Michael's stomach. "I know many things."

Maybe he doesn't know all of it. Play along. "Can I help you with something? Gino and I were about to leave. I have an appointment."

Steffano rose from the couch and strolled to the dark fireplace where a single lamp on the mantel emitted a faint point of light. He took down one of a pair of candles placed on either side and lit it from the lamp. Michael's eyes strained at the flare. When Steffano replaced the candle and turned toward him again, shadows emphasized the sharp features of a predator's face.

"Do I not pay you enough, Michael? Do I not give you enough freedom? Respect?" The words questioned, but the eyes accused.

"No, no," Michael stammered. "You've treated me well. I, I don't understand."

Steffano turned his back on Michael and in unhurried motion retrieved the other candle from the mantel. As he touched the wick to the lamp's flame, he confirmed Michael's fears. "You were seen at the doge's palace today." He set the candle down and faced Michael again. "What did you do there?"

Michael hesitated, considering his next move, whether he would lie again.

What was the use? He let it out. "The doge offered me a job. I couldn't say no."

Steffano pursed his lips and nodded slowly. "I see. To produce more of your inventions, perhaps? What did you promise him?"

"What he wanted most, I guess. Does it matter?" Michael fought the urge to run and stood his ground. Where could he go?

"No, I suppose not." Steffano shook his head and then walked to the front window. He pulled back the curtain to peer out into the evening, up and down the walk. "Michael, what have you accomplished in your life?" He released the curtain. Without a word, he demanded an answer.

Michael looked around the room, at the furnishings he bought himself. "I don't know, I seem to have done pretty well. I started with nothing."

Steffano gave him a mirthless laugh. "Yes, you have accumulated some money and property, but what have you actually produced and finished? Your friends in Caorle are cleaning up your mess there, and now you leave my silk business in disarray to chase another dream." He paused. "What promise have you ever fulfilled?"

Michael thought. He finished college, helped make a few deals that put people out of work, married and divorced. And what about his life here?

Rizzo's accounting. Since college, he had set up a lousy set of books. "You're right." Michael bowed his head in defeat. "I wasn't thinking."

Maybe there's a way.

Michael raised his head and his voice. "I can wrap things up for you. Yes. Benetto's a smart man. I can help him straighten things out. Everything's set in motion anyway, I..."

Steffano cut him off with a look. "No." He shook his head and sighed. "No, it is too late. The council has stepped in. Toma Sandeo has already lost his head over this French affair, perhaps the doge will as well. Now you are involved. I have no choice."

Michael took a step back, his legs unsteady. "Toma, dead?"

"Quite dead. Do you remember my friends Nicolo and Ramaso? The men you had Gino pay a 'visit?'" He shook his head and closed his eyes for a moment. "They are making life difficult for me at a time I do not need trouble. Your brand of politics has threatened me and Venice as well. No, your time here has come to an end." He walked to the couch and retrieved a heavy object from its dark recesses. Luca's book.

Fear tightened Michael's chest. He forced himself to draw a breath. "So, can I go back to Caorle?"

Cecile.

"I am sorry Michael. I really did like you." Steffano looked past him and nodded.

Something slammed into his back. He thrust out his arms to break the fall. *Gino.*

He smacked the floor with a hundred and fifty pound weight on his back and lay still, unable to will his lungs into action.

"Sorry, *padrone*. None of your tricks today," Gino whispered from astride Michael's prone body.

Michael winced at the cord cutting into his wrists, but couldn't make his arms work to fight back. He lay there, stunned, while Gino bound his feet. The *bravo* rolled him onto his back with his bound hands crossed under him. Michael opened his eyes and tried to focus while he caught a breath. He fingered the loose rope ends but couldn't reach the knot.

"Gino," he pleaded. "I thought you were a professional. I'm your boss."

Gino glanced up at Steffano. "The boss of my boss is my boss." He stared down again and shrugged. "Sorry."

Michael struggled against the bonds and twisted his head back toward Steffano. "You don't have to do this. I'll just go away."

Steffano walked over and bent at the waist to stare down at him. "Yes you will. I hope someone mourns you. Goodbye, Michael." Without another word or a look back he strode from the room.

Footsteps receded down the hall. The front door opened and shut. Gino pulled out a scarf and took it by opposite corners to roll it up into a gag.

"No, please." Michael tried to roll away. He saw a boot heel swing toward his head, then a bright light.

His head shook back and forth. An object forced its way into his mouth, choking him. A sharp pain jerked him back to consciousness. Gino had pulled the gag tight around the back of his neck and tied the knot beside his jaw. The nostrils swollen from the earlier impact with the floor restricted his breath to a trickle. He managed to open an eye. Gino reached toward his head holding a cloth bag with a drawstring hanging limp from its gaping end.

No.

Gino wore the same gapped smile he had given Michael back in that garden in Caorle, a man who loved his job.

Gino pulled the bag over his head and turned the lights off again.

Michael twisted his head and tried to pull free, but Gino drew the scratchy bag snug around his neck and tied the drawstring. The coarse cloth retained an earthy smell of old vegetables, potatoes, maybe. Michael's detaching consciousness stirred a vision of Gino packing an empty bag each morning, just in case he got to use it that day.

Something hard and heavy landed on his shins. Pain and shock made him swoon again. Michael heard his own muffled cry when Gino bound the weight to his legs.

Hands grabbed his ankles and pulled. Michael's left palm rubbed across raised patterns in the rug he had delighted in finding. Potential clients would have been so impressed. Then sharp edges of terrazzo tiles tugged at the seams in his clothing and tore at his fingers. He arched his back to get his hands off the floor and bent his neck the best he could to spare his head further abuse.

His feet hit the floor. The front door opened. After a moment, his progress resumed and he felt himself dragged over the threshold and the smooth paving stones of the narrow walk, bumping his head along the way.

Movement stopped again when Gino dropped his feet. Michael relaxed for a moment, but the sound of water against stone seized his heart in terror. Gino intended to drown him in the stinking canal.

Michael mustered all his strength and tried to shout, but the gag muffled his cries. The bag over his head filled with hot, unbearably humid, already breathed air. He gasped in a desperate effort to wring the last bit of oxygen from it. He arched and twisted, strained against the ropes binding him, anything to escape.

Let me go, I won't bother anyone.

A tug on Michael's clothes rolled him over a corner into an abyss. He barely had time to suck in a deep breath.

The piercing cold hit him first, a shock that turned his body into a rigid torpedo headed straight for the bottom. He landed feet first. Dragged along by the currents, his body bobbed like a bowling pin that wouldn't fall. The bag stuck to his face under the pressure and then allowed the cold water to seep in.

Michael tried to push himself back to the surface, but the weight tied to his legs pulled him back down. He would die down here, and no one would ever know. His efforts to free his hands ceased. Why hadn't he listened to Cecile?

"There are serious people in Venice." She had warned him.

Forgive me Cecile.

His hubris had brought him here. It had killed him and left destruction in its wake. He deserved to die.

A sudden calm enveloped him. He had only to breathe and end this agony, but his body would not let him. The pressure on his throat and chest choked him. His ears threatened to implode, but still he clung to that last bit of air in his lungs.

An image of Sheila silhouetted against their apartment window filled with New York City lights replaced the darkness inside the bag. Her lips moved, but the roaring in his ears drowned out the words. The scene flashed to their wedding, to her upraised face, her happy eyes. *I love you*, she mouthed. Blackness returned.

Michael's tortured lungs demanded to expel the poisoned air inside and draw in cool salvation. He struggled to keep his last grip on life.

Sheila.

He made one last fruitless effort, and strained to free the hands bound behind him. His wrists slipped against one another, just a little. Maybe the water gave him a little lubrication, maybe it was his imagination. He pulled against the coils and concentrated on the pain the coarse rope inflicted, a beacon in the cold darkness.

The pain inched from his wrist across the skin on the back of his hand. One more tug and the rope snapped over his knuckles. He reached down and tore at the bindings on his legs and tried not to panic this close to being free.

Michael took a second to run his hands over the object tied to his shins, a vase. Gino had tied the rope around its neck. The bulbous bottom and flared lip kept it in place. He spread the rope over the vase's lip and let it drop away; then he pushed with all his remaining strength toward the surface and clawed at the cord around his neck.

At last his body's urge to breathe would not be denied. He exhaled the spent volume in a raging, gagged scream against the weight that pressed upon him.

God, I'll do anything, just get me a breath of air!

A hint of light seeped through his closed eyelids. Something or someone squeezed his left arm until it ached.

"*Signore, faro' qualsiasi cosa, datemi solo una boccata d'aria!*" Michael gulped in welcome air, relieved to find himself free from the frigid water. He lay in a bed. How long had he been out? He stopped gasping. The ache in his lungs had disappeared, the pounding in his chest subsided.

"Boss?"

Who's there? The voice came in a foreign language, but he could almost understand it. Michael gathered another breath and repeated his thought.

"*Chi va la'?*" The words came out muddled. Why wouldn't his mouth work right?

"Boss, it's me. You're not making sense."

That voice, he knew it. *Settle down.*

Michael concentrated on one task, to open his uncooperative eyes. The lids parted for a second to reveal a form standing in front of the dark window to his right, concern twisting the familiar face. Eyes open again, his unsteady gaze went left to something hanging on a stand, an IV bag. A blood pressure cuff released his left biceps with a sigh and the pent-up anxiety released itself in a flood.

Tears rolled down his face. He savored a deep breath laced with the glorious smell of sterility and struggled against the disorientation. But he recognized his visitor. Bernie. Good old Bernie.

"Boss," Bernie said. "Thought I might not see you again. Glad you're back."

Michael tried to talk, but words wouldn't come. He swallowed against a dry throat and forced out a croak. "Drink."

Bernie fetched water from the sink. "Just a little, Boss. I doubt they want you to have any yet." He held the clear plastic cup to Michael's lips.

A memory of fetid canal water flashed across his senses, but he drank anyway. The cool liquid eased his throat a little.

"What happened?" he whispered. His head hurt. His stomach didn't feel so good either, but he managed to keep his eyes open.

Bernie hovered by the bed. "Somebody hit you on the head and tied you up. Took your wallet and tossed you in the East River. Missed your Rolex, though. Guess he didn't know you never carry much money. Joke's on him, huh?" He laughed a nervous laugh.

Pretty funny. He'd had about enough of people trying to kill him.

"Oh, speaking of." Bernie held out an object. "Thought you might want it."

Michael grasped the watch with his free hand and clutched it to his chest, eyes squeezed shut. Sheila had given him the watch, and what he had done with it in Italy...

Bernie cleared his throat. Michael opened his eyes to catch his assistant staring.

"What."

"Oh. Nothing, Boss." Bernie looked up from Michael's grip on the watch and seemed to remember why he was there.

"Ransel upped the offer like you said they would. We still have till tomorrow morning to beat it. I can get the paperwork from Marshall."

"Fine." Michael cut his eyes toward the table beside his head. "I need to make a call. Hand me the phone. Please."

Bernie cast an uncertain glance at the table. "Uh, sure. Don't you want me to get you anything? I ought to call the nurse and tell her you're awake."

"No, just the phone. I'll be all right." *Go home, Bernie.*

"Okay, here you are." He pulled the set from the table and stretched the cable across the bed rail.

Michael set the telephone on his chest and froze. On the back of his hand, a scar made a ragged diagonal line.

Konrad. He shook his head to chase away the memory that couldn't be. "Thanks, Bernie."

"You bet, Boss. I'm really glad to see you awake."

Bernie stood looking like a lost puppy, waiting. He hadn't caught the hint.

Michael gave him a nod and forced a smile. "Me too. Good night."

"Oh, good night. I'll be back in the morning." Bernie turned to leave.

"Bernie..."

"Yeah, need something else?" Bernie skipped back to the bed.

Michael took a deep breath. "Did I ever learn to speak Italian?"

Bernie's face bunched up in alarm. "Ahh, no, Boss. Remember we had to get that translator last year? You okay?"

I didn't think so. "Yeah, it must be the drugs or something. I'm not thinking straight yet. Hey, I want you to do something for me."

"Sure, name it."

He fought to concentrate. "Remember your accounting classes, that monk they always say invented accounting?"

"Yeah, kinda." The lost puppy face returned.

"I'm working on a project. The guy's name was Luca Pacioli." Michael shifted to ease a cramp in his back and winced. "I need you to see if some museum has the original manuscript of his book. It has to be the *original* handwritten manuscript. There must be scans of it in a computer somewhere. Get those for me if you can." Was Luca's reference to *Michael's method* written there in an educator's elegant script? Michael's thoughts whirled with ways to exploit the events he experienced in Italy.

Stop it.

Bernie hesitated before he answered. "Okay. Anything I need to know?"

"No, never mind." He couldn't get caught up in it again, but he had to know. "Yes, just load the pictures on a laptop and bring it up here." He closed his eyes in dismissal.

"Will do. 'Night."

A couple of seconds went by, and Michael heard footsteps. He waited until the door closed, then opened his eyes and stared at the ceiling. It had really happened. How, he didn't know. He had been given another chance and had failed again.

Addio, Cecile.

He pushed himself up in the bed and received a wave of pain and nausea for his trouble. His wrists and back, even his ankles hurt, but his head pounded in agony. He closed his eyes and lay still while he waited for it to pass. An unwelcome voice from the past whispered.

"What have you accomplished in your life? What promise have you ever fulfilled?"

He had tried so hard to succeed, and what did he have to show for it? Money.

He would have a lot of it after this deal went through. What then? Another deal, and another. An endless cycle of lonely hotel rooms and half-truths and posturing, piling up more money than he could ever spend by himself, a meaningless addiction he could never satisfy.

"I hope you find your peace, Michael." Felix.

"No, I'm done." Michael picked up the phone and squinted at the keypad as he thumbed the buttons.

Please have the same number.

Three rings became four and five and six, then it connected and the sweet voice he thought he'd never hear again made his heart race.

"Hi, this is Sheila. Leave me a message."

Michael slowed his breathing and tried to sound normal. "Hey. It's me. I, you may have heard, I had a little scrape. I'm calling from the hospital, but I'm fine. They have me all patched up. Listen, Sheila, we need to talk. No, wait. I'm sorry. I mean, I've messed things up and I need..." He sighed. "Good night."

He placed the handset in the cradle still on his chest and stared at the ceiling. What was he doing? Sheila had moved on. He tapped a finger on the phone, thought, and picked it up.

"Bernie. Yeah, changed my mind. Swing by my place first thing in the morning and get me some clothes. I'm going to finish this deal."

Chapter Sixty-Nine

Michael marched down the hall toward the firm's office, with each step forcing himself not to squirm. The shoes still felt funny, even though they came from his closet. His feet seemed to remember a different kind of fit. Even the clothes Bernie brought him hung wrong, from his thousand-dollar suit down to his soft cotton underwear.

The dry, manufactured air in this building always reminded him of money, but now he missed the humid dankness of Venice. He shook his head and reminded himself he'd never been there. He resisted sneaking another look at the scar on his hand.

"Got the details straight now, Boss?" Bernie paced to the left and just behind like a good soldier.

Michael nodded. He blamed not remembering on the concussion, but it seemed so long ago. "Yeah."

The double glass doors loomed at the end of the hall, slightly out of square, it seemed. He slowed, and hesitated in front of them. After today his name would probably join the partners etched in frosted print. That had been important once. Maybe it would be again.

"Okay, Boss?" Bernie looked him over. "The doc said the pain pills might..."

"Yeah, I know." That risk-averse doctor at the hospital had lectured him all the way out the door for leaving *against medical advice*. Michael nodded without turning. "I'm fine. Let's get to work." He rested his hand on the mahogany door handle and paused to look into Bernie's questioning eyes. "I'd rather you call me Mike." He pulled open the door and left Bernie staring.

The girl at the front desk, what was her name? She started only a month or so before the attack. A month, only a month.

Janice.

She smiled. "Good morning, Mr. Patriate. I'm glad you're okay."

Michael opened his mouth to correct her pronunciation, but shut it again. She'd said his name right, he remembered it wrong. He mumbled his thanks as he walked by.

A few heads popped up in offices down the hall. He looked into each and found only interested stares. No friends here, he recalled. Only associates who would greet with one hand and swipe a client with the other. He'd done that, too.

The Germans waited in the conference room, standing together, looking very business-like in their gray pinstriped uniforms and identical short haircuts. Michael nodded a greeting and set up camp with the contracts at the head of the long table.

Nussbaum. They had money to buy up another American cash cow. Pharma Centriferix needed capital to expand. A marriage made in business heaven, or something like it. The Pharma delegation swooped in at straight-up 10:00 a.m. and plopped into their seats. Michael stared at his watch for an extra second before he brought the meeting to order.

When it was over, he pushed his chair back and stood while the new partners left, still in two separate, quiet groups. He mentally counted his twenty-seven million dollar bonus. *I should be happy.*

"Well, that's it, Boss, I mean, uhm, Mike." Bernie leaned over the table and straightened a stack of leftover portfolios.

"Yeah, that's it." The ancillary documents nobody cared about looked like scraps of leftover pizza at a teen party.

Michael blew out a big breath and put a hand on his assistant's shoulder. "I've never thanked you for all your help."

Bernie glanced down at the hand. "It's my job."

"You deserve a share in the bonus, anyway. I'll check with Brenda down in..."

Bernie went rigid and spat out a whisper. "What's he doing here?"

Michael followed his gaze to the door and looked into the beady eyes of a weasel. *Wilson.* He straightened and clenched his fists.

Thin, sporting cropped gray hair and an eternal tan, Wilson swaggered into the room. "Well, look who's back from the dead." He grinned, showing a mouthful of gleaming teeth. "I guess I should congratulate you. Pretty good showing for someone impersonating a buoy only a couple days ago."

"Hello, Wes." He forced an even expression. "Slumming?"

Wilson threw his head back and cackled. "Yeah, slumming. Ha. No, I just wanted to come up and tell you to watch where you're going next time. It's a dangerous world out there, you know."

Michael nodded. "Bad things happen, all right. To all kinds of people." He let the implied threat hang.

Wilson stiffened. "What do you mean by that?"

Michael closed the distance until he could count Wilson's eyelashes. He let a hint of an evil smile play across his lips and dug down for his best North Carolina drawl. "Y'all be real careful now, Wes-Lee." He let his shoulder clip the shorter man on his way by.

The Weasel sputtered something, but Michael didn't look back.

Heads in offices may have turned again, but he stared ahead until he got to his door. The adrenaline keeping him going wouldn't sustain him much longer. Plodding footsteps made him turn.

Bernie arrived with the paperwork, still straightening. "Man, that was tense."

Michael pushed the door open and waved him through without an answer. "Just pitch that stuff somewhere. I'll get it later."

The chair behind the gleaming glass and metal desk beckoned him to take his place of honor. Michael expected a gondola to glide by the window beyond. That would be a good trick on the 14th floor. He collapsed into the soft leather and surveyed the sterile décor of his desktop.

Bernie stood on the other side, holding papers in his arms, uncertainty in his eyes.

Michael pointed to a corner of the desk. "Put 'em there. Have a seat." He paused for a second, then leaned to the right and slid open a drawer. There, in the back, it lay on its face. He took the frame, popped out the stand and set the picture in the middle of the desk. He always liked the way that yellow dress set off her eyes. She hadn't answered her phone again this morning. He leaned back and rested his heavy head.

"I can't do it." A black hole hovered where his fight should have been.

Bernie looked back at him with an understanding he hadn't noticed before. "Yeah."

"It's a drug." Michael shook his head. "It's a drug and I'm an addict. If I don't get out," he held out his hand and examined the jagged scar. "If I don't get out I'll drown."

Bernie appraised him for a moment. "Mike, let's take a walk." His eyes made that an order.

Out in the noontime sun the sidewalk seemed at once spacious and crowded. The street noise and press of the pedestrian horde made him yearn for a city free of cars and cell phones. The two strolled in their own sphere of silence.

They turned a corner and fear knotted Michael's stomach. The alley where he last remembered lying against a curb yawned like a canyon that would swallow and refuse to yield him back. The urge to flee peaked when he stepped over the spot and back onto the sidewalk. He drew and exhaled a breath that made Bernie shoot him an inquisitive glance.

Michael had almost calmed again when Bernie drew up and pulled open the door with a pink and white candy cane painted on the front. He gestured inside with an open palm and a guilty grin.

The bottom dropped out again. Michael held up both hands. "No, I can't."

Bernie rolled his eyes. "Mike, just walk in the door."

What was with Bernie all of a sudden, giving him orders? He stepped over the threshold, anyway. It *had* been a couple of days since he had eaten.

"Michael!" Big Rich's voice boomed from behind the counter. "It's been too long!" He wiped his hands on a towel, rushed around and embraced Michael by the shoulders. "*Come stai?*"

Michael missed Rich's enthusiasm. Why hadn't he come back before? A smile forced itself on him. "*Buon giorno*, Rich. *Sto bene, grazie. E tu?*"

The surprise on Rich's face matched the gasp he heard from Bernie right behind.

Oops. He ducked his head. "Oh, I've been practicing just in case I ever made it back."

Rich grinned and gave him a short mock bow. "I'm honored." Then he grew serious and nodded toward the corner. "You have a visitor."

Michael twisted around to look and his knees turned to butter. He reached for Bernie to steady himself. "What..." *How?*

Bernie put an arm around his shoulder and spoke in a half-whisper. "She called me last night, said you left her a message. Sounded like you had changed." He stepped in front of Michael and looked him in the eye. "She said to bring you down here if you really did."

It came at him too fast. Had he? Had he changed, or was he just tired? He sidestepped Bernie to get another look. She wore her golden hair tied back and smiled a nervous smile, just like when he asked her to marry him at that very table.

Bernie got in his face again. "You understand what she wants? Just you."

Michael nodded. He sniffed and wiped away a sudden tear. "How," he cleared his constricted throat, "how can I thank you?"

Bernie smirked. "Well, you can still talk to Brenda in accounting."

Now Michael managed a laugh. "I'll do it." *All those broken promises.* He sobered. "I really will. Tell them I won't be back?"

"Yeah." Bernie nodded. "HR will have some forms, but they'll mail them, I guess. I'll pack up your office and send your stuff."

Michael's eyes went back to the vision at the corner table, hands folded, no ring. "Just the picture. I don't need anything else."

"Okay. What about that special project?"

Michael shook Bernie's hand and looked him in the eye. "I have a new project. Thanks."

He took the first step toward her and the rest of the room disappeared. Michael floated to the table and rested his hands on the back of a chair, lost in those ice blue eyes. Her lips trembled. An unexpected ray of joy brought the first genuine smile he'd felt in a long time.

About the Author

Joe Douglas Trent moved away from his family's West Texas cotton farm, married, went to school and work, reared kids, and found an artistic outlet in song writing. He regaled his wife with brilliant book ideas until she retorted, "Well get off your rear and start writing." So he did.

Joe joined writers groups, honed his craft and won a couple of awards on the way. He reached the first stage of fulfilling his writing dreams with the acceptance of his first novel, *The King of Silk*, for publication.

He shares a good life with his sweetheart, kids, and grandchildren on the plains of West Texas, where he can look out his window and see a cotton farm.

You can reach him at www.jdtrent.com.

MuseItUp Publishing
Where the Muse entertains readers!
www.museituppublishing.com
Visit our website for more books for your reading pleasure.